Black Water

By
Bobby Norman

JournalStone
San Francisco

JOURNALSTONE
YOUR LINK TO ARTISTIC TALENT

This is a work of fiction. All of the characters, names, incidents, organizations, and dialogue in this novel are either the products of the author's imagination or are used fictitiously.

JournalStone books may be ordered through booksellers or by contacting:

JournalStone

www.journalstone.com

ISBN: 978-1-942712-15-2   (sc)
ISBN: 978-1-942712-16-9   (ebook)

JournalStone rev. date: March 13, 2015

Library of Congress Control Number: 2015832364

Printed in the United States of America

Cover Art & Design: Cyrusfiction Productions

Edited by: Dr. Michael Collings

Acknowledgements

No one writes a book alone. I'd like to take this opportunity to thank my wife and best friend, Ilene, and my agent, Leslie Gardner, at Artellus Ltd. in London, then the friends who took the time to help me out with a read. In alphabetical order, they are: James Allen, Clifford Ashpaugh, Kevin Bash, Pamela Blackwell, John Burley, Chelsea Keene, Bonnie Little, Howard and Sue Lowell, Lou Moore, Richard Mullen, and Julia Nunez.

BOOK ONE

The universe is a balance of Good and Evil. Usually, each keeps to its own. Usually. A knock-down-drag-out between the two would be pointless. Because, simply put, one could not exist without the other. Without an up, there is no down. No dark, no light. Regardless, once in a great while, there's a borrowing—a give and a take—needed to maintain the equilibrium. As it was, a favor was owed and Evil came to collect. A deal was struck, and on the night of August seventeenth, nineteen hundred and twenty-four, to rub out the debt, God turned his back on Oledeux, Louisiana.

CHAPTER 1

The witchlet looked like a toad, squatted down with her dirty little toes clenched, bird-like, on a mossy log, her bony back bowed, knobby knees framing her shoulders. Her eyes had a pinkish hue, hair the weight of spider web, and skin, tallowish, the color of a cheap candle you could almost see through. Bluish veins just below the surface crawled like arthritic, cancerous tendrils of ivy. She wore the odor of the decaying, rotting swamp like a shroud. At that moment, she was bothering a terrapin, trying t'mind its own business, eating terrapin dinner, pulling hunks of meat off a water dog. Every little bit she'd giggle and poke it in the tail with a stick, to piss it off.

She didn't know there was a booger hidin' behind a Cypress tree at her back, settin' up to pounce.

The little witch's name was Smoke. Peculiar name, but Smoke was of a peculiar nature. It wasn't a real name anyway, just what everbody called her. 'Cause of her color. Witches didn't let anybody know their real name. A known name was akin to a chink in their armor. A way to get in. Smoke was nocturnal and showed up about the time the bats come out to fill their furry little bellies on muskeeters and lightnin' bugs. She'd come out of a day, but it had to be pretty cloudy. Dark. Like this one'd been. It wasn't that she disliked the sun. It hurt her. And for good reason.

Smoke was albino.

Most things born in a Looziana swamp didn't move much futher than where they's dropped, and if so, she was probly hatched-out in the sluggish, black water swamps northeast of Oledeux, the same year the Great Emancipator was shot in back of the ear.

Half-wild children were as common as bug bites in a Southwestern Looziana wet. Even the ones that lived in houses couldn't be accused of being overly domesticated, and if it hadn't been for the color of her skin or those frogged-out, weird lookin' eyes, she wouldn'ta stood out much either. But, Smoke was like some dead and bloated somethin' or other you might come on alongside the road, all maggoty and puffed up by the sun, legs stuck out, belly-bloated, about to pop, that you didn't wanna look at. But you did anyway. Out the corner of your eye. Like you didn't wantcha to know you's doin' it.

She was like a cat, too, when it rubbed up on your pants leg, hiked up on its tippytoes, with its back all bowed up, makin' little come-and-pet-me sounds like it wanted its ears scratched or belly rubbed, but as soon as you stuck out your hand, lit out. Teasin'. That was Smoke. She was a teaser. If she'd had little gossamer, veiny-like dragonfly wings, she'da looked like a storybook fairy. Delicate and fragile (which she was neither). She had a cute little nose and ears that stuck straight out, a jughead, and when she ran it was always on her toes. It was like she never set her feet down flat. And you couldn't actually call it runnin'—it was more like flittin', her elbow-bumpy little arms stuck out to the side like little wings, and she'd flit. Smoke never walked…she flitted, and she had a thin, squeaky little voice that went along with the rest of her fairyness.

Because of high cheekbones and slight frame, it was a good bet her papa was Sem'nole or Cher'kee, they's both pretty common in Looziana, and poochy-pouty lips and a bubble ass gave credence her mama was Creole. A Creole witch. She coulda been Cajun, they had sizeable hindquarters, too, but Cajuns weren't as witchy as Creoles.

Smoke had no idea what she was. What she coulda been. What she was supposed to've been. Her talents were as natural to her as seein' and hearin' was to regular folk. She'd had no one to tell her different. If things had gone right, Smoke woulda been a Goddess in the witch world, adored and feared by the lowest, revered and hated by the highest.

Achingly careful, the booger leaned down and picked up a rock the size of a tamater out of the water. Half a dozen drops plicked off its fingers and back into the water. Hearing it, the witch jumped up, swiveled around, and the booger helt its foul breath, pretending invisibility.

CHAPTER 2

Witches, like regular folks, had their own particular leanings. For instance, there's them that for enough money could conjure up a hex on a body—make 'em sick or even die if enough had changed hands. But then, if the one hexed come along and offered more to another witch, or even the one who'd done the original conjuring, they could get it unconjured or even bounced back on the original offender. If you were gonna pay a witch to conjure up a curse, you wanted to make sure you paid enough it wouldn't get unconjured. The only loyalty witches had was to theirselves.

There were even some, supposedly, that could turn into critters like wolves, snakes, or bats, but those were probably just tales as there wasn't any actual, factual, hands-on proof.

Then, there were the ones who could bring the dead back to life, and there was buckets of proof of that. The only people that could be brought back from the dead, though, was them that didn't go to Heaven, 'cause once you passed through the Pearly Gates, you were a bona fide, card-carryin' harp-plucker. You'd think it worked the same with the Hell-bound, but common belief was, if you's to be brought back for a purpose evil and nasty enough, Beezlebub'd cut you a pass, but the cost would be just awful. It took a very talented witch to perform somethin' like that. Bringin' the dead back to life.

The eyes was one o' the ways folks knew Smoke was of the anointed. One look at them pale, deep-feelin' orbs, and you turned tail right quick or sure as shit stunk, you got sucked in like iron to a magnet. Smoke had a specialty; she could read people, and men in particular, like a big-print Bible. When the need come on her, most likely from hunger or a fella had a play-pretty she wanted, she'd slip up on him, makin' like a cat with that sweet *pr-r-r-r pr-r-r-r-r pr-r-r-r-r* gurglin' deep down in her skinny little throat, cock her head to the side, and give him that little sidewaysie smile. It made a fella wanna grab her up, close his eyes, and rub his face all over her.

It wasn't 'cause she's much to look at, though. No, sir, not a whit, and especially when first come acrost, before she had time to put on the smoky illusion. The curtain of confusion. At first glance, you saw she was no more than thirteen years old, seventy-some-odd pounds of matted, yellow-white hair. Filthy and smelly as a shithouse rat, perched on scabby and thistle-scarred, heron-thin legs, waxy ears, rotten little teeth, and sure as Sunday's the Sabbath, she was both buggie and wormy. She chawed cut-leaf, dipped snuff, smoked cigars, and abused the Holy Father's name like a gypsy muleskinner. But! If...a man was to make the mistake of catchin' her eye, no more than a sidewaysie squint, he was done for, and in no time the flittin' fairy was all he saw. She started to look all sweet and cuddly, like one of them glass dolls from China, and she smelled of jasmine, or if you preferred, cinnamon.

Smoke was what you mighta called self-employed. She never wore shoes or any kind of underthings and had the habit of hikin' up her tattered dress, advertising as it was, commanding men's lecherous attention. See that and all you wanted was to pick her up, set her on your lap, slide up that dirty little dress—which then appeared made of your granny's finest lace curtain—squeeze her little butt cheeks, spread her legs, grit your teeth, harpoon her little clam, and jack it in her until your noodle dried up. You could want it, yes sir, but it wasn't likely to happen. She'd learned early on how consumed men was with the downy, mysterious little treasure at the juncture of her skinny, alabaster thighs, and for the price of a penny, she'd pinch the hem of her dress up under her armpits, clamp it down in front with her chin, and hold it there while they stared at it.

One of the cutest little things in the world was the tip of a kit's tongue stickin' out of its mouth just a teeeeny bit when it slept. And that's what Smoke's little cooter had. That same fleshy little pink, wrinkled tongue that just barely stuck out between her lips, wrinkled and noodly, like your fingers got when you had them in hot water too long. The fellas'd get a grip on their prong and she'd give 'em a few seconds for their blood to work up and then she'd pull those little vertical lips apart with her fingertips and the men would squirt their guts out, gapin' with their mouth hangin' open, pantin' hard, entranced at the unveiled goodie. Scarce as fangs on a banty hen, a near-hairless albino pussy wasn't somethin' one saw everday.

For two pennies, she got down on her all-fours, looked around her shoulder to keep her eye on 'em, and stuck the rear hatch in the cool evenin' breeze. The two-penny act was a lot better for her than just the extra money, though. With the double southern exposure, her patrons achieved their end much quicker. She'd keep her cheeks spread and stuck in the air until the gruntin' started slowin' down, then she'd stand up, brush off the dirt embedded in her knees, and flit off.

She'd been offered nickels to polish the handle herself, but that meant gettin' way too close, and she'd just shake her head. Some had offered her quite a bit more to let 'em climb on her, but she just laughed it off. She'd seen how big a fella's thing got and knew damn well how little and tight her clam was. She might not've been as pure as the Virgin Mary, but she was ever bit as untouched.

***

Earlier, Smoke had purred little girlie come-ons at the wrong fella—the booger hidin' behind the Cypress that woulda had top billing in a circus sideshow. A six-foot-three, two-hundred-and-ninety-four pound, near-brain-dead mulatto with saggy, hairy titties bigger than most women. His name was Mule, and he had ever bit the smartness of a mealy bug. He was probably forty-five, fifty years old, clad in filthy, raggedy old coveralls, and smelled of pig shit and stinky armpits. He was damn near bald and had huge, bulbous brows like an under-cut, flash-flooded riverbank, lending credence to the theory that Neanderthals hadn't just died out but rutted with Cro-Magnons of low standing.

But the thing that stuck out most about Mule was what didn't stick out at all. A nose. Didn't have one. Not a hint. All there was was a jaggedy hole in the front of his face from just under and between his eyes down to a floppy top lip as useful as eyelashes on a snake that waggled over his mouth when he tried to talk, which, thank God, wasn't often. And, as one would expect, there was a different story from everbody that had ever seen him about how it come to be. Some had the idee he was born without one. Possible. It happened occasionally. Some slid out the chute shy an arm or a foot, stubbly half-legs with little flippers instead of feet. Nubs for fingers. Some born blind or deaf. Harelip. Mute. Cross-eyed. Dead. The often-talked-about-but-never-actually-seen double-headed. But the skin around it was badly scarred, puckered, indicating there'd most likely been one at some time. One of the best stories was that it'd been gnawed off by rats when he was a youngun while he slept peacefully in his crib. That was a real good story, and the visions created by such a thing could keep almost anyone well stocked in teeth-gnashing nightmares for quite a spell, but it seemed unlikely abody could sleep through their nose bein' chawed off by rats, even if they's a youngun.

Another story that got a lot a mileage was that his mama and daddy shared the same last name, but not because they's married. By the laws regarding relationships, that made his mama his aunt, and his daddy his uncle. Which made Mule his own first cousin. That coulda answered some of the questions about his intelligence, or lack of, but it still left considerable possibilities about the missing proboscis.

When Mule knew he was gonna come in contact with people, he had the good sense to fasten a dirty rag over his face to hide the cavity. He kept the two top corners of the thing tucked up tight between the brim of his floppy hat and his head, but loose in the front to allow for just enough dip so he could see. It made him look like a hold-up bandit, but it was better than staring at a hole that allowed you to look right in the front at the juicy parts of a body's head. He spent a lot of time re-situating the rag because it kept slippin' down. The front of it was always wet. If you had a nose you could snuff up snot and such, but if you didn't, it just ran free.

Well, hoping to make a coin or two, Smoke tried workin' him, but lucky for him, and as she was about to find out, very unlucky for her, he lacked the cranial accouterments to be sirened in deep. Seeing pretty quick she was wasting her time, she'd set off for more susceptible prey, but not before she'd stoked the embers in the furnace of Mule's crotchal area.

CHAPTER 3

Mule jumped out from behind the tree, planted his feet, hauled back his rock-chuckin' arm, and launched the thing. That son of a bitch smacked her in the right side o' the head, just above the ear, just as she was turning around, and knocked her into the water. He got to her before she could shake it off, grabbed her around the middle, clamped her up in his armpit, and, gigglin' like a three-year-old, started to lug her off.

Smoke kicked and scratched and clawed, bit his hands and anything else that got in range, the whole time screamin', "Let loose o' me, you fat son of a bitch!" It didn't make any difference, though, 'cause there wasn't nobody around to hear, but she wasn't gonna give up without a tussle. Grab a cat, even a full growed one, by the nape o' the neck like its mama did when it was a kit, and most times it'll quit squirmin'—just hang there with its eyes scrunched back like a Chinaman and its tail tucked up between its legs to protect the dainty parts. But Smoke wasn't a cat, and this was the first time abody'd ever had their hands on her, and she didn't like it a little bit. No matter how Mule grabbed her, she thrashed and scratched so fast it looked like she had five arms and six legs. Unfortunately, one o' them five arms reached up and jerked off the nose-hole-hidin' rag. If she thought she had somethin' to scream about before, she took one look at the ugly pit in the front o' Mule's head, cried "Aaaagggghhhh!" and went plum nuts.

He'd had enough of the caterwaulin', so he helt her out with one hand gripped around her throat so tight it cut off her air, her already bugged-out eyes bugged out even futher, and with his free hand gave her one good whack, slappin' her unconscious. That made her a whole lot easier to handle. He laid her on the ground, readjusted his nose-hole-hidin' rag, straightened out his coveralls, picked her up, slung her over his shoulder like of sack a spuds, and carted her off.

It was still dark when she come to and found herself laid out on a thin, scratchy mattress thing stuffed with itchy horsehair and moldy corn husks, with a headache, a bloody nose, a sore jaw, a bump on the side of her head, and a ringin' in her ear. She was butt naked and latched around the neck with an iron chain securely bolted to the wall post. Seeing the door was open, she jumped up with escape on her mind but hadn't yet noticed the length of the chain and nearly yanked her head off. It only allowed enough room for her to sit up on the cot. Real quick, she flipped herself around, braced her feet on the wall, got a grip with both hands on the chain, clamped her jaw down, and pulled t'beat the band. The only thing that accomplished was rubbing burns on her scrawny little neck and her hands. Her head would come off her shoulders before that chain come off the wall.

Mule sat bassackards on a chair at a rickety table in the middle of the room, with nothin' on but a greasy undershirt, slicing chunks off a raw patater with a big old knife, watchin' her struggle. The knife wasn't much more than a dull blade with two pieces of wood for a grip, leather-wrapped and cinched with thin strips of rawhide. He sipped and dribbled a homemade alcoholic concoction from a dented tin cup and pushed the patater chunks in what she determined was his mouth below the God-awful ugly hole in his face where his nose oughta been. A coal oil lamp in the middle of the table obstructed his view so he moved it to the edge. He leered at her girl parts and nodded his head in appreciation of the fine job he'd done locking her down.

With all that going on, it took a minute before she realized she was sore 'twixt her legs. She saw the rusty color of dried and sticky blood smeared on the soft insides of her thighs and the scratchy thing impersonating a mattress. It was then she realized she'd been done to, and as bad as she was hurtin', determined Mule was sportin' more than a two-finger-and-a-thumber. She was horrified that the noseless, fat piece of shit sittin' halfway across the room shoving patater into its face had stuck his weiner in her.

Mule's gut jumped like a hog in a sack when he chuckled, nodded, and pushed another slice of patater in the hole. She felt bile rising in her throat, but, forgetting she was chained and nearly hanging herself again, hung her head as best she could over the edge of the cot and threw up on the floor. She was now officially a woman. Got that way by an old man.

A fat one that smelled of pig shit and stinky armpits. With a hole in his head where his nose oughta been.

The next few days, Mule did to her whatever come to mind. He was somewhat limited by the length of the chain, but he seemed to have quite an imagination when it come to dreaming up ways to poke pussy. And with good reason. A thousand times over the years, he'd fantasized about stickin' it in a human woman, but what with the hole in his face, he couldn't even rent one by the hour. Even a used-up whore would go without before spreadin' her legs for him. Being that he was getting older and uglier ever passing day, lived out in the middle of nowhere, and had no financial prospects to speak of, he hadn't had a lot of experience with the opposite sex.

Well, that wasn't quite right. Sex he'd had, and quite a bit of it. Just never with his own species. Smoke was actually his first adventure with a human female—he'd discovered it was all he'd hoped it would be and was intent on making up for lost time.

On the very first day she learned he had a tendency to bite, but trying to fight him off just earned her his huge, calloused hands clamped around her throat until her face turned blue, her tongue stuck out, and thousands of sparkly little lights twinkled before her eyes, then everthing went dark.

With her unconscious, he could probe and explore the wonders without all the bothersome squirming.

More than once she had come to, licked clean with painful whisker burns on the inside of her thighs. The source, not somethin' she wanted to think about.

Ever time he come on her she fought like a turpentined cat. She woulda been a lot better off playin' possum or gettin' throttled into blessed nothingness. Conscious or not, though, he was having a great time. If he'd known a human girl could be this much fun, he'da caught one a long time ago. Hell, this one was so much fun, he was giving serious thought about snatchin' up another one. Next time he was in town, he was gonna buy another chain, one a little longer, and keep a lookout for another human.

The girl was a lot better than a sow. He could pin her arms down and look her in the eye and see the fear and the pain. Couldn't do that with a hog. He'd tried to get one of his favorites to turn turtle a couple of times, but discovered that sows was constructed to go in from the back while on their feet. Any other way, the angle was off and his doodle kept slippin' out. A sow squealed and put up a struggle to get loose, but it wouldn't actually what you'd call fight back. He even thought there was a couple of 'em that had learned to like it because when he went to mount up, they'd slip their tails out of the way and brace theirselves against the sty rails, grunt and get all wiggly in anticipation.

He liked to think so, anyway.

He laughed, jamming it inside his new plaything, knowing he had a lot more to give than she had capacity to receive. They were proof you could actually shove a quart's worth of product in a pint-sized jar. It hurt like the devil, but she wouldn't give him the pleasure of knowing how bad, and that just made him pound that much harder. With her size, age, and meager diet, she hadn't developed a hint of tittie yet, but that didn't stop him from pullin' and pinchin' on her little pea-size nipples in the attempt to create some. When he pulled on his doodle it got bigger, so he was determined to prove it worked the same with titties. He tried suckin' on 'em, but with the floppy top lip he couldn't get a secure lock, so he had to settle for licking.

She bit and spit on him and tried to push him off, but never made a sound, other than to cuss and make nasty, although believable and even probable assumptions about his mother and father. His aunt and uncle.

First thing in the morning, he'd have a go at her, then go outside and work for a while, come back in an hour or two later, eat a patater or somethin', have another romp, and then go back outside. He had his way with her three or four times a day, but it vexed him she could take it. Ever time he was done with her, he wasn't happy unless there was blood smeared on the head of his pecker. He even denied her food and water to wear her down, but that just seemed to make her madder. He told her he knew she thought she was better than he was but before he was done with her, nose or no, she'd learn the difference between master and slave and he'd keep it up until she hollered uncle.

"Hell, yeah," she told him one time, "I am better'n you, you ugly ol' fart. I got a nose 'n you ain't." That crack cost her a tooth, a busted lip, a swole-up eye, and an extra hard poking. He grabbed her by the hair, flipped her over on her knees, wrapped his left arm tight around her middle and his right hand mashed her head face down on the mattress, and rammed her from the back until she threw up. It wasn't as good as a scream or beggin' him to stop, but it'd do for a start.

One of his favorite tortures was to eat in front of her while she was near starving. One day he was gnawin' on a piece of meat and she got smart-mouthed and asked him why he'd eat greasy possum when there was a pen full of fresh bacon and ham hocks not fifty feet from the front door. He shook all over and laughed at her like she was stupid and told her that just showed how smart she wasn't. "Possums's fer eatin', pigs's fer sellin'."

***

On the fifth day, mellowed by half a jug of amateur-grade embalming fluid, Mule stood at the side of the cot, goin' at her with nothin' on but his smelly shirt. Smoke was hissing through her teeth because he had her on her all-fours, his big hands clamped tight on her hip bones, taking her from the back. He liked it like that because he could look down and watch what he was doing. He leaned forward, pushed on the back of her head, and blubbered something that sounded like "Bledown." When she didn't move, he slapped her in the back of the head and repeated, "Bledown!" She understood that he wanted her to get down, but at that angle, it hurt a lot more. When she didn't do it, he hauled off and smacked her on the butt with the back of his hand. That hurt. It felt like her cheek was on fire.

She felt his body twist like he was getting ready to give her another and she dropped to her forearms and put her forehead on the mattress. It musta been what he wanted because it felt like his man part got a lot harder. Half a dozen more pushes and he pulled it out. He wasn't done, though. Not by a long shot. He just wanted to keep it from goin' off before he was ready. He was watchin' it bounce when he noticed her other little puckered hole. Lookin' at it, just sittin' there, goin' to waste, gave him an idea. He started running his thumb down the little gap between her cheeks. Thinking. Picturing. And if it'd been possible, grinning.

"Awright! Awright," she squeaked through dry, parched lips. She'd figured where he was going even before he did. "It's over, you win, I give up. I'm done. I'm broke, finished. I ain't no match fer yer manliness." Crocodile tears rolled down her pale, dirty little cheeks and dripped onto the bloodstained mattress. She looked over her shoulder at him. "I've learnt who's boss. Please don't hurt me no more. I honest t' God believe yer tearin' me apart inside. Please, Mista, you're scarin' me s' bad I almost can't stand it. You're 'bout more man than I can take and I promise if ya cut me loose, feed, and take care a me, I swear a solemn promise t' God 'n all th'angels in Heaven I'll stay with ya's long as ya live."

He flipped her on her back. The cot was only inches from the floor so he spread her legs, snugged up close, put his elbows alongside her hips on the mattress, and leaned over, his face three inches from hers.

"D'ya mean it?" he blubbered. At least, that's what she thought he'd asked. His hot breath was as foul as his face, and she was scared shitless he was gonna try to kiss her on the mouth.

She couldn't nod her head fast enough. "Yeah, I promise."

"If ya really mean it, you 'n me'll get married."

It was hard to understand a lot of what he said but she got the gist of it. She just looked at him, unsure of what to do. She had it in her mind that what he'd been doing to her for five days and nights was what married people did, so what was he talkin' about?

"Awright."

Mule was beside hisself with joy. The courtin' was over and he was gonna have a wife!

"Whada we do?" she asked.

"Make promises, I think," he said, earnestly.

"I awready done that. I said I'd stay with ya's long's ya live."

His face contorted with what she assumed was a smile. "Yeah...I guess ya' did! Whadaya want me t' promise?" He was so excited he looked like an ugly, two-hundred-and-ninety-four pound four-year-old. But a lot dumber.

"Bein' married t'you's more'n enough fer me," she lied. It was hardly a way to start a healthy, trusting relationship.

His little bug brain, softened by victory and half a bottle of hearty alcoholic beverage, convinced him she was telling the truth, and gigglin' like a fool, unlocked the chain clamped around her neck but stood between her and the door just in case she changed her mind and bolted.

As of that moment, they were Mr. and Mrs. Mule.

CHAPTER 4

Later that evening, during his second honeymoon poke and with him tanked up with enough inebriant to pickle an adult mastodon, Smoke whuffed out a lungful when he blacked out on top of her. Seeing her chance, she wraggled her top half out from under him, and by bracing her bony little shoulders agin the wall, shoved her new husband's fat, drunk ass off the cot, thudding to the floor on his back. She stopped breathing when he started waving his arms around and raised one leg like he was trying to get up. Then he farted and passed out again. She took a second to catch her breath, and that's when she noticed the big knife stuck in the table. Everthing else in the shack disappeared. It was all she saw. If it'd had arms and a mouth, it woulda been wavin' and hollerin' at her.

She stood up quick and fighting off a dizzy spell from lack of food, stepped to the woodpile stacked up next to the rough rock fireplace and picked up a hunk about a foot and a half long. She didn't wanna take any chance he'd come to, so she got down on her knees, cocked the wood to the right with both hands, like she was about to swing an axe, and let her go, hard, alongside his right temple. Both his arms shot up, but then fell back. The only sign of life was a little trickle of blood from the gash in the side of his head and a blubbery, snottery noise comin' out of his face.

Jumping to it before he could come around, she sat on the floor, braced her back against the edge of the cot, rolled him over on his belly, jumped up, and waggled the knife out of the tabletop. Then she picked up the hunk of wood she'd just conked him out with and laid it on the floor beside his head. She scooted around to the top of his head, sat back on her heels, jammed her knees up against the top of his shoulders, and pinched his head between her legs with his flattened face to the floor. Then she got a good grip on the knife handle and put the rusty blade's pointy end on the neck bone where it fastened to the head bone. She picked up the firewood, gave the knife handle a good whack and then spider-monkeyed off a few feet, ready to bolt for the door just in case he come up bellerin' and hollerin'.

But he didn't.

By Jiggies! That did the trick! His gelatinous bulk had only given one quivery little shudder. She jumped back over, picked up the stick and whacked the knife again so hard that the handle was the only thing sproutin' out the back of his head. In fact, she'd hit it so hard, the pointy end was stickin' out the front of his throat just under his chin. There was even a nick in the wood floor. She stayed right there with both her hands wrapped around that hunk of wood, all cocked and ready to go. She didn't trust the son of a bitch. He had to be playin' possum.

But he wasn't.

She couldn't believe it had been that easy. She waited for him to jump up and come to kill his new bride who had just pounded a rusty knife through his neck bone.

But he didn't.

And she was some little disappointed. Not that he wasn't coming at her, but she'd expected, or maybe even hoped, he'd suffer a whole bunch on his way out.

No such luck.

She moved to his right side, braced her feet, one on the back of his head, the other between his meaty shoulders, and pulled out the knife. Then she turned his head over and jabbed the blade in the hole in the middle of his face where his nose oughta been and wiggled it around like a banger in a bell. Nothin'. Not a dang thing! Shit! Dead as a turd. Oh, well.

But even Mule would have to agree, she was good to her solemn promise to God and all the angels in Heaven—she'd stayed with him the rest of his life.

CHAPTER 5

Being that Mule was damned near three hundred pounds, Smoke knew she wasn't gonna be able to drag his deadweight carcass out of the shack by herself, and she wasn't about to leave it in the middle o' the floor, swellin' up, stinkin', and drawin' flies. Scrabbling around a shed out back, she come on a dull, rusty old hatchet with a cracked handle, and along with it and the knife, put 'em to good use, slicin' and hackin' him down to manageable, draggable chunks.

Four sweat-drenching hours after Mr. Mule's last foul breath, the recently widowed Mrs. Mule was settin' at the table, blood-spattered and tuckered out, smackin' her mouth, runnin' her tongue over her greasy lips, puttin' the finishing touches on what little Mule had left of the possum stew, a raw patata, and a plate of red beans, soppin' up the juice with a moldy biscuit. Seventy-five yards from the shack, a hundred-year-old, hundred-and-fifty-pound mossy-back was pulling meat off what used to be Mule's big butt. The turtle didn't seem to mind at all that his dinner didn't have a nose. Meat was meat was meat.

Smoke assumed that by being Mrs. Mule, she'd earned widder's rights and took up residence in the shack. What with a roof that didn't leak too bad over her head and no tellin' how much worth of Mule's ex-girlfriends gruntin' out in the yard, she was living in high cotton.

The next few weeks slowly oozed one to another and Smoke was getting soft, eatin' regular and sleepin' under a roof. Until one morning it occurred to her that somethin' was wrong. Bad wrong. Having more pressing matters of late, it'd completely slipped her mind. When it did hit her, she sucked up like she'd been doused with a bucket of cold water. Shortly after waking in the mornings, she was gettin' sick, ever day as punctual as the sun's rising. Then later she just couldn't get enough to eat. The little mole-heads Mule had tried to pull off her chest and make into titties were finally puffing up, sensitive and sore, deep inside. She ran her hands low over her belly and felt the slight bulge. She used to be able to suck in her guts to where it looked like she didn't have any. Rib bones and nothin' under 'em. Not now. Just when she thought she was shed of that noseless bastard.

It was *his*! Had to be! Wasn't nobody else. He was the only one she'd ever been done to by. She pictured her guts churnin', twistin' around like a dyin' snake, forming into somethin'. She felt its sharp-clawed little fingers grippin' on her ribs like it was climbin' a ladder. She shoved hard on her belly attempting to push it out like a stubborn turd. She stepped out the door and squatted and pushed so hard her face turned a purply red. She climbed trees as high as she thought she could jump out of without breakin' a leg, hoping maybe she could joggle it loose, like hockin' up a loogie. All that got her was blistery feet from climbin' the trees and sore ankles from hittin' the ground. Finally, too sore and too tired to climb another tree, she hobbled back to the shack, plopped down on the cot, and bawled her eyes out.

The weeks, and then months, following Mule's sudden departure were hard on Smoke as her pregnancy progressed, but she was unaware of the drastic changes in herself, psychologically. Before Mule, she'd made her own way—mostly stealing and gulling the easily manipulated men who paid for her favors, and adding turtles, mud bugs, and fish to her plate when she could catch 'em—but it was different now. Before, she'd kill somethin' without a thought 'cause it was food, 'cause that's what they's for; she neither liked nor disliked it, it was just the way of things. Now, she made the poor creatures suffer first. It started with the hogs, chasin 'em down and hackin' their noses off before they's even dead with that short-handled hatchet she'd hacked Mule up with, but she'd run out of them for some time now. When they were gone, she went back to her old staple of turtles, mud bugs, and the occasional possum. There were instances now, when hungry or not, she caught somethin' and tortured it, slow, just to hear it squeal and thrash in pain, strugglin', wide-eyed while it died. Smaller critters, croakers and water dogs, she squeezed to death, popped 'em with her bare hands, and then just threw 'em away.

Smoke killed for hate. She survived for hate. She lived for hate and revenge. Little by little, her sanity dissipated and evaporated like the early morning mist. Late at night, she struck at her protruding belly in frustration. She'd slap it, picturing the baby asleep and jumpin' up awake, then she'd listen real careful to see if she could hear it crying. She was frightened because there was times she thought she heard it, not crying, but talking. She'd smack her belly and hiss, "Shut up! Shut up!"

When she couldn't get it to shut up (some nights it talked 'til the sun come up), she'd threaten to cut it out if it didn't let her sleep. She hoped the thing couldn't read her mind 'cause it was a bluff. Then she started talkin' back to it; lay on the cot with her dress pulled up, her thumb and pointin' finger pinchin' the knife handle, and she'd casually drag the rusty blade, the one that'd done in Mule, over her belly and whisper babytalk. Coo to it that when its time come, she was gonna stick it with that very same knife before it took a second breath; that she was gonna feed it to the gators and snappers the same as she did with its hog-fuckin', hole-in-his-face-where-a-nose-oughta-been father. That way its death would be a good thing, serve a righteous purpose. The gators and bottomfeeders would eat the demon baby, and then she'd eat them. The cycle of life. Survival of the fittest. Survival of the craziest.

One night, when fearful bad lightnin' jiggered across the stormy sky and boulder-crackin' thunder threatened to level the shack, the unwanted thing growin' inside her made its intentions known. The thought of pounding out the hog fucker's spawn all alone scared her bad, and so, reluctantly, with a burlap carryin' bag over one shoulder, she left the shack. She was gonna go to a Seminole midwife she'd heard of that lived off about three miles to the southeast. She'd get her to help pull the thing out, and then, when the midwife was busy doin' somethin' else, Smoke would stick the knife in the piglet's heart, twist it and turn it and listen to it squeal.

skweeeeee skweeeeee skweeeeee

She knew the midwife probably wouldn't like that, but after she explained how the thing had been started by a hog-fuckin' bastard that didn't have a nose, she'd understand. But, understand or not, the piglet would be dead.

It started raining shortly after she left, thunder and lightning, gettin' worse ever step she took. A hundred feet from the door, she was soaked to the bone. Her water broke with the first hard contraction, and she felt warm bloody ooze sliding down her skinny legs, staining the mud.

She'd always been able to get away from things that tried to pen her in, even if, as in the hog fucker's case, it took a week and a stretch of the truth. This was different. There wasn't any gettin' out o' this mess. Mule's pecker was the biggest she'd ever seen and jammin' it in her little hole hurt like Hell, but that goddamn thing wasn't anywhere near as big as what was about to push its way out. She'd seen horses and cows and hogs and cats and dogs birthin', how bad they'd suffered doin' it, squealin', bleetin', and bleedin', and for the first time in her life she was terrified. Even gettin' caught by hole-in-his-face hadn't terrified her. More than anything, it just made her mad. She knew there was a way out if she just waited long enough. But there wasn't any way out of the shit she was in now, except to see it through to the nasty end. The thought of a thing right up inside her, clawin' and scratchin' its way out, drove her to shiverin'.

She waddled to a tree just off the side of the road, her arm slung under her belly. It'd dropped a lot lower than the day before, and it felt like it was about to pop. She let her bag slip off her shoulder to the ground. Then she grit her teeth, and, writhing in pain, pushed through another gut-wrenching contraction. When it passed, she cursed God, the storm, the hated pig-snouted demon inside her, and the smelly bastard that started it. She wasn't gonna make it to the midwife now and she knew it. She'd waited too long. She knew, too, that sure as shit, she was gonna die under that tree. Ohhhhhh, how she wished Mule was still alive so she could pound another blade into his ugly skull.

She leaned down and picked up the bag, ripped it open and pulled out the knife, tossed the bag aside, gnashed through another contraction, and when it passed, slid down the tree trunk and spread her blood-streaked legs. Because her belly was so big, she couldn't see it, but it felt like the slit between her thighs was ripping apart. Soon, the thing would show itself, then she'd get it. "Come on you little bastard!" It was like waitin' for a gopher to stick its head out a hole so you could knock it off.

Then...it was coming! This was it! She gripped the handle with both hands, pointing at the place where the squirming demon would make its grand appearance. She was gonna stick it right smack dab in the top of its piggy little head, more than happy to end what little was left of Mule, the hog fucker. She wondered, would it be face up or down? Would it have a nose?

Another contraction and something gave way. It felt like somebody was wringin' her guts like a dishrag, and she yelled into the roiling clouds, hoping God was listening. "I HATE you! I HATE you! I HATE you!" She looked back down, ever muscle twitching in anticipation. "Come on," she crooned sweetly. Rain coursed down her face, blood stained the mud. "Thaaaaaaat's right. Come on. Mama's got a big s'prise for ya. Come on, you can do it."

Two hundred yards up the road, a ruddy-faced, hollow-cheeked, hatchet-nosed, skinny-assed, thirty-eight-year-old simpleton by the name of Roach Komes and his plump, homely, forty-three-year-old, much more intelligent common-law wife, Pearl, the Seminole midwife, were huddled up tight on their rickety wagon, grudgingly pulled by a pair of mismatched mules. Almost as mismatched as Roach and Pearl.

Pearl had the cowl of her wrap flopped over her face in a worthless attempt at keeping out the wind and wet. She huddled around a coal oil lamp to keep it from going out. Earlier in the day, she and Roach had taken the wagon into Oledeux to trade what little preserves Pearl had put up and the few measly muskrat and gator hides Roach had trapped for supplies, and now they were headed back home.

Normally, Roach read weather signs pretty good, and he was concerned how he coulda read today's so bad. He had an arthritic left leg he'd broke some years before that let him know a day or two in advance when the weather was turning. Ol' boys'd meet him on the road and ask him what the leg had in store the next few days and he'd tell 'em, and more often than not, it'd be right. Typical of Roach Komes, the leg did all the work while he took all the credit. But this thing tonight, uh uh, noooo, this was different, and it was wrong; goose-flesh wrong. Going into town, the leg hadn't bothered him a'tall, but now it was painin' somethin' awful and he kept stretchin' it out and kneadin' it with one hand while he kept a tight grip on the reins with the other.

It nagged at him that the reason the storm was able to sneak up on him was 'cause it didn't have nothin' to do with weather. It was a thing, a sign, and it was malevolent. Hackles ran up his spine, feelin' like somethin' was about to jump out of the dark woods and bite him in the ass. He was prodding the mules to step it up when, up ahead, a great big ol' lightnin' bolt jigger-jagged its way to the ground. Instantly, ear-splitting thunder nearly finished it for the skittery mules. One of 'em took it so hard it raised its tail and splattered a steamy pile on the road. Roach worked the reins and brought 'em under control, but then, after he did, it took some doin' to get 'em started again.

The mules were still jumpy when they come on the smoldering ruin of a tree that had been split by lightning. It was still smokin' and steamin'. On the next flash, Roach caught a glimpse of a light colored somethin' layin' on the muddy hump in the middle of the wheel-rutted road and reined the mules to a stop.

Pearl saw that Roach was looking intently up the road with his bushy eyebrows scrunched down. "What'sa matter?"

"Probly nothin'," he said, impatiently, and pushed the reins into Pearl's hands, climbed off the wagon, and cautiously approached the thing. When he got to it, he leaned down to get a closer look and when lightning flashed again, he jumped up, shocked at the sight of a scorched human arm with a death grip on a knife. The prickles that ran up his spine told him the muddy, rain-splattered thing and the storm was hooked up somehow, and he didn't like bein' in the middle of it. He figured there wouldn't be an arm layin' in the road all by itself for no reason, and sure enough, looking around, he saw the rest of the chalky carcass, stringy white hair strung over its face, slumped at the base of the tree. He knew it musta just happened because steam was still snaking from the crispy stump where the arm used to belong.

"What is it?" Pearl yelled.

"Shit," he said to hisself. He didn't need these goin's on.

"Roach! You hear me?"

"Yeah, I hear ya!" he bitched back. Then to hisself, "How would I miss it?" Then he barked at her, "You stay there, it ain't nothin'."

Pearl was holding up the lantern, lookin' like a hootie owl, bobbin' her nosy head around.

He was trying to figure out how he was gonna get around the body without her seeing it. She had to know ever dadgum thing. He could turn the wagon around and go back the way they'd come, but then she'd wanna know why, but if he kept on the way they were she was gonna see it and then she'd wanna do somethin' stupid like see if it was still alive and needed help. He didn't understand why she couldn't just mind her own dadgum business.

Although Roach had never had any professional doings with Smoke, he knew that's who it was braced up agin the tree. Even blown apart, he knew an albino when he saw one. Now if he could just keep Pearl from....

"Roach?" She chinned to the body. "What is 'at?"

"Nothin'!" he yelled. "You stay...there!" Then he jabbed his finger at her with each word. "Don't...you...get...off...'at...dad...gum...wagon!"

Translated, that meant there was somethin' he didn't want her to see, so accepting the invitation, she wrapped the reins 'round the brake handle, and holding the lantern tight, descended from the wagon. Slipping in the squishy mud and holding up the light, she started for the thing leanin' up agin the tree.

Roach grit his teeth and huffed and puffed over to meet her. "I thought I tolju t'stay on th'wagon!"

The look she gave him let him know just how much weight that carried. Roach shook his head in frustration and fell in behind her when she walked around him and lowered the lantern to the body. Her hand went to her mouth and her face got all scrunched up like Roach was afraid it would.

"Ohhhhh, my Lord, Roach, it's just a little girl."

Roach took the lantern from her and holding it close to what was left, they saw the full extent of the damage. It seemed parts of her had exploded from the inside out, not the least was a lot of what used to be her face. He pointed his finger from the smoldering tree, down the trunk to the body. "Lightnin' probly hit th'tree up there 'n worked down 'n she's leanin up agin it."

Pearl shielded her face from the rain with her arm and looked up into the shattered tree. Then she looked at where the arm used to be.

Nodding over his shoulder, Roach told her, "Arm's over yondah."

Pearl looked toward the appendage.

"Lightnin' musta blowed it off. Coulda been somethin' was comin' at 'er 'cause there's a knife still clenched in 'er hand." He took Pearl by the arm. "Let's get back on th'wagon. They ain't nothin' t'do."

She jerked her arm away and looked at him like he was crazy. "You don't really think I'd leave 'er here like 'is, do ya?"

"I'll come back 'n get 'er after th'storm's over," he said, hoping against hope that would cover it.

"No, we're here now, we'll take 'er now." She took the lantern back and helt it over the body. "Ohhhhh, Lord, she's pregnant, too. Ain't that a shame. Poor little thing." She leaned down and pushed aside stray hairs off Smoke's ruined face as if she were a baby sleeping in a crib. "It musta just happened, she ain't even cold yet." She shook her head in motherly sorrow. "She weren't much more'n a baby herself. This is such a awful waste."

When she passed her hand tenderly over Smoke's belly, she was stunned by a sharp movement. She set the lantern on the muddy road, kneeled beside the body, and smooshed both her hands tightly alongside Smoke's belly. The baby kicked again.

The midwife in Pearl jumped to the forefront and she forgot all about the storm. She lifted the hem of Smoke's tattered dress, flipped it over her chest, and pointed to the arm in the road. "Gimme 'at knife."

Roach was about to pull his hair out. His leg was killing him, he was hungry and wanted to go home! "Dadgummit, Pearl...."

Pearl turned on him like a rabid wolf. "Get the knife, Roach! If you think I'd leave a baby t'die yer even dumber'n I give ya credit for. Now GET IT!"

Fists clenched up like a spoiled eight-year-old, he stomped stiff-legged to the arm. Then he hesitated, not in any hurry to touch it.

"Hurry!" Pearl snapped, while she rolled the flopping body off the tree trunk and laid it flat on the ground.

Roach picked up the arm and pried the cold, lifeless fingers off the knife handle. He dropped the arm back in the mud and moved over to Pearl.

"Hold th'lamp up," she ordered, taking the knife.

He helt the lantern over the body and Pearl ripped Smoke's dress up the middle. Then she took a deep breath and started cutting her belly open.

"I say we leave it, you cain't even see whatchur doin'. Ain'tcha 'fraid you'll cut it?"

"Whata you think! Shut up 'n let me do this!" She was sawing and ripping more than cutting. "Blade wudn cut soapy water. Move it over here," she ordered, motioning Roach to move the lantern. Determining she had cut a gash long enough, she sat the knife down and commenced to probing inside the cavity, moving the tiny body around to see how it was positioned. Bracing herself, she pulled the bloody little thing out, trailed by the ropey umbilical cord. "Rip off a piece of her dress t'tie off th'cord!"

Roach set the lantern in the mud, and trying not to look at the gutted carcass inches from his shaking hands, ripped a strip off Smoke's dress.

Pearl flipped the baby facedown in her left hand while she carefully, but firmly, slapped and massaged its backside with her right. Its little legs and arms flopped around as lifelessly as a plucked chicken's wings. Concerned that nothing was happening, she shook it up some and slapped its backside again. "Come on! You can do it! Come on, dammit!" Agonizing seconds later, and scared to death it wasn't gonna make it, she screamed, "WAKE UP!" and gave it one more sharp whack on the butt. That did it. The wrinkly little thing clenched its tiny fists, pulled in its little legs and arms into a fetal ball, shuddered, shocked up a lungful of stormy air, and yowled its little lungs out.

Pearl turned it belly-side up and pulled it close, into her. "Get th'knife 'n cut th'cord," she told Roach, then commenced to cooing to it that she was sorry she'd had to whomp it so hard.

Roach picked the knife up and wiped the muddy blade off on his pant leg. From the lamplight he noticed there was a dark splotch that ran from the baby's left cheek, through the eye and high into her newborn, ill-shaped forehead. "What's wrong with 'im?"

"It's a her," she said, impatiently, bunching up the cord. "You mean t'tell me that you didn't look between her legs to see what was or wasn't there?"

"What's wrong with her then," he said, cranky about being corrected and accused all the time.

"I ain't sure," Pearl said, pinching the cord about three inches from the baby's belly. "Might be it's a lightnin' burn, don'tcha think?"

"Lightnin' burn? I wudn think so." He nodded to Smoke's body. "You see what it done t'her." He squinted at the baby's damaged face, figuring what the chances were how a body lightning struck could survive. Unless....

"Roach!" Pearl squawked, nudging his arm with her elbow, snapping him back to this planet. "Down here, come on, cut it by m'thumb, but be careful t'leave enough t'tie off."

Roach moved in and sawed while the baby wailed. It finally pulled apart.

"Awright," she said. "Tie it off, good 'n tight."

Roach double-knotted the cloth to the cord and Pearl pulled the baby to her chest, shielding it from the wind and pelting rain. She looked down at the body. "That's Smoke, ain't it?"

Roach pushed out of the mud and stood up. "What give it away?" The Lantern of Opportunity flickered in Roach's head and he snagged it. "Pearl, th'livin' youngun's th'concern now, not 'er mama's dead body. I don't believe we should worry 'bout somethin' we cain't do nothin' 'bout. I think it's best we get th'baby out o' th'storm."

Pearl struggled to get up. "Got out of it dincha," she said, accusingly. "I c'n see yer just full o' concern, so t'morrow, if th'storm's died down, you'll bring th'wagon back here 'n pick 'er up. I don't care who 'r what she was, she was this baby's mama, and she deserves a decent buryin'. You'll get 'er arm, too." She looked at the body, crossed herself, and said, "God bless you, child," and the instant she did, a three-ring circus of thunder and lightning exploded all around, scaring the shit out a both of 'em. Pearl slogged back to the wagon.

Not one to discard something that might have a little value, Roach picked up the knife and nervously trailed behind Pearl. When they got to the wagon, she handed the baby to him and climbed up.

When she got situated on the seat, she took it back and wrapped it in her coat. Roach ran around to the other side and mounted the wagon, grabbed the reins, and prodded the mules into action. He gave the body laid out at the base of the tree one last look as they passed by.

Pearl pulled her coat back and took a peek at the little thing. "Most likely 'there's nobody gonna claim 'er."

"That's a safe bet," he replied. Then it hit him! Pearl was gurgling babytalk and smiling. He had to head her off at the pass!

"Maybe we c'd keep 'er," she said.

Shit! Too late.

"It's a little hard t'tell in th'dark, but I think she's got color, not like 'er mama." The statement came from a woman who was innately a mother, who never had a child of her own, and, at that very moment, was probably holding her last, best chance of ever having one. She woulda latched on to it if it'd been an elephant-snouted, two-headed hermaphrodite with a hump and a pointy tail, but in Pearl's heart, the fact that the child was damaged was actually a plus. It would need the love and attention she felt she alone could give it, free of charge.

Roach didn't look at it that way. He hated it ever time Pearl helped birth a baby 'cause she'd get in a slump for days afterwards. She'd just park her highly-cushioned rear end in the rocking chair on their front porch, looking off in the distance, fixed on nothing and blow out poor-me sighs. The whole grieving time she wouldn't fix nothin' to eat, the shack would go to pot, and when she looked at Roach, which wasn't any more often than she had to, the look said it was his fault she didn't have any younguns pullin' on her titties. Then she'd sigh and stare off into the distance again. Poor me.

"Forget it, Pearl! We don't need no baby!" Then he jerked his head back over his shoulder. "'Specially one come out o' that womb."

"No! You don't need no baby," she spat back. She knew his objections were coming, and she was fully loaded, cocked, and ready to fire.

"Anyway you want it—you, me, us—but witchin's passed on, 'n that thing layin' in th'mud back there with its guts spilled out's a witch, which means," he jabbed his finger at the bundle on Pearl's chest, "'at's a witch 'n we ain't takin' in no dadgum witch! Now, you listen t'me, God Dammit!" He used "God Dammit" on highly volatile occasions when "Dadgummit" wasn't enough. Unfortunately for him, to Pearl his "God Dammits" were just as toothless as his "Dadgummits."

"I know whatchur plottin' 'n you c'n f'get it! You think you'll wear me down, butchur bad mistook 'n headed fer a haaarrrd fall. I got m'back up 'n I'm tellin' ya! Don't get attached to it! You ain't keepin' it!"

Gritting her teeth, rocking the baby, she said...nothing, not a dadgum word, and Roach knew that wasn't a good sign. Roach would much rather she'd kept argeein'. Not saying anything, he knew she had her feet planted, and he'd have to try another tack.

"Listen. We c'd sell it t'somebody 'at wants one. We'd probly get good money for it. Find somebody that'd treat it good, butchu don't tell nobody its mama was a witch 'r we'll never get shed of it." That didn't work either. She was still tight-jawed, so he tried to make a funny. "On second thought, maybe it'da been better if it was white, too, like its Ma. We'd get more sellin' it to a circus."

"She ain't a it."

Totally frustrated, Roach slapped the reins across the mules backs. "Git up, you sons-o-bitches!"

Pearl pulled the baby closer to her chest and shot Roach a glare. "Not in front o' th'baby!"

The next morning, the storm had shut down considerably. Pearl climbed up Roach's back 'til he hitched the mules to the wagon and rode off to pick up Smoke's body. About a mile from the shack, he stopped the mules, set the brake, pulled out a bottle of hooch he'd stashed under a pile of tote sacks, and layin' in the wagon bed, sipped on the contents in the sporadic morning sun. He closed his eyes and the sun was in one place, opened 'em later and it'd moved quite a bit. On the way back home, he cooked up a story about the body being gone.

CHAPTER 6

Roach and Pearl had an arrangement. An understanding. Pearl made the little, day-to-day decisions, while Roach made the more important big'ns. Roach determined who should be President, whether or not the country should go to war and who with. Everthing else was Pearl's domain, and if the old thing about possession being nine-tenths of the law carried any weight, Roach was had because Pearl had made another of her little decisions. They's keepin' the baby. The second she had her arms wrapped around that tiny little miracle, it was over. Roach had a better chance of waking up handsome than pryin' 'em apart. There was no doubt, though, the child was gonna have a hard row to hoe. The lightning bolt that blew her mama's arm off left the baby with a nasty wine-colored splotch that ran from low on her left cheek to high in her scalp. The eye itself was blue/gray blind, an ugly piece of work. With marks like those, she wasn't gonna have it easy.

When it come to bearing children, the best Pearl had ever done was two or three miscarriages, and one—tiny George, a full-nine-monther, but who'd died within hours of being born—was buried in a shallow hole in the tiny, one-grave cemetery in back of the shack. The sight of that little grave and the faded wooden marker with his name scratched in it bothered her a whole lot.

Within a week Pearl's breasts were swollen and leaking milk and that sweet life laying on her chest while its little lips sucked on her nipple was the most wonderful thing she'd ever felt. No mother, natural or surrogate, ever loved a child more.

She named the baby Lootie after a little snow-white bunny rabbit she'd had by that name when she was a youngster. Unfortunately, the bunny came along the same time a hard winter bared its icy fangs. Her papa'd had to butcher it for sustenance, and poor little Pearl never got over it. Even as an adult, she would tear up ever time she thought about it.

The nastiest part o' losing Lootie, the bunny one, was that dear ol' Papa hadn't mentioned where that night's dandy supper had come from until after the meal'd been consumed, the dishes washed up and put away. He figured it was better to keep quiet about her little buddy's grizzly murder until the meal was over because it was easier to grieve on a full belly than an empty one. He woulda preferred not having to say anything but he knew the next morning Pearl would run outside to play with the unfortunate bundle of fluff, it wouldn't be in the hutch, and Pearl would wanna know where her friend with the twitchy nose was.

So that night, working around a nose dripping watery snot and a flood of tears, dear ol' Papa told Pearl that he was real sorry he'd had to do such an awful thing. He remembered it read somewhere in the Good Book, though, that giving your life for your family was about as good as you could do, and that was exactly what that brave little snow-white bunny'd done—saved their very lives!

Pearl told him the bunny hadn't been brave and it hadn't given up its life, it'd been taken from it and it was pretty much a stretch to call it family, but if that was what he had to do to make it better, it was all right, she understood. A smarter, more compassionate person woulda left well enough alone, but he added, "It did taste pretty good, though, didn't it?" That started a whole new flood of snot and tears and two nights worth of nightmares starring a family sitting around the supper table, clubbing and gnawing on blood-slinging, defenseless little pink-eyed bunnies. Her papa was kind enough to give her the pelt though, and they had a little funeral for it.

Pearl told everbody they knew that Lootie belonged to Roach's non-existent brother and his non-existent wife that lived up north. The brother had come on real hard times so they might have the poor little thing for quite a while. Maybe even for good. Pearl didn't give it much thought that by telling such a whopper she was putting herself in danger of Hell fire. If she had to go around God to find her own baby to love and God didn't like it, He could take a walk!

She learned the hard way not to show her around too much because of folks' reaction to the scars and the blind eye. Early on, she'd made the mistake of telling a couple of women friends that Lootie'd been struck by lightning, but that spooked people where superstition was a hefty part of daily life. A halo around the moon, a bat in the house, or giggin' a two-headed frog were sure signs of nasty doin's, but they were nothin' compared to a lightnin'-struck baby. Over back fences and around supper tables, talk was that it wouldn'ta been the Good Lord that would strike a baby with lightning, and even if it had been, He surely woulda taken it to Heaven rather than to leave it to suffer. The verdict of the majority was passed down—the little Komes girl was marked, and by a lot more than a scar.

***

Pearl took sick in Lootie's eighth year. It started with a nagging cough that turned into a wet, blood-tinged gagger. Then came the fevers that put her in bed, at first just for a couple of days at a time, but later, weeks. Then she couldn't get out of bed a'tall. Listening to her breathe made one feel they needed to clear the phlegm from their own throat. Lootie took to feedin' her, sittin' on a stool alongside the bed, spooning broth in her, talkin' to her and makin' up little stories that always had a happy ending. She cleaned her up when nature called because Pearl either couldn't get up quick enough to go outside, or, as time went on, she was just too weak and there wasn't anything to do but let it go. She had bedsores all over her backside and her chest was just a ladder of bones stickin' out and her poor ol' titties looked like a couple of worn out socks with nothin' in 'em, hangin' off on her sides.

Pearl knew what was happening and it scared her, but not so much the dying—she was more concerned with what would happen to Lootie if she wasn't there to look out for her. Roach was totally worthless and couldn't look out for hisself, how could he possibly take care of Lootie. She'd had so many plans for her. For a better life than she'd had, for damn sure. She hated hers; it'd been valueless and empty. Except for Lootie. Lootie made her entire existence worthwhile.

Pearl had taught Lootie how to pray. To make it simple, she told her it was kinda like writing a letter, and you started it with "Dear God." She said if Lootie needed something bad enough, God would answer her prayers, but she couldn't ask for something like a new kitty or a fancy dress—it had to be for something special. She told her that God was like a father, and like any good father, he wanted his children to be strong and to try to stand on their own, but if things got really bad, they could ask for help. Then she told her how many times she'd tried to have a child and she thought it wasn't never gonna happen. But, she kept praying, "And what happened?" she asked Lootie.

Lootie smiled. "I got borned."

In the last couple of months, Lootie had prayed, day and night. Letter after letter floated up to Heaven. "Dear God. This is Lootie Komes. I'm awful scared. Please make my Mama better. Her name's Pearl 'n she's th'best Mama in th'world. She ain't never done nothin' wrong 'n even if she did, she didn't mean it. Please God. Make 'er better." And with ever letter sent off, she'd run in the house to see if Pearl'd jumped off the bed. She hadn't.

Roach was sending letters to Heaven, too, but his concern wasn't for Pearl. His went no futher than his own hide. He was bad scared. He depended so much on her he couldn't imagine goin' on without her pullin' her share of the load, which had always been pretty much the whole load. Roach declared war and elected presidents, but he'd never cooked a meal or washed out a pair of socks in his life.

One morning he woke Lootie up just before sunup and told her, "I'm gonna see somebody 'bout med'cine fer Pearl." Then he nodded over his shoulder. "I fixed up some biscuits 'n greens. They oughta hold you 'n yer ma 'til I get back. Probly 'bout sundown."

Lootie rubbed the sleep out of her eyes and looked toward the stove. "You cooked somethin'?"

He knew what that meant. "It ain't that bad!" Her face told him somethin' else. "It's that 'r starve." He slapped his sweat-stained hat on his head and left. Lootie rolled over and went back to sleep.

Roach's destination was way back in the swamp to where there was rumored to be a witch who could conjure potions and such, and he detected wood smoke tinged with bacon and eggs two miles before he got to her. His stomach was growlin', and he wondered if maybe she'd ask him to breakfast when she found out how far he'd trekked to get to her. Finally, he spied it through the thinning trees—a rundown, lopsided shack with a slow smoky curl snakin' out the top of the rock chimney.

The skinny old crone was perched on a tree stump just outside the door in the shade of the porch overhang. She had a corncob pipe stickin' out the corner of her mouth and she was bent over, kinda, readin' a book with a busted spine. She wore a dress as shapeless as an old sock and a color that could only be described as disappointed. She had a floppy-brimmed hat on her head that shaded most of her face. Her hair hung over her shoulders and down her back like a greasy old mop. Settin' at her feet was a monstrous thing that had originally been a bristly-coated, Russian Wolfhound, gnawin' contentedly on a bone. Time and circumstance had ground and battered it into somethin' mean, hateful, and cunning. When Roach stepped into the clearing, it raised its head. The scarred old nose sipped the air while its head roamed slowly back and forth like it was havin' trouble seein' him—the lids hung down, pouch-like, like an ol' alky's. It was minus the left front leg clear up to the shoulder. One ear and its top lip had been ripped off the side of its face, revealing a row of long, dry yellow teeth. Its squarish muzzle was peppered with graying hair, and the creature constantly slobbered from the gap in its ruined maw. Finally, the head weavin' stopped and those blood red eyes stared straight at Roach. It growled low and deep.

Roach stopped at what he considered, or at least hoped, was a safe distance. "G'mornin'," he said, nervously, with an equally nervous smile. Then he remembered his manners, jerked his hat off his head, and wrung it in his hands.

She lifted her head, slowly, exposing eyes that looked like black glass.

He waited for a "Good Mornin'" back, didn't get one, and finally told her, "You're Cob."

She waited a second, never takin' her eyes off him, and then croaked, "I awready know that. You want somethin' or 'dju traipse alla way outcheer just t'sell me some eggs?"

He took two jerky steps closer but stopped when poochie's remaining lip curled up. He reclaimed his steps. Then he heard a phlegmy cackle as the woman closed the book, leaned down, and softly petted the monster on the top of its scab-encrusted head. "No, les be patient. See wat it wants first."

The animal looked Roach over then went back to workin' the bone.

"I heard I might could get somethin' from you fer my wife. She's real sick."

"A rec'mendation," the hag said, nodding. "Well, well, 'at's nice, ain't it. From a satisfied customah, was it?" She cut loose with another phlegmy cackle, hocked and spat, then dropped the friendly façade. "Wat's 'er symptoms?"

"She's lost a lot o' weight. Lots o' trouble breathin', cain't hold much o' nothin' down. Coughs a whole lot. Got th'shits."

Cob leaned for'ard and casually passed a death sentence. "She got th'tissick. Don't know 'bout th'shits, though. Might just be th'shits."

"I's told that, 'bout the tissick, but nobody knows what t'do 'bout it. I's hopin' you c'd help." He continued wringin' his hat in his bony hands and kept a wary eye on the dog, which was still eye-locked on him like he was o' slab a somethin' tasty and it was just waitin' for the signal to pounce.

The old woman took another couple of thinkin' sucks on the pipe, snorted up another slug, and spat. She hadn't leaned over far enough or given it enough push. Some of it ended up on her chin and the rest on her dress. She wiped her chin with the back of her hand and then it on the dress. "I got th'cure, fer sure, if you ain't awready waited too long."

"I's told you's a body could do just about anything," Roach said with a mite more cocky than he actually felt. "Maybe I's tol' wrong."

She gave him a look and hissed, "You take off yer ol' hat but ya ain't got no more mannahs'n t'stand way off outchonder, makin' me yell, not showin' no respek, but come scratchin' 'round, jerkin yer doodle 'n beggin' favohs."

Roach was at a loss with a comeback because he didn't want to make her or the dog mad.

"I doubt you got 'nough t'pay me t'work mir'cles nohow," she said with a dismissive wave, "'n a mir'cle's probly what it'd take. Ten dollahs 'n three bottles o' good whiskey 'n I'll give ya th'cure fer the tissick. But...," she jabbed a lethal-lookin' finger in his direction, "you betta b'lieve I know th'dif'ence 'tween good whiskey 'n bad."

Roach shuffled his feet like a kid that had to take a pee. "I ain't got ten dollahs 'n I ain't got one bottle o' whiskey, good 'r bad, let alone three, 'n I don't know nobody that'd go 'em for me."

"What 'bout a book? Got any books?"

"Books?"

"You do know what a book is, doncha?"

"Yes," he said, haughty, "I know what books is. We got a McGuffey Reader 'n a Bible."

"Awready got th'one 'n don't want tother. No Mock Twain or Shakespeah?" The look of mass confusion on his face told her everthing she needed to know. "Aw, f'get it." A low growl gurgled up the dog's throat and the old woman kicked it in the rump. "I tolju t'wait!" The cur whuffed and lowered its massive head to rest on the knobbly end o' the bone. She gave a couple more thoughtful pulls on the pipe. "'At's awright...'at's awright, although I p'fer th'money 'n th'likkah, maybe we c'd work somethin' else out. Watcha got we c'd bahtah ovah?"

"I ain't got nothin'. All they is's me, th'wife, 'n a youngun, a girl. Times's been hard...real hard. I's thinkin' maybe this one time you c'd give it to me out o' th'goodness o' yer heart or maybe I c'd work it off somehow."

The witch nearly fell off the stump, laughing. "I traded off m'hawt f'a sack o' p'tatas long'go. They cooked up real good with some onions 'n a lib'ral pinch o' peppah." She finally stopped laughing, wiped her teared-up eyes, and, sucking on the pipe, looked him over, severely. In fact, she looked at him for so long, he didn't know if the interview was over or what, but, finally, "Tell me 'bout th'girl. She ain'tchur daughtah?"

"No," he said, wringin' his hands, "she's m'niece, m'brother's child. We had 'er so long now, though, she thinks we're 'er Ma 'n Pa. Me 'n th'wife's takin' care of 'er 'til they get back on thr'feet. They's had hard times."

"Seems t'run in th'family, don'it...hawd times." She took a pull on the pipe and asked, "Wat's yr'brotha's name?"

Roach's eyes rolled through the back of his head lookin' for somethin' and then spat out, "Frank."

She looked him over, then, quietly, threateningly, "No it ain't! You ain't got no brothah. You a lyin' sack o' shit, 'n I don't take kindly t' bein' lied to, 'specially comin' 'round with yer hand out, beggin'.'" Roach started to say somethin' but she cut him off. "'At child ain't no blood o' yourn or yr'wife's. Noooo...'n futhamoah, 'at woman's notcho wife. Now...," then, looking like she was soooo proud of herself, "watchu think o' that?"

Poochie growled again. From the way Cob was talkin', it hoped she'd finally had enough of the blowhard, and pretty quick he'd get a crack at him. It had no doubt its three legs could outrun his two.

"You don't know nothin' o' th'sort," Roach told her, puffin' up and puttin' on a show. "Yer just guessin', 'n I reckon I'll go now," and while shivers crawled up his spine, he turned to leave. Putting the hound to his back was probably the bravest thing he'd ever done, but his ragged nerves were payin' for it. Had the beast barked right then he woulda packed his drawers with the hot and steamy and turned into a pillar of salt.

Before he took his fourth step, she called after him. "Somethin's wrong...with'at child. Wat is it?"

With fresh shivers up his spine...—*Lord, I hate witches!*—'n he turned.

She'd dropped her face to hide behind the hat brim.

"What'd make you think anything's wrong with 'er?" he demanded, trying his best to sound indignant. He wished he could see her face. As much as those black eyes made him nervous, not seein' 'em made him even more so.

Cob sucked on the pipe and waited him out. Finally he got flustered enough and said, "She's struck by lightnin' 'fore she 'scaped th'womb 'n she's blind in one eye, but other'n 'at, they ain't a good...God... Dang...THING wrong with 'er. She's a good girl, but I don't know where 'at's any o' yer business!"

The dog started to rise. Cob put out her hand, and it settled back with one last low, growly, frustrated threat.

"Who's th'chile's muthah?" she asked. It sounded like a casual question but it was actually much, much more than idle curiosity.

"Little albino girl, kilt by th'same lightnin' strike. Why?"

Cob's heart pounded wildly but she hid it well, her face concealed under the hat brim. "If you 'n I c'n strike a deal," she told him, calmly, "you come back in two days 'n I'll give ya th'med'cine."

"I don't know if th'wife's got two days," he said, picturing what Pearl'd looked like when he left.

"If she ain't got two days left in 'er...even I cain't hep 'er." Then she lifted her head just enough to make eye contact, "But, until she crosses ovah, there's a chance...." She trailed off, shrugging her bony shoulders.

"You'd give it to me?" he asked, suspiciously, noting the change in her tone, "'n what kind o' deal? I awready tolja, I ain't got no money 'n no whiskey 'n no likely way t'get 'em."

"Come back in two days...'n bring the girl with ya."

"The girl? Why'd I do that?"

"If you ain't no mo' int'rested in gettin' th'med'cine'n t'make me yell alla way 'cross th'yawd, you c'n leave. But...if yoah intrested in workin' somethin' out, praps somethin' ben'ficial t'us both...praps.... come closah 'n I'll tell ya how."

Roach blinked, swallowed hard, and looked at the distorted lump at her feet.

She noticed and jabbed the dog's rear with her big toe. "Git!"

With the deformed mouth, the cur always looked like it was snarling, and Roach was sure, because of the way the thing looked at him, that its having to go to the trouble of getting up was Roach's fault, it'd remember the intrusion...and it had a long memory. The monster chomped on the bone, picked it up, and hop-stepped hop-stepped hop-stepped off what it musta felt was distance enough, and with a laborious whump, plopped back on the dusty ground.

Warily, keepin' his eye on the nasty lookin' thing, Roach moved closer...

...and the witch made him an offer.

CHAPTER 7

After kickin' around all the why-he-shoulds and why-he-shouldn'ts about going back to the witch, Roach drug hisself out of bed and, by the feeble light of the coal oil lamp, fixed a bite to eat. After washin' it down he wished he hadn't. He worried more about Pearl's condition ever time he fixed his own eats. Ever time he had to put on the same dirty pants. Ever time he had to traipse to the crick for a bucket of water. He stepped to Lootie's little cot, pinched her big toe pushing up from her one thin blanket, and shook it. "Lootie, get up, but keep quiet, don't wake yer mama."

Lootie mumbled something, sat up, bed-headed and groggy, knuckled her sleepy eyes, and looked out the window. "It's still dark!"

"I know that. We gotta start early if we wanna beat th'heat." He pushed her on the shoulder. "Get up. We got a long way t'go."

She yawned, dropped her chin to her chest for just a second....

"Hey!" Roach snapped the back of his hand on her shoulder. "Don't go back t'sleep!"

The shack was cold. Lootie scratched her head, crawled off the cot, pulled her nightgown up over her head, tossed it on the cot, picked up her dress, and shivered while she pulled it over her head and down. She wheeled around and sat down with her eyes closed, still half asleep, and put her socks and shoes on.

Roach bent over Pearl's bed to check on her. He wouldn't touch her, though. The day before she'd wheezed like her throat was squoze nearly shut, fightin' for ever breath. Right at that minute, she musta been doin' better because she wasn't wheezin'. He thought about rousin' her up to let her know they were leavin' but that woulda meant touchin' her. He justified passin' on it, convincing hisself she needed the sleep. It didn't take much convincing. He'd even gone to sleepin' on a makeshift palette on the floor. He couldn't stand the thought of wakin' up to find she'd passed in the night while layin' next to him. The physical discomfort of the floor wasn't nearly as great as the thought of layin' next to a flat-eyed, slack-jawed corpse all night. He stirred up the near-dead embers in the pot-bellied stove and put on a couple more little sticks. He closed the stove door and saw Lootie was dressed, her chin resting on her chest.

"Hey!" he whispered harshly.

"Huh?" Her head snapped up.

"You ready?"

"For what?" she said through a yawn. Then, "I'm hongry."

"Quiet down. We ain't got th'time now. We'll eat later on."

Scratching her head, she looked at the stove and noticed the pan he'd fixed his eggs. "You et. How come I can't?"

"I thought I's bein' good lettin' ya sleep 'n then ya try t'make me feel bad for it. I'm sorry, maybe I shoulda woke y'up, but we ain't got the time now. You'll eat later at th'nice lady's house. She's fixin' somethin' good. Come on now, let's go!" He pushed her to get up and then out the door into the dew-dripping morning.

All Lootie had on was her thin little dress, underpants, holey socks, and worn-out shoes. She noticed Roach was all bundled up tight in a coat buttoned nearly to his neck with the collar turned up and his hands in the pockets. "I'm cold," she said, crossing her stick-thin arms to her chest and scrunchin' up.

"Walk faster. That'll getcha goin'."

Cob had also been up since before daybreak, making preparations for the big doin's. For one thing, she had some baking to do. It was gonna be a busy day, and she'd brewed a cup of strong, dark tea to help get her sluggish blood pushin' through her veins. She was sittin' on a three-legged stool lookin' out the shack's one greasy, wiggly-paned window, one leg over the other, nervously wagglin' her ugly foot.

There were shelves on the walls with various sized bottles and jars. Some of 'em had seeds, and others, beans. Gnarled, rooty lookin' stuff. Critter innards. One had a two-headed terrapin. It looked spooky. That was the intent. She even had a cracked crystal ball stuck in a box somers. It was all foofoo, circus sideshow stuff, meant to impress the easily impressed. Of all her possessions, though, her favorites were the well-worn books stacked up in the corner; thirty-five, maybe forty of 'em, and when business was slow, which was mostly what it was, they helped pass the time.

She took a sip from the chipped china cup and looked over her shoulder. She already had one visitor layin' in bed and was expectin' six more before long. Two of 'em bein' the jittery fella who'd come sneakin' around, tail-tucked and ears down, and the little girl he'd promised to bring with him. All her thoughts had been on that little girl. Cob wasn't motherly. In fact, she didn't like children a'tall—too noisy and too needy—but she was lookin' for'ard to seein' this'n. She took another sip and looked out the dirty window, thinkin' the nubbly-faced fool claimin' t' be her father was far too simpleminded to make up the stories he'd told. Other than the one about the child belonging to a brother goin' through hard times. She saw through that one as easy as the sun through a lace curtain.

But the one about the child bein' cut from the fresh-dead womb of a lightnin'-struck mother. Better yet, an albino mother. She knew all about her. The one they called Smoke. It all added up. The lightnin' that killed her mother shoulda killed her. But it hadn't. Then there was the blind eye. The left. Not the right. Yeah, it all added up, and no, the ignorant blowhard hadn't the knowledge or the imagination to concoct somethin' like that. He had no idea what he had.

Cob smiled. She was lookin' for'ard to this day like she hadn't in a long time. She, bein' a witch herself, was a rarity and was lookin' for'ard to meetin' a kindred spirit. Then she chuckled at the thought of considering herself a kindred spirit. To that one? Not hardly. No, she had to be honest with herself. She'd spent a lifetime developing her talents, feeble as they were. Her bloodline had been severely watered down over the generations. That's why she had to practice on the fringe. But, if the child was who...what she believed her to be....

She swallowed hard and waggled her foot, imagining. Slowly, another idea was takin' shape. She looked in the cup and swirled around what little dark tea remained. The corners of her mouth rose and she started laughin' so hard the tears coursed down the gullies of her wrinkled old face. Then she remembered her slumbering guest and looked over her shoulder, hopin' she hadn't disturbed her, but other than the faint rise and fall of her sunken chest, she hadn't moved. She doubted there was anything left there more than the body. No, there'd be no more sunrises for that one.

Her eyes rolled over the shelf and stopped at one of the small, seed-filled vials. She set the cup on the floor, reached up and pulled the little bottle off the shelf, twisted the cork stopper off, and shook the seeds out on the floor. Then she leaned over and picked up her tea cup.

CHAPTER 8

Without going into any great detail—in fact, deliberately leaving out most of it—Roach told Lootie the day before where they were going and about the nice old woman…

"Her name's Cob. Ain't that a funny name?"

…who was gonna give 'em the medicine that could make Pearl all better, but the old woman had somethin' she wanted Lootie to do first. She had somebody who needed help, another nice old lady who was feelin' low, and Lootie could help the poor thing, and if she did, they'd get the medicine for free. Lootie asked him what it was she wanted her to do. Roach cooked up a whopper about how the old woman's children hadn't come to see her, even with her bein' so sick and all. How she'd cared for 'em all the years they were young, but it didn't make any difference now that they were grown up and moved off. She was sick and lonely. She might not even get better, it might well be the end. It was one of the saddest things Lootie'd ever heard. She thought for sure everybody loved their mamas like she loved hers. It woulda been a pretty good piece of fiction, except that Roach'd dragged it up out of his own conscience. He'd done his mother thata way, and even heartless, didn't-care-for-nobody-else Roach Komes felt guilty about not bein' with her when her time come, and maybe, although through somebody else, namely Lootie, he could come clean…kinda. Sorta. Somethin' akin to gettin' into Heaven, taggin' along on somebody else's good deeds.

He told Lootie the old lady'd heard what a nice little girl she was and she wanted to meet her. She was bakin' a fresh loaf of bread she wanted to share with her, and after she'd eaten it, Cob would give 'em Pearl's medicine.

Lootie asked him how somebody she never met knew she was a nice girl, but after a left-handed baring of his soul—and bereft of the intelligence to cook up something remotely logical—Roach told her, "Don't ask silly questions, she jes does, don't worry 'bout it!"

What was making Lootie more nervous than anything was how nice Roach was being to her.

It was just before noon when they reached the witch's shack. The day had warmed considerably, and the humidity was so high they looked like they'd just clumb out of the crick. Roach had taken his coat off and draped it over his arm. His shirt was soaked and Lootie's hair was plastered to her head like a stringy helmet.

The witch was outside the shack in the shade of the little porch overhang, bare-footed, sittin' on the tree stump with one leg over the other, suckin' on the pipe. Because of the heat, she'd pulled the raggedy hem of her long black dress above her knees and Roach noticed how ugly her legs were, especially her feet. Long and bony, and— except for the coarse, dark hair—they looked like a frog's.

The Devil Dog was curled up at her feet mouthing another bone. A thinner one than before. It was a leg bone, but it wasn't one Roach was familiar with. He knew cow bones; it wasn't that big. Sheep, hog, and goat, too, but it was bigger than them. Then he sucked in a lungful; he knew what it was. He looked in the mongrel's eyes and a low, slow growl clawed up its throat.

The witch raised her head, and Lootie was unnerved by the old woman's face, mostly veiled in the shadow of the wide, floppy-brimmed hat. She only had two teeth Lootie could see. Her face and hands were more gray-white than regular hand colored, and her eyes were black as pitch. It frightened her how it seemed that eyes she couldn't look into at all seemed to be lookin' clean through her. The only other times Lootie'd ever felt that naked was when she didn't have any clothes on. Blood was thumpin' through her heart, and her head but felt like it'd dried and caked up everwhere else.

The witch toed the dog in the rump, "Git!" Reluctantly, it picked up the bone and hobbled off.

When the old woman turned her attention back to Lootie, she felt like she'd been squeezed around the throat, gasped, and grabbed Roach's pant leg.

"Now don't be like 'at," he told her. "This's th'nice lady I's tellin' y'bout. The one with the med'cine that'll make yer Mama all better." He dug his fingers into Lootie's shoulders and turned her to face the witch. "This's my little girl, Lootie."

The old woman took a long time to look her over, like she was a mule at auction, and the whole time, Lootie was tryin' to get her breath. The old woman's bottomless black eyes roamed over the scar, followed it up into Lootie's scalp and then back down to her one good eye. The choking feeling stopped the instant the old thing faked a smile. "G'monin', little sistah," she crooned, hoarsely. "My name's Cob."

Lootie swallowed and blinked. "How do, ma'am. I ain't got no sistah."

Cob rocked back, slapped her bony knee, and cackled hard. "No," she said, hawked up a gob and spit it on the ground, "notchet." She laughed again. "Ain't she jes th'most precious thang evah was?" She cocked her head toward the shack door. "Didjer..." she glanced at Roach, "...yer Papa. Did he tell ya I had a lady friend inside wantin' t'meetchew?"

Lootie nodded, cautiously.

"You'll like 'er, mm-hmm, yesssssss, yes, she's a nice lady, but feelin' a mite pohly of late, 'n yer Daddy 'n me, we thought mebbe a little girl bein' nice to 'er'd make 'er feel so much bettah."

"Did 'er children come t'see 'er yet?" Lootie asked, innocently.

Cob and Roach locked eyes. Roach could always think 'em up, but had no talent at follow-through. Thank God, Cob could think faster than he and put two and two together. "No, dahlin, notchet, poah ol' thang. Don't 'at beat all? But we'a still hopin'." Then she put her elbows on her knees and leaned for'ard, her eyes piercing into Lootie's like needles. "I betchew got up early this monin', dincha ya? Had a long trek? I betchur hongry, too. You ain't had nothin' t'eat this monin', have ya?"

"She ain't had nothin'," Roach jumped in. "Nothin' since yestedee. Not a crumb."

"Is 'at right, you ain't had nothin' t'eat?"

"Yes, ma'am, I mean, no, ma'am," Lootie replied, politely. "I ain't."

"Yes, ma'am," Cob said, convinced. "Such mannahs. Yes, well, 'at's a long time for a little'n t'go 'thout eatin' somethin', ain't it?" She gestured over her shoulder. "Th'lady inside's fixed somethin' special, jes f'you." She pushed her flat ass off the stump, stepped to the edge o' the porch, and helt out a knuckly hand. "Why donchew come inside with me now 'n I'll inaduce ya, then we c'n eat, awright?"

Lootie still had a deathgrip on Roach's pant leg.

"Dahlin', I thoughtchu said you hadn't et. If ya ain't, you mus' be hongry. You'd like somethin' t'eat, wuncha?"

Roach nudged Lootie from the back.

"Yes, ma'am," she said.

"Yes, ma'am, no, ma'am," Cob cackled. "Ain't 'at jes th'sweetest. I c'd jes hug you in half."

Roach felt Lootie press into him when Cob again approached with her hand helt out, scared to death the old woman was gonna try to hug her in half. Lootie just looked at her hand. "Lootie!" Roach said, and gave her a sharp nudge.

Lootie took Cob's hand, shocked and appalled by the cold, clammy, waxey touch. Cob led the way to the door. Roach started to follow but Cob turned her black orbs on him. "You'll wait outchere."

Catching Roach's reaction, Lootie started to balk. "I want my daddy t'come with me."

"I blieve it might be bettah if I went in with 'er," Roach said, while a nervous smile twitched his face, "If it's awright."

"It ain't," Cob said, leaving no doubt. "I b'lieve...it'd be bettah...if you's t'wait. Outchere."

Roach gave it half a moment's thought while the witch gave him the evil eye, and, finally, he got down on one knee in front of Lootie. "It's awright. You go on in with Cob 'n I'll be right out here, and after you meet th'othah lady 'n eat a bite...." He looked up at Cob like maybe he was reconsidering their agreement. But then, steeling his resolve, "You have a bite...then we'll take th'med'cine 'n go back home."

Lootie was more scared than she'd ever been in her short little life. There was somethin' about Cob, besides the obvious, and whoever, or whatever it was in the shack, that made her head itch.

Roach clenched his jaw. "Lootie! Listen t'me! If you don't do what th'lady wants, we don't get th'med'cine, and Pearl needs it...bad."

Lootie's love for her mother and the need for the medicine was stronger than her fear of the unknown, and so, without taking her tear-laden eyes off Roach, allowed Cob to pull her through the door and into the dark recesses of the shack. From just inside the door, she watched Roach wringing his hat in his hand.

"I'll be right heah."

He waved, Lootie thought, like he was wavin' goodbye, and the door closed.

CHAPTER 9

The door latch clicked, and the Hound from Hell took it as an invitation to pick up the bone and take up his duties back at the door. Roach saw it hop-stepping his way so he thought he might like to go somers else to wait and moved off to the shade of a tree a good thirty yards from the front door. Devil Doggie got to the very spot Roach had vacated and whumphed onto the dusty ground. Roach looked at the hateful thing and thought for sure the animal's earlier surly sneer was now more a kind of a smile.

Cob tugged Lootie through the shack. Because her eyes hadn't yet adjusted to the darkness, Lootie couldn't see the candles themselves, just the flames of the dozen or so set about the room. They looked like they's floating. Neither did it register to her that they'd all bent toward her, like compass needles, the second she came through the door. Cob had, though, and wondered: were they bending...or bowing? It was just one more proof of Lootie's dark royalty.

Slowly, her eyes adjusting, Lootie saw that the only other light was what knifed in through the loose, splintery skeleton of weathered, hand-hewn planks poorly passing for walls. The hovel was so decrepit it looked like the dust-ladened cobwebs in the corners were helpin' hold it together. Besides the dark, there were unfamiliar smells. Thick, smoke smells. They weren't like the smoke at home from the wood stove, though, but stronger, and they burned her eyes, her nose, and her throat. She swept her free hand from side to side like a blind man with a stick to keep from bumpin' into somethin' while Cob hauled her through the shack. They came to a stop when Lootie's shins banged into somethin'. Instinctively, she put her hand down to keep from fallin' over, but jerked it back when she touched somethin' cold. Somethin' not wood, or metal, or glass.

She found herself at the foot of a narrow cot just off the floor. She knew she was comin' to see some sickly somebody, but she didn't know she was gonna be accompanied by four other age-ravaged, toothless old biddies sittin' on rickety little chairs alongside the cot, two to a side, all dressed in black shawls draped over their scarce-haired skulls. They were all cocked away, lookin' at her like she was a double-headed, stubby-legged fetus floatin' in a jar in a carnival freak show. Lootie wondered if they might be family members. Cob said the lady's kids hadn't showed yet, so maybe they were her sisters or cousins, or even friends.

She couldn't tell what they were sayin', but they were quietly mumblin' to theirselves, and as her eyes got more used to the dark, she saw they were fiddlin' with somethin'—necklaces with little crosses on 'em. The necklaces looked like they were made up of black beans.

Cob took one of the candles from a shelf and brought it in front of Lootie's face, clamped her fingers onto Lootie's chin and turned her head this way and that. The old women moved their faces all around to get a good gawk. Lootie didn't know Cob was givin' 'em the opportunity to peruse the scars and the blind eye she'd told 'em so much about. The desiccated old lizards, who'd never laid eyes on Lootie, knew far more about her than she knew about herself.

After starin' and weighin' for a few seconds, they looked at each other, then, as if coming to a mutual agreement, turned their creaky, turkey-wattled necks to Cob and nodded. Cob smiled and nodded back, like she was relieved. She let go of Lootie's chin and put the candle back on the shelf.

Lootie's eyes were finally used to the dark, and she saw, layin' on the cot, the purpose for this strange gathering. The lady's eyes and cheeks were sunk way down in the skull that seemed to be shielded by no more than a thin layer of parchment. She was laid straight out, her head on a little pillow, her emaciated, meatless arms straight down to her sides. Her hands were horribly twisted, like tree roots, all knuckles and joints. She had a kind of rag looped from the top of her head, down to and tied under her chin. Her flappy cheeks puffed in and out as she pulled in hard-fought breath.

Lookin' down her body, it hit Lootie that the cold thing she'd touched with her hand had been the old thing's bare foot. Although she couldn't tell what color it was—black, blue, or purple—she could see it was much darker than the rest of her leg. The hem of the dress they had her in only went down to just below her knee. Knee. As in singular. Her other leg was gone.

If this was the lady Cob had been talkin' about, there wasn't any way she was gonna know Lootie was there, let alone eat with her. The poor old hag had the death rattles and the room was filled with the rancid, musty smell of a body takin' a long time to die, yet had wait only moments to live.

It was when Lootie's eyes worked their way back up the old woman's body that she noticed the little loaf of bread, the size of a muffin, restin' on the wretch's slatted chest, risin' and lowerin' with each wheezie breath. It was the wheezin' that made Lootie look at the old woman's face. She almost took a step back. Somebody'd already placed pennies on her eyes. Pearl'd told Lootie about the pennies. How they were put on the eyes of the dead. How they were payment for the ferryman to take the souls across The River. But it was frightening to see 'em on one who wasn't yet dead.

Lootie jumped when Cob nudged her toward the old woman, and the two women on the closest side of the cot stood up and moved off a little to give her room. She felt Cob's hand at her back, pushing.

"Eat th'bread, Lootie," she said, her voice catchin'.

Lootie helt back. "No, thankee, Ma'am, I ain't hongry no more."

The Old Testament priests made sacrificial offerings to God, a God of Abstinence, using the unblemished calf, kid goat, or lamb as payment of a sort for the forgiveness of sins; and any sign of a blemish, an affront, was punishable by an instant, fiery death.

There was another world, ruled by another Supreme Being, some say lesser than God, but they'd be sorely in error. He was a God of Indulgence and went by many names. Beelzebub. Scratch. Lucifer. Satan. For the forgiveness of sins in His domain, there was also the requirement of a sacrifice. One blemished. When Cob learned that

Lootie'd been struck and marked by lightnin' while still in the albino's womb, it was all she could do to maintain control.

Like the Christians watching for the return of The Messiah and the Plains Indians for the White Buffalo, Cob and her ilk waited for the likes of a Lootie Komes. Cob had been paid exceptional money — twenty times the going rate — for today's holy, but unholy, ritual. The oathing and chanting of the spells had all been baked into the bitter bread, and the recipient, the sacrifice, the blemished...

—The Sin Eater—

...was, at that very moment, standing alongside the bed in the guise of an innocent little girl.

CHAPTER 10

Cob'd lied. The old woman's children had come to see her, and it was they who surrounded her now. That putrid, vile old bitch on the cot was their hated mother and that putrid, wiry-haired slash below her belly had been their entrance into sixty years, give or take, of Hell on Earth. She wasn't somebody they loved, honored, respected, admired, or revered, but one they hated hated hated and were deathly in fear of. Their lives had been soaked and saturated with the physical and psychological tortures lovingly and joyously administered by the dried out husk laid out between 'em.

They continued to carry her surname because no man would have 'em. All four had a different father, and all four men had died horrible deaths, their need over and done, before their daughters had taken their first breath. The first died of a broken neck, falling in a well. The second screamed to death in a barn fire. The third, supposedly trampled by a horse, and the fourth…well, he'd merely disappeared. When the old woman was dead, her remains would be hacked and burned, the bones pulverized to dust and spread to the four corners.

So why all the effort to ensure she went to Heaven instead of a more just sentence to an eternal, fiery Hell? Because of the belief that the Hellish could be conjured, revived, even from death.

Her imprisonment behind the Pearly Gates was worth the weighty cost of an innocent's soul.

When Lootie said, "No, thankee, Ma'am, I ain't hongry no more," the old women had gasped, clutched their bean necklaces and looked to Cob. *Do something!* was etched on their faces. After being sanctified and placed on the old woman's chest, the bread couldn't even be touched by anyone other than the one sacrificed or it lost its power. Lootie had to take the bread and eat it herself.

Cob knew they were at a crossroads. There was one alternate course she could take, but she would much rather not. If Lootie failed to eat the bread, Cob would kill her, right there, right then, and use ever precious drop of her blood and various body parts for future spells and curses. She was worth far more alive, but if Cob had to....

She took Lootie by the shoulders and jerked her around with no pretense of niceness. "No! They ain't no 'No, thankee, Ma'am, I ain't hongry n'more!' You will eat th'bread. We went t'all th'trouble o' bakin' it jes f'you. All we want is f'you t'eat one bite. 'At's all! One bite!" When Lootie hesitated, Cob pinched her chin, jerked her face up to hers, looked deep in Lootie's eyes, threateningly, and warned, "If you don't eat it, they won't be any med'cine f'yer poah, sick mothah 'n if not gettin' it's th'cause of 'er death, you hafta live with 'at all th'rest o' yer days." She reached over to a shelf, snatched up the small, corked vial, and helt it out to show Lootie. "This is it!" Lootie watched her set it back on the shelf. Cob chinned to the bread. "Pick it up, Lootie. You don't hafta eat all of it. One bite'll be enough. It was baked f'you! You hafta pick it up 'n you alone hafta eat it."

Lootie looked at the vial one more time, then edged to the old lady's side and cautiously reached for the loaf. The last thing she wanted was to accidentally touch the old woman. Lifting the hard-crusted loaf, she brought it to her mouth, and as she did, she noticed that, depending on which one she looked at, the four old crones were either holdin' their breath or breathin' like they'd been runnin' up a hill. They gaped at her like she was a bug in a jar, crossed theirselves, pinchin' and fingerin' the bean necklaces with the little crosses.

Lootie opened her mouth and raked her upper teeth over the bread's hard corner and broke off a piece. She started to chew.

Immediately, a coldness swept through the room, clenching teeth and turning expelled breath to a foggy vapor.

The one-legged sack of bones on the cot gasped and gurgled.

The four old ladies pulled their scrawny arms under their shawls, and lookin' from one to the other, wrapped them tightly around their shoulders.

The last breath slowly bubbled from the old woman's withered, pulpy lungs.

Cob looked around the room and at the walls that were growin' a ghostly crop of hoarfrost like mold on an old peach. She turned her attention to the dirty window when she heard it crackin' and watched it freeze over from the outside in, shuttin' out even more light than what little there'd already been. Then the door creaked like a bone bein' twisted. This was more than she'd been expecting. The feeling invading the room reeked of evil. And more...the absence of life. Eternal nothingness. Any happiness or peace embedded in their souls leached out.

Then it hit Lootie, the saltiest, most bitter anything she'd ever tasted. She scrunched up her face, bent over, and started to spit.

"NO!" Cob demanded, and quicker than a snake, grabbed the hair at the back of Lootie's head with one cold hand and clapped the other over her mouth. "EAT IT!"

Lootie tried to peel Cob's hand from her mouth, but Cob flailed her around like a rag doll. Hot yellow urine dribbled down Lootie's leg and splattered, hissing, on the cold floor, creating the only warmth in the room—a swirling, lip-curling steaminess.

"EAT IT, DAMN YOU!" Cob demanded, takin' a second to look at the steam, considering the unknown, but possible, ramifications of breathing it in. "Don'tchu dare spit it out!"

Being jerked so violently, Lootie dropped the rest of the loaf on the floor, and the hags gasped, clenchin' their fisted hands around their shawls, their breath comin' in quick little puffs. That was it! If Lootie spit it out, it was all for naught. The remainder of the loaf hittin' the floor had ruined it, and there was no time left for Cob to either bake another or find another sacrifice. And never, as long as she lived, one as unique as Lootie Komes.

Having no other choice with Cob's cold hand clamped over her face, Lootie swallowed.

"Swaller it!" Cob demanded, venomously. Lootie tried to nod, to let her know she had. Having felt the movement, Cob removed her hand, then jerked Lootie's face to hers. "Ju swaller it?" She knew she had, though. The room'd already started to get warmer—the ice on the window was receding from the center out. Fright-induced tears ran down Lootie's cheeks. Cob grabbed her by the ears, yanked her face even closer, and yelled, "Answer me! Ju swaller it?"

"Yes," Lootie said.

Cob wrenched Lootie's head back and ordered her, "Open yer mouth!" Warmer or not, she wasn't gonna take any chances. When Lootie didn't comply, Cob slapped her on the face four or five times. "Open! Open! Open!"

Shocked, Lootie opened her mouth and Cob rummaged all through it with a foul-tasting finger. The horrified quartet huddled around the cot had stopped breathin'. Satisfied the bread had been swallowed, Cob nodded to the others, let go of Lootie's hair, collapsed to one of the two vacated chairs, and wiped her finger on her dress. Exhausted, she put her elbows on her knees and hung her head while she got aholt of herself. Hardly the time or the place, she'd damn near taken the Lord's name in vain.

"I don't wanna eat no more," Lootie said, choking back sobs. "Please."

"Oh, quit actin' like a baby," Cob hissed. "You don't hafta eat no more." She huffed and puffed like she'd just won a wrestlin' match with the Dark Lord hisself. Then, realizing the deed'd been accomplished, she sat up, shook it off, looked to the other old ladies, and cackled, "I'm gettin' too damn old f'this shit." She stood up and grabbed the vial off the shelf and thrust it into Lootie's hand. "You do have a sistah now." She pushed Lootie toward the door, and as she opened it, the light streaming in momentarily blinded her.

Roach was waitin' under the tree, but jumped to his feet when he saw the shack door jerk open. The Devil Dog was still standing guard. Cob dragged Lootie outside, kicked the beast into makin' room, leaned down, and took Lootie by the shoulders. "Someday, little sistah, we'll see one'nothah 'gin."

Working up a false bravado now that she was back outside in the bright sunshine, the ordeal behind her and Roach standin' not too far off, Lootie turned on Cob and with a fist full o' clench and a face full o' grit, "I ain'tchur sistah!"

Cob exploded with gurgly laughter and without even a "Goodbye," a "Thank You Very Much" or a heart-felt "Go t'Hell," spun around, stepped back into the shack and slammed the door.

CHAPTER 11

The Devil Dog hadn't moved off far enough for Roach to feel comfortable, so he beckoned the whimpering Lootie to the tree. The bright sunshine blinded her so bad it almost hurt. She had to cover her eyes with her forearm, and when she got to him, he took the vial from her hand. "This th'med'cine?" Lootie ground her knuckles in her eyes and nodded. "You awright?" he added, putting the vial in his pants pocket.

"I'm cold 'n th'light hurts m'eyes."

"That's cause it was dark inside. You'll get used to it in a minute." He picked up his coat off the ground, laid it over her shoulders, and took her by the hand, shocked at how cold it was. He looked back over his shoulder at the shack and the triple-legged terror gnawin' on the bone. "Let's go."

He hadn't dragged her a hundred yards when she started gaggin'. She was bent over, kneading her cramping stomach. She scrunched her eyes shut and told Roach, "Papa, I'm gonna be sick."

"Try t'hold it down. I wanna keep movin' as long as we can. I wanna get home 'fore sundown." Too, the futher he could get from the witch and her yellow-fanged minion, the better. He started to pull her along, but she slapped her hand to her mouth and fell to her knees. Her body contorted and she wretched like her guts were gonna come out. Roach knelt to her, pattin' her on the back. That and givin' her his coat was a whole gob of concern for Roach. When the attack finally abated she raised her head, and when Roach saw her eyes, he fell back and scuttled off like a spider.

Her hair was plastered to her head, she was deathly pale, lips purple, and her one good eye was no longer brown, but black as liquid tar and fathomless as Cob's. There was somethin' else, too. The pact made between Roach and the witch wasn't anything he woulda put much stock in. It was simply tit for tat. The medicine that could possibly save Pearl's life in exchange for a simple favor, and when she told him what it was, he couldn't believe it.

That was all?

Naturally, Roach had heard all the goosebumply tales about witches, spells, hexes, haints, and nasty child-gobblin', wooly and scaly boogers inhabiting the swamp. He thought most of 'em were silly. Some he wasn't so sure about. He did believe in witches. Hell, there was mention of them in the Bible. But he didn't believe in Sin Eaters. Stories o' folks consuming the sins of the dyin', takin' on the weight of their life's transgressions before they went to meet their maker, all ceremoniously baked into a loaf of bitter, salted bread. And as the story went, the Sin Eater's unpardonable soul was sentenced eternally to a fiery Hell and no reprieve. There was no such thing as a Sin Eater for a Sin Eater.

Puckie! They were great stories when you wanted to scare the Hell out o' skittery niggers and little kids...that was always fun, but anybody with a lick o' sense knew they were nothin' more than that. If he had to put Lootie through some backwater superstition to get the medicine needed to cure Pearl, it was worth it.

Now, though, he wasn't so sure. The child in front of him was still Lootie, but not. There was a hardness, a coldness, an oldness, in her face. Still the child, but not the child. Well, whatever it was, it was over and done now, and they had the medicine. They'd be home in three or four hours, and in a couple o' days everthing'd be better, back to regular. It'd all work out. He got Lootie back on her feet and for the next few miles he kept tellin' hisself it'll work out. It'll work out. It'll work out.

CHAPTER 12

They got home just before the sun set, and bangin' in the front door, all excited that he had the medicine, Roach saw that Pearl was layin' just as he'd left her that mornin'. If the sun had been up, or if he'd helt a lantern to her, if he'd taken a good look at her before he and Lootie left, he woulda seen it was already too late. And now, unlike the old woman on the cot in Cob's shack, Pearl's mouth hung open, her jaw hung over like it'd slipped out o' joint, and her half-closed eyes were lookin' at the ceilin' but not seein' it. Flies buzzed around her face and in and out of her mouth. Her nose. Her ears. Lootie's black eye blinked in empathy as one of the hateful things walked right acrost Pearl's half-open right eye. She'd already started turnin', stinkin'. Lootie recognized the smell. Just like where Cob lived.

The next mornin', Roach hitched up the mules and took the wagon into Oledeux. He had to make arrangements for the undertaker man to come out and fix up the body for buryin' and the preacher to say the words. Lootie noticed he'd said *the body* instead of *Pearl*. She didn't wanna be left alone. She asked if she could go with him but he told her he didn't think it'd be a good idea. He didn't want the body left alone. What'd he think, somebody'd steal it? He told her he'd be gone no longer than he had to.

They'd covered the body with an old sheet so they wouldn't have to look at it. Too, it helped keep the flies off. Covered or not, though, Lootie wasn't settin' foot past the door frame until Roach come back. Lootie may have loved her, but a dead body was a dead body was a dead body. She just sat on the porch in the sun, her clammy little hands in her lap, nervously holdin' onto each other, or practicin' writin' her name in the dirt with a stick. Ever so often she'd get up and walk in the direction Roach would be comin' back from, hopin' to hear the harness, the wheels, or a bray. For the first time in her life, she was lookin' for'ard to seein' him.

Ever little bit, she thought she heard somethin' from inside the shack. A crackin', a creakin', or a poppin'. It was actually nothin' more than the shack contracting from the day warmin' up 'n coolin' down. But she'd get up and cautiously step to the door, expectin' to look in and see Pearl walkin' around in her ol' moth-eaten nightdress, her mouth hangin' open, eyes half closed, and her hair laid flat to the back of her head from layin' on it for so long. Lootie wished she might be. Kinda. But scared she would be. Mostly. Settin' on the porch by the door, she did hear a gurglin' one time. Like a belly that needed somethin' t'eat. She cautiously stepped to the door, planted her hands on the jamb, leaned in, and saw there was a kinda roundness under the sheet where Pearl's belly was.

He finally come home and they skipped supper.

Come morning', Roach told Lootie he wanted her to take a walk before the buryin' man got there with the box. He wanted her to run down to the crick and play with the croakers or somethin', and he'd fetch her after the fella was gone. She figured it was because Roach didn't want her to see 'em load Pearl's body up in the box, but actually, what'd happened was, the buryin' fella said he wouldn't come out if Lootie was anywheres about. If he even thought he saw her peakin' around a tree or somethin', he'd pack up and leave. Right then and right there. He warned Roach that if they had Pearl's body halfway in the box and he saw Lootie, he'd walk out the door, get on his wagon and that'd be that. Workin' with a dead body while a witch-in-training hung around made for a bad combination.

The next day, Roach, Lootie, the Preacher, and two black gravediggers stood around a rough hole in the ground that housed the cheap wooden box where Pearl was, and in which Roach told Lootie she was gonna spend the rest of her life. The comment made Lootie think that if Pearl was in the coffin, and dead, the spendin' the rest of her life thing didn't make much sense, but she wouldn't pursue it. Pearl had told her more than once that Roach only ever talked about two things: things he didn't know much about and things he didn't know nothin' about. She said she coulda had a more meaningful conversation with a stick of firewood than with Roach.

Cornelius Demacles Lusaw was the black-suited, multiple-chinned, holier-than-thou pulpit-pounder from Oledeux who was gonna say the words. Preacher Lusaw was weavin' from the influence of half a dozen shots of liquid courage, a dangerous thing to do standin' beside a six-by-six-by-three-foot hole.

Lootie looked around while he droned on, and thought that it woulda been a nice day for her and Pearl to work in the vegetable garden. The Kentucky Wonders and squash was ready to pick, and it wouldn't be long before the melons would be ripe enough to drop. It was so hard for Lootie to think about Pearl not bein' around any more. Ever time she turned around she saw somethin' she wanted to show or tell her. More than once she'd jumped up and started for the shack, sometimes even callin' out "Mama, Mama" while she was runnin' and then she'd remember. Like runnin' face-first into a wall.

She was standin' alongside the hole, next to Roach, wearin' Pearl's old shoes. They were so big on her she'd had to wrap her feet in cloth and stuff leaves in the toes so they wouldn't just fall off. She was hopin' the extra wrappings would help warm her feet, but it didn't. That was all right, though—the shoes were Pearl's, and they helped comfort her. Not far off stood the weathered board that had George scratched on it. George was the baby that'd only lived a couple o' hours. The board had split and *Geor* was on one side and *ge* on the other.

Lookin' down the hole at the box, she wished Pearl would push the lid open and sit up, gaspin' for air and madder than a scalded chicken at Roach for not makin' sure she was all the way dead. She also wished Pearl'd looked a little more like the old lady at Cob's, with the rag tied around her head, instead of her mouth hangin' open and her dead-lookin' eyes starin' up at nothin'. She knew better than to ask, but she hoped that either the buryin' man or Roach'd thought to close 'em and her mouth before hammerin' the lid down. Pearl was worth more than to go through eternity with her mouth hangin' open. She wondered if he'd put pennies on Pearl's eyes.

She looked up at Roach's lumpy, unshaven face, his turkey neck, ears that stuck out, the hair in his nose, and thought, I'm alone now. All by myself.

She was still daydreaming, waitin' for Pearl to push the lid off the box when she heard the Bible Thumper mumble somethin' about abody walkin' through a valley somers, with shadows o' dead things. Gettin' forgiven for doin' people wrong and forgivin' people who'd done them wrong. She hoped he wasn't talkin' about Pearl, 'cause the only thing Lootie could think of she'd ever done wrong was dyin' and leavin' her alone, all by herself. With Roach. She didn't think the Preacher was talkin' about his ownself either, 'cause he was so big and fat and looked like he'd break an easy sweat, she doubted he'd ever walked anywhere, let alone some far-off valley with shadows o' dead things. Fat scardey cat.

Ever little bit, the Preacher snuck a wary eye in Lootie's direction. He knew the rumors about who the little girl's real mother mighta been and didn't like the look of her lightnin'-scarred face or the eyes, one blue/blind and the other, black as a chip o' tar. His lip almost curled back in disgust, lookin' at the dirty dress, and he thought that surely she had another pair of shoes. He mighta spouted Holy Scripture from the Good Book and carried a raggly one with him everwhere he went so everbody could see him wavin' it around and poundin' it on the pulpit, makin' his point, but underneath he was as superstitious and demon-minded as everbody else.

He finally said the *Hallaloo* and *Amen* words, pressed the Good Book to his puffed-up chest with his left hand, and helt his right out toward Roach, palm up. Roach reached in his pants pocket, pulled it out, slipped him somethin', and then, lookin' at the ground, toed the dirt like a little kid caught in the act. The ol' boy looked in his hand, like a chicken'd shat on it, then back at Roach. Roach was still lookin' at the ground and blinkin' like a sleepy toad. Fat Boy shook his head disgustedly, slipped whatever it was in his vest pocket, and waddled his big ass off to climb on his poor old sway-back mule.

Cornelius Lusaw couldn spur it away from the evil-eyed, Devil-possessed brat quick enough. Ever once in a while, his faith slipped some, and he wondered if there really was a God or a Heaven, there was so much evil in the world, but he'd never doubted whether there was a Devil or a Hell. And that putrid little heathen, Lootie Komes, that little bitch with the Devil's eyes, was the absolute, perfect example, proof o' their existence. That innocent demeanor might fool some, but he was a man o' God, dammit, and he knew evil when he seen it. She was a forked-tongued, demon-in-training if there ever was one. He was sorry he'd ever agreed to grace them with his presence. And then Roach had slipped him half a dollar. Half a dollar! God Damn! What the hell kind o' service had he been expectin' for half a dollar? This was the last time he'd allow his soft-hearted, good-naturedness get the best of him! He'd made up his mind about the Komeses. The Lusaws'd never never *never* have a damned thing to do with the Komeses again. Never!

Just before Lootie and Roach turned to leave and let the diggers earn their pay, Lootie took out the little vial that Roach had traded her soul to the Devil for, and dropped it into the hole. The vial into which Cob had laughingly dribbled the last few drops of her tea.

CHAPTER 13

It was six years later that the war which began some months earlier was coming, inexorably, to its final battle. The war between lust and guilt. Winter had moved in, and when the sun went down, it took what feeble warmth there'd been during the day. Lootie sat at the dinner table with a thin blanket laid over her lap and wrapped around her legs, studyin' her McGuffey while Roach heated up a big pot o' water on the squat, pot-bellied stove.

"I'm heatin' this up," he said, his speech slurred, "so you'cn take a bath. Gettin' too cold t'take 'em in th'crick anymore."

The cold of the weather didn't bother Lootie like it used to. Ever since the trip to the witch's shack. She hadn't been truly warm one time since. Engrossed in the book, she was only half listenin' and nodded. She was settin' on one of the two straight-backed chairs, with her legs drawed up and her bare feet propped on the other, warmin' 'em by the stove. Roach's courage, pumped up by tippin' the bottle all day, he tried to get into position to look up her dress by pretending to get more wood for the fire. She put her feet on the floor to give him room.

"You didn't need t'move," he said, slippery. "I coulda got it."

She was growing up. Her pea-sized nipples, pushin' against the dress's thin material, and her thighs, too long for the dress, drove him to distraction. Just the day before, she was sittin' on the porch, leanin' over a basket, stringin' and snappin' green beans. Although cooler weather was comin' on, the midday sun warmed her up enough that she'd hiked the dress well above her knees and stuffed it 'tween her legs to keep her underpants hid. There were a couple o' buttons missin' on her shirt at her chest, and ever so often Roach was lucky enough to be standin' beside her when she bent over for another handful o' beans and caught a glimpse of a wrinkled little nipple fronting a tight young tittie. More than once, between then and that evening, he'd had to relieve hisself, rubbin' out the swelling, and his thing was gettin' raw. He'd done it so much, the last couple o' whackins he'd had to use a pinch o' lard to cut the friction. His right hand smelled like stale urine and chitlins.

Pretty quick, the shack was hot and Roach poured the steaming water in the tub they used for washing clothes. He laid a lumpy cake of lye soap and a cloth on the floor beside it. "Okay," he said, like it was nothin' out o' the ordinary, "it's ready. Gitcher clothes off 'n hop in."

She closed the book, set it on the table, pulled the blanket off her and stood up.

"Come on," he said and clapped his hands, impatiently. "Gitcher clothes off. Let's go. Water's gettin' cold 'n I ain't agonna heat it up agin."

She noticed he'd said, "Gitcher clothes off" twice in the last ten seconds. "I ain't takin' m'clothes off with you standin' there."

"Whadaya speck me t'do?"

"If I'm takin' m'clothes off, I speck ya t'go outside."

"It's cold out there. If I's takin' a bath, you think I'd ask you t'go out?"

"You never take a bath, but even if ya did, you think you'd hafta ask me t'leave? You nekkid's 'bout the last thing I wanna see." She sat back down and started to rewrap the blanket around her. "I'll wash up in th'crick t'morrow. It ain't that cold."

"Awright, I'll go," and easy as that, he opened the door and stepped outside.

She waited a few seconds, unwrapped the blanket, set it on the chair, stepped to the tub, and swished her hand around in the water. It was hot. It felt good. She hadn't had half a dozen hot baths, 'n none since Pearl died. She quickly unbuttoned and slipped off her dress, holey underpants, dropped 'em on the floor by the tub and oozed in. She reached over the side o' the tub, picked up the soap, the washrag, and after workin' up a lather, started on her arms. She jumped when Roach's voice muffled through the door.

"It's cold out hyere! You in yet?"

She smiled, picturin' him turtled up, tryin' to keep warm. He'd been nice enough to fix her a hot bath, the least she could do was hurry it up. "Yeah," she replied and went back to washin'.

Then the door opened...

Lootie dropped the soap and the rag in the water...

...and he stepped in...

...wrapped her arms around her knees, and slunk down.

"What're you doin'?"

"Whadya mean, what'm I doin'?"

"You said you'd go outside!"

"I did! You didn't speck me t'stay out there!"

"I meant when I's takin' th'bath, too."

"Oh, shaw, 'at's silly," and with a dismissive gesture he closed the door and stepped to the tub. He picked her dress and underpants up off the floor and Lootie watched him casually drop 'em in the bath water. He felt a lot better now. Yes, sir, the plan was finally comin' together. And a fine plan it was, too. He had her where he wanted her, in the tub. He had her how he wanted her, nekkid. And best of all, there wasn't a dadgum thing she could do about it. Before she could say anything, he was on his knees next to the tub. "Don't make no sense t'take a bath 'n then put on th'same dirty clothes, does it? This way we kill two birds with one rock."

She tensed up when he stuck his hands in the water, swishin' the dress around and brushin the back of his furry fingers over her legs. "Yeah...we'll get this real clean." He made a show of scrubbin' the dress between his knuckles, lifting it up, and wringing the water out. Then he stood up, shook the dress out, laid it across the chair by the stove, and went back to repeat the process with her underpants. Lootie was still hunkered down. "Ain'tchu gonna wash up? Water's gonna get cold."

"What'm I gonna wear when I get out?" She nodded to the dress-draped chair. "My clothes's all wet."

"That's awright," he sloughed it off. "They'll dry drekly 'n you'cn stand by the fire 'til they do." He took the washrag and soap and started for her shoulders. "Here, I'll hep ya."

"No!" she chirped, leanin' away from him like he was the troll that lived under the bridge. Then, from the surprised look on his face, she wondered if maybe she'd jumped too quick. "Thank you, but I can do it."

He laughed nervously, rubbed the soap into the washrag, and asked, "How ya gonna wash yer back, silly? Monkey's is th'only things can wash their own back. You ain't a monkey, are ya?" He pulled a chair beside the tub, pushed the blanket to the floor, hiked up his pants legs and set down. "Come on now, stand up."

She just looked at him, scrunch-eyed. He couldn't be serious.

But he was.

Very.

Like a boil fest'rin' to a head, he'd invested a lot o' time and energy fantasizing about those little nubs, so tight they could barely jiggle, and he'd never been more serious about anything in his life.

"Lootie? Git up. Now. I ain't foolin' 'round n'more. Yer Mama give ya a bath 'n it ain't no differnt with me. I went t'th'trouble o' fixin th'water 'n you ain't got a dang thing I wanna see," while the sight of her puffy little breasts, smooshed up against her thigh was drivin' him crazy.

There are few times in one's life where they can honestly say they'd come to a crossroads. For Roach and Lootie, this was one of 'em. Roach'd drawn a line in the sand, and he was waitin' to see what she was gonna do. With the help of the bottle, he'd already crossed the fine line between reality and fantasy. Lootie had no idea how close she was to losin' not only her virginity, but quite possibly…her life. She could be raped, strangled, and buried in a mulchy hole fifty yards from the house before the sun came up and no one would ever know. It was damn sure no one would care.

She'd never stood up to an adult before and she wouldn't start with her father tonight. Pearl had told her many times, "He's lazy 'n he ain't very smart, but he's still yer Papa, ya do what he says 'n don't sass 'im no more'n ya would me." Lootie'd taken her lessons to heart.

It saved her life.

Givin' in to his demand, she pushed herself up with her right arm clamped across her chest and her left hand cupped 'twixt her legs. She only had two hands and bein' that they's occupied, that left her well-rounded, blood-boilin' rear end exposed.

Seein' her compliance, he softened his tone. "At's better," he said, swishin' the washrag in the warm, soapy water. He brought it up to the back of her neck and wrung it out over her shoulders. He watched the warm sudsy water run down the curve of her back. "Now, don't that feel good?" Soapy bubbles slitherin' between her tightly squeezed butt cheeks made his pecker moan. It was either look away or fill his pants.

"Ya know, I been athinkin'…when spring comes back around, we'll hafta plant us some veg'tables like you 'n Pearl used t'do. Jes you 'n me? Wouldn' 'at be fun? Whadaya think'd be good? Maybe some t'matas," he continued, trying to get her mind off what he was doin' and slyly movin' the washrag down her back. "Okra…"—along the outside of her legs—"…a few o' them sweet yella onions. You like them don'tcha? Maybe some sweetaters." Then his soapy hand slid between her thighs well above her knees. "A little bit o'…."

She abruptly squeezed her legs together and looked over her shoulder. "Thank you. I can do th'rest." She slunk back into the water, rewrapped her arms around her knees and turtled up.

She hadn't moved fast enough, though, and he'd caught a glimpse of her little clam and the fuzz, far too little yet to cover it. The fuse was lit, and it was a short one. He pictured draggin' her out o' the water, throwin' her on the bed, spreadin' her legs, and fuckin' her. Hard.

"Papa?"

Papa was lookin' at the cleavage between her legs that was already seared into his brain.

"Papa? Look at me. Please."

He did, and for whatever reason, caught as surely as a fly in a spider web, he couldn't look away. The black eye had him nailed.

"Thank you. Now, go outside 'n let me finish."

He blinked, fighting to do as she asked.

"And stay out there this time. Please."

She'd asked so sweetly, it affected him. Maybe he'd pushed it enough for the first time. He'd had his hands on her. Given her a little taste of what could be. In the next couple o' days she'd be thinkin' about it and wonder what it woulda been like if she had only let him go a little futher. He knew her reluctance was just ignorance. She was still pretty young. There'd be many, many more opportunities like this'n, and she'd eventually warm up to it.

"Awright," he said, with one last, longing peek, and dropped the washrag into the water. He pushed hisself up off the edge o' the tub and turned quickly so she wouldn't notice the throbbing protrusion in his britches. "Holler when yer done."

She watched him leave and close the door. Then she looked to the window alongside and saw the poor excuse for a curtain was closed. She heard his voice, muffled through the door.

"You hurry up, now. It's cold out hyere."

"Thank you, I will," she said, but kept her eye on the door for a few seconds just in case he decided to jump back in again. The water was startin' to get cold so she got up and quickly finished scrubbin', unaware that Roach was outside in the dark, peekin' in the tiny crack between the curtains, while his hand slid over his pecker like there wasn't no tomorrow. She drug the washrag between the lips on the near-hairless little slit and his cucumber exploded, spittin' goo on his shoe.

Pearl was in the cold, hard ground six years, two months, one week and two days the first time Roach and Lootie shared a bed. All Lootie'd ever slept on was a cot, the kind army soldiers or prospectors used in tents. The only thing beneath her was the rough, canvas, sling-like bottom, and with winter comin' on, it got miserable cold at night. He explained that the reason for havin' to sleep in the same bed, together, was to save on firewood and keep each other from freezin' to death.

Sharing a bed come to a head not long after it started. Lootie'd seen enough of her little animal friends rasslin' and ridin' piggy-back to know that the growth between Roach's legs wasn't caused by roomatiz like he claimed. As time went on, he got bolder and bolder, until one night in mid-February, with his brain anesthetized from a snoot full of whiskey, he started runnin' his hands clumsily over her legs. He'd touched her before, but always made like it was a slip o' the hand when he turned over. He turned over a lot. That night, it wasn't a slip; one hand boldly moved to her crotch while the other stroked his legless Cyclops.

She grabbed his hand before it reached its destination, threw his arm back, yanked the thin covers off, and jumped out o' bed.

"STOP IT! You ain't doin' that no more! I know whatchu want 'n it ain't gonna happen! You ain't givin' me no more baths...," she spat, her little fists clenched, "'n you 'n' me ain't sleepin' in th'same bed no more, either. I'll sleep on th'cot 'r th'floor 'r standin' up like a horse if I have to. Yer my Papa, 'n it ain't right!"

It'd happened so fast, the booze took aholt of Roach's mouth way ahead of his soggy brain, and it was his turn to jump up. "Well, I'll tell you somethin', you think yer s'dadgum smart. NO! I ain'tchur papa. 'N Pearl? She weren'tchur mama! Yer real mama was a dadgum albino witch, bitch, whore everbody called Smoke 'n she was bad fucked b'th'Devil hisself 'n that's th'festered pecker 'n th'stinkin Hell hole you come from!" He clapped his arms over his chest and jutted out his jaw. "So, whadaya think o' that?"

"You're a liar!" she barked.

"Bullshit I am!" he boasted. "Pearl 'n me come on yer mama...fried as a fish in a skillet 'n jest's dead, but Pearl wouldn't leave it alone. Noooo, no, God jabbed a stick o' lightnin' up Smoke's witchy, snow-white ass, but Pearl knowed more'n dadgum God. She sliced up yer mama," he pointed to his crotch, "from here..."—and drug his thumb up to his breastbone— "...t'here 'n fished you out."

Then he thought of something and pointed his finger at her. "You know what?" He stepped off the bed and stalked carefully in the dark to the table, snatched up the knife with the leather-wrapped handle, and brought it back to her.

"That's th'very dang knife Pearl gutted 'er with. I pried it out o' th'dead fingers o' th'dead hand on th'dead arm that'd got blowed clean off 'n laid in th'muddy road." He waggled it in front of her face, then tossed it back to the tabletop. "Your real mama had six fingers on her dadgum hands." He shivered at the memory.

Lootie looked at it, imagining. "My mother?"

"Yep!" he said, smartassey. Then he chinned to her face. "How'dju git them scars? What was it blinded yer eye?"

She didn't understand why he was asking. He knew what it was.

"Come on...tell me...," he pushed. "What was it?"

"I's lightnin' struck."

"When?" he demanded, thrusting his chin out.

"I don't understand why yer sayin' these things 'r why yer askin' me this. You know when."

"Yeah," he said, smartalecky, "I do, but I don't think you do. When was it?"

"I don't know zackly how old I was. I's a baby."

"Ha!" he chirped. "No, you wasn't! You wasn't no old! When Pearl cutchur mama's belly open, you come out lookin',," he jabbed a finger at her face with every word, "...jes...like...'at! Th'lightnin' 'at gotchur mama 'n blew 'er arm off in t'th'road's th'same one fried yer face." He put his hands on his hips. "So...therrrre ya go...noooow ya know. You 'n me ain't no blood kin a'tall! But, 'spite all th'trouble you been, I been takin' care o' ya all these years 'n Good God Dangit, I oughta get somethin' for it! I'm a man 'n I got a man's needs tooken care of, 'n YOU ain't gonna get nobody else."

Lootie was struck dumb, both at what he'd said and the venom in the telling. How could he talk to her like that, knowin' he was in the wrong? He was wrong! He was storyin' 'bout another woman. Another mother. He was lyin'! He had to be.

Didn't he?

Then she remembered. Of course he was lyin'! He'd slipped up! Pearl herself said she was the first to hold her. She'd talked about how hard the birthin'd been, but Lootie'd been worth ever painful second of it. She wanted to scream back at him and tell him he was a big ol' liar again...

...but was he?

Nothin' Roach said went against what Pearl'd told her. She *had* been the first to hold her. She *had* suffered through the painful birth, *had* been a part of it. Pearl hadn't lied to her, she just hadn't told her the truth.

Pearl wasn't her mama.

Roach calmed down some and tried another approach. "I know yer actin' this away 'cause yer changin', turnin' to a woman. Y'all go a little nutty when it happens. It's natural. I can see it." He sniffed animatedly and nodded to her crotch. "I can smell it. Yer sproutin' titties 'n I know ya'started th'bleedin 'n with th'bleedin' comes th'needin', butcha see, that ain't nothin' you oughta feel bad 'bout 'cause it's natural, and ya oughta know that I wantchu ever bit as bad as you want me."

Her eyes goggled in astonishment. "Are you crazy? You can't really believe that. Wantchu? Me? Lord, no, I don't wantchu. Why would I? You're old 'n I ain't, 'n you been my papa all my life, 'n even now, learnin y'ain't, it don't make no dif'ernce."

Not one to cut a good argument short, Roach jumped back in. "I told you y'ain't gonna get n'body else. Yer ugly, face full o' scars, you only got th'one good eye 'n it's black! Everbody knows ya come out of a witch."

Lootie was shaking in rage and confusion but she couldn't deny the accusations.

Roach helt out his hands. "Listen, there ain't nothin' left t'argee 'bout. You think on this. I can't stand it no more, I'm up agin th'wall! Startin' t'night…'n I mean you spreadin' yer legs 'n satisfyin' my needs *t'night*, or t'morrow, when th'sun comes up, you get out. You pack yer clothes 'n get out 'n find somers else t'live. Drive somebody else crazy. I'll tell ya th'truth…if ya do, I'll pine for ya no end, but I can't go on this away.

"I don't like sayin' it, but matin' with you's all I think about. Don't let on like you don't know whatchur doin' either. Prancin' 'round, bendin' over in 'at little dress, drawin' yer shoulders back, stretchin', pushin outchur titties. I can't git nothin' done fr'thinkin' about it. Now, I ain't lied 'bout where ya come from 'n I humbled m'self barin' m'soul 'bout how I feel for ya. I'm sorry 'bout some o' th'things I said here, m'back was up, but if ya stay with me, I'll love ya ever bit like I done Pearl 'n I'll take care o' ya just's good, but we ain't goin' on th'way it's been no more." He took a step back, folded his arms on his chest, and toed another line in the sand. "So…what's it gonna be?"

Lootie thought about all the concern, love, devotion, and caring he'd given Pearl, and it made her as mad as a scalded cat. But before she could slap him silly or scratch his eyes out, she jerked the one and only blanket they had off the bed, wrapped it around her shoulders, and without givin' him another look, stomped to the door, yanked it open, stepped outside, and slammed it shut.

The cold was almost physical. She gripped the edges of the blanket and pulled 'em around her, tight, her head turtled down into her hunched-up shoulders. Her fisted hands wrapped in the blanket were bunched under eyes that darted here and there, lookin' for an answer. There wasn't one, and nowhere she could go beyond the porch to find one.

The woman she'd believed all her life to be her mother, wasn't. The rut-ravaged weasel she'd believed to be her father, wasn't. All she was to him was a thing. A thing to do with as he pleased. She was no more than a dog he could kick out anytime he wanted. She was property. If she wanted to stay, she had to agree that he owned her. A slave he could have his way with anytime he wanted. Fork it over, or when the sun come up, pack up and get out. But, pack up what? She had nothin' to pack up. She didn't even have her own name.

Then a moment of clarity washed over her and she asked herself what would be th'diff'rence between t'morrow mornin 'n right now? Hours? That's all. Nothin' more. Almost like it was a sign, her body stopped shakin'. She took three steps and clenched her toes over the edge o' the cold, rough-hewn porch planks. She looked into the cold night and wondered: How long would it take t'freeze t'death?

Tears she didn't know were coming ran down her face. They felt hot against her freezin' cheeks. She didn't know exactly why she was cryin'. Fear? Humiliation? A life unfulfilled? She hadn't felt this low, this lost, this helpless, since Pearl's death. Then she thought of somethin' Pearl'd told her, and her pulse quickened. It was a last resort. She looked up into the sky and said, "Dear God…"

…and then she stopped.

"Dear God…"

…she tried again, but she didn't know what to ask. Maybe make Roach not wanna…but a memory, a picture come to mind. Pearl's tortured face and lip-curlin' stench of rot and decay. A lot o' good beggin' to God'd done Pearl. The hopeful spark in Lootie's eye shut down and her jaw tightened. She looked up, once again, into the star-flecked sky.

"Dear God…"

…and this time, she had no trouble findin' the words.

"…go t'Hell."

Lookin' into the cold dark woods, she took a deep, steadying breath and dropped her arms to her side. That allowed the blanket to slide off her shoulders and fall to the porch in a crumpled pile at her heels. She waited a couple more seconds, and when lightnin' didn't strike her dead like Roach said it had her mother, wearin' only her thin nightshirt, she stepped off the porch, and melted into the cold, dark night.

Roach'd expected her to come right back in. When she didn't, he blinked a couple o' times, got back in bed, pulled up what scant covers that were left and laced his fingers in back of his head.

A quarter hour later, and thoroughly ashamed of herself, having discovered that she was a pitiable coward, Lootie slipped back in the shack and threw the blanket at Roach. She pulled the bottom of her nightshirt up to her waist and got in bed. Her teeth were chattering and her body quivering. She clenched her arms tightly to her side and spread her legs without sayin' a word. With no pretense of love-making, Roach hiked up her legs, her heels to her butt, got on his knees between 'em, and wrapped his hands around her cold knees. The skin on his pecker was as tight as a drum, ready to romp, but before he could take it any futher, she put her hands on his.

"I ain't givin' you nothin'," she hissed, her lips drawn back. "Yer takin' it. 'N I'm allowin' it only 'cause I got nowhere else t'go 'n not 'cause I owe you anything. As long's I'm here, you can take it. I'm agreein' t'all that. But…you stick it in me now, yer agreein' t'what I say, too."

He'd never seen this Lootie before and he was some spooked. She was a witch, after all. "T'what?" he asked, lookin' in that depthless black eye.

Calmly, and without any doubt she meant it, she told him, "You ever say anything nasty 'bout Pearl again," she nodded in the direction o' the table, "that knife over there? I'll stick it in yer heart…'n I'll kill you over 'n over 'n over."

"You'd kill yer own papa?"

"You ain't my papa. Yer old, yer stupid, ya stink, 'n I'd stick you faster 'n quicker'n you'cd blink. Even if you was my papa. I got nothin' t'lose. You awready give 'way my soul."

He gave it about three seconds deep thought, and she grimaced in disgust when he rubbed his thumb lightly between her downy little lips, brought it to his nose, and sniffed. "Agreed," he said, shifted his knees, lifted her hips, and pulled her to him. Just like Lootie's real father'd done her real mother, Roach was gonna show her who was boss. He licked his thumbs, pulled her little lips apart, and pushed it in with no more purpose than to inflict pain. And he succeeded. She felt somethin' pop and a fiery bolt shot through her, but she just gripped the covers, grit her teeth, and, like her real mother, took it. Any satisfaction on his part would have to come from him.

He pulled her nightshirt up futher with the intention o' suckin' on her nipple. But when he leaned down she grabbed a handful of the hair on the back of his head to steady it, slapped his whiskered face, hard, then yanked the shirt back down. "That wasn't part o' th'deal."

He backed off, rubbed his whiskered cheek, and concluded that for now, he'd leave well enough alone. His pecker was in her. She didn't look real happy about it, but he knew it was only a matter of time before she learned to like it and crave it as much as he did. He was lookin' for'ard to watchin' her squeeze her tits in delight, beggin' him to suck and bite on 'em. He mighta been stupid, but he had an incredible imagination.

After poundin' as hard as he could for another seventeen seconds, his lizard spilled its guts and all his fantasies came true. He pulled it out, deflated and blood-smeared, wiped it off on her nightshirt, and rolled off, suckin' air, spent. He did it three more times before the sun come up.

The only difference between Lootie's and her mother's first time...although ugly, Roach had a nose.

Lootie was fourteen.

Roach was fifty-two.

The war was over.

The bad guys won.

Two years later, Lootie was pregnant with her second child. The first was a boy she named George after the only one Pearl carried full term. The one yet to be, if a girl, she'd name her Pearl. If a boy, he'd be called Matthew from one o' the fellas Pearl read to her about in the Bible. There were nine or ten others. There was a James, a Tom, and a Peter, but she liked Matthew the best. George was cute as the devil, and Lootie thought she understood what Pearl musta felt. Livin' with Roach, she'd given Pearl as much reason to survive as George gave her. He was a smart little shit. Lootie'd sing and George'd dance. He liked playin' in the dirt with bugs and chasin' chickens. He and Roach had an understanding. They both stayed away from the other as much as they could.

Not long after Roach and Lootie made their pact concerning the matin' process, Roach found it wasn't anywhere near as exciting as he'd anticipated. He discovered that fantasizin' about somethin' he couldn't have was much more exciting than gettin' what he could anytime he wanted it. He'd climbed his mountain and found it cold. Now what?

After she swole up big with George, the sight of her belly stretched to its limit didn't do much for his sexual appetite. In the last few weeks, he resorted to wrappin' his fingers around it, imagining sneakin' looks up her dress back when she was eight or nine.

After George slid out, Roach went back to usin' Lootie, but after a while, the only thrill he got out of it was poundin' it in her. He wanted to get somethin' out of it, even if it was nothin' more than hurtin' her. What shoulda been his Heaven ended up bein' his Hell. She'd be doin' somethin' in the shack and he'd get the urge, step in back of her and pull his pants down. Lootie gave no more thought about pullin' her dress up over her back, spreadin' her legs and bendin' over with her forearms on the table than she'd give doin' the dishes. He'd try his damndest to work it up, but most o' the time it wouldn't cooperate. Frustrated, he'd try to shove it in limp and she'd look back over her shoulder and laugh at him. Humiliated, he'd shove it back into his pants and stomp out the door. He started thinkin' again about sendin' her off. The only reason he didn't was because her not bein' there'd drive him crazy. He was addicted to the memory of what she used to do to him.

He finally figured it out. In his mind anyway. She'd hexed him. That explained everthing. She was a witch and she'd made him want her, then she put the hoodoo on his man part so it wouldn't work. She'd hexed him to Hell on Earth. All the pussy he wanted and no way to get it. It was like a big ol' plate o' meat and taters and no mouth to eat it with. That's why she laughed at him. She'd put a hex on him.

One day when he went to town for supplies, Lootie packed up what few clothes she had in a tote sack, but other than that, all she took was four other things. She wanted something of Pearl's. She didn't have a necklace, a ring, a bracelet, or a fancy dress, so she took the shoes she'd worn at her funeral. It wasn't 'cause she needed 'em. It was just that they'd been Pearl's. The second was Roach's last name. He wouldn't miss it; it didn't have any value. The third, George, who Roach didn't give a whit about, and the fourth, the baby in her belly, who wouldn't mean any more to him than George did.

Then she thought that if it was a girl, she'd probably end up replacing Lootie as Roach's next slave.

She went out back o' the shack to say goodbye to Pearl 'cause she couldn't think of any reason she'd ever be back. She went back in the shack, slung the tote sack over her left shoulder, cocked George up on her right hip, and left. But then, just as she was leavin', a strange thing happened. She was no more than twenty feet from the front door when she flat stopped, jolted. It was like a rope was tied 'round her middle and snapped taut. A voice came in her head—a thin, squeaky little girl voice that said, "Ain'tchu f'gettin' somethin'?"

The voice had enough weight that she looked around for who mighta said it. Then the image of the knife came in her mind. The thought was so insistent, she went back in the shack, grabbed it, and stuck it in her bag, just as her real mother'd done. It was the only thing she had that both her mothers had touched.

She didn't know it, but sixteen years earlier, her real mother had left a shabby cabin just like she was doin'. Lootie was less than three years older than Smoke'd been, but she was just as pregnant and just as eager to escape her prison. She didn't leave a note. Roach couldn't read nohow. He'd figure it out. She wondered how long he'd spend foolin' hisself, thinkin' she'd change her mind and come back. She wondered if he'd know where she was goin', and if he did, would he have the nerve to come after her.

She had nothin' to eat but two biscuits and an onion. The biscuits were for George. She set off knowin' that bein' pregnant, havin' to lug George and the tote sack, it'd take most o' the day to reach her destination.

CHAPTER 14

Pearl and Lootie used to practice writin' and fig'rin' numbers in the dirt with a stick. Lootie took to it pretty good. Pearl knew she could only take her so far, though, so early one Fall morning, just a couple o' years 'fore she died, Pearl walked Lootie the nearly three miles to a little makeshift schoolhouse. Pearl was already showin' the early signs o' the tissick and had to stop ever so often t'catch her breath.

The schoolhouse was a simple, white-washed, one-room affair nailed up to the side of a barn, and the lessons were given by a local farmer's wife who could read and knew a bit about cipherin' numbers. It had a little wood stove inside, three long, uncomfortable benches for the students, a chair and homemade desk for the teacher, and a one-holer out back.

More than the education, though, Pearl wanted Lootie to have some little friends to play with. She knew they were up agin it tryin', but she wanted something better for Lootie than to end up like she had, with a never-gonna-do-nothin', never-gonna-be-nothin' wastrel like Roach.

They got to the little schoolhouse before anybody else showed. Pearl thought it'd probably be best if she didn't come while everbody else was already there, maybe get to know 'em one at a time as they showed up. They also concluded that Pearl wouldn't stick around like a banty hen protecting her brood. Hampered by the tissick, Pearl only got 'bout halfway back home when Lootie caught up with her, tears streamin' down her scarred little face. Pearl picked her up, and despite the tissick, carried her all the way back home, so mad she wanted to hit somethin'. That was the end o' Lootie's formal education.

But now, at sixteen, she was about to get it, after all. When she showed up at Cob's shack, luggin' a baby on one arm, a tote sack on the other, and another baby packed solidly in her belly, the old witch recognized the scarred face and laughed so hard she peed. "I tolju we'd see one 'nother agin!" She grabbed the porch post, bent over, and hawked up a gob. She'd lost all her teeth, which made it look like her face had caved in on itself. That same old, three-legged hound was layin' by the door. Lootie thought dogs must live a long time. Actually, it had a lot to do with who owned 'em.

Lootie thought it was odd that all the way to the shack, she felt less and less like she was leavin' somethin', and more and more like she was goin' to somethin'.

Cob taught Lootie how to read and do her numbers and that the only truth, the only value, was power. She explained that, thanks to her, Lootie'd already been initiated into the world of power, without her even knowin' it. Initiated the first time she ate sin. And because o' that initiation, she couldn't go back. Heaven's door was closed up tight as a nun's pussy and never to be opened, so whatever time Lootie had on this miserable orb, she may as well take advantage of it and have herself some fun. She didn't feel bad about what she'd done to Lootie. Born a witch with a scarred face, Lootie never stood a chance nohow. Cob also taught her what little she could of the dark arts. Lootie only had to be shown something once. In no time, she was beyond Cob's puny limits.

As Lootie's reputation grew, Cob became her agent, her familiar, linin' up the dyin' sinners like wagons at a cotton gin, and with each loaf consumed, Lootie became stronger and more fearful. She experimented, and through trial and error, gleaned the uses and abuses of various herbs, body parts, and blood. Eventually, Lootie Komes, with her will alone, had the ability to kill off the living and bring the dead back to life.

When Lootie was twenty-seven, Cob's days came to an end. She was both shittin' out and coughin' up blood. The Devil Dog died; just laid its head down one night and stopped livin'. Cob didn't have the power to keep the beast alive anymore. Just before she died, as her adopted sister, she made Lootie promise one thing. Lootie complied. Cob died. Lootie used the same knife that'd sliced her from her mother's belly to cut out Cob's heart and eat it.

BOOK TWO

CHAPTER 15

Six and a half miles from Cob's shack, and as many years after George's little brother, Matthew, slipped out of the womb, another baby was born, but unlike George and Matthew, he had a mother and a father who paid him a lot of attention. The father's name was Paul David Lusaw and the little boy's name was Hubert Marshall Lusaw, but everybody called him Hub. His mother's name was Iva Jane and she loved Hub with everthing she had. He was just the cutest, smartest little baby ever.

Iva Jane lived in the real world and didn't believe in make-believe. She didn't believe wishes wished came true—nevertheless, she had one, and she'd wished it many times. She wished with all her heart and soul that Hub had never been born. And the reason was Paul David. Somebody else she wished had never been born.

Paul David Lusaw considered hisself one Hell of a man and was determined to make the same of his son. Not that he wouldn't've anyway, but Paul David wasn't gonna take any chances. When Hub was old enough to pick up a hoe, Paul David taught him what it was for. Same with a shovel and a muckin' rake. By age three, Hub's little hands were padded, thick, full o' calluses. At four, one of his daily chores was to make sure there was plenty of firewood, which involved swingin' a double-bit axe. Iva Jane's jaw clenched with ever swing of the thing, fearful that someday it was gonna eat one o' his little feet or a finger.

Paul David taught him how to get on a horse by first tyin' it to a fence rail, shinnyin' up the fence post, and slidin' onto the saddle. It didn't matter his little legs weren't anywhere near long enough to reach the stirrups. What did matter was, when he fell off, he led the horse back to the fence, shinnied up the splintery post, and got back on again. Slow to compliment and quick to discipline, Paul David was the opposite of Iva Jane. She believed Hub could be a man and still be kissed and hugged. And she did. Just not when Paul David was around.

There were two things Paul David really liked. The first was any kind of alcohol and the second was any kind of woman. If they were willin', he was able. Iva Jane knew about it, but after countless arguments and broken promises, she'd quit caring. She'd given up on everthing but Hub.

Just because Paul David was handin' out goodies to ever woman he found receptive didn't mean he wasn't still dishin' it out at home, though. Iva Jane knew that ever time Paul David got lustful toward her, which was mostly when he was too drunk to ride the horse somers else he considered more exciting, she could come up pregnant, and she didn't wanna bring another child into that house. But, as luck would have it, five years after Hub, she gave birth to a girl. Loretta Abigail, who everbody called Ret. Paul David was disappointed it hadn't been another boy. The way he looked at it, Hub was his and Ret was Iva Jane's.

There was one thing that Iva Jane hated even more than Paul David's drinkin' and runnin' around. And that was...once he made up his mind about somethin', he never went back. Depending on what the subject was, that could be a good thing. But if it was a bad thing, it was really bad. If Paul David started somethin' or said somethin' was or wasn't gonna be, everbody else had to live with it.

When Hub was nine, he asked Paul David if he could have a dog. Paul David told him, all right, but nothin' in life came without a price and a dog was a valuable thing. What was Hub willing to give in return? He told Hub to think about it a couple o' days and see what he came up with. Hub told him he didn't need to; he'd keep the woodpile stocked. Paul David told him he was already doin' that. In fact, it was one o' the things he'd been doin' that kept a plate at the table for him. That idea pretty much squelched any other chore he was already doin'.

After two days and Hub hadn't come up with anything, Paul David said he had somethin'. He'd let Hub have a puppy if Hub'd take care o' the family's killin' and skinnin' duties. That meant the rabbits, chickens, possums, fish, and whatever else was to be consumed. Too, the dog could have the guts. The chore woulda been a handy thing for Hub to do, but the real reason Paul David mentioned it was 'cause he knew how bad Hub hated killin' anything. Skinnin' and cuttin' 'em up was even worse. But Hub wanted a puppy. He gave in, and after a while, learned to handle the chore without throwin' up ever time. The dog was all Hub'd hoped it would be. Buddy was his name and he was an ugly thing, a mixed-blood mutt of the first order, but he was fun and Hub loved him.

One Sunday afternoon, the family was sittin' around, and Paul David asked Ret if she'd get him a cup o' coffee. She was sittin' in the middle o' the floor playin' with her dolly and told him "In a minute." Iva Jane and Hub heard her, and both their hearts nearly stopped. The only time you told Paul David anything but "yes" was when you knew that was what he wanted to hear.

He told her again, and again she told him "In a minute." That woulda been enough, but the second "in a minute" she sounded like she was a little put out havin' to tell him twice.

Paul David pushed hisself out of his chair, yanked Ret off the floor by the arm, and headed for the front door. Ret was already squealin' in terror. Paul David's face was red, and his jaw was clamped down. On the way out the door, he told Hub he could follow, which meant he was supposed to follow. He told Iva Jane she could stay in the house, which meant she was supposed to stay in the house. Ret knew she'd made a real bad mistake, but it was too late. Paul David'd done it—made up his mind. He drug Ret to the henhouse, jerked her up short, and asked, "Which one's yorn?"

Ret pointed out a little Banty hen, and Paul David turned to Hub, "Get it!" Then he dug his fingers into Ret's shoulder hard enough to get a squeak. "I'll show you what sassin' me gets ya."

As scared o' Paul David as he was, Hub still took the chance. "Papa, please don't."

Paul David was shocked all to Hell. First, Iva Jane's daughter told him "in a minute," and now his own son was tellin' him what to do. "She sassed me 'n this family's eatin' that chicken t'night."

Hub listened to his little sister's howlin' while he stepped into the coop and chased the hen down. Paul David wouldn't let her go until Hub wrung its head off. The rest of it ran around the yard, slingin' blood, until it bled out, and she had to watch. When it finally keeled over, still flutterin' its wings, Paul David asked her, "Didju learn anything t'day?" She nodded while tears dripped off her chin. "T'marra, you come out here 'n pick yerself out another chick, 'n let's us hope we don't hafta do this again." Paul David let her go and she ran for the house. Then he turned to Hub. "Go gitchur dawg." Without waitin' for a response, Paul David headed for the house.

Hub knew better. He shouldn'ta tried to talk Paul David out o' killin' the hen. He couldn't imagine what he'd do if he tried to talk him out o' this, so he went to look for the dog. He had him in his arms when Paul David stepped out the back door with his gun in his hand. A .45 revolver with a six-inch barrel. Hub's lip curled in pain. Paul David waggled the barrel toward the dog.

"Set 'im down."

He did and Paul David didn't give it a second before he shot the dog in the right flank. The blow swung it around a hundred and eighty. The poor thing yipped pitifully and tried to run, but it just turned in circles, draggin' its bloody backside, convulsin' in pain. Paul David walked to Hub and helt out the gun, butt first. "You'cn finish it 'r let it bleed t'death. Whichever you think's best. And when it's dead, you dig a hole 'n bury it. Then you fashion a cross for it, so that ever time you look out in th'yard, you see it."

Hub took the gun. Paul David turned and walked toward the house. Hub's first inclination was to thumb back the hammer and shoot Paul David in back o' the head. He wondered if he knew it.

He did, but he didn't think it would happen.

Hub cocked the pistol and put Buddy out of his misery.

Next day, Paul David brought home another puppy. Hub didn't bother to name it, he just called it Puppy or Dog or Hey. Ever three or four months, Paul David would bring home another and then let Hub get attached to it. Then he'd drink up some cockamaymie excuse and shoot it or beat it with a stick bad enough to cripple it beyond repair and then Hub'd have to kill it.

CHAPTER 16

Oledeux's Meeting Hall was on the west side of town. It was big and sturdy and that was about all one could say for it. Years earlier it'd been a combination blacksmith and livery, but because of Mr. Ford's noisy damn contraptions, the need for horseshoes and the critters that wore 'em got scarcer and scarcer. When the old boy who'd owned the place kicked the bucket, his son tried to take it over, failed, and abandoned the building to possums, pigeons, and rats.

It used to be just outside of town, but with time the town had spread out, and eventually the building found itself right in town. One day one of the city fathers brought up the idea of an official Meeting Hall. The bigger cities had one 'n, God Dammit, Oledeux oughta have one, too. Well, instead of goin' to the expense of puttin' up somethin' new, they junked the smithy's forge, shoveled out the horsey stuff, bat and rat droppin's, and slapped on two or three coats o' whitewash, put up a raised platform they called a stage, hung a couple o' criss-cross lines of eye-waterin' two-hundred watters, and called it The Meeting Hall.

In the early evening of August seventeenth, nineteen hundred and twenty-four, the big rolling doors were open and the place was jumpin'. On the heavy plank stage were two farmers, an undertaker, and a pharmacist, known far and wide as The Band. It was comprised of a guitar, fiddle, banjo, and the little fella, the pharmacist, slappin' the strings on a dog house, which was what they called the stand-up bass.

One o' the more popular revelers was a raven-haired, drop-dead beauty named Ret Lusaw. Her eyes were wide-set, near black and sparkly, like the moon reflected in a pond. She had dimples you could push peas in. She wasn't the ain't-she-pretty, glamorous Hollywood or classic beauty, but the raw, nasty, Boy-howdy-I-sure-would-like-me-some-o'-that kind. She was nineteen years old, slim and flirty; slim on the slim, heavy on the flirty. The term 'full of herself' was made for Ret Lusaw. She sported one o' them bobbed hairdos popular in the big cities. She'd seen a picture of it in a magazine and had the local hair girl cut it for her. She knew it'd create a lot o' talk at the dance and that's why she did it. Ret Lusaw liked bein' talked about and looked at. The fat, dumpy, grumpy, and envious prune-faced old biddies sittin' on their flabby asses on the benches linin' the walls all agreed she looked like a boy with too big teeth and too little titties.

Watchin' her, a body woulda sworn she was totally natural, but truth be told, everthing she did was highly choreographed. Ever wink, ever twirl, ever giggle—rehearsed to the hilt. Ret's best friend had always been the swing-wing mirrors on the vanity in her bedroom. Ret Lusaw knew what she had and how to use it.

Two others enjoying the production was thirty-two-year-old George Komes, the kind that kept an invisible chip perched on his shoulder, currently nursin' a whiskey and rubbin' the end of a twiggy little stick over his teeth. Where babies had a banky with a frayed end they brushed under their nose or a dry-puke-flaked doll they drug about, George Komes had a little twig end he constantly rubbed over his teeth. He kept half a dozen spares in his shirt pocket.

At his side was his peanut-chompin', dim-witted, thirty-year-old, almost bald-headed brother, Matthew, a good argument for mandatory, mental-hospital-steppin'-in-for-the-sake-of-mankind, sterilization. Where George's teeth were dazzlingly white, Matthew's were disgusting. Filthy, discolored, and the left top front was missing. He had the constant habit of playin' with it with his tongue. It also gave everthing he said a *th* sound. "Tho what? Thath mine!" And, like almost everthing else about Matthew, it was annoying. "Hey, George! Look at thith. Whadaya thay?"

George was big, well in excess of two hundred pounds, quiet and secretive. He was a fighter, too. Not a good one, but he didn't have to be. He had two things goin' for him. The first was an extremely high pain threshold. The second was perseverance. A deadly combination. He'd get hit time and time again but kept on comin'. He could take it until the other fella was completely worn out. Eventually, he'd get in that one punch and that was all she wrote. Once his opponent was on the ground, George finished him off. Then he'd finish him off some more.

Matthew wasn't near as big as George, but what he lacked in size he more than made up for in stupidity. He was ever bit as scary as George, though, but in a different way. He was as conniving, too, but in a creepier way. George never smiled, and meant it. Matthew never stopped smilin', and didn't.

The Komes Brothers were a surly duo you didn't wanna mess with, with or without alcohol, but more than that, they were sons of the witch, Lootie Komes.

Across the room, leanin' up agin the wall, was Hub, Ret's big, twenty-four-year-old, overly-protective brother, and he was watchin' George and Matthew watch Ret. When the music was over, Hub caught sight o' George knockin' back the last of his drink, and Matthew grabbin' two handsful o' roasted peanuts and shovin 'em in his pocket. They gave one last lustful look at Ret and sauntered out the back door.

Oblivious to it all, a perspiration-glistening Ret glided toward a group o' young men, part of her admiring throng. Before she got to 'em, though, one, a crimpy-haired red-head name of Nud Beaumont, took the initiative, leaped from the anxious herd, jumped to her side, and slipped his arm around her waist. Then he swung her around and headed for the dance floor, tellin' everbody, "My turn!"

Roscoe Bowles, who figured it was his turn, followed 'em onto the floor and playfully but purposefully pulled Ret from Nud's grasp. "Hell y'are, boy," and he yelled to the band, "Fire up another'n, fellas!"

Nud grabbed her back. "Don't be grabbin' th'woman's gonna marry me 'n have my babies!"

"Who died 'n left either o' you rich?" Ret asked, lookin' at 'em like they's crazy.

Fakin' heartbreak, Nud clutched his chest and whined, "Why Ret, is monetary riches so important when ya feel for one another th'way we do?"

"Yeah, I think so!" she said. "First, they ain't enough money in all Looziana t'get my interest, 'n two, I ain't havin' noooobody's babies. 'Specially yorn."

Roscoe grabbed her around the waist and told Nud, "Yeah," then to Ret, "Let's go!"

"Uh uhhhhhh. That's it," she said, pushin' away from Roscoe, "ya'll're gettin' way too grabby. Ya'lla rurnt my night. I'm goin' home." They circled her, pleading with her not to go, and she told 'em, "Don't beg, it ain't manly." Then she casually pulled a hankie out o' LeRoy Ledbetter's coat pocket with her fingertips. The boys stopped breathin', watchin' her run the hankie over her throat and the back of her neck. Then she drug it through the barely perceptible indentation separatin' her small but tantalizing breastages and handed the moistened keepsake back to LeRoy. He was already thinkin' 'bout runnin' home and puttin' it in a Mason jar to keep the moisture from escapin'. She started away, and lookin' over her shoulder, gave 'em the Poop-Poop-a-Doop, ain't-I-just-the-cutest-little-thing-you-ever-seen, and gushed, "Good night, boys." She exited, and once outside, took off her shoes, supremely satisfied with her performance.

She was half a mile from the Meeting Hall, walkin' down the middle o' the dirt road, straight into the face of a custard-yellow full moon hoverin' just above the h'rizon, bright enough to read by, imagining what the boys were sayin' about her, when...

Snap!

...she jerked to a stop! Like she'd run into a brick wall. All her senses come to life while she scanned the dark woods at her left, listenin'. While the moon lit the road in front of her well enough, it couldn't penetrate a dozen feet into the woods. Maybe it was just a possum or some other woodsmate, so why had she reacted that way? She'd heard critters in the dark before. Keepin' a wary eye to the woods, she continued on her way, tryin' to shake it off, but she couldn't shake the nigglin' feelin' that somethin' was wrong.

Suddenly, she squeaked a squirrel-like yip. Somethin' had ricocheted off her chest and bounced to the ground. She rubbed her hand over where it'd struck. It hadn't hurt her. It wasn't big enough, but where had it come from? She bent over and picked it up. A peanut! Where the Hell....

A silly giggle in the woods to the left brought her straight back up. "Who's there?" she chirped, and then realized her voice sounded choked, and that made her feel she'd betrayed concern to somethin' she shouldn'ta. She was owlin' her head back and forth, lookin' in the woods, when she was struck with another peanut. "Come on now, this ain't funny. Who's out there? Nud? If that's you, I'm gonna skin you alive, then I'll get Hub t'beatchu t'juice!"

Again, the muted giggle. She jerked her head to the sound of another stick snappin'. This time, though, it wasn't from the giggler's position. She cocked up, set for fight or flight. Her head jerked to another snap, and this time she saw somethin' movin', comin' out o' the trees to the road, just up ahead and to her left. When it stepped into the road, the light o' the full moon blinded her from the front so that she couldn't make out the face, but she did recognize it for its size and the way it carried itself.

Her lip curled back and her stomach seized up like she was gonna vomit! Boy, oh boy, how quickly things could go south. Twenty yards to her front, George Komes sauntered, slowly, to the middle o' the road. She'd noticed him and his stupid brother leerin' at her at the dance, but with dozens of people around, she'd passed it off. But now she didn't have the crowd to protect her. Or her brother. Her ever instinct screamed at her to run. Everbody'd heard rumors o' George and Matthew doin' nasty things to girls, sex things, but nobody ever admitted to it 'cause gettin' sexed up by George wasn't anywhere near as bad as tellin' on him and gettin' nearly beat to death. Then, too, there was the witch.

There was always the God Damn witch.

She glanced around, lookin' for the stupid one, knowing full well that where you saw the one, the other was close by. George without Matthew was like a body without a shadow. She didn't see him, and that made her more nervous than if she had. She turned her attention back to George and started backin' away. He didn't make a move to follow her, so now she felt stupid. Maybe there wasn't anything wrong after all, he was just bein' scary ol' George. He liked bein' scary as much as she liked bein' cute. "What're you doin', George?" He didn't say anything. That didn't help her nerves. She chewed her bottom lip, glanced around. "Where's 'at brother o' yorn?"

He still didn't say anything. She was up to there with whatever the joke was, and she wanted out. She spun around to go back the way she'd come, and stuttered to a stop. Matthew, with that stupid goofy smile plastered on his ugly face, was standin' in the middle o' the road, the moon full on him, poppin' peanuts in his mouth.

"Boy, you're a quiet one, ain'tcha?" she said.

"Yeah," he agreed, friendly, and gigglin' like a snake if a snake could giggle. "Wanna peanut?" and he flipped another one. It bounced off her chest, and to the ground. "Hold still," he said. Then, miming what he wanted, "push yr'tittieth t'gether 'n I'll thee if I'cn pitch one 'tween 'em," and pinched another in his fingertips like he was about to toss it at her.

"I'd rather ya didn't," she said. If she ever knew anything in her life, she knew this—she was in trouble. Real. Bad. Trouble. This was what people felt just before they died. She quickly surveyed her situation. George in front, Matthew in back, and the dark woods to the side. The choice was obvious.

George had read her mind, brought his hand up to his mouth to remove his tooth-rubbin' stick, and asked, "What'cha gonna do, Lowwwretta Lusaw? Gonna run?"

Then, behind her, she heard Matthew's insane chortlin', "Runnnnnnn, Ret! Run 'r I'm gonna gitcha in th'tittie with a peanut!"

Ret dropped her shoes and was in the woods before they hit the road.

CHAPTER 17

George had his eyes scrunched down, concentrating hard on something up the street, rubbin' a twig over his teeth with one hand, a lit hand-rolled in the other. Ever few seconds he'd take a pull and then blow the smoke out his nose. He and Matthew were sittin' in a beat-up Ford shortbed parked at the curb in the middle of the industrial section of Lecerne, Louisiana, which was pretty much all Lecerne was. They'd been there about half an hour and it was miserable cold and wet. George was nervous 'cause he couldn't see for shit through the fog. They had to keep the windows rolled down to keep their breath from foggin 'em up. Ever little bit George would stick his arm out the driverside window to wipe the front glass on his side off with a rag, and then pass it to Matthew to catch the other side.

"Thit, it'th cold," Matthew bitched for about the millionth time. He was slunk down in the seat with his coat collar turned up, arms crossed over his chest and his fingers tucked in his armpits. He didn't notice George give him the stink eye, tired of his complaints.

Matthew was worryin' a rubbery thingamabob in his mouth about the size of a cashew. It wasn't a cashew, though. Far from it. He'd pass it back and forth between the gap in his teeth with his tongue for a little bit, pull it out, mash it in his fingertips to flatten it out and then, when he let go, watch it reshape itself. Then he'd smell it and stick it back in his mouth. He noticed George was watchin' and helt it out to him. "Wanna chaw?"

George laughed and shook his head. "No, thanks, that's an acquired taste."

Matthew didn't know what a *kwired* was and didn't really give a shit, so he let it go. "Firtht one I had'n a long time," he said. He pinched it out again, brought it to his nose, flared his nostrils, and took a slow whiff. "Don't tatht no more, but it didn't have much t'thtart with. You'd think it'd have more, wudncha, 'cause o' where it come from." He put it back in his mouth, took a deep breath, blew it out, and the vapor gave him an idea. He clenched his fists and pistoned his arms back and forth. "Chka-chka, chka-chka, chka-chka, chka-chka." Then he tilted his head back and out the window, blowin' vapor. "Wooooooo, wooooooo, woo-woo, wooooooo. Chka-chka, chka-chka, chka-chka, chka-chka. Wooooooo, wooooooo." He looked over at George and grinned. "Thounth like a train, don't it?"

"Right," George said. "How 'bout pullin' it in th'station 'fore somebody hears ya."

Matthew looked around the deserted street. "They ain't nobody around."

"Let's not take th'chance, okay?"

Matthew smiled, clenched his fists, pistoned his arms, and chka-chkaed slower and slower until he sshhhhhhhhhed to a stop. "Everbody out!" The ride over, he wrapped his arms over his chest and stuck his fingers back in his pits. "Fuck, it'th cold!" He turned to George, looked over his face and grinned. "You done motht o' th'payin', I feel awful guilty gettin' all th'joyment."

George adjusted the rearview mirror with a knuckle-skinned right hand, leaned for'ard and, as best he could in the truck's dark confines, examined his fresh, deeply-scratched face.

"Theyth gonna latht," Matthew teased.

George looked over his face in the mirror. "Yeah, well," he picked up the .45 resting in his lap, flipped open the chamber, checking the load, "I got my share." He flipped the chamber back and, imagining something dark, said more to hisself than to Matthew, "'n I got a lot more t'come."

"We got a lot done t'day," Matthew said.

"Yep, I think we did." He put the gun back in his lap, pulled a watch out of his pants pocket and flipped it open. 12:15 a.m.

"'Bout time?" Matthew asked.

"Should be," George replied. He put the watch back and felt somethin' hang up on his knuckle. He rubbed his finger over it. A flap a skin. He brought it to his mouth and gnawed it off with his front teeth. Then he pinched it off the end of his tongue and helt it out to Matthew. "You want this, too?"

Matthew squinted at it. "What ith it?"

"Flap o' skin."

Matthew shook his head and parted his lips to show he was still occupied with the current prize. George flicked the flap out the window.

Nestled in the warm, cozy office of one of the warehouses half a block up and on the other side o' the street, Jack Hoff, mid-fortyish, a fearless security guard with a Southern States Security patch sewn on his sleeve, checked his watch. 12:16 a.m. He snapped it shut and stuck it back in his pocket. He and thirty-five-year-old Randolph (Snotty) Snodgrass, another highly-trained example of securial guardatory ferocity, relaxed after a grueling day of waitin', sittin', and readin'. Randy had a three-week-old newspaper spread out on the small table in the middle o' the room, but it hadn't kept him from nodding off.

The purpose of this deadly duo on duty at a non-descript warehouse in the middle o' nowhere was because somehow, earlier that afternoon, their armored truck ran into engine trouble on the road and they didn't get into town until long after the bank'd closed. They'd picked up the strong box on time from the train whose tracks didn't yet swing anywhere near Lecerne. It was their job to bring it into town and to the bank. It was a run they'd done ever month or so for a couple o' years, so just another day at the office.

A few miles outside o' town, Randy'd been droning on and on 'bout somethin' that was goin' in one o' Jack's ears and out the other, when Jack skorked up his face, cocked his good ear to the front o' the truck, and told Randy to, "Hush up!" Randy didn't know pucky about motors and Jack knew it. If he told Randy the rackety-soundin' motor had Rocky Mountain Chicken Pox he'da believed it. Randy listened real hard, said he didn't hear nothin', but Jack said he was gonna pull over anyway and take a gander under the hood. He pulled off the road, turned off the motor, climbed out all huffy-like, propped up the hood, and stuck his head in. He twisted and wiggled and waggled first one thing and then another. Then he kicked the bumper hard, pulled off his official Southern States Security cap, scratched his head, and spat out, "Shit! I's afraid o' that! God Dammit all t'Hell!"

While Randy scanned the motor, lookin' to see what the that was that Jack was so concerned about, Jack told him, "Jump back in 'n when I say, give it a crank 'n keep yr'fingers crossed." While Randy was gettin' in, Jack unhookled a couple o' spark-plug wires and yelled, "Make sure it's in neutral 'n let 'er rip!"

Randy pushed in the clutch, took it out o' gear, and punched the starter, kickin' it over. It sounded like it was grindin' rocks. Jack jumped back like he'd been snake bit and yelled at Randy to, "Shut it off, quick, quick! Jesus H!" He jumped around, slingin' his hand. "Damn thing nearly took m'hand off!" D.W. Griffith woulda been poundin' his pud, Jack's performance was that good. Randy started to jump out o' the truck. "No," Jack said, "stay there, I might wantcha t'try it again."

"Are you nuts?" Randy asked, shocked beyond belief at Jack's bravery.

"Listen," Jack snapped, full of manly responsibility, determination, and company pride, "We gotta get t'th'fuckin' bank 'fore it closes. Just gimme a second." Jack cautiously approached the hand-gobblin' machine and after makin' sure Randy couldn't see, rehookled the spark-plug cables and backed out.

"Ready?" Randy asked, stickin' his head out the window.

"Naw, changed m'mind, we jes better leave it."

Randy climbed out o' the truck and came to stand beside Jack. "That sounded like Hell," he said, ping-pongin' back and forth between Jack, Jack's hand, and whatever the Hell it was that made the hand-grabbin' racket in the engine.

"Yeah, well, I's right. It's th'God Damned Heckle Shaft. Burned clean up! I never woulda thought it'cd happen twice in th'same lifetime." He was so into the moment, immersed in the part, he was havin' trouble backin' out.

"You had it happen b'fore, huh?"

"Once, but that was twice too much." Randy was such a great audience, it was hard to pull the curtain down. "Tryin' t'get it lit probly just fucked it up that much more." He kicked the tire. "Shit!"

Randy took a quick look through the engine compartment, like he'd know the difference between a burnt Heckle Shaft and a cracked Speckle Joint. Then, he looked at Jack and asked, hopeful, "We got a spare?"

Jack looked at him like that might possibly be the dumbest thing he'd ever heard another human bean ask. "Are you kiddin' me? Not on this fuckin' planet! Them damn things's scarce's hen's teeth. And expensive? Whoooooooee are they ever! They almost never blow, but when they do, well, shit, you heard it yr'self. They ain't somethin' ya keep layin' 'round in th'glove box, waitin' fr'one t'crap out on ya." He scratched his head and looked up and down the road. "Shit, we ain't gonna get there in time, God Dammit! There goes a perfect God Damn record!" He pulled out his pocket watch, took a disgusted look, snapped it shut, and put it back in his pocket. "That jes beat's all! Fuckin' bank's gonna close. Come three o'clock them double-breasted sons o' bitches snap th'front door shut faster 'n tighter'n my sister-in-law's hairy pink snapper." Then a funny popped in his head and, laughin' out loud, he said, "But, unlike th'bank, if th'sister-in-law had any idee I had fifty G's hunkered in m'front pocket warmin' th'Trouser Mauser, she'd swing th'gates open," he snapped his fingers, "jes like 'at."

It was about three hours before they got a tow, and now, there they were, sittin' it out with fifty thousand sheckles in a locked box in a little coat closet in a warehouse the bank'd had to take back from a company that'd went belly up, waitin' for the sun to come up and the bank to reopen. They weren't too worried, though. They were armed and knew how to use 'em. How many people knew they were there? Industrial area, quiet, no problem.

Jack'd made two phone calls earlier. One to the bank tellin' 'em what'd happened and linin' up the warehouse for the night, then another that Randy assumed was to Minnie, Jack's old lady, tellin' her what'd happened. Randy'd met her one time. She was bossy. She was fat. Had more rolls than a German bakery.

Jack chuckled to hisself remembr'in' when the guy with the tow showed up, he'd asked if they had any idee what might be wrong. He said maybe he could fix it right there and get 'em back on the road. Randy jumped up real quick, more than a little anxious to show he knew more than a little about truck motors, hiked his thumb over his shoulder t'ward the hood and informed the fella, "It's probly th'damn Heckle Shaft. Can ya believe that?"

The tow truck fella goosed up his face and, behind Randy's back, Jack gave him the "Don't pursue it, he's a fool, just tow us in" look. The fella nodded and winked knowingly, hooked up, and hauled 'em off.

Thinkin' about it now and tryin' not to laugh out loud, Jack stood up, laced his fingers behind his head, and stretched out the kinks. "Ohhhh, boy, I'm gonna get some air 'n try t'wake up. Why don'tchu see if you'cn shake us up a pot o' coffee," he said, and headed for the office door to the warehouse proper.

Lookin' through the office cupboards when they first got there, they'd found half a can o' ground Arbuckle and an electric hot plate in a cupboard. No tellin' how old it was, but when you're up to your ass in alligators....

"I need sumpthin'," Randy groaned, standin' up. He stretched so hard somethin' popped in his low back. "Oh, Hell, what was 'at?" he gasped, twistin' carefully to see if anything was busted.

"Shit, Randy, I heard that clear out here," Jack said from just inside the warehouse. "Maybe ya busted yer Heckle Shaft."

Continuing to flex his back, Randy farted and did a little jig. "Woops! Maybe that was it." He lifted a leg and fired off another one. "Bark, bark. Nice Froggy."

Just before Jack got to the warehouse's outside door, he looked over his shoulder, checkin' on Randy. Contented he'd probly stay in the office, Jack unlocked the door, pushed it open, and the cold, damp night air hit him. He hunched up in his coat, stepped outside, closed the door, and pulled out a cigarette he'd rolled earlier from his shirt pocket. He looked through the fog to the lonely shortbed parked half a block up the street and strikin' a wooden match, lit the cigarette.

George caught the flare and back-slapped Matthew's leg. Matthew popped straight up, gawked goggle-eyed out the front window, workin' the thingamabob for all it was worth. George purposely took two long drags off his weed to fire up a good glow, stuck his arm out the window and flicked the weed in the air. It arced through the puffy fog and landed with o' shower o' twinkly sparks, then hissed out in the wet street.

Jack saw the little meteor, took two healthy drags on his own, and launched it in the same manner. He owled around like there might be an insomniac walkin' his bulldog, then pulled a small wedge o' wood from his coat pocket and placed it under the door to keep it from closing completely. One more last look up the street to the truck and he re-entered the warehouse.

George stuck his tooth-rubbin' stick in his shirt pocket. "Let's go." They climbed out o' the truck, George with a heavy, double-handled leather satchel and Matthew with his gun drawn and cocked, battle-bound. George halted and nodded to the gun. "Why don'tcha wait'll we get inside?"

Feeling stupid, Matthew stuck the gun in his belt.

George nodded to it again. "Y'might wanna uncock it."

Feeling even stupider, Matthew pulled it out, notched the hammer back, and stuck it back in his pants.

"There ya go," George said, and they headed across the street for the warehouse, lookin' 'round for the same dog-walkin' insomniac.

Anxious after settin' things up, Jack entered the office, eased into his chair, and took a big breath to calm his nerves.

"That was quick," Randy said. He had the coffee pot in one hand and was slappin' the base of a hot plate settin' on a side counter with the other.

"It's too cold fer a smoke," Jack replied.

"That ain't th'only thing cold," Randy bitched, referring to the uncooperative hotplate. "This thing ain't worth a shit. Plugged it in 'n a little red light come on, but the plate only gets warm. I don't wanna go through th'whole fuckin' night sippin' luke-cold coffee."

The lights bein' on in the office made it difficult to see in the darkened warehouse unless you knew what to look for. George and Matthew were creepin' stealthily through the machinery, inchin' their way to the office while Randy's voice filtered through the office wall.

"Didja?"

"Did I what?" Jack asked. Concerned with what was about to take place, he hadn't been listenin' to Randy's droning.

"Know that frogs'cd talk?"

"Frogs?"

"Yeah. Ask one how much water there is in th'pond 'n whadaya think he says?"

"I dunno. What?"

"Kneedeep. Kneedeep. You know what a horny frog says?" but before Jack could answer, Randy added, "Rubit. Rubit." He howled with laughter. Then he repeated the punch lines again.

"Ha ha ha," Jack faked. "Yeah, 'at's pretty good, didn't see 'at comin'," when in truth, he'd heard both of 'em all his life. Stupid Snotgrass wasn't capable o' tellin' a stupid joke without repeating the stupid punch line. Jack thought that if everthing went right tonight, though, he'd never have to put up with another one. Lookin' out the corner of his eye, he saw George and Matthew crouched at the other side o' the office door, ready to pounce. He glanced back at Randy foolin' with the hot plate and then to George and nodded the "go for it."

George rared back on one leg and put everthing he had into kickin' in the office door, nearly blowin' it off the hinges. He coulda just opened it, it wasn't locked, but kickin' it open would show Randy how dangerous he was.

It worked. Randy's spinchter just about gave up the ghost, dropped the coffee pot and fumbled for his .38. Jack jumped up in a play-pretend, half-assed attempt to pull his.

"Do it," George growled, his revolver cocked and aimed squarely between Randy's eyes, "'n I'll blow yer fuckin' head off!"

"Yeah! Do it," Matthew repeated, denied from birth the cranial micro-inchage to come up with his own threat. Worked up as a ferret in love, he feverishly chomped on the thingamabob, wavin' his gun back and forth between Jack and Randy. Heatin' up like a runaway boiler he pushed, "Come on! Do it! Do it!" He didn't know exactly what the *it* was he was waitin' for one of 'em to do, but figured he'd recognize it when it happened. It didn't make much difference to Matthew though, he thoroughly enjoyed bein' worked up over anything.

"Calm down," George said, recognizing the signs.

"I'm calm," Matthew said, wound up tighter'n an eight-day clock, "I'm calm."

He wasn't, but at least George had put a gov'nor on it. "Get' th'r guns," he ordered.

Matthew stuck his gun in his belt and started for Jack.

"Hey," George said, pointin' the end of his gun barrel at Matthew's belt. "Un...Cock...It."

Matthew rolled his eyes, turned his back to Jack and Randy, pulled out the revolver, uncocked it, and stuck it back in his pants. Then he collected their guns and handed 'em to George, who placed 'em in the satchel.

"How th'Hell'dju get in here?" Randy snapped.

"What dif'ernce does it make?" George barked, wagglin' his gun at a chair.

"Yeah," Matthew repeated, slammin' the heel of his hand hard into the back o' Randy's head, "What dif'ernth doth it make, you thimpledon?" Then he grabbed Randy by the back of his shirt collar and shoved him onto the chair. He was about to clobber Randy again but George cut it off.

"No, not now," he said and produced pre-cut lengths of thin cord from the satchel and tossed 'em to Matthew.

Matthew wrenched Randy's arms to the back o' the chair and started tyin' him down. "You'll lemme know, wont'cha, if it'th too tight," he said and looked at George, gigglin'.

"Where's th'money?" George asked Jack.

"Money?" Jack came back. "There ain't no money in here! I don't know what th'Hell yer talkin' about!"

George pressed the end o' the gun barrel to his temple.

"You can't get away with it," Jack growled.

"Is it worth dyin' for?"

They were puttin' on the show they'd discussed days earlier so that Randy would unknowingly cover Jack's ass and brag to the authorities later how incredibly brave he'd been during the holdup.

Juttin' his jaw out, Jack delivered one of his best lines. "I ain't tellin' you shit!"

George cocked the hammer and Randy nearly peed his pants. "Fer Christ's sake, Jack, are you nuts? It ain'tchur money, give it to 'em!"

Jack seemed to be mullin' it over, milkin' the moment.

"JACK!"

Jack finally nodded to the desk. "It's in th'closet. Key's in th'desk. Bottom left. In the back." He looked to the floor, so ashamed. He hoped Randy noticed.

George stepped to the desk, opened the drawer, and pulled out a key ring and a near-full bottle of Jack Daniels.

Matthew noticed the bottle and smacked his lips. "Mmmmm, Uncle Jackth Cure-All."

George sat the bottle on the desktop and tossed the keyring to Jack. "Open it."

Feigning reluctance, Jack walked to the closet door, unlocked it, and swung it open, revealing the non-descript metal box shoved in the back corner on the floor.

"Git it out," George ordered, kickin' Jack in the leg.

Jack thought the kick was a realistic addition to the act, but he didn't think George had to kick quite so hard. He pulled the box out o' the closet and stood up.

George'd had it with all the stupid playacting. "I ain't got time fer no more o' these monkey-shines! Open it!"

Jack set the box on the table and opened it, revealing mucho bundles o' money.

"Oh, Lordy," Matthew exclaimed.

George waggled his gun at Jack and told Matthew, "His turn."

Matthew yanked Jack to a chair and commenced to tyin' him down.

With Randy tied and Jack gettin' that way, George took the satchel to the cash box and started transferring the precious bundles.

Suddenly, Matthew grabbed his throat. "Aw, Thit!" he croaked. "I thwallered it!" He bent over makin' an awful racket, tryin' desperately to cough the thingamabob back up.

George couldn't stifle a laugh.

"Well, God Dammit," Matthew snarled, "you wanna laugh? You think it'th funny? It ain't funny!"

"I wasn't laughin' atcha," George tried to cover, "I's laughin' with ya."

"Bullthit! I ain't laughin'! You thee me laughin'? I ain't laughin'! It ain't funny! They'th hard t'come by. I thoulda got both of 'em while I had th'chanth, but noooo, you'th in thuch a big dang hurry, I had t'leave it! Thit!"

George brought the satchel to Matthew, grabbed him hard by the back o' the neck, and forced him to look inside. "Tell me if 'at don't ease th'pain some."

Immediately forgetting the recently consumed, hard-to-come-by thingamabob, Matthew stuck his hand in the satchel and ran it through the bundles. "Boy, 'at'th a lot o' money, ain't it? How muth ith there?"

"S'posed t'be fifty thousand 'n I reckon that's about what it is."

"Fifty thouthand? Boy, oh boy! How muth ith that in money?"

"I ain't got th'time t'explain it right now," George said, used to such questions. "We'll talk about it later."

"Okay," Matthew said.

"You know," George said, steppin' over to Jack, "if we's t'do in this fella," he tapped the end of his gun barrel on top o' Jack's head, "we wudn hafta split the money with 'im."

"I don't know what th'Hell he's talkin' about," Jack said when Randy snapped a look at him. Then, back to George, "I ain't got no idee what th'Hell yer talkin' 'bout!"

"Sure ya do," George said, and then to Randy, "He's in on it with us. That's how we got in. He jammed a stick in th'door so it wouldn't close."

Randy glared at Jack. Didn't look like he'd be standin' up for him at the big inquisition. George took the one step to Randy, raised his gun, and without flinching, shot him in the forehead, blowin' him back'ards. Runny, bloody brain stuff splattered and glopped down the wall.

"Hoooooo, Yeah!" Matthew yelled, excitedly. That was the spontaneous shit he lived for.

"What th'Hell're you doin'?" Jack blurted. "That wasn't part o' th'deal!"

"Yer right." And one half second later, Jack's brain and blood created more wall-bound artwork.

"Fooled him," Matthew said, grinnin' like a maniac.

"Yeah, well, he's figgered it out now," George said, watchin' Jack's body give one last involuntary twitch.

Matthew pulled a large pocketknife from his pants, peenched it open, and stabbed it in the tabletop. Then he got down on one knee and started to undo Jack's belt.

"What're you doin'?" George asked.

"Gettin' their weenerth."

"No, we ain't got time f'that."

"Aw, George," Matthew whined, "I hate t'watht'm. Freth oneth'th hard t'come by."

"Whada you get outa that?" George asked, pinch-eyed.

"I dunno," Matthew replied, shrugging childlike. "I juth like playin' with 'em." Then, not totally believable, he added, "It ain't thex thtuff. I don't kith 'em 'r nothin'." He didn't want George to think he was a sissy or a queer or a queer sissy.

George wasn't so sure. If Matthew could deny it, it meant he'd imagined it, or...oh, well, what the Hell, he could do worse. Brotherly love kicked in and he relented. "Awright, but hurry up. I'll get th'truck 'n meetcha outside." He put the whiskey bottle in the satchel.

He was halfway to the office door when Matthew called out. "George?" George turned back, and with a face full o' brotherly admiration, Matthew said, "I thure had a lotta fun t'day."

"I know," George said and headed for the office door.

CHAPTER 18

The full moon, now well up in the sky, shined on the darkened shack set back off a rutted road, nestled in moss-bearded trees. The only sounds were the crickets, night birds, and croakers broadcasting reproductive invitations. It was the same shanty that years earlier had housed Roach and Pearl Komes and their scar-faced little girl, Lootie. The shack where Pearl died. The shack where Lootie had reluctantly forked over her virginity. The one where Roach had eventually died alone, of malnutrition. Committed suicide from eatin' his own cookin'.

It used to be quite a ways outside o' town. It was closer now, and when the Komes boys got of an age when they could live away from their mother, they left Cob's and took up in the old place. Pearl and her little baby George's bones still filled a space in the mulchy ground out back, although their names were no longer advertised on short slabs of wood. Tonight, another dead body lay within.

The silvery moonlight slanted through the open front door as big Hub Lusaw spread half a raggedy blanket on the sittin' part, and the other half, draped over the back o' the smelly, dusty, threadbare couch. Sighing heavily, he bent to the floor and easily lifted his little sister's naked, battered, butchered body. It shocked him that the arms and legs that dangled and flopped like only a dead somethin' could do, had only a few hours earlier been so very much alive and happy.

She was so young.

Had been.

She was so pretty.

Had been.

He laid her on the blanket. He felt self-conscious, embarrassed even, as he ran his eyes over the ruined little body and thought how much his little sister had grown into a woman. Then he tenderly pulled the part o' the blanket that hung over the back o' the couch over her. He could only imagine how embarrassed she'd be bein' seen in this condition; naked, and her new hairdo, a mess. He wished now he hadn't teased her about it.

He started to tuck the edge o' the blanket under her to keep her warm, but then he remembered…it wouldn't make any difference. She was dead. He'd never seen anything deader. He tucked it anyway. Groaning to the floor with the couch to his back, he pulled a tobacco pouch and papers from his shirt pocket, separated one paper from the pack, and set the rest on the floor. He pulled at the neck on the pouch and shakily filled the paper with leaf, spillin' as much on his crotch as landed on the little square. He pulled the pouch strings with his teeth, set it on the floor beside the other papers, tamped the leaf around, rolled the paper, and licked it down. His licker was pretty dry, and he had his doubts it'd hold.

That done, he pulled a wooden match from his shirt pocket and snapped it to life with his thumbnail. Lighting the cigarette, he started to shake the match off, but instead, pinched the cigarette in his lips and stuck his leg straight out so he could dig his pocket watch from his pants pocket. He flipped it open to see the time – 1:45 a.m. He pinched it shut, shook the match out, and set both the watch and the spent match on the floor next to the pouch and papers. After a couple o' pulls, he looked over his shoulder into the half-open, dead eyes that couldn't look back any more, and he imagined all the things that coulda been, that now never would, and he promised silent promises.

He reached over and pressed her eyelids closed. Not hard, he didn't wanna hurt her, just enough to close 'em. He helt 'em down a few seconds then let go. They didn't close completely, but it was better. It almost looked like she was peekin' at him on the sly. He turned back around, and while starin' at the glowing ember on the end o' the cigarette, flipped through the mental scrapbook of his and Ret's lives until the fire reached his fingers. Then he got up and stepped out on the rickety porch to shake the pins and needles out of his legs. A wispy carpet of mist lay on the ground. He leaned on a porch post, and while the lightnin' bugs twinkled, rolled another smoke and made his plans.

The off-kilter headlights flashed on the front o' the shack and the truck scudded to a stop. The engine died, and a second later the lights went out. The drained Jack Daniels bottle clinked to the ground when Matthew pushed open the squeaky shotgun door. Drunk as a skunk, his foot glanced off a rock and he stumbled into the side o' the truck. He heard George laugh and told him to fuck hisself and go to Hell. Then he pushed off the fender and stumbled around the nose o' the truck, headed for the shack like he didn't have a solid bone in his body. George slid out on his side, laughin' his ass off. Swayin' next to the driver-side door, he hauled out his pecker and commenced to empty his bladder all over the runnin' board. He looked over his shoulder and laughed at Matthew lumb'rin' toward the front door while the smelly, yellow stream bobbed and jerked with each alcohol-induced chuckle.

Matthew entered the shack, and, with no time to register a complaint, his ill-equipped brain box exploded, literally, like a ripe watermelon, from the full go of a three-foot length of two-by-four to the back of his ugly head. George heard the commotion and chuckled at the picture o' Matthew fallin' flat on his face, havin' tripped over the turned-up edge o' the dirty rug just inside the door. He shook off the last lingering drops and jammed the turtle-necked lizard back in its smelly shroud. Then he, too, stumbled his way into the dark shack.

On the dirt road a hundred yards to the east, scrawny, twenty-two-year-old LeRoy Ledbetter was walkin' off the effects of too much o' the home-brewed consumed at the dance. If he entered his mother's house with liquor on his breath—and she would still be up just to make sure—she'd remind him he was still livin' under her roof and not a bit too old to be slapped silly. That's what he was thinkin' about when he heard the screams and shrieks filterin' down from the shack. Concerned, although not near enough to get personally involved, he hot-foot it down the road.

Just before sunup, a reluctant LeRoy accompanied an uncomfortably over-weight, nearly-bald, fifty-year-old Sheriff Bernard "Bernie" Rowe to the Komes shack. LeRoy was shoved over as close as he could get to the Dodge Brothers passenger-side door. He had his right arm stuck out the window while his left was crossed over his chest, his hand grippin' the window frame. Rowe had a short fuse and a lot o' powder and he'd threatened LeRoy that by gettin' him out of a warm bed that early, this call'd better be a damn sight more than George and Matthew gettin' drunk and fightin'…again. Another thing was, just before the sheriff got in the truck, he pulled off his gunbelt and set it on the seat between him and LeRoy. Then, when he got in, he unsnapped his pants to make room for his gut and it was makin' LeRoy nervous.

Ever time Rowe looked over at him with his jaw clenched down tight, LeRoy expected a whack upside the head. It was known for miles around that LeRoy Ledbetter was a card-carryin' fuckup.

Rowe finally pulled up in front o' the Komes shack, nose to nose with George's old Ford. He turned off the engine. Instantaneous nothingness. Egyptian-tomb quiet. No bugs, birds, or croakers. LeRoy pushed his head back when Rowe owled across the cab and out LeRoy's window to the shack. It was dark inside and out. After LeRoy's description o' the holocaust, he'd expected numerous casualties layin' about and construction destruction on a grand scale.

Then he looked out his own door window, and there sat the empty whiskey bottle layin' in the dirt up agin the Ford's right front tire. He looked back at LeRoy and gave him another jaw clench, pushed in the knob on the dash, switchin' off the headlamps. From past experience Rowe knew he'd probly find the infamous Komeses draped across their bed, passed out in very uncomfortable positions, or on the floor, swimmin' in a puddle of their own vomit and shit, and that picture made him work up a mad on LeRoy.

LeRoy wasn't nervous, though. He was way past that. He wished now he'd just gone home and got mother-slapped, but he was a ferrety little shit, addicted to mindin' everbody's business but his own. If it turned out to be nothin', he'd get a lifetime extension on his fuckup reputation. But! If he was to be the one that found the Komes Brothers in a bad way, it'd be all over town, and he'd be the one tied in with it. Everbody'd remember it.

"It was LeRoy found 'em!"

"Well, LeRoy was tellin' me...."

"Go ask LeRoy if you don't believe me."

Yeah, if only. The sheriff was huffin' and blowin' and shootin' nasty sidewaysie glances at him, because so far, there wasn't nothin' at the shack that said any more than that George and Matthew had knocked back a bottle or two of JD, punched each other's lights out, were layin' in vomit, and had shat their drawers. If they were even wearin' drawers.

He was right; Rowe's biggest concern was findin 'em layin' in shit. And vomit. And butt-ugly naked. If the dumb bastards were naked, he'd just spin on his heels and leave—they could sleep it off. That was a possibility, but because o' past experiences with other sheriffin' happenings, not the only one. He couldn't take any chances. He was gonna have to go in. "Yer sure it was more than George 'n Matthew agoin' at it?"

LeRoy shook his head. "No! I didn't say it was them, but it is their place. I said I thought it was them 'n somebody else, 'n that somebody else sounded like Hub Lusaw. That's what I said. And they wasn't just scrappin', they's yellin 'n screamin' like they's killin' each other. That's what I said."

Rowe looked to the shack, then back to LeRoy. "You hunker down 'n keep yr'God Damn mouth shut. You get shot 'n bleed all over my truck, I'll beatchu t'death."

LeRoy slunk down 'til the only thing showin' was his eyes and the top of his head. He didn't sport a badge or a gun and was more than willing to follow the orders o' the one that did.

All ridge-backed and fuzz-tailed, Rowe opened his door and slid out. He sucked in his gut, hitched up his pants, and re-cinched his belt. Then he reached in and pulled out his gunbelt. He wrapped it around his gut, sucked it in as much as he could, and pushed the little dogoodie in the last hole on the belt. Another few pork chops and he was gonna have to pound in another hole or buy a bigger belt. He waggled the belt down, pulled the gun up by his face with his finger hooked on the trigger. He closed the door quietly, gave LeRoy one more nasty look, took a deep breath, and crossed around the front o' the Dodge, headed for the shack.

Reason for the gun at all was 'cause o' George and Matthew's reputation. Gettin' drunk and shootin' up the shack wasn't a common occurrence but it was a possibility. He'd known 'em for years, but if one of 'em came at him, bleary-eyed and squeezin' the trigger, he'd put him down. He'd try for a leg first, but if that didn't do the trick, he'd put one in their chest. Very carefully he crossed the porch and laid flat on the outside wall just to the right o' the black hole of a door and called out. "Hey! What's goin' on in there?"

As quiet as it was, his sudden yellin' scared the snot out o' LeRoy.

No answer came from the shack.

Rowe tapped the end o' the gun barrel on the wall and called out again. "George!"

Nothin'.

"Matt!"

More nothin'. Still quiet as a graveyard.

"Shit!" he said under his breath. Grittin' his teeth and with fire in his eyes, he looked over at the pickup. LeRoy's bugged-out, froggy-lookin' eyes peeked back at him from just over window frame.

"God Damn you, LeRoy, if I don't find a dead body, I'm gonna kick yer worthless ass 'til Sundee!" Workin' up his courage, he pulled the gun up and jumped spread-eagled to the middle o' the open door. Finding he hadn't been shot at, he worked up the gumption to enter the shack.

LeRoy, cocked and ready to bolt at the first sign o' trouble, watched as Rowe's bulkitude slowly dissolved into the shack's blackness. The sheriff was in the shack only a few seconds when LeRoy saw the soft orange glow of match light flare up and filter through the front door and the window just to its right. He saw the light bend from the match light movin' around. It snuffed out, and three seconds later another one took its place, and like the first, shifted around the shack. Then it went out.

Rowe'd been sheriffing long enough that he'd seen a bunch o' bad stuff, but shortly after the second match light went out, LeRoy saw him come back out the door all wobbly-legged, white-faced, and holdin' on to a porch post with shaking hands. He lurched over the edge o' the porch and hockled up the porkchops, beans, and apple pie he'd had for dinner just a few hours earlier. LeRoy figured he wouldn't be gettin' his worthless ass kicked 'til Sundee.

LeRoy left from there to walk home. Figuring the Komes brothers weren't goin' anywhere, Rowe drove over to the Lusaw house to talk to Hub. Raeleen, Hub's wife, said, "He ain't been home since he left for the dance. I'm worried about 'im. How come yer lookin' for 'im?"

"Looks like he mighta done in George 'n Matt Komes."

Before noon, Rowe and a couple dozen hurriedly deputized locals, heavily-armed with a multitude of various explosive implements of destruction, accompanied by an excited pack of bayin' bloodhounds and buoyed by the consumption of various alcoholic accouterments, fanned out in all directions from the murdered brothers' shack.

CHAPTER 19

Tr'tl Garnier (pronounced Garnyae)—a waddlin', beetle-browed, bubble-butted, little-bitty-armed, stumpy-legged dwarf—was shovin' a securely-tethered boar off the back o' the wagon parked in front of Lootie Komes' shack. Cob's old place. Thudding to the ground, the pissed-off boar squealed, forcing Tr'tl's fearful attention to the shack's door. Quickly, the same fate as the boar was followed by a ham-strung, four-foot gator and a full-growed cottonmouth imprisoned in a dirty flour sack, lookin' to empty its fangs on somebody dumb enough to get close.

Tr'tl's little legs scuttled across the wagon bed to a ladder attached by hinges to the left side o' the wooden seat and descended to the ground. Keepin' the ever-watchful eye on the door, he scampered to a wad o' bills pinned under a small rock on the same stump Cob had used to park her flat, wrinkled ass on. Snatchin' the money in his poorly impersonated fingers, a bill flittered away, comin' to rest right next to the door. Tr'tl started for it, but after half a second's thought, figured maybe he'd let it go rather than get any nearer the door.

He had good reason.

Twenty-some years earlier his mother'd made the mistake o' pissin' Lootie off while Tr'tl was still in the womb, the size of a pollywog. He, more than most, knew what the witch was capable of.

Although the butt of a lot o' jokes, he'd more than survived. He was intelligent, resourceful, hard-working, and worth enough to've bought a wife. A beautiful white girl, although blind and deaf. A mismatched set if there'd ever been one, but they made it work. There were also a lot of jokes how he'd pulled off gettin' her pregnant. They had a girl. Jubilee was the baby's name. Although not overly pretty and a far cry from dainty, she was Tr'tl's pride and joy.

He scuttled back to the wagon, wriggled up the ladder onto the seat, and, using a rope attached to the bottom o' the hinged ladder, hauled it up and into the bed. He grabbed the reins and hyaw-hyaw'd the mule into action.

Lootie Komes had been much too preoccupied to pay any attention to Tr'tl. She was consumed in the preparation of a potion comprised of mysterious and deadly ingredients. If she'd not been so involved in her current project and had given it a thought, she woulda recognized the irony in Tr'tl's deliverin' the still-living ingredients to be used in the concoction of a curse. Although, as opposed to Tr'tl's, a death curse.

The years hadn't been kind to Lootie. Consuming the sins o' the dyin' had taken its toll. Heavily. At forty-eight, she looked seventy-eight. She was the epitome of a nightmarish, storybook ogress, with a ragged scar runnin' from her left cheek, through the milky, blue/blind eye, and up into her scalp, creating a streak o' snow-white, stringy hair. Although, now, her whole head was white. As she ambled about, she drug one leg, the by-product of a degenerating hip, scratchin' out a memorable sound. Step-drag, step-drag, step-drag. Her mind was as sharp as ever, but thirty-four years o' bein' a Sin Eater'd destroyed her body, and just stayin' one step-drag ahead of death had become a full-time job.

She had to be careful raisin' an arm because done too quickly, her shoulder kind o' popped and was sore for days. She had to watch where she stepped. She'd fallen she didn't know how many times, and tryin' to get up with a bum leg and weak shoulders was Hell. It took her an hour or two each day to collect enough vegetable matter to make it count. Meat was actually easier to come by, as she still had the power to pull a rabbit, a squirrel, or possum right to her front door. They'd come squealin' and kickin', like they had a noose snugged up tight about their necks. But there wasn't any noose. Only the power of her mind. She'd stand in the shack door and keep her one eye trained on 'em 'til they got close enough she could club 'em with a stick, then ask for their forgiveness for takin' their life so she could have one more painful day. She wouldn't thank God. It wasn't Him 'at had to give up his life. She knew God didn't think much o' her, but she didn't think much o' Him either. What kind o' coward did it take to create a Son to die, nailed to a splintery cross? Someone else to do the dirty work. If God was so tough, why didn't he do it Hisself? Lootie did believe in God, though. She had to. Because she believed in the Dark Lord, and ever force in the universe had an opposite and equal.

The very people who damned her and her name in public paid handsomely in private to have theirs and their loved ones' souls cleansed. Everbody believed she had an iron pot filled with the gold she charged, hidden in the shack, maybe tucked in a hole under the floor. Not so. It was in a wooden box without a lid, and set along the wall in plain sight. Just a box. She had no use for gold, although she did think it was pretty. No, gold was power only to them that had none.

Lootie, being born of a witch, had innate abilities, but over the years, with the addition o' the consumed sins, her power had increased many fold. With her reputation, no one came to her to purchase a cure for warts or to get even with a lover proven false. Lootie Komes had become a specialist, and in her final years, all she offered was death. If you had the gold, Lootie Komes had the power, and you didn't subscribe to her services unless you were serious. With her will alone, she had the power of death over life. But today? Today was the climax, the apex of her career. She was preparing for her final act, her biggest ever.

Completing the first part o' the potion, she set it aside, allowing it time to work. It set in a pot on the stove with no fire, bubblin' of its own accord. To the uninitiated, the fumes alone were lethal. To Lootie, no more than a nose-runnin', eye-waterin' annoyance. Over the next two days, her knobby, arthritically tortured hands hung up the boar, the snake, and the gator, and slit their throats, allowing the blood to drain into ancient wooden bowls settin' under 'em, one apiece. Each one gave freely more than the required few ounces, except the cottonmouth. She'd had to wring it out tight so she could get ever drop.

Her poor ol' hands.

Next, she cut her own left wrist with her knife, enough to allow her life force to drip into each o' the others'. Finished, she wrapped a rag around her wrist and added the potion prepared earlier to hers, the boar's, the snake's, and the gator's blood. After she'd given 'em time to work, she filled two little bottles with the concoctions, one with the boar's, and the second, the snake's. A third little bottle she filled with a mixture o' the potion, her blood, and verminous, fetid swamp water. It was also finished and went on the shelf with the other two. The blood from the gator she set aside and left to work a little longer—for a special project.

With the aid of a walkin' stick, she struck out for the woods, and with her one good eye closed, she let the third eye lead her to a cypress branch about three foot long, felled and scorched by lightnin'. She lugged it back to the cabin, took her old knife to it, and slowly, the end started to take on the crude shape of an alligator head. In what would be taken for the mouth with no lower jaw, she burrowed out six holes, three to a side. That alone took her all day and half the night. (Her poor ol' hands.)

She gouged out six teeth from the dead gator's maw and with a sticky goo made of tree sap, pushed 'em solidly into the holes bored into the wooden gator's mouth. The next couple o' days she sat in the dark, dank cabin, kneadin' and rubbin' the gator blood potion into the wooden gator's teeth. While she worked, she thought about her life, the four people she'd loved, and why.

Pearl...her first mother, because Pearl had loved her. Unconditionally.

Cob... her sister and second mother, because Cob had taught her how to survive in a barely survivable world.

And finally, George and Matthew...simply because they'd erupted from between her legs. Unfortunately, like pus from a boil. She tried not to think about the men they had become, but remembered the snot-nosed little scamps who'd scurried about out in the yard, playin' in the dirt, chasin' bugs and each other. The smart one watchin' over the feeble-minded one.

Pearl. Cob. George. Matthew. They were gone now, all of 'em—and soon, very soon, so would she.

CHAPTER 20

The sheriff's hastily deputized posse lasted all of two days. The fun of the chase lasted as long as the bottle and the jug, and then they went home. Three days after that, a mud-caked and bedraggled Hub Lusaw walked down the streets of Oledeux, headed for the sheriff's office. Passersby were shocked not only at his condition but at seein' him at all. Everbody figured him long gone after sendin' the Komeses to answer for their sins.

Rowe was bent forward, perched on the edge of his squeaky swivel chair, takin' aim with a switch-blade knife at a badly scuffed boot worn by Toad, his one official deputy—mid-thirties, skinny, pock-faced, head back, gurglin', sound asleep. Toad's real name was Ernest Froget (therefore, the nickname), pronounced *Fro-jay* with a mushy *j*. Rowe was tryin' to see how close he could come to ol' Toady's boot without hittin' it. Splintery puncture marks on the floor attested to his progress.

Suddenly, the office door banged open and Hub entered just as the sheriff launched the knife. The shock created a hitch in the launch, causin' a slight alteration in its intended trajectory. Just enough. It harpooned Toad's boot toe, jerkin' him from whatever Hellish landscape he'd been inhabiting in his sleep.

"God Damn," Toad yelled, jumpin' up. He lifted the blade-festooned boot and pulled the knife out with a little screech, and pressin' on the boot toe, noticed that neither Rowe nor Hub seemed to be overly concerned that he'd been shishkabobbed.

Rowe slowly opened a desk drawer and, without takin' his eyes off Hub, pulled out and cocked one o' Mr. Buntline's long-barrel .45s. While pointin' it at Hub's heart, the sheriff had a thought. He uncocked the cannon, laid it back in the drawer, and closed it. "What th'fuck're you doin'?"

"Turnin' m'self in," Hub replied, casually. "I didn't have anything t'eat and got tired o' waitin' f'you t'come 'n get me."

"I don't want it like this."

"I awready give ya five days, you think five more'd make a dif'ernce?" He nodded toward the street. "Gimme a fifteen minute head start 'n you'cn try again."

"You're a fool."

"And you're a fat piece o' shit," Hub countered, tired of the verbal swordplay. "Now what?"

Rowe grabbed the key ring off the desk and tossed it toward Toad, who by that time'd pulled off his boot, vigorously massaging his blood-stained sock. Rowe motioned to the back. Toad stuck his boot under his arm, picked up the keys, worked up a face, and hobbled off.

"I'da gotcha," the sheriff informed Hub.

"Not settin' on yer big ass in here, stabbin' Toad's foot."

Rowe wheeled Hub by the shoulder and shoved him roughly through the back door. Toad was standin' beside an open cell, rubbin' his foot, put-out that still nobody was payin' attention to him or, in his mind, what'd already become known as the knife wound.

Hub entered the cell and Rowe braced hisself by grippin' the bars on either side o' the door and slammed his boot heel hard into Hub's low back, smashin' him face-first to the back wall. Blood was already runnin' from his split brow when he turned around. Rowe nodded for Toad to lock the door. Then he exited, followed by a limping, pissed-off Toad.

Hub lay on his bunk when, an hour later, Rowe entered, followed by Hub's big-bottomed wife, Raeleen, and their two sons, six-year-old Harvey and three-year-old Henry. "Don't take all day," he growled. He gave Raeleen's back-side the once-over on the way out. He liked 'em a little on the meaty side. Hub rolled off the bunk and stepped to the bars. Raeleen noticed the swolen, blood-caked brow.

"Whad ya do t'yer eye?"

Hub passed it off with a nod to the front office.

"I been worried sick. You okay?"

"Time'll tell."

"Papa," Harvey inquired with six-year-old innocence, "What'cha doin' in there?"

"Hush, Sugar," Raeleen said, pattin' him on the head.

"Why'd ya bring them here?" Hub asked, like she didn't have a brain.

"Well, I was gonna leave 'em at home with a book o' matches 'n a butcher knife t'play with, but I thought I'd bring 'em so they'cd see their papa in jail. Whadaya think I oughta done with'm?"

"Awright, awright, keep it down."

"You wanna talk about it?"

"What's there t'talk about? They killed her 'n I killed them."

"The funeral was nice. You oughta been there."

"Don't tell me I oughta been there, Rae. I had other things on m'mind."

"You heard anything about a trial?"

"Sheriff says it could be anywhere from two weeks to a month 'fore they get to it. I'm 'sposed t'get a lowyer."

"I'll do that."

"It'd help."

"You scared?"

"Not a whole lot. What they done to 'er? Ju see her?"

"I's told I didn't want to. Doc Ben signed the papers identifyin' 'er so I wudn have to."

"He done ya a favor, b'lieve me. They ain't nothin gonna happen t'me f'killin' them bastards."

"You don't know that! The way I see it, they's a chance our life's maybe shot t'Hell!"

"Whad you expect me t'do? Huh? Let 'em get away with it? What if it'd been you 'stead o' her? You think I wouldn'ta done the same thing? I'll tell ya what, I ain't in th'mood f'yer negativeness 'n yer scardiness 'n if that's th'best you'cn do, you'cn go!"

"Don't get short with me, God Dammit! I'm doin' th'fuckin best I can!"

"Don't say *fuck* 'round th'boys."

"You said Hell 'n God Dammit!"

"*Hell 'n fuck*'re two dif'ernt things. *Fuck*'s a sex word 'n I don't wanna hear no more sex words 'round 'em!"

"Fine," she barked. "What if you don't get off? What'm I gonna do? I cain't b'lieve this is hap'nin'!" She started shakin' and looked like she was gonna cry…or maybe she was gettin' mad, he couldn't tell for sure, but then she brushed away a tear.

"What's people sayin'?"

"I been bothered s'much by newspaper people, I'm scared t'leave the house. Couple of 'em come right up on th'porch, bangin' on th'door 'n twistin' the latch like they's gonna walk right in. What few people I talked to, though, said they had it comin'."

"Well, there ya go. It'll go t'court 'n it'll come out how they done 'er 'n I'll get off, you'll see. They might not be able t'let me go clean, so I might get a little time, but it won't be much. Listen, they ain't nothin' you'cn do here, 'n th'boys's scared. Take 'em on home."

He got down on one knee and asked, "Y'all wanna stick o' Black Jack?" They nodded. "Well, come 'ere, gimme a big hug 'n I'll give ya one." They came to him sheepishly. "Don't act like 'at," he scolded. "Are you roly poly bugs 'at curl up 'n hide like sceeredy cats 'r pincher bugs, givin' what for?"

"Pincher bugs," the boys dueted and giggled.

"Awright then. What's bugs do when they greet one another?" The boys pushed their little faces through the bars, snorted, and rubbed their noses over his like they's smellin' him. "'At's better," he said. He reached through the bars and mussed their hair, then he pulled a pack o' Black Jack from his pocket and gave 'em each a stick. "Y'all be good 'n mind yr'mama 'r I'll blister yer b'hinds good when I get home."

The boys nodded, already smacking gum. Raeleen motioned toward the door. "Y'all wait out there a minute. Ask th'sheriff t'show ya 'is gun." The older boy took his brother by the hand and started for the door. Once they were around the corner, she stuck her hands between the bars and took his. "I'm sorry. I'm just scared."

"I know, but if I had to, I'd do it again. Don't worry." He squeezed her hands. "Everthing's gonna be awright. And when it's over, things's gonna be a lot better."

There was somethin' in his face and the way he said it. "What makes you think so?"

"I can't talk about it now. But things's gonna be a lot dif'ernt. Come 'ere." She stepped closer and he kissed her.

"I wish this was over 'n you's back home. I ain't never been so worried 'n lonely in m'whole life. It's a big bed when yer in it alone."

"I'm sorry, Sugar, but everthing's gonna be okay. You go on, now."

"Okay. I'll be back as soon as I can." She kissed him one more time and left. From the office he heard two little voices. "Bye, Papa," followed by bug snorts.

"Bye," he called out, snortin', and lookin' longingly at the door.

CHAPTER 21

Toad was leaned back in the sheriff's squeaky, swivel office chair with his eyes closed, exhausted from the exertion of trying to stay awake. His fingers were laced behind his head, legs crossed at the ankle and propped up on the sheriff's desk, one foot with a boot on, the stained sock, obvious as a flag, on the other. He coulda changed socks, but the wound had stopped bleeding—he couldn't even squeeze out any more blood—and there wouldn't be anything to brag about with a clean one. All of a sudden, the front door opened and in strode Luther Knox, a real Dapper Dan in his mid- to late-twenties, little toothbrush mustache twisted in a curl on the ends. Toad nearly fell out o' the chair jerkin' his legs off the desk, scared shitless it was the sheriff.

"Good afternoon," Luther said, recognizing the stir his entrance had created. Toad tried to compose hisself while Luther flashed a mouthful o' pearly whites. "Sheriff Bernard Rowe, I trust?"

Totally confused, Toad wondered *What th'Hell's that s'posed t'mean? Who gives a shit?* "So what?" he exclaimed. It was obvious Toad wasn't an elected official.

Then it was Luther's turn. "So what...what?"

Toad's brain was gonna start smokin' any second. "What?"

Seeing he was getting nowhere, Luther offered, "Let's start over. You are Sheriff Rowe?"

"No!" Toad replied abruptly. "What in tarnation would make you think that? Do I look like 'im?"

"I wouldn't know. I've never met the man."

"Well, I ain't him. He ain't here," then he lowered his voice, gettin' all biggety. "But I'cn hep ya, I'm 'is dep'ty, th'only dep'ty. Whadaya want?"

It only took a second for Luther to figure out what he was working with, pull a card from his inside coat pocket with a flourish, and hand it to Toad.

Not used to the approach, Toad was slow to take it.

"Luther P. Knox, Attorney-At-Law, defending Mr. Hubert Lusaw, who, unless I'm badly mistaken," he took a look around the office and attempted a little levity, "is a temporary resident of your fine establishment."

Toad didn't like the smooth talk, the fancy dress, or the fancy card, and still didn't understand why he said he trusted the sheriff, someone he just admitted he'd never even met. "He's boxed up in th'back but I doubt it's tem'prary."

"May I see 'im?" Luther asked, still flashing that toothy smile. "Please?"

"What for?" Toad asked, suspiciously. "You know 'im?"

"No."

"Well, y'ain't related. I know 'is whole famly 'n you ain't one of 'em."

"No, it's his right," Knox attempted to assure him.

"Says who?" Toad demanded. With the sheriff away, if anybody was gonna be handin' out rights, it'd be Toad, and he didn't like a smart-mouthed city thing tellin' him what he had to do.

"The Bill of Rights," Luther said, way too cocky for Toad.

Now Toad'd done it. Put hisself in a box and snapped the lid shut. It wasn't the first time. He had no idea what a *billarites* was. It could be somethin' important Sheriff Rowe forgot to tell him about. This was startin' to smell like one o' them 'tit-in-th'wringer' things the sheriff was always blamin' him for. He chinned toward Luther's coat. "You got'ny weapons?"

Luther opened his coat, showing he was minus any implements of destruction.

Begrudgingly, Toad grabbed the keys off the desktop and pushed out o' the seat. "Back here," he said and started hobblin' toward the cellblock.

Luther fell in behind and noticed the favored, shoeless foot. "How'd you hurt your foot?"

Finally! Somebody asked! "Knife wound," Toad announced proudly. "Line o' duty. No biggie." He tried to make it sound like it wasn't a big deal, but desperately hoped Luther thought it was.

"In the foot?"

Shit! Toad hadn't thought about that so he handled it the only way he knew. By ignorin' it. They entered the cell area.

"Oh, Hubert," he sang out, "you gotcha'sm comp'ny."

Hub rolled off the bunk and approached the cell door.

Luther extended his long-fingered hand through the bars. "Mr. Lusaw, I trust?"

Hub just looked at it with his eyebrows all scrunched down. Then, it was Toad's turn to eyebrow-scrunch. Again, he wondered why the Hell the dude had to tell everbody he trusted 'em. Did he honestly think anybody gave a shit?

Hub looked him over. "Who're you?"

Retracting his hand along with a lot o' the warmth he'd brought in with him, Luther looked to see if it had shit on it. "Luther P. Knox, Attorney-At-Law. Mrs. Lusaw has retained my services as your defense attorney."

Hub backed up to get a good look. "How old're you?"

Luther'd had just about enough of smart mouths and bad attitudes from ignorant backcountry inbreds. "My age has nothing to do with my abilities."

"'Bil'ty takes time," Hub replied with a smirk that said he'd been around the block more than once.

Luther slapped on his Smile of Superiority. "If you'll notice," he pointed out Hub's side o' the bars, "you are on that side of Incarceration," then pointed out his side, "while I, on the other hand, am on this side of Freedom." He then pointed to Toad and added just for chuckles, "Even *that* is on this side."

The jab was lost on Toad 'cause he was busy tryin' to remember where Incarsurashun was.

"It would seem," Luther continued, "initially at least, that I'm smarter than you. Also, Mrs. Lusaw only had fifty dollars and I was willing to take a drastic reduction from my usual fee. I need the experience." Then he stuck his chin in the air. "You have the distinction of being my first murder trial."

"How 'bout that," Hub said, givin' Luther his Smile of Smartalecky, "Mine, too."

"Soon," Luther said, "I will be victorious, and famous, and you'll be free."

"Or in prison," Hub said.

"Or maybe even dead," Toad sniggered. He gave both of 'em his Smile of Smartassiness, displaying a mouthful of disgusting chompers.

"What a jovial little rat," Luther said.

Hub rattled the cell door. "Come on, Toad, let 'im in, I'm startin' t'like 'im."

"Ah, Toad," Luther said, looking him over like he might be the dumbest Homo Sapiens he'd ever come across. "An amphibian. My apologies to the rodent community."

Toad unlocked the cell door. Luther entered, and Toad gave him the evil eye. "Smart ass."

Toad relocked the door, started off, and out of earshot, Luther countered, "Dumb ass." Then he pointed to Hub's bunk. "Sit, we have a lot to do."

Lootie Komes completed the last of her tasks, and she was spent. She had one final mission, and she was fearful of not having strength enough to carry it out. She stood next to the table in the center of her cold little shack. She was naked, and a horrible sight it was. Her nose and ears were disproportionate to her head. Her eyes were sunken, her face, skullish. She was humpty-backed, her spine twisted, forcing her to stoop and lean uncomfortably to the left. Sitting, standing, or laying down, the pain low in her back never let up. She couldn't straighten out her legs. Her feet and toes were as warped as her hands and fingers. She hadn't been able to wear shoes for years. Her tits and butt cheeks sagged like melted candle wax.

More than once that week, she'd weighed passing on cursing Hub and his family. After all, George and Matthew had murdered Hub's sister. More than murdered. They'd defiled her. Badly. In the end, though, regardless o' what George and Matthew had become, they were still her children and that was what had shifted the fulcrum point. Hub Lusaw and his family were gonna pay.

She spooned a decades-old gourd into a bowl on the table, the dark contents the consistency of blackstrap molasses. When she raised her arm over her head, her shoulder popped and she yelped. Pain slashed up her neck and exploded in the back of her head. It was yet another reminder that her life was approaching the midnight hour.

Luckily, she hadn't spilled the gourd's contents. Steadyin' herself with half a dozen deep, careful breaths, she raised her arm again, slower, not quite as high, and anointed herself, ritualistically, with the thick, foul potion comprised of the remainder of fetid swamp water, and blood from the gator, the snake, and the boar.

Mumbling her chants, she worked the goo into her scarred scalp and pushed it over her wrinkled old face, stinging her eyes. She traced her finger along the scar that jaggered from her cheek to well into her scalp like she'd done all her life. All within the discoloration was dead. The lightnin' had destroyed the nerves. As a child, she used to sit, trance-like, and trace its dead line without havin' to see it.

The ooze rolled down her humped back and bone-slatted chest and globbed off her withered breasts hangin' like rotted squash, onto a bulbous belly and down her spindly legs. She dipped the gourd into the stinking morass until it was gone.

CHAPTER 22

All the town's hotels, restaurants, and saloons were packed. The only things in any abundance was beer, whiskey, and rumor. Three-cent watermelons were goin' for a dime. Hookers were charging fifty percent more than usual and still didn't have time to stand up between appointments. Reporters scurried about like rats, interviewing any and everone who'd had or even claimed to've had anything to do with the Komeses or the Lusaws.

It was standin' room only outside the courthouse. Anybody passin' out from the heat had to wait for the crowd to thin out 'fore there was enough room to fall over. But if it was bad outside, the inside was just awful—everbody drenched in sweat, worthlessly swishin' fans. The only air to breathe in was what somebody else'd breathed out, and if you got up to go outside for some fresh or to answer nature's call, somebody grabbed your seat, so most people just sat it out, simmerin' in their own juices and crossin' their legs real tight.

Raeleen woulda preferred bein' inside but she didn't have anyone to watch the boys. They ran around jumpin' and squealin', gripin' about bein' hungry, havin' to wet and wantin' to go home. The waitin' was Hell, not knowin' what was goin' on until the end o' the day.

The bailiff, a vulturesque, Ichabod Crane-lookin' thing with a prominent and active Adam's apple, sat by the judge's bench, lookin' the crowd over and tryin' not t'nod off.

His Honor, the ruddy-faced Almer Parks, sixtyish, occupied the Bench of Honor.

Totally out of his element, Hub Lusaw sat uncomfortably at the defense table alongside Luther P. Knox, Attorney-At-Law.

Sheriff Rowe, in new duds that weren't gut-stretched all to Hell, was on the witness stand as the prosecuting attorney, Sam Dimwiddie—fiftyish, a well-padded, local good ol' boy—paraded back and forth, stretchin' out his suspender straps. This trial was his ticket to fame and fortune and he was gonna milk it for all it was worth.

"Now, Sheriff," he began, lawyerly, "how was it you learned about the hap'nin's on the night of August the seventeenth o' this year?" Two days earlier, he and the sheriff had gone over all this and both knew it by heart.

"I's at home, asleep," Rowe replied, "and LeRoy Ledbetter come poundin' on th'door blabbrin' like a ravin' idyit about trouble down t'th'Komeses."

LeRoy was sittin' in the gallery hopin' t'God his name would come up. Now he was sorry it had. He had a headache, was sweatin' like a draft horse, thirsty as a sponge, and had to take a piss so bad it hurt...and bein' labeled a ravin' idyit was all he had to show for it. Everbody craned their neck in his direction and snickered. He knew the whole town considered him a boob, and he'd hoped that bein' The One Who Started The Ball Rollin' On The Murder Of The Decade would turn that around, but now he'd been referred to as The Ravin' Idyit in front of ever rumormonger and blabbermouth in town. He thought he may as well had I-d-y-i-t tattooed on his forehead.

"Did he say what that trouble was?" Dimwiddie continued.

"He didn't know, just that they's a ruckus he thought I oughta see 'bout."

"Would you please tell the court what you found upon your arrival at the Komes home?" If he'd been the defense attorney instead o' the prosecution, it woulda been the Komes shack, but since he wanted to make the poor brain-pulpalized brothers look like they'd been wrongly done on, it was now the Komes home.

"When I got there it was quiet. Four 'clock, give 'r take, still dark. Their truck was parked out front 'n th'front door was open. I called their names a couple o' times but nobody answered so I pulled m'gun 'n went in." The questions and answers may have been scripted but he twitched nervously, bein' reminded o' the scene. "They's two bodies on th'floor, just inside th'front door, 'n one alayin' on th'couch."

"And they were...."

"George 'n Matthew Komes 'n Ret Lusaw."

"When you say Ret, you are referring to Loretta Lusaw? Sister o' the accused?"

"Yessir."

"Which one was it on the couch?" Anybody woulda assumed the one on the couch woulda been the girl but Dimwiddie was attempting to set the stage.

"Ret."

"Was she settin' up or layin' down or just exactly what was her position?"

"She was laid out on 'er back, covered with a blanket, tucked up under 'er."

"Tucked up under her, mm-hmm," Dimwiddie replied, his eyes scrunched down like he was tryin' to picture it. "And the brothers?"

"Like I said, in the front room, just inside th'front door, on th'floor, 'parently where they fell." The scripted crap and Dimwiddie's bullshit demeanor was wearing thin. Rowe much preferred a stand-up fight and not all the legal fertilizer and dancin' around he was bein' forced to take part in.

"Mm-hmm," Dimwiddie replied again, and then actin' like he was thinkin', he asked, "Did you happen to find anything queer or out o' place?"

"Yessir," Rowe said after a long, unscripted sigh, "a t'bacca pouch, rollin' papers, spent matches, 'n a pocket watch was settin' on th'floor in front o' th'couch."

"A pocket watch you say. Have you since determined who that watch belonged to?"

"Yessir, it was Hub's. He admitted it."

"I see, well, that seems to simplify things doesn't it? Was there anything else besides the pouch, the papers, and the pocket watch?"

"Yessir. Rubbed-out ceeg'rette butts."

"Cigarette butts," Dimwiddie repeated off-handedly. "Hmmm." Then, puttin' on like he'd miraculously put two and two together.... "Butts? Plural?"

"Yessir. Four of 'em."

"Sheriff, what would four rubbed-out cigarette butts tell you?"

"That he'd had time t'roll 'n smoke four ceeg'rettes waitin' for th'Komeses t'...."

"Objection," Luther chirped, jumpin' up, "Your Honor, unless cigarette butts've learned how to talk, he doesn't know that."

The crowd laughed and the judge gave 'em the evil eye. "Objection sustained," he declared, but the damage'd already been done. Everbody pictured a relaxed Hub Lusaw, his back to the couch, puffin' out a chain o' smoke rings, flickin' ashes, and pickin' his nose, waitin', red-eyed and plottin'.

Luther sat down and Dimwiddie asked the sheriff, "What was the condition o' the house?"

The sheriff glanced over at Hub. Two o' the badly mutilated bodies in the shack—their heads and faces completely destroyed—had been done to by him. It was still a heinous sight. For the rest o' his life, he'd be reminded of three mutilated bodies, pulverized brains, eyes hangin' outside sockets, missin' parts, and the smell of iron-rich blood mixed with piss and shit. "It was a mess. They's blood evawhere."

"Had they been shot with a gun?"

"No, sir," the sheriff answered, robotically.

"Stabbed with a knife?"

"Ret'd had a knife used on 'er, but I don't know that you'cd actually say she'd been stabbed. I'd call it more cut than stabbed. They's," he tried to think of a better word, but none came, "parts. Removed. Missing."

The sheriff's last statement was ad lib, not somethin' they'd rehearsed. Dimwiddie wanted to get away from it quickly and the best way to do it was to borrow Toad's out—ignore it.

"Well, if they hadn't been shot or stabbed, how'd they meet their end?"

Luther rolled his eyes and stood up. "Your Honor? Would you please instruct the prosecuting attorney to save his playacting for the stage and get on with it? If he doesn't know how they died, he's the only one within two hundred miles."

The courtroom busted up, and Parks looked at Dimwiddie over his glasses. "You are slatherin' it a mite." He pounded his gavel. "Let's keep it down, folks."

"Sorry, Your Honor," Dimwiddie apologized and turned his attention back to the sheriff. "For the record, would you please tell the court how they died?"

"Beat t'death. All of 'em."

"At that time, did you know who the perpetrator was?"

"Only idee I had was what LeRoy'd said. He thought it was Hub agoin' at it with 'em. He said he couldn't hear good 'nough at what was said, the exact words, but he heard 'em yellin' 'n he said one of 'em sounded like Hub."

"And what happened when you went t'question Mr. Lusaw?" Dimwiddie asked while he passed the defense table and looked at Hub.

"I couldn't. He'd lit out."

"Lit out, huh? Then, how did you ultimately apprehend him?"

Rowe was reminded of Hub's tellin' him he never woulda caught him if he hadn't surrendered. "He turned hisself in."

"When he was confronted with the deed, did he deny doin' it?"

"No, sir. He volunteered sole respons'bil'ty."

Dimwiddie stepped to, and picked up a paper off the corner of the prosecution table and waggled it in the air for the jury and spectators to see. "Yes, he did. In fact...Hub Lusaw signed a confession...a full confession...for the cold-blooded murder of George and Matthew Komes." He slapped the paperwork back on the table. "Was this the first time Hub Lusaw'd been at odds with the law?"

"Nope."

Parks popped up like a Jack in the Box. "Come again?"

Assuming Parks hadn't heard him, the sheriff sat up straighter and spoke louder. "I said, 'No, sir.'"

"That's not what I heard. You said 'nope.'"

"Same thing ain't it?"

"Not in this court. Try again."

"No, sir," Rowe said. "Sorry, Your Honor," then to Dimwiddie, "No, sir."

"You're a public official, dammit, and this is a court o' law," Parks chirped, hotly. "You don't use that kind o' language in here. I'd better not hear 'yep' either." He pointed the gavel handle to Dimwiddie. "Go ahead."

"Thank you, Your Honor. He'd been in trouble before. How many times d'you think?"

"I don't know exactly, a lot."

"Well, three? Half a dozen? A dozen?" Dimwiddie drilled.

"More like a dozen."

"How many times would you say were for fightin?" Dimwiddie asked, swiveling toward the gallery.

"All of 'em."

"All of 'em? My goodness. So...what?...he gets too much to drink...."

"No, I don't know that he drinks much. He's just got a temper. It cuts loose 'n he don't know how t'cap it off."

"Thank you, Sheriff," Dimwiddie said and turned to Parks. "Prosecution rests." He sauntered back to his table and plopped into his chair.

"Mr. Knox," Parks said, "your witness."

Luther stood without leavin' his table. It was meant to imply that anything the sheriff had to say wasn't worth comin' all the way around the table for. "Thank you, Your Honor." He had a paper in his hand that he rolled and unrolled into a tube while he talked. The sheriff watched it like it was a snake. "Sheriff, I only have a couple of questions." He pointed the tube at him. "You don't like Hub, do you?"

"Not much," the sheriff admitted, and shifted nervously in the seat. "He's mean 'n...."

Luther waggled the tube back and forth to cut him off. "Thank you," he said. "Just answer the question." He crossed his arms over his chest, but the tube was still evident. He was glad to see it was makin' the sheriff nervous. "Weren't you close to the deceased, the brothers?"

"I knew 'em. I don't know as I'd say close."

"No? That's odd. I heard different. I heard you were very close. In fact, I heard you were one o' the few that got along with 'em. Went hunting together and such. They ever spend time in one o' your cells?"

"Once 'r twice, maybe."

"It was more than once or twice," Luther said, and the sheriff watched while Luther unrolled the tube. He took his time to look the paper over, then raised his eyebrows a couple o' times as if somethin' special'd caught his eye. "Quite a few more than once or twice. Isn't it also a fact, that in your younger, more mischievous years, you and the Komes brothers all slept off a few bottles? In the same cell? At the same time?" Rowe looked trapped. Luther rolled the paper back up. "That was a question, Sheriff." Rowe glared at him. "Requiring an answer. Don't make me swear up your predecessor. He's old and lives outside of town, but I will if I have to."

"We were just kids blowin' off a little steam," the sheriff finally said, "'n we didn't beat nobody t'death."

"Right. But then no one had raped...tortured...or murdered your sister. Ethel. Had they?"

The sheriff looked like he'd been kicked in the gut. Luther had just earned his fifty bucks and then some. It was a brilliant move and so simple. Every man in the room who had a sister, pictured her butchered, gutted like a fish, layin' on that couch, and vicariously pictured themselves, as Hub had done, exacting bloody revenge.

"That'll be all," Luther said and sat down.

Parks nodded to Rowe. "You can step down now."

The sheriff rose and on his way back to the spectator gallery, Luther helt out the rolled paper to him and winked. The wink caught Rowe so off guard that he took the paper without thinkin'. He pushed through the squeaky little spring-loaded gate in the ornate railing separating the gallery from the business end o' the court and continued down the aisle.

He pushed through the back door in dire need of a water closet and a stiff drink. Hurryin' across the floor, he unrolled the paper. He stopped dead and looked back at the closed doors as if he could see through 'em and to the back of Luther Knox's head. His jaw muscles rolled up to his temple. There was only one word on the paper, written in a nice hand.

Thanks.

Back in the courtroom, Parks jabbed the gavel handle to the prosecution table. "Mr. Dimwiddie? Your next witness."

"Your Honor," Dimwiddie said, standing, "I'd like to call LeRoy Ledbetter."

LeRoy jumped up like he had a spring in his ass. His shirt was soaked in sweat and his hair plastered to his head. It seemed to take an eternity to excuse and apologize hisself past the gauntlet of his fellow gawkers' knees. He finally got to the aisle, walked down that massive gap separating the spectator gallery, feelin' ever eye on the back of his head. He pushed through the squeaky little gate and approached the witness stand, hopin' to God he didn't trip. He finally got to the bailiff waitin' with a big black bible in his hand.

"Putcher left hand on th'book 'n raise yer right."

LeRoy did so, and the bailiff buzzed through a blistering rendition of "Do you swear t'tell th'truth, th'whole truth, 'n nothin' but th'truth, s'hep ya God?"

"Yep," LeRoy stammered.

Parks exploded. "Whad you say?"

Some fellas, no matter what they do, it's the wrong thing.

"Yeah, I mean yes, Yes, sir, yeah, No, I mean, Yes, Yes, sir, I do. Swear. I swear. Yes, sir!"

"Statechur name for th'court," the bailiff said.

"LeRoy."

Parks rolled his eyes. The court busted up. Parks banged the gavel and after they'd calmed, the bailiff said, "Yer whole name?"

"LeRoy Thadeus Ledbetter," he said. Ripples of laughter trickled up the benches. *Thadeus* wasn't really all that funny, but it was hard not to kick a man who was already on the ground, beggin' for it.

The bailiff nodded to the witness box. "Take th'seat."

LeRoy slid in. Parks looked like he'd enjoy bitin' a big chunk out of his ass.

"Mr. Ledbetter," Dimwiddie said, approaching the box, "you've known the Komeses and Lusaw's most o' your life, isn't that right?"

"Yep," then before Parks could roast him again, he said, "Yes, I mean Yes. Yes, sir, I have. Most o' m'life. All m'life. Yes, sir, I sure have."

"You know 'em well then?"

"Much as anybody, I reckon," LeRoy replied, then he looked at Parks hoping reckon wasn't another "Yep" or "Nope." Parks glared at him but didn't yell or point the dreaded gavel handle.

"Would you consider yourself a friend of Hub's?" Dimwiddie asked. "From what the sheriff said, you know him well enough to recognize his voice."

"Sure, we're friends," he answered, none too sure if he was supposed to be a friend of a mass murderer.

"Good friends?"

"I don't know 'bout good, but we're friends."

"Were you a friend o' the late Ret Lusaw?"

"Sure, everbody liked Ret." He was startin' to feel better now. Things seemed to be goin' pretty good.

"You think everybody liked Hub as much as they liked her?"

"Your Honor?" Luther said, standing, "Is anybody driving this bus?"

Parks looked at Dimwiddie. "Where're you goin', Sam?"

"Your Honor, allowed to continue, my purpose will become evident."

Good enough for him, Parks pointed the gavel handle to Luther. "Siddown."

Luther sat. Dimwiddie looked at him, shook his head, and chuckled. "Anybody drivin' this bus. Ha! That's rich. You're a funny fella." Then he turned his attention back to LeRoy. "Well?"

"Well, what?" LeRoy asked, blankly.

"Did you...or did you not...like Hub as much as you liked Ret?"

"I liked 'em...dif'ernt," he said, and the spectators broke up. Parks pounded the gavel and rolled the evil eye over the crowd.

Dimwiddie laid his arm on the witness box and leaned in. "Which one...were you...dif'ernt...closer to...do you think?"

LeRoy shot another nervous look at Hub. "Maybe Ret. Only maybe, though."

Dimwiddie caught the look. "Would that be because she's closer to your age, you think?"

As best he could, LeRoy weighed every question, wonderin' which ones would trap him into trouble. This one sounded safe so he gave a very decisive, "Maybe."

"Could it'a been because she was smart?"

LeRoy pinched his eyebrows together in deep thought. "I don't reckon she's any smarter'n most."

"Well, then, maybe because she was a girl? Because she was pretty? She was a pretty girl. Did she like to have fun?"

"Sure, who don't like t'have fun?" he replied, thinkin' that sounded logical.

"You ever have fun with her?" LeRoy's face went slack. "Out behind the barn so t'speak?"

LeRoy was struck dumb. The son of a bitch slipped one in on him. He couldn't answer any way that wouldn't get him in dutch.

Dimwiddie stared at him, waitin' for an answer.

Parks stared at him, waitin' for an answer.

He looked at the spectators, all starin', waitin' for the Ravin' Idyit to make a fool of hisself again.

"Ever play doctor and nurse?"

Luther stood and demanded, "Your Honor!"

"Overruled!" Parks snapped. "Siddown!"

Luther sat, knowing this was more than a little out of order.

"You're under oath, LeRoy," Dimwiddie pushed, "answer the question. Did you ever diddle with Ret Lusaw?"

Luther jumped out of his seat. "Your Honor! Diddle? I have to object. And then, what does this have to do with anything?"

Parks was very interested, and from much more than a judicial view. He aimed the gavel handle at him. "Over...ruled! Sit...down!"

Luther sat, reluctantly. This obviously wasn't a New Orleans court!

Dimwiddie pushed on. "Answer the question, LeRoy. Did you ever have fun with Ret Lusaw?"

LeRoy squeaked out an unbelievable, "I don't remember."

Parks threw his hands in the air. "Oh, for Christ's sake!"

The spectators groaned in unison, grossly disappointed. Dimwiddie's eyes nearly popped out of his head. "You don't remember if you ever messed with a girl that looked like Ret Lusaw did? Have you had a stroke or somethin' I ain't heard about?"

Parks pounded the gavel, nearly propelling poor LeRoy to the ceiling. "Answer the God Damn question or I'll jail you in contempt!"

LeRoy grabbed his head in his hands and whined, "We's kids, f'God's sake! Shit!"

"You don't say *shit* in my court you dim-witted pud-pounder!" Judge Parks yelled.

LeRoy was about to cry. "I'm sorry. We's just touchin', lookin' 'n lickin'. But I never done 'er!" Then, Holy Shit, it hit him what he said and shot a look at Hub. "NEVER, I swear t'Godamighty, Hub, I NEVER done 'er!"

Dimwiddie looked at Hub then back at LeRoy. "How come you keep lookin' at Hub ever time I ask you a question?"

Caught with his pants down, LeRoy lied. "I ain't!" Then squirming, he said, "Listen, I don't feel good, maybe I..."

"You can feel bad later," Dimwiddie snapped. "Right now, you answer the God Damned question. Why're you afraid o' Hub Lusaw?"

"I ain't! Maybe a little, but everbody's some 'fraid of 'im, it ain't just me!"

As the day went on, Dimwiddie continued to badger numerous witnesses. What he was attempting to show was that Ret Lusaw had been a shameless, conniving flirt, a hussie, a floozie o' the first order, and although bein' murdered was a heavy price to pay, she'd been playin' a dangerous game, and it finally caught up with her. He wanted to show the jury that the Komes brothers'd been lathered up beyond control.

When asked how many times he'd had his own share of Ret, Nud Beaumont confessed to, "Four 'r five." Roscoe Bowles put up his hand, took the oath, said his whole name, sat in the witness chair, and admitted, "Once't," even before he'd been asked the question. Dimwiddie asked Bob Beaudoin, "If Hub's so scary, how come you kept comin' around?"

"Ret turn it on," Bob said, grinnin', "she's haaaaaard t'turn down."

With Hub basically tied down at the defense table, the witnesses' long-standing fear slowly diminished. Ike Messick was a good example.

"Hell, I ain't ashamed of it. She turned me no way b't' on 'n ever way bt'loose. Yes, sir, Ret'd make th'little general slap on 'is helmet 'n stand right up straight."

Parks pounded the gavel tryin' to kill the room's laughter.

"Boys was a game," Ike continued, "'n she knew how t'play 'em."

"She ever play that game with the Komes brothers?" Dimwiddie asked.

"Hm!" Ike snorted. "Did they have a snake in their pants?"

"Hub ever find out about any a y'all foolin' with 'er?"

"Once in a while."

"What would happen?"

Ike looked at Hub. "You stayed home from work fer a couple o' days, lickin' yer wounds."

"Hub seemed to be very protective of his little sister."

The picture flashed in Hub's mind of Paul David draggin' Ret, squealin', across the dirt yard for the hen house.

"Mm-hmm," Ike replied easily.

Parks leaned over the bench. "Yes or no'd be more appropriate."

"Yes, sir."

"Did you know their father?" Dimwiddie asked.

"Paul David? Sure, I remember him."

"He died," Dimwiddie said.

"Yes, sir," Ike replied, "he sure did. Hard."

Hub saw hisself walkin' in the woods with a cheapass, single-barrel, six-gauge in the crook of his arm. Sixteen years old. He and Paul David'd been huntin' rabbits. Earlier that day, the old man'd slapped Hub's mother for makin' the mistake of standin' up for herself. Hub thought about the blood dribblin' out the corner of her nose, brought the scattergun up, aimed it at dear old dad's back, right where his heart would be, and pulled the trigger.

"A hunting accident," Dimwiddie said, shaking his head. "Accidentally killed by the person he was hunting with. Do you recollect who that was?"

Ike nodded to the defense table. "Hub."

Paul David dropped his own gun, his arms flew in the air, and he fell face-first in the dirt, his back a bloody mush. Hub laid his shotgun in the dirt, next to a gopher hole, then slowly walked to Paul David and squatted down beside him. The old man wasn't dead. Yet. Layin' with the left side of his face in the dirt, he looked at Hub. He looked surprised. Neither of 'em said a word. Hub sat beside him, Indian style, and watched until he heard a last gurgly breath and the body relaxed. Kinda flattened out. He stood up and slowly walked back to the house, cookin' up a story about trippin' in that gopher hole.

"Must be a terrible thing," Dimwiddie said, "killin' your own father. Even if it was accidental."

Everybody turned their attention to Hub. Many were familiar with the story and had heard the rumors about the possibility it hadn't been an accident, but now, after his killin' the Komeses, it'd moved possible up to probable. What Dimwiddie was tryin' to do was put doubt in the jury's mind that it'd been his first go at murder. A lawyer winning a murder trial and the murderer gettin' fifteen or twenty years was all right. Gettin' life was a lot better. But winning the death penalty was the brass ring.

"I have no more questions for this witness, Your Honor."

Parks pointed the ever-present gavel handle to Luther. "Mr. Knox, you're up."

Luther stood up. "I have no questions for this witness, Your Honor." He sat down.

Hub grabbed his arm and growled under his breath, "Do yer job! Ask 'im somethin'!"

"What do you think I should ask?" Luther asked, quietly. "I've asked around and from what I hear, you're not much more liked than the Komeses. Anybody I put up could and would be cross-examined, and they'd all make you look bad. This is a battle, Mr. Lusaw, but your enemy, the prosecution, has all the ammunition." He glanced down at Hub's hand gripped on his arm and then back up. "You don't frighten me, and it looks to me like the people who you used to scare aren't any longer. Your chickens have come home to roost, so to speak. The whole room is watching. You're not improving your reputation. Let...go...of my arm."

Frustrated, Hub complied, and again, Luther told Judge Parks, "No questions."

"That's it, Ike," Parks chirped. "You can step down." Then he looked at the clock on the wall. "It's gettin' late. Mister Knox, we'll reconvene with your side tomorrow mornin' at ten o'clock." He pounded the gavel.

"Everbody rise," the bailiff shouted, and everbody jumped up and pulled their pants and panties out of their sweaty cracks.

As Luther packed up his paperwork into his case, he told Hub, "Tomorrow morning, I'm putting you on the stand." Hub looked surprised. "You are the only chance you have, and if you don't pull it off...and you'd better believe it...you're going to prison. Make it good."

The bailiff came to the table for Hub and Luther walked off.

CHAPTER 23

It was 10:00 a.m. the next morning, and the courtroom had been packed since 7:15 a.m. Finally, the door behind and just to the right of the judge's bench opened. The bailiff stepped through, left it open, and walked to the center o' the room in front o' the judge's bench. He cleared his throat and ordered, "All rise."

Everone stood. Judge Parks sauntered in, robes swaying majestically. He climbed the two steps to his throne and plopped down in the big chair. "The State o' Looziana," the bailiff announced, "versus Hubert Marshall Lusaw. You may be seated."

Everbody sat back down, and Parks gave the room the once over. "Mornin'," he said pleasantly. He was a happy man. He should be. The biggest danged three-ringer in the world had come to his town, his court, and he was the man with the tall hat. He yanked up the robe's sleeves, laced his fingers, laid his elbows on the bench, and nodded to the prosecution table. "Good morning, Mr. Dimwiddie."

"Good mornin', Your Honor."

"How'd you sleep last night?"

"Like a baby, thank you."

"And how'd you sleep, Mr. Knox?"

"Not well, Your Honor, but thanks for asking."

Parks gestured to the prosecution table. "He didn't either."

Dimwiddie chuckled.

"You ready?"

Luther stood up. "Yes, Your Honor, we are."

"All right," the judge replied, and he leaned back to get all comfy. "Let's go."

Without any further hubbub, Luther announced, "I call Hub Lusaw to the stand, Your Honor."

Hot! Dog! That's what they wanted to hear! The courtroom thrummed with excitement.

Hub tried not to show how nervous he was as he pushed his chair back, stood up, walked around the defense table, and approached the witness stand. Everbody heard ever step. The bailiff met him with the bible. Hub laid his left hand on it and raised his right.

"Do you swear t'tell th'truth, th'whole truth, 'n nothin' but th'truth, so hep ya God?"

"I do," Hub replied, stiffly.

"Statechur whole name."

"Hubert Marshall Lusaw."

The bailiff nodded to the witness stand. "Have a seat."

Hub took the one step up into the right side o' the box, pulled his britches legs up, sat down, took a long, deep breath, helt it a second, and then blew it out. He was the picture of uncomfortableness.

Luther stood up and walked around to the front o' the defense table. "Hub? You ran...and you were successful for five days. In that time, do you think the law came anywhere near finding you?"

"No," Hub answered, easily.

"Do you think you could've gotten away with it."

"Probly."

"But you didn't. You turned yourself in. Why? If you honestly thought you could get away with it, turning yourself in doesn't make any sense. You knew you'd be tried for murder."

"I didn't wanna be on th'run th'rest o' m'life." He seemed almost demure, tired. "But more important, I got a wife 'n kids, two little boys. I couldn't drag 'em along with me, 'n I couldn't just walk away from 'em. My family's everthing."

"Your sister included," Luther added.

"Yeah." He seemed to deflate a little more. "Yeah. She was."

"Were those your only reasons?"

"I don't know. I ain't thought much 'bout why."

"Would you please tell the court what happened on the night of August seventeenth and the early morning hours of the eighteenth?"

One coulda heard the proverbial pin drop when Luther walked from the witness box and perched one hip on the defense table, handing the stage over to Hub.

Hub'd never spoken to over a dozen people at one time in his whole life. "We's at a dance. Looked like th'whole town was there."

Many in the room had been. They turned their faces to their benchmates and nodded. They pictured where they, Hub, George, Matthew, Ret, even LeRoy'd been. For decades to come, time in Southern Looziana would be measured between before the Komes murders and after the Komes murders.

"George 'n Matthew'd been drinkin' most o' th'day."

All the men pictured George and Matthew, their backs to the temporary, makeshift bar, knockin' back a glass and lookin' mean.

"I don't rec'lect what time they took off. Ret left 'bout nine 'r so 'n they'd left a little 'fore she did, so maybe eight thirty." Dark images of the night of the murder was affecting him. He was tryin' to save his skin, tellin' his story and actin' all hang dog, but he was also being pulled back into the horror.

"I left t'go home somers about midnight. I'd gone, I don't know, maybe half a mile, I come acrost a pair o' shoes in th'middle o' th'road 'n picked 'em up. I thought they's Ret's but I didn't know why she'd leave 'em settin' in th'middle o' th'road. They's brand new. I went another fifty yards 'r so 'n I heard a kind o' mewlin off th'road a bit." He swallowed and licked his lips.

"Take your time," Luther said, quietly.

Hub took a deep breath and backarmed his shirtsleeve over his forehead. "I followed th'sound, th'whim'prin 'n..." his eyes seemed to focus on an invisible something in front of him. He bit his lower lip and blinked. "It was awful." There was a quiver in his voice. He looked over to Luther, up at the judge, and then back to Luther. His eyes were glistening. "She's layin' in th'dirt. Both 'er eyes was swole nearly shut." He wiped a tear running down his cheek, embarrassed that he'd allowed his emotions to slip up on him.

Luther couldn't believe it, but God knows he wanted to. He almost felt sorry for him. He peeked out of the corner of his eye to the jury box. They were hooked. Big, bad Hub Lusaw was in pain and everbody was riveted. Never would they've believed it, not one of 'em, that Hub Lusaw could be hurt.

Hub helt out his arms as if reachin' for somethin' he alone could see. "I tried t'pick 'er up out o' th'dirt, but no matter how easy I was, she hollered in pain. She cried 'n begged me not t'move 'er. It hurt s'bad t'have t'leave 'er lay in th'dirt." He took a big shuddery breath and continued. "I asked 'er who done it. She told me she's goin' home 'n George 'n Matthew jumped 'er on th'road. They chased 'er through th'woods 'n she thought she might coulda outrun 'em, but she tripped over somethin, wrenched 'er foot 'n 'fore she could get up, George jumped on 'er. She said she raked 'is face with 'er nails 'n got loose, but hadn't no more'n stood up when Matthew knocked 'er back down again.

"She said Matthew stood 'er up 'n locked 'er arms from behind while George grabbed 'er legs 'n told 'er she's a whore th'way she flirted at th'dance 'n that lightin' fires in boys was one thing, but heatin' up a man was another. Said he'd put a fire in 'er she'd never forget."

Now he was beyond hiding his feelings. He didn't care about puttin' on an act any longer, he wanted everbody to know what they'd done to Ret; how they'd butchered her. "Then she said Matthew bit down hard on th'back of 'er neck 'n yelled *I got 'er bleedin George, I got 'er bleedin*. She was tryin' t'get loose 'n George whacked 'er face s'hard he knocked 'er out."

The court was mesmerized, waiting breathlessly for the next deliciously hideous description.

Hub grit his teeth and looked straight at Luther. "After they tore 'er clothes off, they lugged 'er back t'their place. She said one time she come to 'n George had a hammer handle jammed up inside 'er." The women gasped and clutched at their throats. "She come to another time feelin' like she's afire. Matthew was astraddle of 'er, cuttin' on 'er with a knife. She tried fightin' 'im off but George kicked 'er in th'head. When she woke up she found they'd drug 'er off t'th'corner 'n shoved 'er up agin th'wall like a sack o' meal. They's gone 'n I swear I don't know how, she's beat up s'bad, but she managed t'crawl t'the road 'n that's where I come on 'er."

He stopped, spent, tryin' valiantly to put hisself back together. "Then...she give a little groan 'n I heard th'breath kinda wheeze out of 'er." If he'd whispered it, the whole room would still've heard. He took another long, ragged breath. "She couldn't be hurt no more, so I picked 'er up...took 'er t'th'shack...theirs...'n laid 'er on th'couch. I covered 'er over with a dirty ol' blanket. She didn't deserve 'at. First, layin' in th'dirt 'n then that filthy blanket. She was nekkid 'n dirty 'n I knew she'd hate it if anybody seen 'er 'ataway, but th'blanket was all I'cd find t'cover 'er up with."

Finally, taking a cleansing breath, he looked first at the jury, then at Parks. "I killed 'em." It seemed he couldn't stop nodding. And blinking, like he was lost. It was mesmerizing. "I ain't denyin' it. I know I did it. I killed 'em. They wasn't nobody else there. Jus' me...'n them...'n her." He looked at Luther. "But I swear, I don't remember it. I don't remember 'em comin' home. But they musta. I do remember, 'fore they come back, of settin' on th'floor with 'er, I didn't want 'er t'be alone...'n then...next thing I know...I had a hunk o' wood in m'hand...'n' George 'n Matthew's both on th'floor, dead."

Grave yards weren't any quieter than that courtroom.

"Then," he said, spent, "I's out in th'woods runnin' t'beat all. It took me t'sunup t'figure out where I was, 'cause I hadn't run t'nowhere in paticklar. Just run."

Luther P. Knox, Attorney-At-Law, wanted in the worst way to turn around and get a look at the gallery. He could actually hear 'em breathin'! Hard! He looked at Hub and thought, *He's either telling the truth or that beat any performance I have ever seen*. Figuring he'd milked it as far as he could, and reminded of the old stage adage, "Leave 'em wantin' more," he merely said, "Thank you." You could hear it clear to the back o' the room. Then to Parks, "Defense rests." He pushed off from the table and walked around to his chair.

Parks nodded to the prosecution table. "Mr. Dimwiddie?"

Now came Luther's next concern. As impossible as it'd seemed yesterday, there was now the possibility Hub'd pulled it off—if he could just get through the next few minutes without....

The quiet was shattered when Dimwiddie's chair scraped across the floor, pushin' it back from the table. He stood up and slowly approached the witness stand. "Mm, mm, mm," he said, shakin' his head. "Boy howdy, Hub, you had me sorry for your pain. I couldn't even imagine what you coulda felt, but I have absolutely no doubt you did." Then he looked Hub square in the eye, cocked his head, and winked. "Imagine it, that is. Because I don't believe one little word of it." Then on second thought, "Well, no, I take that back. Some I do. I do believe you were shocked at the sight of her. I do believe you picked her up and brought her to the cabin and I do believe you sat with her. I don't believe it was just t'keep her company, though. No, sir! She was keepin' you company while you waited for George and Matthew Komes to come home so you could bash in their heads!"

Luther couldn't believe Hub hadn't catapulted hisself out o' the box, latched his hands around Dimwiddie's throat, and throttled the life out of him. He wondered if that wasn't what Dimwiddie was trying to accomplish. He saw the veins in Hub's forehead poundin' all the way from the defense table. Dimwiddie'd cocked the gun and stuck it in Hub's crotch. Now, could Hub keep from blowin' off his own pecker.

"Boy, what a waste," Dimwiddie went on. "What a waste! When I think of all the money we coulda made sellin' tickets to this show."

"Your Honor," Luther said as he stood up. "Is there going to be a question any time soon?"

Parks looked over his glasses at Dimwiddie.

"All right, all right," Dimwiddie said. "I'm gonna let you off light, Hub. I'm gonna ask you but one question. I believe I already know the answer, but I'd be very interested in hearin' it anyway. Are you sorry you did it?"

Luther's objection had given Hub time to calm down some, and now he seemed to give Dimwiddie's question thought. "I'm sorry I had to."

Luther closed his eyes and dropped his chin on his chest. Speaking for the prosecution, Hub couldn'ta said anything better. Dimwiddie hadn't expected it to be anywhere near that easy. All Hub woulda had to say was "Yes," and he mighta got off. One tiny, little three-letter word! "Yes!" But he hadn't.

And now, Dimwiddie was a screamin', fiery-eyed eagle, talons spread, on a broken-backed little mouse. Kidnapping the opportunity before it could slip away, he asked, "You'd do it again? If it happened again, you'd do it?" The gallery was so glad they'd had a chance to catch their breath 'cause it looked like the game was goin' into extra innings.

Hub saw his mistake and tried to back up. "I couldn't do it again. I only had one sister."

Dimwiddie had him on the ropes and almost ran to the witness stand, white-knuckled his fingers over the edge o' the box, and pounded home. "That's your answer? Ohhhh, Hub," he groaned, "I was told you weren't afraid o' anything." He pushed off the box, swung around dramatically with his arms helt over his head. "Ohhhh, my, how the mighty have fallen!" He came back to the box, gripped the rail, and looked Hub hard in the eye. "What if you did have another sister. And what if George and Matthew was to somehow come back to life and do the same thing t'her. Would you do it again?"

"Your Honor," Luther said, jumpin' out of his chair, "This is ridiculous. The prosecution is goading…."

But it was too late. Dimwiddie was rollin down hill and he smelled blood.

"What if they'd had another hammer handle jammed up inside her, too, Hub," he growled, spittle fleckin' the air.

"Your Honor, I object!" Luther demanded.

"Order! Order! Order!" Parks yelled, pounding the gavel like he was drivin' a rail spike.

"Yes, you weak-kneed son of a bitch!" Hub growled over the crowd's hubbub, creating dead silence.

It worked! Dimwiddie had his proof it'd all been an act, and he thought *Oh, Thank You, Sweet Jesus*. The room waited, hungry for the next act. And Hub didn't let'm down. It was like Sheriff Rowe'd said earlier, when Hub got goin', he didn't have any idee how to stop. And Dimwiddie had him goin'.

"I'd gladly spend time in Hell if I'cd stoke th'furnace t'keep them screamin'."

Dimwiddie just smiled.

"Your Honor?" Luther whined, but it was too late.

Parks pounded the gavel. "Order! Order! Order!" but he was beatin' a dead horse—the crowd had gone crazy.

Luther collapsed back to his chair and thought *All that's lacking is an elephant, a clown, and hot roasted peanuts*.

"I SAID ORDER, GOD DAMMIT!" Parks aimed a lethal gavel handle at Dimwiddie. "You're out of order!"

"My apologies, Your Honor," Dimwiddie said above the ruckus, and actually bowed. Then he turned to Hub and bowed to him. "To you, sir, I say, thank you. Very much," and on the way back to his chair, he winked at Luther. He sat down. "Prosecution rests."

Parks glared at Hub and jabbed his finger at the defense table. "Go back there and siddown!" Hub left the witness stand and walked to his chair. When he got there, Luther's back was already to him.

Parks pounded the gavel one time. "Court's adjourned until summations tomorrow mornin' at ten!"

It was 10:02 a.m., and once again, the courtroom was packed beyond capacity. The bailiff had everybody stand up and he said his thing. Parks parted the waters, climbed the mountain, and plopped onto his throne. The bailiff told everybody to sit down. The judge pounded the gavel one time, real hard, passing on "Good mornin'."

"Mr. Dimwiddie? Let's get this over with. Your summation, please." Then he waggled his finger at him to approach the bench. When he got there, the judge leaned for'ard, looked real mean and quietly warned, "If you pull any o' that happy horse shit like you did yesterdee, I'll walk you to the jail m'self." Dimwiddie mumbled something that sounded contrite and Parks told him, "Go ahead."

Dimwiddie turned to the front with the air of a Southern Baptist Pulpit Jumper with the weight of a sinful world settin' squarely on his shoulders, when actually there was a pre-victory breakfast of three greasy eggs, over easy, a thick slab o' pan-fried ham, hashbrowns with finely diced onions and parsley, heavily festooned with coarse-ground black pepper, two flaky biscuits submerged in chicken gravy seasoned with sausage, and a butter-slathered sweet roll under his belt. And for dessert, two shots o' bourbon. He didn't normally imbibe before noon, but it looked like it was gonna be a long day, and he needed all the fortification he could get. This was a big case, and a big victory could mean a big payoff in future fees. It could also help landing a cushy position somewhere in government work. He'd like that 'cause he was gettin' awful tired o' havin to actually work for a livin'. He approached the jury box prepared for war.

"Ladies and gentlemen," he started, "what happened to Loretta Lusaw was a horrible, horrible thing. Just horrible. But…that…and the Komes brothers…are not on trial here." He swung around and thrust a finger in Hub's direction and, as with one mind, the jury followed the accusing digit. "But, Hub Lusaw, their murderer, is. A cold-blooded, calculating, premeditating"—he turned his attention back to the jury—"murderer. Yesterday, we all heard the grisly account o' what happened to Ret. It was real, folks, and it was grisly. No doubt about it. But what you haven't been told was how the brothers Komes met their end. Oh, yes, they'd been beat to death. Hub Lusaw even admitted standing over their pulverized bodies with a blood-soaked two-by-four clutched in his hands.

"But...here's something I want you to think about. I want you to think about all that was done to Ret Lusaw, and how she died. Put it in your mind and look at it. Now, let's say that Hub Lusaw hadn't come on her. And hadn't killed George and Matthew Komes. Let's say he was on vacation in Mobile and didn't even hear about it for a week. Then let's say the Komeses did the deed, lit out, been apprehended, and was settin'"—he pointed to Hub's chair—"in that chair right there, alive, standin' trial, accused o' killin' that poor girl." He looked hard at one of the two female jurors as if he was talkin' just to her. "And now, let's say they admitted to it, just like he did. Now here's my question. Would you have any trouble findin' them guilty o' murder?"

Totally unsettled, the woman fidgeted nervously, lookin' around at all the faces lookin' at her.

"No, of course you wouldn't! They did it, didn't they? They admitted it?" What a stroke of genius. He was assured of one vote. Then he shifted his attention to the man seated next to her and said, "I wouldn't!" Insinuating that if the juror didn't feel the way Dimwiddie did, he was an idiot and didn't give a shit about the victims. Dimwiddie now felt confident of two votes. "No, sir," he said, shifting to the next juror. "I'd do the right thing, as I know you would."

He gave 'em a second to think about it and then continued to the second woman. "Do you think a man-killer should be treated any different than a woman-killer?" She was so flustered she almost answered, but Dimwiddie turned to face the gallery. "No! A life is a life, and any way you look at it, a cold-blooded killin' is a cold-blooded killin'! And that man"—gesturing to Hub—"that man right there, beat not one, but two other men to death...with his bare hands!"

He shook his clawed hands in front of his face, showing the jury. "My God, can you imagine? His bare hands. It gives me the shiv'rin' fits just to think about it. How much d'you have to hate a body, how Devil-possessed d'you have t'be, to kill someone…rob 'em o' their life…with your hands?" He closed his eyes and shook his head like he was trying to exorcise the image from his mind. He approached the defense table and chinned to Luther.

"In just a minute here, Mr. Knox is gonna tell you how Hub'd lost 'is mind, or somethin' to that affect…that and he didn't know what he was doin', but…," he swung back around to the jury box, "that's a sucker punch, because Hub Lusaw did know what he was doin'. As he stated hisself, yesterday, he had 'presence of mind'"—he mimed picking somethin' up—"to pick up his sister's body"—he acted like he was carryin' it—"the 'presence of mind' to carry it to the house"—mimed layin' the body on the prosecution table—"the 'presence of mind' to carefully lay 'er down"—then like he was pullin' the blanket over her—"and cover 'er up. And then…what did he do? He waited…. Waited and plotted! For his victims…t'come home."

For effect, he spun on the jury. "He laid in wait! Just like a lion or a wolf! It wasn't a knee-jerk reaction! Nobody snuck up behind 'im and scared 'im to action. No, sir! No, ma'am! He waited an hour! A whole hour! Hell, over an hour"—he looked toward Hub, disgustedly—"rollin' cigarettes like he was waitin' for a bus…waitin' and smokin' and plottin'." He raised his hand displaying four fingers. "The time o' four cigarettes, plannin' his revenge." He acted like he was totally blown away by the human condition and how cruel it could be. "That, ladies and gentlemen, is," he punctuated each syllable with a back slap of one hand into the other, "Pre…me…di…ta…ted…MURder!"

He took a deep breath and continued. "Now, I do personally believe there is such a thing as insanity, and I'll even go so far as to say I also believe in temp'rary insanity. I do! But, either one of 'em means that forever, or for a certain amount o' time, a body didn't know what they were doin'. Had no idea! The nut house is filled with those poor souls settin' around peenchin' dust motes out o' the air with their fingers, and they don't know the difference between Thursday 'n a bowl o' clam chowder. Just as crazy as they can be, and there ain't no comin' back for 'em.

"On that dark and dreary mornin' of August eighteenth, if the sheriff'd entered the Komes home and found Hub Lusaw settin' on the floor in wet pants, blubberin' to hisself, pickin' boogers and eatin' 'em, I'd say he was probably a likely candidate for full- or part-time insanity. I'd have to agree that he probably didn't know the difference," he raised his hand, stuck up his thumb, and waggled it to starboard, "between right..."—then to port—"and wrong." He leaned on the jury box. "But that wasn't the case, was it?

"You know what makes the difference? It's as plainnnnnn as the nose on your face. The one and only difference you need to know. You ready? He ran." He helt his arms out as if to say *voila*! "It's just that simple. Do you think that mote-peenchin', bugger-eater'd know the difference? No." He took two steps toward Hub and looked him in the eye. The room was stone-dead quiet. "But he did. He knew the difference...'cause he ran." He turned back to the jury box. "It's the very thing I mentioned to you just a few minutes ago when I described what he did with his sister's body. What'd I say?" He looked down the line of the jurors, expecting them to remember. "He had 'presence of mind.' Remember that? Sure ya do. An insane person doesn't know that difference. But a sane one does," and without lookin' at Hub, pointed in the direction of the defense table, "and did."

He approached one end o' the jury box and looked each person in the eye as he walked to the others. "Y'all have a very weighty decision to make. There are tools...tools you can use to make that decision. You know what we call those tools? Facts. That's right, facts. Fact number one—tool number one—Hub Lusaw killed two men. He freely admits it. Admits the fact. And then, fact number two—tool number two—he freely admits that given the opportunity, he would do," he smacked one hand in the other with each word, "*The Same Damn Thing Again*! He said he was sorry he had to do it? Does that sound sorry to you? Contriteness? Doesn't t'me. Yesterday the truth come to the top when he said he'd be more'n happy to stoke the furnaces o' Hell to keep 'em screamin'. Remember that? His very words. Turned my insides to butter, it did.

"Your job, as jurors, is to use those tools, those facts, to determine whether or not he is guilty of cold-blooded, premeditated murder. And he is! There is no other verdict you can possibly come to. If the brothers hadn't already been murdered, and if it was them on trial, you woulda found 'em guilty, guilty, Guilty! Well, what's good for the goose, so to speak...so's he."

He slapped the jury box railing like it was a done deal. "I thank you very much, you're good people." And with that, he walked to his chair and plopped down, exhausted from another day of slayin' Satanic dragons.

After listening to that, Luther believed Sam Dimwiddie was absolutely right about one thing. They shoulda sold tickets.

"Mr. Knox?"

CHAPTER 24

Luther pushed his chair back, rose, and approached the jury box clutching another paper. "Ladies and gentlemen, naturally we've heard all about what was done to the Komes brothers. That's what this trial's about. It was a bad thing. I'm not slighting that. It can't be slighted. And...as much as I hate to give anything to the prosecution, Mr. Dimwiddie's right about my wanting you to think about what was done to Hub Lusaw through the savage murder of Loretta, his nineteen-year-old sister.

"Nineteen...," he slowly shook his head, imagining. "I have a sister. Eighteen. And I can't begin to imagine what Hub Lusaw's gone through. I'll be honest with you, it scares me to think what I would've done...if something like this had happened to her. If I had found her like Hub did Ret."

He'd just committed perjury. He didn't have a sister. Or a brother. He was an only child whose parents'd doted on him all his life.

"This," he said, holding up the paper, "is the coroner's report on Loretta. I'll start at the top. Hair had been yanked from her scalp, probably from being drug about. These are the coroner's own words. She had a concussion. Facial bones crushed. A broken jaw. Five of her teeth had either been broken or knocked completely out. The coroner found one in a lung. Bruises at her throat indicated she'd been strangled. A dislocated shoulder, five busted ribs, bitten on her neck, her belly, high on the inside of both thighs. Her backside. Raped and sodomized. Every time I look at this, it just makes me sick. Multiple internal damages from severe blows to her midsection, probably from being kicked. He says down here at the bottom, that any one of these could have been the cause of her death. But what had she actually died from? She bled to death. It goes on, but, because there're ladies in attendance...we've already heard more than enough about the hammer handle." He took a long breath and then, almost as if talking to hisself, "Two big, grown men. One little girl."

"Now, here comes the part the prosecution calls the sucker punch. I prefer to call it your conscience punch. Contrary to what Mr. Dimwiddie would have you believe, the law is not black and white. It actually allows for those occasional gray areas. And it gives you, a jury, the...freedom...the latitude...for give and take. It's not the tools or even the facts...but *you* who will not only determine his guilt or innocence, but to what degree. I don't want to get long-winded here, but I do want you to try and put yourself in the same place Hub was on that night.

"It'd been a hot, sweltering day, but the evening had cooled down and Hub was walking home after the dance, when he came on his pretty, nineteen-year-old sister. She was laying just off the side of the road. In the dirt. But she wasn't pretty anymore. Was he surprised? Was he confused? Was he stunned? Was he shocked beyond belief? Could this possibly be his little sister? What if it'd been a favorite dog or a horse? What would he have felt? What would you have felt? But it wasn't his favorite dog, and it wasn't his favorite horse."

He gave it a second. "He wasn't dreaming...but it was a nightmare. Worse than any nightmare he'd ever had. It was his little sister, and somehow, she'd managed to drag herself out of that shack, where she'd been nearly beat to death...the brothers may have even believed she was...and made it to the road." He helt the paperwork up again. "And even after all this...this horrible...damage...she was still alive. A good hundred yards from the shack to the road! How did she do it? It was nothing short of proof that there are still miracles in this wicked, wicked world. Through that poor busted face she managed to tell Hub it was the Komes brothers. And then," he looked like he was picturing it, "while in his arms...she died. Hub actually saw...and heard...her last breath. The life in her eyes, there only a breath before, began to fade like a last tiny ember. And then...other than that horribly tortured little body, his little sister didn't exist anymore.

"Ladies, gentlemen, ask yourself, would that be enough—or was it more than enough—for anyone to be affected? Think about how it would've affected you, and then make your decision. Hub Lusaw has already served time in Hell, please don't send him to prison. I thank you for your consideration. You are good, honest people. I have no doubt you'll do the right thing."

That was another bit of artistic fabrication. He walked back to the defense table, hemorrhaging doubt.

"Thank you, Mr. Knox," Parks said, sittin' up. Then he looked to the jurors. "That's it, folks. Let the bailiff know when you reach a verdict."

He pounded the gavel one time, and the bailiff called out, "All rise."

Everbody stood up, glad for the opportunity to stretch their legs. The judge stepped down from the throne and passed into the little room in the back. The bailiff motioned for the jury to step out. They shuffled out o' the box and moved into another little room in the back, and Luther noticed that not one even glanced at Hub. The jury room door closed. Luther saw Sheriff Rowe comin' to take Hub back to jail. "If you've got a lucky rabbit's foot," he whispered out o' the corner of his mouth, "you better start rubbin' it."

At the same time Sheriff Rowe was escorting Hub back to jail, Lootie Komes was some miles away, depositing the gator stick and the three tightly corked vials in a heavy cloth pouch. She had a long way to go, and it'd probly take her the rest o' the day and most o' the night to reach her destination, but before she set off, she took the time to step outside, set the pouch in the dirt, and park her skinny butt on the old stump just off the door. The same one she saw Cob sittin' on the first time Roach brought her to this decrepit hovel she now called home. That thought gave her an internal chuckle. She wondered if Cob had felt as frail and used up, then, as she did now. *You're born*, she thought, *struggle through a life o' pain 'n regret, 'n then you die. Amen 'n Amen.* She and Cob. Different characters, same story.

She heard crows cawin' and little birds twitterin'. Their kin had been cawin' and twitterin' before she was born and their kin'd do it after she was gone. Did any o' the feathered ones remember their forebears, or did their caws and twitters just dissolve into nothingness? Her parents, both real and adopted, were dead. Her own children, dead, and she wondered: what had her being accomplished? What was a life without purpose? What had been her purpose? Any more than the birds? She massaged her gnarly, arthritic fingers. They were cold. Had been since handing over her soul. Regardless o' what she had on or how warm the weather, she was cold. She heard another crow caw and looked around, but she couldn't see it. Her one eye was too far gone to discern much more than dark and light. She knew where the table, the chairs, and her bed was so she hadn't fired up a lantern to see her way in some time, but she did have one settin' on the table, burnin' low, right now.

She couldn't believe she could feel this old and still be alive. Her wrists hurt. Her elbows hurt. Her shoulders. Her feet. Her calves cramped and kept her awake ever night. Her knees popped and creaked. Her hips. Her back. Her neck. Her nose had a scabby growth that bled, continually. Drip drip drip. Her eyes hurt. She'd been oozin' 'tween her legs for weeks, both front and back. Bloody pus from the back and pusey blood from the front. Had she been a hog or a horse, some good-hearted soul woulda shot her and put her out of her misery.

She wasn't the kind to make wishes, but if she had been, she woulda wished for a different life. She woulda wished she wasn't ugly. That Pearl'd been her real mother. That she'd never given birth to George and Matthew—they probly wished they'd never been squeezed out of a witch. Even worse, a sin eater. She was their mother, and simply because o' that, she loved 'em. And, simply because she was their mother, they loved her. As children, they'd been as cute and loveable as kittens or puppies. But kittens grow up to be cats; and puppies, dogs. As children, they were difficult to control. Grown, impossible. They were mean, they were lazy, they were liars and thieves and fornicators, and although the subject had never been brought up, she'd always assumed they'd raped and murdered. Ret Lusaw was undeniable proof. From what they'd done to her, it was obvious she hadn't been their first.

Add to her bein' a witch and that Roach Komes was their father—they never stood a chance. Genes filtered down like a plate o' stale leftovers. Matthew was particularly unbalanced. When he was still a child, she'd occasionally discover a stash o' maggoty heads: birds, squirrels, possums, dogs, and cats. But his favorite parts were more of the procreative. Collections of animal peckers, stuck in a box, desiccated and stinkin'. Then, out o' the blue, he'd bring her a fistful o' flowers with that stupid grin on his face. He was sneaky, conniving, warped, and sadistic and never would be anything more...but he loved his mother.

Part of her feelings about Hub was simply the fact that he was a Lusaw. She'd put up with grief from that hateful bunch her whole life. She and her doins'd been fodder for many o' Cornelius Lusaw's fire and brimstone pulpit rantings. Although she'd had nothin' to do with his cottonmouth-bitten demise, she'd been accused and was given full credit. She didn't give a shit. Although it was good advertising. But Hub Lusaw killin' her boys was the final straw.

Another crow cawed, bringin' her rudely back to the moment. She wiped her face brusquely with the back of her hand. The time for tears was passed, and the next-to-last chapter in her life was about to start. She had one purpose left on this side o' being, and it was best to get goin'. She gave one more long sigh, blew it out, pushed her creaky bones off the stump, and stepped into the shack. Reachin' for the lantern settin' on the table, she cranked up the flame, gripped the wire handle, casually swung it a couple o' times, and tossed it to the far corner. She'd already doused the wall and the floor with the last of her coal oil. Almost immediately, a small blue flame reared its hungry, feathery little head and licked greedily up the wall and across the floor.

She stepped outside, draggin' her bad leg, leaned on her walkin' stick, reached down for the pouch, and hoisted it over her bony left shoulder. It hurt. Dark smoke began curling out the top o' the front door and wafting back over the roof. The crows raised a ruckus 'cause o' the smoke. Before she got very far, she heard the shack begin to crackle and pop.

That was all right, though, she wasn't comin' back.

***

It was 10:25 a.m. and the bailiff stood expectantly beside the judge's chamber door. Ever minute or so he wiped the sweat off his upper lip with his finger, then off his forehead with his shirtsleeve. Twelve sets of butt cheeks squirmed uncomfortably on the hard wooden seats in the jury box. They'd been waitin' for almost twenty minutes for his royal judgeness to make his grand appearance. They coulda done this yesterday. The jury's first vote was taken ten minutes after they were sequestered in the jury room, and the score was twelve t'nothin'. They called in the bailiff and told him, but the judge and the hundreds o' gawkers'd already gone to dinner, and a dozen clock-watchin' hookers were already on their backs, faking interest.

Finally, there was a slight tapping from a fingernail on the other side o' the judge's door. The bailiff opened it, leaned in, listened for a second, and nodded. He left the door open and, knowing ever eye in the room was on him, stepped to the front o' the bench and called out, "All rise!" Everbody jumped up, their eyes glued to the judge's chamber door.

Parks, falsely impersonating godliness and goodliness, sauntered in, his black silk robes billowing obediently behind. He ascended the two steps to the throne, hiked up the robe, plopped into the big judge chair, pulled up the sleeves, laced his chubby fingers, and rested his forearms on the bench. He was wearing underwear and had throughout the whole trial. It was hot and humid, and the cloth helped absorb the moisture.

There'd been many times, though, especially when the temperature and humidity cooperated, when he didn't wear nothin' but a shirt and his boots under the robes. He thought it was funny he could pound the gavel and send abody to jail for a week, or the rest o' their lives, while twiddlin' with his turtle-necked doodle. Besides, there were times when judgin' was boring and having somethin' to pass the time with made a shorter, more endurable day.

"The court reconvenes," the bailiff bellowed, "in the case o' the State o' Looziana versus Hubert Marshall Lusaw. Be seated," and everybody sat.

Parks nodded through the *good morning*s to Dimwiddie and Luther and they *good morning*-ed back. He then looked over to the jury box and, judgey-like, asked the lanky, bald-headed drink o'water sittin' in the first chair, "Mr. Foreman? Has the jury reached a verdict?" This was bullshit formality—if they hadn't reached a verdict, they wouldn'ta been in there—but it was a great chance to stretch out the trial o' the decade.

There were a number of reporters in the audience, and the judge wanted to give 'em as much to write about as he could. No tellin' how long it'd be before another howdy-do as heinous as this one come along. He was really hopin' the reporters got his first name right. They'd fucked it up more than once. It was Almer, not Elmer. He'd wondered more than once what the Hell his folks had been thinking when they came up with Almer.

The Foreman played his part, stood up, pulled a slip o' paper from his coat pocket, and proclaimed, "Yes, Your Honor, we have." Standing in front of a mirror, he'd rehearsed those lines at least a hundred and fifty times last night and again this mornin'. Five little words. Eighteen letters 'tween 'em, and they were all his. God Damn! They'd probly be engraved on his headstone when he was finally laid to rest. He'd thanked God a thousand times that he'd been given the opportunity to lob the first stone during the vote. There'd been a whole bunch o' *shits* and *God Damn*'s from the unlucky and envious rest when he was designated foreman. He was a veterinarian, and as coincidence would have it, Judge Parks had a bunch o' cows, horses, and hogs, most requiring medical attention at one time or another. One and one was two. When the vet was dead of old age, and the worms 'n beetles'd stripped his bones clean, he'd still be known as the Foreman at the Komes Brothers Murder Trial.

The bailiff strode to the jury box, took the coveted script, carried it back to Parks and, reachin' over the bench, handed it to him. From that day for'ard, he'd be known as the bailiff who handed the piece o' paper with the verdict written on it to the judge at the Komes Brothers Murder Trial.

Parks helt it up so everbody could see. He unfolded the paper and read the verdict to hisself. After draggin' it out as long as he could by scrunchin' up his eyebrows, puckerin' his lips, and noddin' most judgely, he looked over his glasses at the defense table, cleared his throat and said, "The Defendant will rise." Hub and Luther stood up. Knowin' everbody was watchin' Hub and Luther, Parks slipped the paper in his pocket. Next week it'd be framed and hangin' on his office wall next to his various certificates of accomplishment. "Mr. Foreman, would you please read the verdict to the court?"

Hesitant and nervous that he'd blow it, the Vet unfolded a copy o' the paper given to the judge. "We...the jury...in a vote...o' twelve t'nothin'...find the defendant...Hubert Marshall Lusaw"—and he let it hang in the air. Time stopped. The Earth quit spinnin' 'round the Sun. "Guilty," he finally declared. "On both counts."

Hub was flabbergasted it hadn't gone his way. Dimwiddie was intoxicated it had gone his; his two lucky bourbons had come through. Luther wasn't anything. It went the way he'd feared, and the rest o' the cheering courtroom had a cud to chew on for the next decade. Parks regretted wearing underwear. He'd dreamed of rollin the head of his pecker in his fingertips while passing such a sentence as this for years, and now he'd let it slip away.

He pounded the gavel, alerting the crowd to the next act. "Hubert Lusaw, for the murder o' George 'n Matthew Komes, this court sentences you t'forty years hard labor at Angola State Penitentiary. Court's adjourned."

The courtroom exploded, and the judge banged the gavel hard one time, stood up, and descended the two steps. The bailiff met him at, and opened, the back door.

Hub turned to Luther, dumbfounded. "Forty years?" Two guards started for Hub while he grabbed Luther by the collar and screamed in his face. "Forty years? You good f'nothin', why didn't you do somethin'?"

With help from the guards, Luther pried Hub's hands from his coat. "Dimwiddie gave you the rope, you dumb shit, and you stuck your head in it!"

The guards helt Hub's arms and he growled back. "'Cause o' you, you prissy little bastard, I'm goin' t'prison!"

Luther calmly straightened his coat, and then surprised the Hell out o' Hub and the guards both when he jumped in Hub's face and spit all over him, yellin', "Because of you, you backwoods, brain-dead pud-pounder, I lost my first murder trial! We're even!" Luther Knox, Attorney-At-Law, was the only person present in the courtroom that day who would never, ever brag about bein' any part o' the Komes Brothers Murder Trial. He stuffed his paperwork in his briefcase, yanked it off the table, and huffed off while the guards drug Hub away.

On the way out, Dimwiddie met Luther in the aisle and offered to shake his hand. "Young man," he said, friendly, "considering what you had t'work with, I believe you did an admirable job." Then he looked around to see if anybody could hear, "And, I was thinkin' I might write a book about this, and if it's all right with you, I might like t'use that bus drivin' line in it. I'd give you full credit, of course. That was a humdinger."

By the time the guards got Hub through a side door to the outside, he was shackled with one set of irons at the wrists and hobbled by 'nother at the ankles, forcing a stutter-stepped shuffle. Raeleen approached, draggin' a whining Harvey and Henry behind her, dread granitized on her face. She already knew about the sentence. The verdict had been shouted to the waiting throng outside the courthouse two and a half seconds after bein' announced.

"Hub?"

The guards stopped, allowing time, but Hub said nothin'.

"Hub, say somethin'," she pursued.

"Like what?"

"Like what're we gonna do?"

For a second it looked like he was gonna tell her somethin, but then licked his lips and shook his head. "I can't tell ya what t'do Raeleen. Looks like yr'on yr'own."

Before they could say another word, a haint-like visage pushed through the crowd and, before Hub could do anything, raked the wooden gator head across his left forearm. Lootie'd gripped the tail end of the thing in her right hand and pushed the poison-laden teeth down and into his arm with the left, slicin' it badly.

Instantly, the arm felt like it was on fire, and he jerked it to his side. Bits of skin and flesh hung from the thing's curse-hexed teeth. She dropped the wooden gator head to the ground, pulled one o' the vials from her bag, popped the cork, and before Raeleen could jump out o' the way, splattered her in the face with the dirty, fetid, swamp-water concoction. Immediately, her eyes burned and she was temporarily blinded. One o' the guards put his hands on Lootie's shoulder, but when she turned that one depthless black eye on him, he let go and backed off.

Lootie turned to Hub. "You killed my boys!" She rummaged in the bag hung on her shoulder and gestured to Harvey and Henry. "One o' these days, I'll collect these two in payment." She popped the cork off the snake blood vial and flung it across Harvey's face. He fell to the ground, screamin' and roilin' in fiery pain.

Although she could hardly see, Raeleen tried to step between Lootie and the boys, begging, "No! Please, no! Not my babies." She bent to pick Harvey up and pull him to safety, but because o' the depth o' the gossip-mongering gawkers who'd gathered to watch the guards haul Hub off, she couldn't push through.

Lootie twisted the cork off the third and final vial, the boar blood, shoved Raeleen aside, and splashed it across Henry's face. Now both boys screamed like they were bein' boiled alive, the black, cursed potion drippin' from their little faces.

Lootie pointed to them all. "Th'day th'first dies, y'all die," then she pointed to Hub, "and th'lowest o' th'low'll fight over yer bones." She reached in the bag one more time and pulled out the knife. The same one ol' hole-in-his-face-where-a-nose-oughta-been cut taters with. The one Smoke pounded in the back o' the noseless pig fucker's head. The one Pearl used to free Lootie from Smoke's belly. The one the squeaky little voice told her to take with her from Roach's cabin. Pointin' it at Hub, she cast her last spell. "My life f'yours." Never taking the black eye off Hub, she gripped the knife handle with both gnarled hands and placed the tip under her ribcage. Then she deliberately fell on it, burying it in her heart and cracked the front of her head open when she hit face-first in the dirt. In seconds, black blood circled her head like a hellish halo.

The crowd pushed back like a drop of oil on water, and for ten seconds, the only sounds were of shufflin' feet, Harvey and Henry squirmin' on the ground, and Raeleen pleading, "No! Somebody do somethin'! Don't let 'er die! Please don't let 'er die," but no one moved. No one spoke.

Finally, one o' the guards cautiously knelt beside the inert, emaciated lump and checked the pulse in her neck. He looked up. "She's dead." He stood up, wiping his fingers on his pants leg.

Blood rivered down the toothed grooves on Hub's arm, over his hand and off the ends of his fingers, puddlin' beside his left shoe. No one paid any attention to the thickening tributary that inched sluggishly from the pool at the front of Lootie's head to the one at Hub's feet.

It took a dozen law enforcement officials twenty minutes to push the crowd away enough so that one o' the guards could back his Ford short-bed pickemup to the scene. Sheriff Rowe guided him until the back bumper was about eight feet shy o' the body. He helt his hand up, and the driver killed the motor and set the brake. He got out and walked to the sheriff and another guard standin' beside him. They looked at the corpse and then at each other. Rowe gave 'em a look that said we need to get it in the truck.

The truck's owner recognized it, stiffened, and shook his head. "Uh-uh. No, sir! I'll use m'truck. I don't want to, but I will. But that's's far's I go."

Rowe looked at the other guard.

"I'll turn in m'badge first, 'n I ain't funnin'."

Rowe looked around and noticed a couple o' colored boys, Bob McDonald and Phillipe LaRue, standin' around lookin' like do-nothin', shiftless, lazy-assed niggers. "Hey, boys. I'll give y'all fifty cents t'load 'er in th'truck."

They sauntered over, and the oldest, Bob, looked at the body and then the Sheriff. "Two dollahs."

"Apiece," Phillipe added.

"Yeah," Bob agreed. "Apiece."

Rowe didn't have to think about it much. "Awright, but f'that, you load 'er up, ride in th'back, 'n unload 'er at th'morgue."

Bob and Phillipe shared a nod and walked to the body.

CHAPTER 25

Sweatin' like a plow horse in July, Hub bounced and rocked from side to side in the center of a hard metallic seat welded along the driver-side wall of a smallish, dirty, drab-green bus bound for his new home. Angola Penitentiary. The worst rat trap in the whole world. Every bump touched off a searing flame of pain. His arm felt so heavy it was like somethin' was pullin' it to the floor. His leg irons snaked through a heavy-duty eyebolt welded to the floor 'twixt his feet. The guards had passed on the wrist manacles 'cause of Hub's mangled arm, cupped in a hastily contrived sling double-knotted around the back of his neck.

He was leaned for'ard, head hung and eyes scrunched in pain. His right elbow rested on his knee, so the slung left arm could hang between his legs like a hammock. The pain throbbed like a rotten tooth, and even tightly wrapped, the blood-saturated sling leaked and dripped, puddling molasses-like blood on the dented and scraped metal floor.

Besides the driver, there was one-armed guard on the front seat o' the prisoner section, back to back with the driver, and another all the way in the back, facing the front. Both were as far from Hub as they could get, and neither was very big on conversation. They knew who he was and who Lootie Komes was, and that was all they needed to know. They watched the bloody puddle spread with each drip.

Halfway to the prison, Hub's mouth dropped open, his eyes rolled up, he turned to linguini and toppled over head-first to the dirty bus floor. Another smaller puddle started from a new gash over his right eye in the same place he'd been cut when Sheriff Rowe slammed him against the cell wall. The guards looked at him, then at each other, shrugged their shoulders, and shook their heads as if to say "not me." They'd let somebody else handle it when they got to Angola.

Hub opened his eyes. Stunned. He didn't move. Except his eyes. He helt his breath and looked around. Then he closed 'em, squeezed down real hard, rolled his eyeballs around behind the lids like he was cleanin 'em off, and then opened 'em again. It was the same. It was still there.

He blinked, confused.

First he'd been in a bus, goin' to Angola Penitentiary with his arm on fire, and then...he looked at the arm. It was unslung and undamaged. He bent it, wringin' it around, and straightened it. Nothin'. He slapped it with his other hand. No pain. He was dreaming! Yeah, that was it. That had to be it! But he'd never had a dream that looked this real. Then, just to be sure, he checked the other arm. Nothin'. It wasn't like he could just forget which arm had about been destroyed and ready to rot off, but the one he thought shoulda been...wasn't.

He looked around again. His surroundings were familiar. Very familiar. Too dang familiar. He waited for the skip-jump of a dream, the weird stuff. Flippin' from one place t'nother. It wasn't happening, though. It wasn't a dream. But how could it be real? He was on a bus, goin' to Angola Penitentiary. He looked around again, wonderin' where he was and, better yet, how the Hell he got there. It looked so familiar, but....

Then it hit him—he was dead. Yeah. That was it! He was dead. Died on that God Damn bus! He didn't hurt anywhere. He didn't smell smoke or hear anybody screamin' or beggin' for ice water, but there wasn't any other explanation. He was dead. Dead and sittin' on the edge o' the front porch o' the Lusaw family home. The same house where he was raised. But it wasn't there anymore. That old house wasn't anywhere anymore. It'd been torn down. Caught fire, burned, gutted, torn down, and hauled off, what was salvageable used on another house or a barn. But there it was. Here it...is.

"My name's Hub Lusaw," he said, out loud. He said it to see if it would sound as strange as his bein' there. It didn't. It sounded like him. He was still hangin' on a little some to the dream idea. It was easier to accept than that he'd died and gone to Hell, toppin' off his life by killin' the Komeses.

"It's nineteen-twen'y-four 'n I'm twen'y-five-years old. I'm married 'n got two younguns. I killed George 'n Matthew Komes fer killin' m'sister. I went t'court 'n got forty years. I's on a bus goin' t'th'pen. I got sick 'n...."

And here he was, feelin' silly, talkin' to hisself, sittin' on the front porch o' the house he's raised in. The one that burned down when he was sixteen. Yeah, sixteen. And Ret was eleven. His mother and father were both dead. In fact, it was the house burnin' down that forced him and Ret to move in with an aunt and uncle until he got a regular job and was able to pull in enough for him and Ret to move out on their own.

He shaded his eyes and looked up. It seemed to be late mornin', with the bright sun in a clear blue sky. He felt its warmth. The soft breeze pleasantly wafting over his face also rustled the leaves in the trees. He closed his eyes to feel it. Then he heard a scufflin' and opened his eyes. Just off the porch aways, not ten feet from him, with her back to him, squattin' barefoot in the dry, dusty yard, with her knobby knees tucked under her chin, was a skinny little six-year-old girl with dirty, black, shoulder-length hair. Now it was startin' to feel more like a dream. She hadn't been there two seconds ago. She wasn't payin' him any attention, although he had the impression she knew he was there. And even with her back to him, he knew who she was. He'd seen her just like that, hundreds o' times. But not recently.

It was Ret. His sister. The dead one.

Then he reminded hisself again, the dead one. But here she was. And she wasn't dead. And she wasn't nineteen.

He looked all around the porch, left and right. It was then he noticed all the dust. Dust everwhere, like a thin, fuzzy carpet. He looked to his back, at the screen door behind him, and right of that, to the rough-hewn wooden bench that'd always set there, pushed up tight agin the porch wall. To the rusty old coffee can at the end o' the bench, its bottom rim duned with dust, that his father'd used as an ash and chewin'-t'bacco-spittin' can. The rusty nail on the edge o' the steps that'd been hammered over but still stuck up just enough that it'd caught his toe when he was nine and almost tore the dang thing off. He still had the scar.

It was all there—the thin, worn, faded curtains his mother'd put up just 'fore she died of female problems; ever board on the porch; ever mark on ever board; the broken, cracked, heavy plank that served as the one step. Everthing, except for all the dust, was exactly the same. Without havin' to get up, go out back, and look, he imagined the thin cord clothesline would be there, hung between the back o' the house and the dead tree. The screen door off the kitchen with a notch rubbed into the frame from the spring's slidin' back and forth from hundreds o' thousands of opening's and slammening's. The hook/latch with a dark, half-moon stain that looked like the bags under an old man's eyes, from years o' swingin' back and forth. They'd be there, too. He could still hear his father yellin' "Quit slammin' that God Damned door" when he or Ret was foolin' around and runnin' out of or into the kitchen and forgettin' to keep it from slammin' shut.

His mother and father were dead, so they wouldn't be there. But Ret was dead, so what was she doin' there? What was she doin' here? Maybe his folks were there. Here. Then a shiver run up his spine. If his father was there, here, would he remember that Hub'd killed him? He was ashamed of hisself for feelin' the same old fear.

When he looked back, the Ret child wasn't sittin' in the dirt any longer. She was perched right beside him, on the porch, hip to hip, gigglin' and playin' with a scruffy little black-and-gray-striped kitten layin' on its back between her pressed legs, playfully grabbin' and bitin' at her finger. But now she had to be ten years old. Her dark hair hung below her waist and over her shoulders, framing her face, like it had at that age. He was reminded of all the time she spent brushin' it out after acquiring the knowledge that she was pretty. She was wearin' a pair of worn coveralls and was still barefoot, her feet dirty, a big toe stubbed and scabbed. She'd always hated wearin' shoes. The kitten bit a little too hard and Ret jumped and slapped her hand to her mouth, stifling a giggle. She hadn't actually giggled out loud— it was just that she looked like she had. Hub took the chance and baby-talked, "Did he bitecha?"

She hunched up her shoulders like she was fixin' to get slapped, pinched up her eyebrows like he'd sinned by voicing somethin' out loud, and pressed her finger to her lips. She looked around, secretively, put her hand on his shoulder, pulled him towards her, and cupped her hand to his ear. He felt her hand at his temple and her lips brush over his ear, and although she seemed to whisper, he didn't actually hear her say anything. Nevertheless, the message had been conveyed and understood. She wanted him to go into the house. She turned and stuck her dirty little pointin' finger over her shoulder. He understood she didn't just want him to go into the house but to go to one specific room, one o' the two bedrooms. He wanted to ask her why but she just pointed, more forcefully, impatiently, to go. He felt her say, *Don't ask, just go.*

Nodding to her command, he got up and started for the screen door, then felt her tug on his britches. She helt the kitten to her chest, used his pants leg to help herself up, and crooked her finger, beckoning him down again. When he did, she cupped her hand to his ear and whispered in the same manner as before. He understood he wasn't to go in the bedroom, but only to peek in the door. When he straightened back up, she winked at him and put her finger to her lips, reminding him he must be quiet.

She back-handed a wave to the door like she was shooin' gnats, hefted the kitten to her neck, and stepped back for the edge o' the porch. He pulled the screen door open, and the spring squeaked. He looked to her, expecting to see her finger pressed to her lip again. But it wasn't. She wasn't there. He looked down at the steps and noticed the mussed circle his butt'd made in the dust on the porch's edge, and his footsteps to the door. But there was only the one set. The little girl, and any sign of her, had vanished. He eased the door closed, walked back to the edge o' the porch, and looked around the yard, but she was nowhere to be seen. He stepped off the porch, crossed the yard to the left o' the house, and looked around the side. She wasn't there so he crossed back to the right side. Not there, either.

She'd told him to go in the house, to his old bedroom, and peek in, so he went back to the door, opened it, and stepped into the front room. He allowed the door to close behind him and took the time for his eyes to adjust before he went any futher. He looked around and, other'n all the dust, it was perfect. The same Spartan furniture, same old pictures on the otherwise bare walls, same old worn-out rugs on the floor. Everthing as he'd known it as a child and young man. It even smelled the same.

The house's construction was simple, a rectangle. The combination front room and dining ran the full length. There was a fireplace at the far left front room wall. The right third was the dining area. One got into the kitchen from there. The two bedrooms were to the left o' the kitchen; the one at the far left was his parents', and the one he'd shared with Ret was between it and the kitchen. Both bedroom doors were closed. Before trying the door, he crossed the front room and to the right, entertaining the thought of possibly finding his mother or father in the kitchen, drinkin' coffee.

He stopped at the kitchen door with his hands on the doorjamb, leaned in, and looked around. No one. The door at the back o' the kitchen leading to the backyard was open, but the screen door was closed and latched. He looked at the floor. Dust. No footprints. The slight breeze filtered through the screen, and sure enough, he saw the sagging clothesline trailing from the back o' the house to the dead tree trunk. He pushed off the doorjamb and walked through the kitchen to the screen door, lifted the little hook, unlatching the door, pushed it open, and stepped out to the back porch.

There wasn't anybody out there, but there was somethin' he'd forgotten about. Well, he hadn't exactly forgotten—he just tried not to think about it. Seein' it now brought back a lot o' pain. It was another reason he was still afraid o' seein' his father. All the little graves. One for each o' the puppies Paul David'd killed. One ever two, three, maybe four months, until Paul David had a grave marker all his own in the Oledeux Cemetery.

He went back in, closed and locked the screen door, followed his footprints into the front room, and crossed the floor to the bedroom he'd shared with Ret. He stood in front o' the door a few seconds, apprehensive about what he'd find on the other side. Finally, he took a deep breath, wiped his sweaty hand on his pants leg, wrapped it around the doorknob, and turned. Slowly pushin' it open, he saw the bed he'd slept his growin' up years in. Pushin' futher, he noticed the thin, white curtains hangin' from the window in the middle o' the wall between the two beds, billowing gracefully, like they's breathin' with the soft, warm breeze passin' through the room. He pushed the door open futher and saw Ret's bed.

And she was on it!

On her back, arms drawn up over her head and sound asleep. This newer version was more like twelve years old, and her long, dark hair was splayed out over the pillow. She was wearin' a thin little dress, and her right leg was drawn up so that the bottom of her foot pressed against the inside of her left knee. Her feet coulda used a good scrubbing, and there was a crusty scab on the outside of her left knee. The hem o' the dress was bunched halfway up her left thigh.

He looked around the room. No dust. It was clean. He looked at the girl on the bed and his heart pounded, drawn between two frightening thoughts. The first was the recurring, *what'm I doin' here? What's she doin' here?* The second was more a desire, a hunger, a craving, than a thought. He wanted to lift the bottom o' the dress, but he was afraid. Afraid o' doin' somethin' he knew was taboo, but more, afraid a bein' caught. That was nothin' new. Shit no! From the first moment he became aware of the differences between him and Ret, between male and female, he'd been drawn to her. As all men who ever saw her were. Countless times, he'd done as he was doin' that minute. Sneakin' looks at her while she slept. While she played. While she sat. When she walked. Ran. Ate.

When he fought with her, most o' the time, it was an act. Fightin' and argeein' proved to everone that he felt no more for her than any annoyed brother did for a bratty little sister. No one knew about the Hell he lived in ever day. Ever hour. Ever minute. Livin' in the same house with her, and even worse, sharin' a bedroom. Always lookin', never touchin'. Wantin' and never havin'. Hub Lusaw'd never heard the word *obsessed*, but he knew the condition intimately and lived his early years in fear he'd be found out. That same crushing fear rushed over him now. He looked into the front room, half expecting to see somebody, see that he'd been found out. They'd catch him standin' in the door, lookin' at her, and his face'd tell it all. There was no one right there, but he couldn't be sure there was no one else around.

He turned his attention back to the bed and Ret. Should he take another second to look? Should he move closer as he'd done hundreds o' times to get a better look? Could he bend down enough to look up the dress, catch a glimpse of her underpants? Should he take the chance of movin' closer, as he had back then...or take the sensible route and leave?

Finally, the fear of bein' found out won out. He backed away and started to pull the door closed when he felt a sharp tappin' in the middle of his back. Startled he'd been caught, he turned to see the ten-year-old Ret, the one who'd been playin' with the kitten on the front porch—the one who'd disappeared—standin' by his side, kitten 'n all, shakin' her head like she was put out. He started to ask her where she'd gone, but before he could, she raised her brows and pressed her finger to her lips.

Takin' the bull by the horns, she tucked the kitten into her left armpit and pushed the bedroom door open. Then she took his left hand in her right and gently but purposefully pulled him into the room. The next thing he knew, he was standin' at the foot o' the bed. She moved to the side and looked from him to the Ret on the bed and back again. When it looked like Hub wasn't gonna take the hint, she rolled her eyes. She reached over the bed, pinched the hem o' the dress, pulled it up, and gently laid it on her other her's belly.

Hub sucked in a lungful. The Ret on the bed wore nothin' under the dress and there was a dark, downy fuzz poorly concealing her pouty-lipped little slit and the soft curvature of the pubic mound. He wanted to look, but ten-year-old Ret's presence made him extremely uncomfortable. Then, to his surprise, she scrunched up her shoulders and cupped her hand over her mouth like she was stiflin' another giggle.

She nodded toward the near naked Ret, and he felt her say, "It's awright. Look at it. It ain't gonna bite 'n I ain't gonna tell." He was still reluctant, but the look on ten-year-old Ret's face told him he was bein' silly. This was the reason she'd brought him in, and if he wanted to get closer, go ahead. Live it up. When he didn't, she put the kitten on the floor, leaned over the girl on the bed, and put her face just inches from her older self's crotch. She turned to Hub and wiggled her eyebrows. Then she closed her eyes, lowered her face just enough that she brushed her lips lightly over the other's furry down.

Hub jerked when he saw the girl on the bed react to the touch. Her belly tightened, her pelvis kinda pushed out, her toes curled up, and her hands clenched. A second later, she seemed to relax. Then the younger one leaned in and breathed deeply, pullin' in the scent. She rolled her face to Hub, wrinkled her nose and he heard, *smells like pee pee.*

Engrossed, Hub unconsciously breathed along with her, watchin' one Ret do to another that which he'd dreamed of so many times. She turned to him and ran her eyes over his face, then turned back, closed her eyes, and kissed her vaginal lips. Then, she stood up

her nasty secrets and taking all her clothes all the way off. She didn't even have socks on!

Keeping her eyes riveted on Hub's, twelve-year-old Ret seductively ran her shaking fingertips over her tummy, slid her hands down the inside of her thighs, spread her legs apart and....

And ten-year-old Ret took him by the hand and pulled him from the bedroom.

NO! NO! NO! NO!

Why, when his most impossible fantasy was about to come true, was she pullin' him away? She hauled him through the door and he looked back, hungrily, over his shoulder. The bedroom door was closing of its own accord, but just before it did, he saw that the curtains that had been billowing so softly now hung in desiccated, rotted tatters, the floor and the bed were shrouded in dust, and the girl on the bed...was gone! The bed was empty. All made up. Not a wrinkle on the bedspread. No discarded dress on the floor. Just footprints. One set. Large. His. He looked at the girl pullin' him through the front room. She wasn't the ten-year-old with the kitten any longer, but the one who only seconds before, had been on the bed, naked...now fully clothed. She dragged him through the front room toward the screen door.

She stopped him at the door, pulled him down, and, with her sweet voice again goin' to the middle of his brain, told him she had a surprise for him. He was to close his eyes and not open 'em until she told him to. She was lookin' up at him expectantly, smiling. Her face said she had a gift he was really gonna love and she couldn't wait to show it to him. Before he'd be shorted another fantasy-come-true, though, he leaned down, closed his eyes and kissed her on the lips. When he opened his eyes, she was still there, still holdin' his hand and smilin' at him. He'd never kissed her before, but he'd fantasized about it over and over and over. It was better than he'd ever imagined. Her lips were soft and warm and moist, and bein' that close to her, she smelled musky. Earthy. He kissed her again. He didn't push into her, or pull her into him, but just helt it, his lips on hers.

He started to kiss her again, but she put her fingers over his lips, shook her head, and nodded to the door. Her smile was so sweet, so enticing, so exciting, so...innocent, he was more than willing to cooperate. After all, ever step so far had been better than the one before. He closed his eyes like she'd asked. He heard the screen door squeak and felt the breeze on his face as she led him on to the porch. She led him to the steps and helped him sit. He felt her squat down behind him, pressing her chest to his shoulder blades and her tummy on his low back. She squeezed her knees at his sides, wrapped her arms around his shoulders, and then, with the same internal voice, whispered that he could open his eyes.

There'd always been a small creek about a hundred yards west o' the house. It now burbbled not ten yards from the porch. It hadn't been there when he first watched the six-year-old play in the dirt, but it was now. It reminded him again, this was a dream. And there was another Ret. In the creek. Not six, ten, or even twelve years old, but fifteen or sixteen. She stood in the cool, six-inch deep water, barefoot, with the hem of her dress bunched up to her knees as she playfully flicked water in Hub's direction with her toes. Hub turned to look at twelve-year-old Ret, but she was gone. Again. He looked at the porch and saw only one set o' prints in the dust. Boot prints. His.

When he looked back at the Ret in the creek, she was steppin' out o' the water and walkin' in his direction. That saucy, flirty little walk she used on the boys. She stopped just in front of him, ran her fingers through her black hair, displaying herself. She wanted him to look her over, like the little girl on the bed had, and he took advantage of it. The three or four year difference between the Ret on the bed and this one was miraculous. Taller, more and better physically developed, somewhat more adult, although still young. But the most captivating aspect was the nervous smile and the look in her eyes. They radiated the same sexual cravings the twelve-year-old had displayed. After a few seconds, she took a step for'ard, bent down, placed her hands on the inside of his knees, spread his legs, and stepped between 'em.

She gripped a fistful o' the dress and pulled it up, achingly slow.

His eyes flitted from one leg to the other while the hem rose like the curtain in a picture show.

Then...there it was. His breath caught in his throat. More feminine, more mysterious, more glorious than he'd ever imagined. In fact, what he was lookin' at could only be imagined. Skin like felt, and as hairless as the day she was born. Dream or not, he had as much chance of pullin' away as a drunk sittin' at a bar with o' glass a whiskey under his nose. She bunched the dress at her waist, lifted her long, silky right leg over his left, and placed her foot on the raised edge o' the porch. The lips parted just enough to reveal the wrinkled edge of the prize tucked inside.

It's all right, he heard in his head. Her voice sounded kinda husky, but unmistakably inviting. *Nothin t'worry about. There's nobody else here but you...'n me. Do whatchu want.*

When Hub had sat on the Komes shack floor with Ret's tortured body at his back, one of his strongest emotions had been regret. He'd ached for her for years. Fantasized about havin' her, but George and Matthew'd stolen any opportunity of that ever hap'nin'. As he sat with his back to that dirty couch, he wished he'd gone after it. He woulda suffered through any consequence if he coulda slaked that thirst. Now, for whatever reason, he had that opportunity, and he wasn't gonna make the same mistake a second time. He ran his hand up the back of her calf, closed his eyes in ecstasy, and kissed her thigh just above the knee. Then he pinched a tiny bit of her thigh between his front teeth and felt a shudder pass through her body. He kissed and licked, higher and higher. She pushed her pelvis to him, invitingly, and his tongue finally gave in to her soft, warm, wet lips. He was so immersed, he'd completely set aside the impossibility of its reality. Even if he had recognized it, he wouldn'ta had the will to give it up. He ran his tongue the length o' the crease, and she moaned and dropped the dress over his head, and he felt her hands through the material, kneading and pressing the back of his head, guiding his hungry tongue to satisfy her own rising carnal longings.

Both of his hands ran up the back of her legs to the tight little butt. He pulled her cheeks apart, kneading, drowning in ecstasy. She moaned in response and pulled his mouth in tighter. He heard her fun-filled giggle, while his tongue explored every fold and crease. All the years of fantasy had come true; he was lost in the sensation, the scent, the taste, the feel of her body. His tongue found the little button at the top o' the crease, and it made her moan. He felt it pulse and grow, almost as if it was reachin' out to be massaged and sucked, like a cat, stretchin' its neck to be scratched.

He felt her desire building, the urgency in her breathing, in the way she guided his mouth, tensing, tensing, tensing, quivering, until finally, she moaned, and when she cascaded over the edge he tasted the salty, pulsing, orgasmic secretions. She moaned with each pulse.

Totally enveloped in the moment, he was ready to explode hisself, but then…slowly…he became aware of a change. She continued to move his face over her body, but now she helt his head pressed so tightly, he couldn't breathe. It was as if the labia had grown, like cabbage leaf, and created a seal around his mouth, halfway over his cheeks. And it was cold. One second it'd been warm and alive. Now it was cold and sluggish. Cold as death. Then she was pressing his face so hard against the pubic bone he was actually concerned she'd break his nose. He was suffocating, it hurt, and the taste was wrong. The secretion became a flowing! Pee pee woulda been much better. What'd been sexually salty and exciting, now tasted…Decayed? Rotted? Dead? He opened his eyes and the tender, silky alabaster thighs had withered horribly. Sagged. Purple veins zigzagged under the surface o' the skin on her bulbous belly, and the hairy, nasty crevasse between her legs oozed a putrid, bloody pus, squirming with maggots and wriggling grubs.

It was Lootie Komes, and he was trapped under her smelly robes! He heard her gurgly cackle while she ground his face in the filthy, bloody, maggot-squirming morass. The harder he tried to pull away, stronger was the pull back. Like iron to a magnet, hauled into a hellish maw of wrinkled hide, yellow teeth, and black, bristly hair. Her vaginal lips waved seductively, back and forth, like pond moss, beckoning him back, and the putrid crevasse was filled with rounds of hellish, pointed teeth, churning like a meat grinder. He placed his hands on her bony hips and shoved with all his might, but the nasty thing's pull was more than his push. Just when he thought his face would be chewed up, it just let go, and she jerked the filthy dress from over his head, laughing.

"No, not yet, boy," she cackled.

Desperately sucking for air, Hub saw the hideously scarred face of his worst nightmare, the blind eye, the depthless black one.

"Mayhaps not fer a long time. Not until I've had my fill o' pesterin' you. And yer family."

Never taking her eyes off him, she raised the dress to her waist, squatted, spread her legs, raked her gnarled fingers across the gaping hole between her legs, scooped out a handful of the rancid mess crawlin' with masses of the squirming filth, and slathered it across his left forearm.

He gnashed and hissed like it was acid. The arm festered and the skin bubbled, the flesh writhing and wrigglin' with maggots and fallin' off in clumps onto the ground.

"I let ya go now," she told him, her image dissolving into a roiling cloud of black smoke, "but we, me 'n my little girls, we be back, now 'n then."

Her hellish screech and cackle fading like steam from a boiling cauldron, he slowly came to his senses, trying to pull away and get up, but he couldn't move. His arms were securely chained to two eyebolts anchored to the porch. He thrashed and thrashed, jerking frantically on his tethered arms. He closed his eyes, took a deep, ragged breath, and blew it out, then another. His face pruned up. Somethin' stunk, bad. Somethin' left over from the nightmare.

He raised his arm to wipe the stinging sweat from his eyes and discovered that he *was* tethered, securely. To a bed. In a large room. He raised his head and noticed two other beds at the far end, inhabited by men starin' at him like he was nuts. Let 'em stare, he didn't care. They didn't scare him. Who were two grown men he could pound to a pulp compared to a ninety-pound Creole witch who'd handed him, and his wife and kids, a death curse. And then given her own life as insurance that the curse would be carried out.

That scared him.

He tested the strength of the heavy leather straps, painfully reminded of the ravaged left arm, as a man in his mid-forties approached his bed.

"Welcome back," he said, friendly enough, "and welcome to Angola." Then, casually, "Bad dreams?"

"Yeah."

"Well, at least you're alive enough to have nightmares. For a while I was concerned we were going to lose you. I'm Dr. Kamarata. You were poisoned," he said, as if Hub'd asked. "A couple of times I considered taking the arm, but you started to turn around." He looked at the blood-soaked bandage and added almost to himself, "I still might." He unbuckled the straps. "Do you know where you are?"

"Hell."

"I guess so, from your perspective. Where were you born?"

"Oledeux. Southeast o' Opelousas." He groaned when the doctor lifted his arm.

"Sorry," Kamarata said, and it sounded like he actually meant it. "Oledeux. Yes, I know where Oledeux is. Everyone does. Big things doing there recently. Thanks to you, from what I hear." He started to remove the bandage. "When?"

"When what?" Hub asked, wincing.

"When were you born?"

Hub let out the breath, "October tenth, ninety-nine."

Kamarata gingerly unwound the gauze wrappings, but Hub grimaced all the same. The pain was extraordinary, and the stink was startin' to turn his already weakened stomach. "Do you know what day today is?" the doctor asked. He had to turn his face away to breathe.

Hub strained to think, and finally, "October fifth."

"All right," the doctor replied, congenially. He picked up a pair o' scissors off a nearby table, and cut some o' the blood-and-pus-soaked bandage. "But that was when you came in. It's actually the tenth. Happy birthday, and like I said, you're lucky you're alive." He finally removed the last wrap and carefully turned the arm one way, then the other. The wound was still horribly festered. Hub got his first good look at it and grimaced. He'd seen rotted animal carcasses that didn't look that bad.

"I was told an old woman did this. She must be a tough old bird."

"Was. She's dead. She didn't cotton t'me killin 'er sons."

"I read about it. You're already quite a celebrity. Heard you were gonna be here quite a while, too. Forty years. Long time."

"Yeah," Hub said, imagining.

"It looks a lot better," Kamarata said, looking the arm over. "Doesn't smell much better, though." He rested the arm on the bedside. "I'm gonna have t'rewrap it. That'll be o' lot a fun, too, but before I do, there's something else you need to know, and now's as good a time as any." He unhooked the leather strap on Hub's right wrist. Then he picked up a hand mirror from a nearby cart. "You're gonna love this." He put the mirror in Hub's hand. "Prison's hard on a body, and I've watched men age, some quicker than others, but you, Mr. Lusaw, you take the cake."

Hub turned the mirror to his face, astonished to see the unfamiliar reflection of an aged, hollow-cheeked, sunken-eyed, silver-haired stranger with half a dozen stitches over a still-swollen right eyebrow.

"I assume it was the poison," Kamarata said, "and considering how much you had running through your system, I have no idea why or how you're still alive."

Hub looked at the reflected image and thought...*I think* I *do.*

CHAPTER 26

Ten days later, twenty-three pounds lighter, and his arm still heavily bandaged, Hub shuffled dizzily along the prison chow line. He was so weakened, his heart pounded from just that little exertion. He used both hands to hold the tray, but most o' the weight was on his right, undamaged arm. The left was little more than help to keep the tray balanced. There were two gaps in the line. One at his front and one at his back. Hub was his own island. It was his first day in the prison proper, and his reputation had preceded him. No one looked him in the eye—if they looked at all, it was no more'n a wary glance. The same look they'd give a body hangin' from a tree, head bent at an uncomfortable angle from the snap o' the rope.

Here was the man who'd beat the Komes Brothers to death. The one the old witch had hexed right off the courthouse steps. Nobody wanted to be anywhere near him when a bolt o' lightnin' jiggered up his ass. Truly, a dead man walking. None o' the guards could remember it ever being that quiet in the mess hall. Hub got his portion, and ever footstep he made echoed off the walls as he moved to a table with an open seat. The men at that table, and then at the ones surrounding it, silently picked up their trays and moved to another.

Robert Dewberry, a big, forty-year-old, no-nonsense career guard with cauliflower ears and a humpy nose, noticed the inmates' reaction and approached the table. Hub flinched when Big Bob tapped his injured arm with a nightstick. "You! Hop up! You got all th'coons 'n half th'white boys' knees knockin' wi'this nigger voodoo shit. I ain't gonna have it. From now on," he jabbed his nightstick in the direction of a corner table, "you getchur chow 'n park yr'ass ova yondah." He banged the side o' the table impatiently with the stick. "Let's go."

Robert Dewberry used to be a professional rassler and went by the name o' "The Manitoba Mauler." Actually, Uricky Springs, Arkansas was as close as he'd ever been to Manitoba, but the moniker sounded good. He won ever match but the last one. That one earned him two weeks of blindness. Scared the shit out of him. It came back, slowly, but not all the way. The doctors warned him if he wanted to keep walkin' without tappin' a cane with a red tip, he should look for a less robust line o' work. He liked pushin' people around, so he put his application in at Angola. The Warden took one look at the scars, his size, the cauliflower ears, his win/loss ratio, and hired him on the spot. He could fill out the job app later.

Hub picked up his tray and, with inmates leanin' out of his way as he passed, headed for the corner table while Robert and his nightstick followed. Hub noticed Shadrach, a sixty-some-year-old black man sittin' at the table with his chin on his chest. Emaciated, scarred, bald, blue-blind eyes, with little bitty ears, he fumbled with a spoon while bubbly threads o' spittle drooled to his plate. Scraps of food hung from his chin, his shirtfront, on the table, his lap, and the floor.

Hub pulled up short. "I ain't sittin' with him!"

Robert poked Hub between the shoulder blades, hard, with the fully-loaded nightstick. "Listen, Cotton, you think you got some rough bark on you, but I'll shave 'at off. You don't tell me whatchu ain't agonna do. This's my house 'n you do what I say, 'n right now th'magic word is Sitchurfuckinassdown."

Hub reluctantly laid his tray on the table and perched on the edge o' the seat opposite the old man.

Robert looked between the two and laughed. "You two look like God Damned salt 'n peppah shakahs!" Hub looked Shadrach over. "You 'n 'at ol' go-rilla's got things in common. He usta preach Holy Rollin' down in Bugaloosa 'n made th'mistake of accusin' a Creole witch in Oledeux o' bein' a Hell-bound sinnah."

Hub snapped his attention at the mention of a Creole witch out o' Oledeux.

"Maybe th'same one gotchu. Anyway, next thing ya'know, he's one deader 'n dead ol' spear chuckah. Yowza, yowza, deader'n a lumpy turd 'n buried deep. He's down 'ere wi'th'worms f'days."

Shadrach seemed to be there in the physical only. Because his chin rested on his chest, Robert had to lean over to look in his face.

"Butcha wudn stay dead, wudja, Shaddie? No, suh." Robert stood up. "I don't hold wi'this dead-niggahs-comin'-back-t'life shit, but th'story goes, a week 'r so aftah buryin' 'is ugly face, he showed up back at home bangin' on th'door, wantin' in, dirt in 'is shoes 'n weeds in 'is hair 'n more'n a couple o' fingernails missin' from diggin' 'is way out o' th'box.

"Family's scared to 'n scared not to, but once in, it's too late t'change their minds. He went t'chokin 'is ol' lady t'death with 'is bare hands 'n hackin' up three o' th'little monkeys with a butchah knife. When they come on 'im, they's parts missin' on th'Misses 'n th'hacked-up little'ns blood was drippin' off 'is chin." He leaned back down to Shadrach's face and grinned. "They said it looked like monkey blood, didn 'ey, boy?" As if all he had to do was mention bleedin', and Hub and Robert both noticed that very same drippin' onto Shadrach's plate, mixin' in with the tasteless rice and mushy dumplins. "Shaddie? You gotchasef a nose bleed?"

Witches follow the same adage as regular folk. Waste not, want not. Shadrach'd made a witch mad. A witch just outside Oledeux. Shadrach'd been killed, brought back to some imitation o' life, and put on a shelf until needed. That time had come. Slowly, Shadrach raised his head. Fog-gray, sightless eyes stared across the table at Hub, while blood burbled like hot cherry-pie filling from his mouth and nose. He grinned a demonically exaggerated smile, as if the corners of his mouth were pulled back by fishhooks, displayin' blood-stained teeth.

"Hullo, Hub," he said.

Impossibly quick, his hand snaked out over the table and grabbed Hub's bandaged arm. Hub's first thought was that he was in another nightmare. But the pain screamin' up his arm like hot lava told him different.

Shadrach pulled Hub to him, opened his bloody mouth, but it wasn't his voice that growled, "Yours f'mine." His hot, foul breath reeked o' the same death and decay he'd been nearly strangled with in the nightmare, and what little Hub had in his stomach rushed up his throat like an oil rig comin' in. It splattered, hot and lumpy, all over Shadrach's face and shirtfront, but the ol' nigger didn't seem to notice. Never even blinked. With the strength of pure evil, he stood up, stepped around the table, bent Hub's arm back, and forced him to his knees. That same demonic, hook-lipped smile, baring red-tinged teeth stretched tightly across his face. Robert was just movin' in to pull 'em apart when Shadrach's bloody vomit erupted all over him and Hub. Ever inmate within thirty feet scattered like a floor full o' cockroaches when the kitchen light goes on. Robert jumped away while inmates scrabbled, screamin' appropriate cursings, creatin' an ever-widening circle.

Shadrach was about to twist Hub's arm off. His eyes, nose, and earholes pulsed gloppy black blood while Robert blew on a riot whistle like he was heralding the end o' the world. More guards flooded the area, jumped Shadrach and tried to pry his hand from Hub's arm. Shadrach craned his neck around and bit one o' the guards on the hand, growled, and shook it like a dog. The guard screamed in pain. Shadrach finally let go when another guard pounded and pounded and pounded him so hard on the back o' the head with his nightstick it shoulda killed him, but whacks on the head don't faze a zombie. Apparently, you can't kill somethin' that ain't clinically alive.

Finally, they got Hub's arm pried loose, and he skittered across the floor like a three-legged spider. The guards wrestled the writhing, blood-and-bile-belching Shadrach to the floor, struggled to wrench him onto his belly, pinned him down with their knees on his neck, and manacled his arms behind his back.

All Hell had erupted, but as suddenly as it started, it stopped! Shadrach's blind eyes opened wide, jaw clenched down like he was tryin' not to fart, frothin' at the mouth and his body tensed, vibratin' ramrod straight. Everbody else was just as still as he was, waitin' for...nobody knew. Suddenly, blood and shit exploded out his ass, stainin' the butt of his pants. The vomit-and-blood-plastered guards jumped up when he flip-flopped like a cat in a gunnysack that knew it was goin' for a dunkin' in the crick. Finally, with one last, hellacious scream, his body stuck straight out like he had a hot poker jammed up his ass, and he died. Flat died! And this time...it looked like it was probly for good!

"Great Godamighty!" Robert gasped, grippin' his nightstick, ready for another go, just in case. "What th'Hell was 'at? That sumbitch ain't said a God Damned word in fifteen years!" A freight train o' shakes, accompanied with prickly goosebumps, started at his feet and whooshed right up to the top of his head. "God Dammit!"

Another wave of guards rushed into the mess hall, nightsticks, rifles, and handguns at the ready. All they saw was blood, vomit, shit, scared guards—one cradlin' a blood-soaked hand—scared inmates, one of 'em, the new fish with the white hair, off in the corner, rockin' back 'n forth, rubbin' a sore arm. And layin' smack dab in the middle of it all, a nigger with what looked like his ass blown out. The show was over, but the latecomers'd be hearin' about it for weeks from the one's who'd lived it.

Robert motioned the guards to lower their weapons. "It's awright, it's ova now." He looked at the prostrate Shadrach. "I think. I sure's Hell hope so." He looked around at the mess. Time to get back to business. "Get this shit cleaned up." He chinned toward the quaking inmates lined up agin the far wall. "'N get them fuckers back t'their cells!" The guards started to roust the inmates. Robert noticed blood surging from Hub's bandaged arm and motioned to one o' the other guards. "Get him t'th'Infirm'ry." The guard helped Hub up, and as he walked him away, Hub took one last look at Shadrach.

"You!" Robert yelled at his back. "You keep 'at fuckin curse t'yer self!"

***

Hub sat on the cell floor with his bunk at his back. His left leg was drawn up, heel-to-butt, knee pressed against the bars at the front o' the cell, his right leg stuck straight out. His left arm was still bandaged but healing, the healing slow going. It'd been a month since Shadrach'd tried to rip it off. That old nigger hadn't done it any good. It was still raw and oozing, but Dr. Kamarata had cut the re-wraps from twice a day, to once, and finally, ever other. Ever unwrap pulled off skin, pus, and yellowish, squishy, scabby pieces. It was gonna leave a very nasty scar. Actually, more a deformation. He'd lost so much fleshy material, it left ugly depressions and runnels. Kamarata told him that with all the scar tissue, the skin'd probly have very little give but he should consider hisself lucky that it hadn't affected the tendons.

At that particular moment, he was drawing. His medium, dark chalk and paper; the artwork, rough but recognizable. It was after lights out. There was still enough from ever third, wire-caged bulb way up high that the guards could make their rounds, but not enough that Hub could use to draw. He had a small candle perched just off his shoulder on one o' the flattened horizontal cell bars.

He didn't have his mind on what he was doin'. He felt guilty. Real guilty. That afternoon he'd been taken to the visiting area. Prisoners were allowed one a month. This was Raeleen's third time and it started like the first two with her askin' the same question. *What'm I gonna do?* and he gave her the answer today he gave the first two visits. What d'you 'xpect me *t'do?*

"I need help, Hub. The boys're hungry 'n I ain't no money! I've looked f'work, but th'name Lusaw's spelled s-h-i-t."

He looked like he was thinkin'.

"What?" she'd asked.

"D'you love me, Rae?"

"What kind o' question is 'at? Course, I do!"

But then, another thought popped into his head, and his brows hunkered down. "You ain't got any money?"

"No!"

"Then, how'dju get up here?"

"I got somebody t'drive me."

"Fer free?"

"It don't make no dif'ernce, Hub. Tell me what you's thinkin'."

"If our name's shit 'n you ain't got no money, how'd you get somebody t'drive y'up? Was it a man 'r a woman?"

"I toldju it don't make no dif'ernce!"

"Whadja hafta pay, Rae?"

"Whadayou think?" she hissed, press-lipped.

"Who is it?"

"I ain't tellin'. I don't needju killin' nobody else."

"Don't come back. You do, the only one gettin' anything out of it'll be th'one broughtcha."

She cried, and he told her again not to come back. She got mad, and he told her again. She begged, and he told her again. She was still beggin' when he had the guard take him back to his cell.

One o' the night guards, Dan Entwhistle, came by, makin' his rounds. "Hey, Hub, how's it goin'?"

"Okay," Hub replied, tappin' cigarette ashes in a mayonnaise jar lid, 'thout lookin' up.

"My wife told me t'tell ya she's prayin' for ya."

"Yeah, well, you tell 'er I said praise th'Lord."

"She told me t'tell ya."

"And you did."

"I just wanted ya t'know it came from her. I ain't as big on that stuff as she is."

Hub thought Dan coulda passed on tellin' him. The little woman never woulda known.

Dan musta read his mind. "If I hadn'ta told ya, she'd know 'n I'd never hear th'end of it. She's got a way 'bout 'er." He stuck his hand through the bars, chinned to the artwork, and asked, "Y'mind?"

Yes, I do, Hub thought, but with nothin' better to do, he set the cigarette in the lid and helt the drawing up. Dan pulled it through the bars and adjusted it to the candle so he could see. Nodding appreciatively, he glanced through the bars at the other dozen or so Hub had pasted to the walls.

"Not bad. Damn sight better'n I could do, I'll tell ya that much. I couldn't draw a straight line with a ruler. I mean it, Hub, you got a real talent."

"Yeah," Hub replied, without a lot of enthusiasm.

Dan looked back at the one in his hand; a swamp scene with moss-festooned cypress and an old fallin'-down, two-room cabin. No smoke from the chimney. It clearly stated nobody lived here, hadn't for a long time, and probly wouldn't in the future. The other drawings on the wall were of varying locales. Some swampy. Some dry. Most were of tall Cypress trees. The only structure was the same old cabin, but from different angles.

Dan passed the drawing back through the bars. "Is 'at where ya live?"

'No," Hub replied. He had to pull back on somethin' sarcastic. Where the Hell did he think he lived and would for the next forty years? Dan wasn't a bad sort. Obviously, all you needed to be a prison bull was to have a total lack of ambition, be content with a small paycheck, and a just-above-starvation-level pension at the end o' God only knew how many years. "I lived off aways. Quite a ways. Acshully, I holed up there a couple o' days when they's lookin' for me."

"Looks lonely."

"Yeah, well," he reached over, picked up the cigarette and took a drag, "I had a lot on m'mind."

"I'll bet. Well, I gotta be goin', make sure all you fellas're accounted for." Hub raised his hand in response and went back to his drawing.

An hour or so later, he'd put it aside and was laid out on his bunk. He'd get back to the drawing later, or he wouldn't. Whatever. God knew he had time. It only took a minute or two before he dozed off. There was no draft and no one'd walked by to stir the air, but somethin' made the little candle dance a little jig and shortly after, Hub found hisself perched on the old Lusaw house front porch lookin' at the back of a little black-haired girl.

CHAPTER 27

September, 1925, in Louisiana was a permanent sauna. Parked in the shade of a large Cypress dripping mossy tendrils, a prison road boss sat astride a state-supplied horse with a state-supplied, double-barreled twelve-gauge nestled in a scabbard on his state-supplied saddle. He kept a bored but watchful eye on his charges, also state-supplied—a troop of a dozen or so inmates clearing brush alongside the county road. Off aways, under another tree, a team of lethargic mules, harnessed to the stakeside flatbed that had delivered the black and white striped throng to this weed-clogged thoroughfare, dozed, their tails wastin' their time swishin' at the hordes of relentless, bothersome, butt-biting insectoids. A second twelve-gauge-totin' Angola Penitentiary employee inhabited the wagon bed, legs danglin' off the side, a hand-rolled pinched in his fingers, watching. He was a watcher. That was his job. Watching. Alllllways watching. And he did it well. They both did. They were a team. Masters of Ambition.

One o' the pick-swingin', sickle-swishin', hoe-hoein', shovel-shovelin' candy-stripers was twenty-five-year-old Hubert Marshall Lusaw. His shirt was off; he was dirty, sweat riverin' little lines in the grime, and hard as nails. He stood out from the rest o' the pack 'cause of his sun-baked hide, close-shorn, stark-white hair, and deeply scarred left arm. He'd been in the big house one month shy a year, and the other prisoners still gave him a lot o' room. Only one time, fairly early on, did someone profess possession of an over-sized sack o' nuts to challenge him and his supposedly fearful murderous resume. Other than the newspaper stories and tall tales, no one had seen actual proof of his cold-blooded ferocity. He was big and he looked mean, but apparently that wasn't enough for one.

They beat the livin' shit out o' each other. For three and a half minutes. Following the embarrassing pummeling, one o' the other combatant's pethy reproductive accouterments had to be surgically separated from its bagmate by Dr. Kamarata, having been too irreparably damaged to keep. He also had quite o' bit o' trouble chewin' anything more substantial than apple sauce, or seein' just one o' anything for 'bout five weeks. It cost Hub a month in a place where the sun actually didn't shine. The enhanced reputation garnered from that one incident undoubtedly kept many other mountain oysters where they belonged.

It wasn't a bad job, workin' the road. Outside in the fresh air, in the sunshine. Three squares a day and a comfy place to sleep at night, paid for by the state, guarded day and night by people who…well, you were guarded. You got free transportation with your cohorts, to and from the worksite. And, again, the ever-watchful, protective somebody constantly lookin' out for you.

Constantly.

It wasn't perfect by a long shot. No, sir, but no job was. You had to put up with the heat, the humidity, bitin', burrowin', suckin' bugs, numerous reptiles of both the multi- and non-legged varieties, all which were sharply toothed, none o' which were very friendly. The old you-don't-bother-them, they-won't-bother-you thing didn't work in and around a Looziana swamp. They would come lookin' for you, with evil and hungry intent.

BOOK THREE

CHAPTER 28

Same humid Looziana, thirty years later, a different road boss, comfortably situated in the shade of another droopy, moss-bearded tree. But instead o' sittin' astride a horse, this one was slouched in the passenger seat in the cab of a new Ford pickemup truck, his crossed ankles on the dashboard, the prison logo emblazoned on the door. The radio was on, Hank Williams warblin' about a woman with a cheatin' heart. He pulled on a little green bottle o' Coca Cola, deliberately brought up a carbonated belch, and then took a suck on a Camel. He turned his wrist to look at his watch. Four more long hours, and he could put another day closer to retirement to bed. He kept the same bored eye on his charges as his predecessors had—a troop of Angola's black and white-striped finest, clearing brush alongside the same road. The same twelve-gauge lay nestled within arms reach in a gun rack acrost the back window. The old road was dirt; this one was paved. Some things change. Some don't.

Case in point: fifty-five year old Hubert Marshall Lusaw. Still one o' the gang, but still not. His shirt was off. He was still dirty, still sweatin' muddy rivers down his grimy back, and still swingin' a pick. It coulda been the same one, maybe not, he hadn't cared enough for it to scratch his name on it. But, if anything, he was harder than the nails of thirty years past. He still stood out 'cause o' that close-shorn, stark-white hair, and the scarred arm, and the other prisoners still gave him room. The reputation had endured. One o' the first questions asked by new craney-necked recruits was, "Which one's Lusaw?"

He'd just about put Raeleen and the boys out of his mind. She came up to see him two more times after he told her not to, but he never went down to see her. He got an official paper from the court shortly after sayin' she wanted a divorce. The paper said he could fight it if he wanted. If he didn't, he'd lose his wife and sons. But, he reminded hisself that he'd told her not to come back. What had he expected? That she'd sit around the rest of her life and mourn like a grieving widow? He signed the papers and never heard from her again. She might be dead for all he knew. He couldn't even remember what Harvey and Henry looked like.

His only other reminder of a past, now, besides the art gallery in his living quarters, was the nightmares. Same one damn near ever night. Over and over and over. After the first few times findin' hisself perched on the Lusaw family front porch, he began to recognize it for what it was and knew it wasn't real, but had no power to end it. He'd tried. God knows he'd tried. He'd stand on the porch and scream and punch hisself tryin' to wake up, but to no avail. All he got out of it was Little Ret givin' him mean looks and pressin' her pointin' finger on her lip to shush him up. He knew he wasn't sittin' on the porch in the sunshine, but layin' on his bunk in prison in the dark. He'd pound his head on the porch post or the back wall, but all it gained him was a headache when he finally woke up, screamin', and his arm on fire. It was like a movie, always the same fuckin' movie—Lootie was the projectionist and she saw to it that it always ran to the end.

He tried foolin' her and climbed on the bed with the twelve-year-old, bypassin' the sixteen-year-old, and they romped like a couple o' sex-starved weasels. Ret, her smell, her feel, her response, so real he'd lose hisself in the act and end up under the bed covers, his face buried 'tween hers, and then Lootie's, festered legs. It was the same with the six-year-old and the ten-year-old with the kitten. Each time, Lootie ended up grindin' his face in her crotch and rakin' her rancid fingernails over his arm. Ever time he woke up with a bleeding arm. It bled...even after thirty years, it bled. No scab, no laceration, but it still bled.

His own Hellish stigmata.

After the days work was completed and he was chaperoned to his cell, Hub relaxed, starin' at the walls and pullin' on a hand-rolled.

He had the wherewithal to barter for machine-made, but any fool knew it wasn't the same. Machine-made tasted like shit, probly tainted by the grease on the machines' wheels and cogs, and anybody who succumbed to 'em was either lazy, stupid, or both. He'd suck on his first machine-made right after he sucked his first dick.

After thirty years, almost ever inch of his walls was plastered with the chalk-and-paper memories. Rend'rin's o' the swamp. Some were so old and desiccated they'd cracked, the torn edges and corners patched up with multiple layers o' Scotch tape. Most were Cypress behemoths and that same run-down old cabin. Interspersed willynilly was the occasional image o' what looked to be the same young girl, but at different ages. Six, ten, twelve, maybe sixteen. He was better with trees and cabins than the human form. The girl's body parts varied depending on the image. Legs a little longer in some, arms a little shorter, the neck, sometimes long, other times almost nonexistent. In a couple, she helt a little kitten. In all, there was a head, but no face. A dozen images o' the same girl, sittin' on a porch, standin' barefoot in a little creek, some layin' on a bed, but all faceless. Faceless 'cause the memory o' broken limbs didn't haunt him as much as the distorted, busted face.

He was immersed in memory when he became aware of somebody or something comin' down the catwalk. A step, then a drag. Step-drag, step-drag. He'd heard it before. When it was almost to his cell, he wondered, whose face would it wear this time?

Lifting his head from the bunk, he turned to see the guard, Mr. Pickering—large on intimidation, short on personality—as he approached the cell door, flippin' his nightstick like a one-handed juggler. Hub watched him work the stick—the hiss as it left his hand that sounded like the drag, and the catchin' it, the plop to his palm, which sounded like the step. God, but that old bitch was sneaky. These days, it was usually Pickering, manipulated, unknowingly shackled with the threat. She'd chosen others in the past. Occasionally, one o' the other prisoners, but more often, a guard.

"What'sa matter?" Pickering asked off Hub's look.

"Nothin'."

"You ain't goin' out tomorrow. The Doc wants t'see ya."

"What for?"

Pickering pulled a pack o' Luckies out of his uniform breast pocket, shook one out to his lips, and pressed the pack back into his pocket. He stuck his hand down his pants pocket, pulled out a Zippo, flipped the lid open, slid his thumb over the striker, bringin' up the little flame, and brought it to the end o' the weed. He sucked it to life, flipped the lid shut, and shoved the lighter back in his pants. Asshole! Pulled that crap all the time. Ask 'im a question 'n then he made ya wait f'an answer. Filter-smokin' asshole.

He tilted his head back and blew out a plume o' smoke toward the ceiling. "They're takin' six at a time, checkin f'TB."

"TB?" Hub snorted, derisively. "I ain't got TB."

"I DK, Hub. DK, DC. Don't know, don't care. Tomorrow mornin', 'fore chow. They wantcha fasting. Be ready." He grimaced, looked at the end of his cigarette, nodded to Hub's and asked, "You got another o' them awready rolled?"

"Sure," Hub said and rolled off the side of his bunk. It was always a good idea to stay on a guard's good side. 'Specially this dipshit. The Boss Hog. He reached up over to the shelf above his bunk and picked one of a half dozen already rolled. As Hub reached through the bars to give him the weed, Pickering pulled the Luckies out of his pocket.

"Here. I'll trade ya. Mine f'yours."

Hub looked like he'd been slapped, but then he started laughin' like he'd heard a good one. Pickering looked at him like he was nuts.

"Let's go! Let's go!" Pickering hollered, impatiently bangin' the nightstick on the horizontal bars outside Hub's cell, glaring down the catwalk and motioning to the guard monitoring the opening and closing of the cell doors. "Morgan! Come on, God Dammit, let's go." He looked at Hub. "I hate fuckin' rookies. Can't even open th'God Damned door! We get a prison break, 'at son of a bitch'll huddle up in a corner cryin' 'n peein' 'is pants." He pounded on the cell again. "MORGAN! It's a handle f'Christ's sake. Just wrap yr'fuckin' fingers around like it was yer cock 'n pull!" The cell door finally opened, jerkily, and Mr. Pickering stepped back. Hub was barely through when it slammed with a clang. Mr. Pickering shook his head. "Fuckin' rookies."

Fifteen minutes later, Hub and five other shirtless inmates were lined up agin the wall in the doctor's office. Dr. Wade, in his early fifties, and an orderly, like they were on an assembly line, checked the inmates' eyes and listened to their hearts and lungs with a stethoscope, while Pickering and another fuckin' rookie stood at the door.

Wade pressed the stethoscope to Hub's back. "Big breath." He moved on down the line repeating the order. When he got to the end, he took six little bottles off the counter and handed one to each man. "Fill 'em," he said with less warmth than he'd give a ham sandwich. The inmates turned their backs to one another, holding their reluctant appendages over the bottles. Hub stepped to a corner and milked a few drops.

"I cain't git it started," one o' the inmates griped.

"You'll be there til ya do," Wade threatened. Finally, all six turned in their yellowish/orangeish offerings. Wade placed 'em on the counter and nodded to his assistant. "This gentleman'll be taking a blood sample, then you fellas can go back to your cells."

The assistant picked up a syringe and a rubber tourniquet used to tie off their arms. The inmate who couldn't get his thing workin' got real nervous. "With a needle?"

Wade looked at him over his glasses. "You know another way?"

"I don't like needles."

"There's nothin' t'be afraid of. We ain't puttin' in, we're takin' out."

"In 'r out, yer still stickin' somethin' in me."

"You took three slugs in a bank job and you're afraid of a little needle?"

"I didn't hafta watch th'slugs comin'."

"Well then," Wade replied, sarcastically, "don't watch it come this time either."

The assistant approached and Mr. Chicken started to back away. "I don't wanna do it, I tell ya!"

Pickering handed his rifle to the fuckin' rookie and motioned the rest o' the inmates to a wall. He approached Mr. Chicken. "Don't gimme any trouble."

The inmate helt his hands out defensively. "Aw, Mr. Pick'ring, can't I skip th'needle? I ain't got TB."

Pickering took him by the arms as the assistant approached with the needle. His arms pinned behind him, the inmate's eyes got bigger and bigger as the needle got closer and closer. Just as the needle hit his skin, he whimpered, his bladder emptied of everthing he'd failed to put in the little bottle, his eyes rolled up, and he passed out. Pickering let him slide to the floor and patted the top of his head. "'Atta boy."

"Get it before he wakes up," Wade said. The assistant slapped the tourniquet around his arm, jabbed him, and Wade looked over his half-glasses at the next man. "You gonna sissy-up, too?"

Hub was in the prison garage layin' on a greasy creeper under an old jacked-up Dodge Brothers double-clutcher, pullin' the transmission and listenin' to Tennessee Ernie Ford on the radio singin' about how he'd worked his ass off but still owed 'is soul t'the comp'ny store. Hub understood his frustration. After thirty years, he'd become somethin' of a trustee, and although didn't hold the keys to the gate, he pretty much had his run o' the place and his choice o' work. His back on a creeper under a truck listenin' to a radio was better than breakin' his back, swingin' a pick in the hot sun.

He jumped when somebody tapped the bottom of his shoe. He looked down past his feet and noticed a pair o' highly shined shoes. He rolled out from under the truck and Pickering chinned in the direction of the main building. "Doc wants t'see ya again."

"Again? What for now?"

"Same don't know, same don't care," Pickering said and motioned him up. "Let's go." Hub got up, pulled a rag from his back pocket, and wiped his hands as they headed for the door.

Minutes later they entered the doctor's office. Wade was seated behind his desk. "There you are," he said, rising, "Sorry, Hub, but we need t'do your tests again."

"How come?"

Wade motioned him to the counter, picked a tourniquet and syringe from a tray. "Roll 'er up."

Hub unbuttoned his shirtsleeve and rolled it up. Wade snapped the tourniquet tightly around his arm, tipped a bottle of alcohol on a cotton swab, rubbed it across the inside of Hub's arm, and harpooned him with the subtlety of a bull dyke with a turkey baster. To Wade, it wasn't an arm connected to another human but a job connected to a paycheck. Hub watched it fill up with what used to course through his veins. After a bit, Wade pulled the tourniquet loose and tossed it to the counter, letting the syringe fill. Topping it off, he pulled it out, set it on the tray, and stuck a cotton ball on Hub's arm. "Hold that." Hub pressed on the ball while Wade pulled a piece o' tape off a roll.

"How come we had t'do it again? I got TB?"

Wade laid the tape across the ball and pressed the ends down. "Just a p'caution. I doubt it's anything. Most times it's just a tainted test."

"If I had TB I'd be coughin' 'r somethin' wouldn' I?" Hub asked while he rolled his sleeve down and buttoned it.

"You don't have TB," Wade said, as he filled out the form to go with the blood.

"How d'ya know?"

"'Cause I went t'doctor school half my God Damn life! That's how I know."

Hub wanted to say *and you ended up workin' in a prison*, but instead o' pissin' him off, he nodded to the form and the syringe. "Then what's 'at for?"

"I said it was probly nothin'! You don't have TB, so don't worry 'bout it. The first test come out a little funny's all, and I'm just makin' sure!"

"What was funny 'bout it?"

"If I knew that I wouldn't be doin' it over, would I! God Dammit, Hub, I'm the doctor and you're the prisoner. I'll act like one 'n tell you what t'do, 'n you act like th'other and do it!" He handed Hub another little bottle. "Don't ask so many God Damn questions, and fill 'er up this time."

Hub started to turn his back to Wade, but that put him facing Pickering so he turned back. He'd rather pee in front o' the doctor than Pickering. Wade stepped up uncomfortably close and squinted in Hub's eyes, first one, then the other. "Your eyes look a little yella. How ya been feelin'?"

Hub'd just got the waterworks started when the question pinched it off. "You ain't makin' this easy. Other'n havin t'do this shit, I feel awright." Hub tried to get it goin' again, but it was difficult with Wade starin' him in the eyeball and breathin' raw-onion breath all over him.

Wade pulled a flat stick from a little box settin' on the counter. "Open your mouth."

Hub opened his mouth. He couldn't have felt any more conspicuous. One hand gripped the little bottle and the other stuffed his dick head in the bottle's mouth so he wouldn't pee all over hisself.

"Say *Ahhhh.*"

"Ahhhaaaaa..."

Wade looked all around, pulled the stick out, and stepped on a little foot-pedal doohickie stickin' out the bottom of a can. The lid flipped up, and he tossed the stick in. He slid his foot off the foot-pedal and the lid slapped back down. Then he looked at the bottle. Hub hadn't done much more than moisten the bottom.

"Hub? I don't have all day, come on." Hub closed his eyes, hopin' that would help, but just as it started to dribble, Wade asked, "You havin' reg'lar BM's?"

Hub opened his eyes in time to detect Pickering tryin' to squelch a smile. "How th'Hell would I know. What's reg'lar?" He'd run out o' pee and patience. "You know what? That's it." He shook the dew off the lily. "You shoulda told me you's gonna need it" — set the bottle on the counter — "'fore I come in, 'n I would'nta" — stuck his dick back in his pants — "drained it first" — and zipped up.

Wade picked up the bottle, helt it to the light, and examined it. "Hmmm..." he said, dubiously. "What little there is looks cloudy. You go ever day? You always have this much trouble gettin' it goin'?"

"What if I's watchin' you?"

"Don't get smart," Pickering warned.

"Well, Hell," he said, exasperated, "it ain't somethin' I keep records on. Why're ya askin' me this shit? You didn't bring nobody else back? Mine the only one you fucked up on?"

Other than shooting Hub a nasty look, Wade ignored the question and set the bottle on the counter next to the blood sample. "Notice any blood in the stool?"

"Stool? What stool?'

Wade's patience had run out, too. "God Dammit, Hub, when you push one out, do you notice any blood in it?"

"You mean when I take a shit? Why didn't you just say that? Uppity son of a bitch."

"Hub?" Mr. Pickering warned.

"No, I don't...didn't...I don't know. It's shit! Why th'Hell'd I look at it 'cept t'check f'worms?"

The presence of worms was a distinct possibility. As were lice. And fleas. And ticks. But those were just the varmits you could see. A prison was a pharmacopoeial supermarket of parasitical probabilities.

"Your gut ever burn?" Wade pushed on.

Hub looked to see if he was kidding. "On prison food? Whada you think?"

"Don't get smart-alecky, Hub," Pickering warned again, "just answer th'man."

"Yes," Hub said, very pointed. "Like a fuckin' clock, three times a day. After breakfast, after lunch, 'n after dinner." He thought he heard Pickering tryin' not to giggle.

Wade opened a glass-fronted cabinet above the counter and removed a small pill bottle. "Now, listen t'me good," he warned, holding the bottle so close in front o' Hub's face his eyes crossed. "I'm gonna give these to ya just t'be on the safe side. I want you to take one a day, but only if you really need it."

Hub squinted at the bottle, mullin' over 'just t'be on the safe side.' "What is it?"

"Dammit, Hub, you are one o' the most argumentative sons o' bitches I ever met!"

"I ain't argeein'. I just asked a simple question!"

"Somethin' to ease your stomach," Wade chirped. He tapped his fingernail on the new test's paperwork. "If these results come back same as the first, I think ya might have the beginnings of a stomach ulcer." He said it with all the warmth of tomorrow's weather report. He reached for a glass and started to fill it at the faucet. "I'm gonna have ya take one right now."

"Ulcers? How th'Hell'd I catch ulcers?"

Wade shook out a pill, handed it and the glass to him. "I didn't say you did, I said you might, and you don't catch ulcers! They sprout from a guilty conscience." Hub eyed the pill suspiciously. "They work better," Wade said, "if ya swallow'em. Come on, Hub, I got better things t'do than stand around jawin' with you all day."

Hub popped it in his mouth and washed it down. Wade took the glass, set it on the counter, and helt the little bottle in front o' Hub's face again. "One a day! No more." He stuck the bottle in Hub's hand. "If it does start t'hurtin' more, you still don't take more than one. You understand?" Hub nodded, concerned. Wade looked to Pickering and jutted his chin to the door. "He can go."

Pickering helt his hand to the door as if to say, *After you,* and Hub exited.

CHAPTER 29

Mr. Pickering escorted Hub back to Wade's office. Upon entering, they noticed the doctor seated behind his desk and another man in an official doctor's white lab coat sittin' 'longside the desk. He had an open folder layin' on his crossed legs, rubbin' his chin, studiously perusing the contents. When Hub entered the room, he closed and tossed the folder on the desk, then he and Wade stood up. Wade made the introductions. "Hub, this is Dr. Ball. He's a...specialist."

"Mr. Lusaw," Ball said, extending his hand, "I'm pleased to meet you. Have a seat, please."

Hub looked at Pickering, not just a little suspicious—a specialist and all the pleasantries. Prisoners didn't often hear words like *please*, less often *pleased to meet you* and never *have a seat*. Never introduced to, or shook hands with. Belief was if you shook hands with a prisoner, you just might find the next day you got worms in your stool and/or little tight-clawed bugs in your dickie hairs.

Wade, Ball, and Hub sat while Pickering remained standing beside the door, his arms crossed over his chest. Ball scrunched his eyes up, conveying doctorial concern. "Dr. Wade asked me to take a look at your tests. Unfortunately, the second set confirmed his suspicions." He leaned toward Hub, his elbows on his knees. "Now, I want you to know that at this point, there's nothing to get overly...."

"I got ulcers?"

Taken aback, Ball sat up and blinked. "Ulcers? What would make you think you have an ulcer?"

Hub fired a finger in Wade's direction. "He said I did!"

Wade jerked back. "I did no such thing! I said there was the possibility and no more!"

Ball jumped in. "Mr. Lusaw, it's all right, you don't have an ulcer. The tests were concerning your blood. That's why I was called in. I'm a hematologist." Then, from the look on Hub's face: "My specialty is blood. Your white cell count's a little haywire, and I believe it would be a good idea, purely precautionary you understand, if we took some X-rays. Just to be on the safe side. To try to determine what might be causing it."

Hub got his hair up. "Whoa whoa whoa, pull up a minute!"

"Take it easy, Hub," Pickering threatened.

"No, that's all right," Ball jumped in, "he's got a right to be concerned."

"What's this cell count stuff," Hub wanted to know, while *he's got a right t'be concerned* ran around in the back of his mind right beside the ever-lingerin' *just t'be on the safe side.*

"Everyone has red and white blood cells," Ball explained. "The white cell's main function is to counter infection. The first test's low white-cell count being off could've been caused by any number of common things. Something you'd ingested, a drug, even a stressful day. But after a second test, with the same results…it warrants looking into." He shrugged and followed with the second, "Just t'be on the safe side."

Hub's heart rate picked up dramatically thinkin' about the one "he's got a right t'be concerned," and now *two* "just t'be on the safe sides"!

Ball picked up and leafed through the folder he and Wade had been looking over when Hub first entered. "Now, I see here that Dr. Wade's already given you something." He looked at Hub. "Did it help?"

"No."

Ball took a deep breath, and he and Wade shared a look of concern. Ball then looked back to Hub as if mulling something over. Finally, he made a decision and slapped the desk top with the flat of his hand. "Dr. Wade? I don't want to wait on this. I want the X-rays done today; in fact, if we can, right now! The clock's ticking. I want more urine and blood samples, also. And it wouldn't hurt to make a couple of follicle and dermatological tests. I want to get to the bottom of this!" He turned his attention to Hub. "It'll take a couple of days to get everything back, but in the meantime, if the pain increases, I'll authorize the use of two pills a day. But I can not warn you strongly enough, no matter what, you do not, under any circumstances, take more than two in a twenty-four-hour period. Have you taken one yet today?"

"You want more blood 'n I gotta pee in 'nother bottle?" Hub asked, astonished. "And what's that fockel 'n dermawhatchamacallit shit?"

"Yes, Mr. Lusaw," Ball said sharply, "I want more blood, I want more urine, and I want it now! I'm sorry, but this could be important. Now, answer me, have you taken one of those pills today?"

"One, early this mornin'," Hub replied. He nodded in Wade's direction and added, tersely, "He gave me one yesterdee 'n I upchucked last night, 'n I hadn't done that 'fore I took th'damn pill."

"No no no no," Ball said, shaking his head. "You can't do that. Dr. Wade did the right thing. The timing of you taking the medication and vomiting was purely coincidental. If anything, it confirms our suspicions. The last thing I want to do, Mr. Lusaw, is frighten you...but we need to move on this. Now." He stood up, crossed to the counter, and poured a glass of water. He pulled another pill bottle from the cupboard, shook one out, and handed it and the water glass to Hub. "I want you to take another one right now."

Hub reluctantly helt his hand out, and Ball placed the pill in his palm. Hub took the glass, and Ball watched him wash it down.

"I apologize for being short with you," Ball continued, "and I know you think this is all happening too fast, when actually, it's probably been coming on for some time and it's just been so gradual you didn't notice it 'til it's too late."

If he thought that was gonna help, he was badly mistaken. The only thing Hub heard was, "til it's too late." Somethin' else to add to "he's got a right t'be concerned" and the two "just t'be on the safe sides."

"Sorry," Ball said, "bad choice of words," but it was too late to yank 'em back. It was like when Judge Parks told the jury to forget what Sam Dimwiddie'd said about a hammer handle bein' shoved up between a young pretty girl's legs. Ball took the glass and set it on the counter. "There are actions that can be taken to fight it, but until we get the results back we don't really have anything concrete to discuss." He stood up and nodded to Pickering. "X-ray, now, please."

Pickering stepped to Hub's chair and tapped him on the shoulder. "Let's go." Hub rose, trance-like, and he and Pickering went into the next room.

Forty-five excruciating hours later, Pickering ushered Hub yet one more time into Wade's office. Wade wasn't there, but Ball was behind the desk. He stood and offered his hand. "Hub, come in, come in, sit down." Pickering took his customary position beside the door. Ball looked Hub over, doctor-like, and asked, "How're you feeling?"

"Awright," Hub replied, worried-patient-like.

"Is the discomfort better? About the same? Worse? What?"

Hub'd always been reluctant to let his feelings show, but that was before he'd been told he could possibly be in a world a shit. "I b'lieve it might be a little worse."

"Yes, well, nature o' the beast."

"Listen," Hub said abruptly, "you didn bring me back here t'yammer about th'nature o' th'beast, whatever th'Hell 'at means, so let's have it."

Ball took a second to sift through his thoughts and then, "No, you're right. I didn't." Then, right smack between the horns, he clobbered him. "You're out o' road, Hub. You got a cancer." He swallowed nervously. "A bad one."

Hub woulda sucked in an involuntary lungful of air if he hadn't quit breathin' altogether.

Then Ball hit him with the capper. "A real bad one."

Naturally, Hub hadn't known what to expect when he walked through the door, but whatever he'd imagined, it wasn't any shit like that. He thought maybe he'd have to take more pills, or possibly get whittled on—some little blackened, malfunctioning hoomahotchee somewhere in his guts, somehow gone bad and had to be removed. But...out o' road? Cancer? A bad one? A REAL bad one? His heart was poundin' like a bass drum. His bunghole twitched like it was gonna unload on him, and he was afraid he was gonna fall off the chair and smack his face on the floor. Finally, he remembered how to make his mouth work. "I'm dyin'?" It was a desert-dry croak.

"Yes," was all Ball said. It was all he could say. It didn't seem sufficient, but he didn't have a lot o' leeway. It was definitely a yes-or-no thing.

"How's 'at happen?" Hub asked, swirling in a tornado of confusion.

"I could give you a hundred answers, Hub," Ball said, compassionately, "but cancer isn't that simple. Other than this, you're as healthy as a horse. You see, everyone has cancer cells. It's a natural part of the system. You could go your whole life, and they don't mean a hill o' beans. Then, for some unknown, unfathomable reason, they'll turn on you. Some do—some don't."

"Me...," Hub started.

"They did," Ball finished. "Hard."

"You're really sure," Hub pushed. He hadn't heard much o' what Ball said after "Yes" had followed "I'm dyin'?"

"I ran the tests every way I could." He gestured at Hub's file layin' open on his desk. "There's absolutely no doubt. Not a whit."

"How long've I got?"

Ball looked back over his shoulder at Pickering. "Sir? Could I ask you to leave us alone for a bit?" Pickering wasn't supposed to leave a prisoner unattended. "I won't tell if you don't. Please."

Pickering, the soft-hearted humanitarian that he was, mouthed that he'd be right outside and exited. The door clicked shut.

"The way it works," Ball almost whispered. Both of 'em were leaned for'ard with their elbows on their knees and their hands clasped, one looking like a preacher and the other, a man who needed one. "It'll get progressively worse. Slowly at first, for three or four months."

Hub sat up real quick, bug-eyed, this bein' the first he'd heard of an approximate time. The dark at the end o' the tunnel. The finish line. Literally. "Three 'r four months," he mumbled, another shade lighter. He felt like lookin' for a clock so he could watch his life tick away.

"At most," Ball continued. "After that...it'll pick up dramatically. But the last month...." He just shook his head slowly, imagining the pain-riddled end. He was reluctant to go on, but it wouldn't be fair to Hub to drag it out. "The last month, Hub, you just won't die quick enough."

"Oh, shit," Hub hissed through bleached lips. Tiny little muscles twitched all over his face. "Oh, shit!" He slid down in the chair, leaned his head over the back, put the heels of his hands to his temples, and pushed. Then he quickly sat back up and pounded his knees. "Shit! Shit! Shit! God Dammit!"

Hub was takin' it ever bit as badly as Ball had anticipated. "I'm sorry," he said, then stepped to the sink for a glass o' water, filled it up, and handed it to Hub. Hub's Adam's apple jumped up and down like a monkey on a stick, gulpin' it down. Ball took the glass back, set it on the counter, and went to his chair. "Listen," he said, but Hub wasn't. "Hub, listen to me." Hub looked up. "I don't want to get your hopes up, but Dr. Wade and I had an idea. We talked it over, and he said you'd been up for parole three or four times."

Hub's mouth said, "Four," of its own volition.

"Okay. In thirty years, your record's been pretty good. Dr. Wade and I want to give the board a recommendation that you be released so you don't..."—again, he was reluctant to continue—"so you don't have to die...in here...in prison."

"You think they'd go with it?" Hub asked, slathered in a cold, clammy sweat.

"Well, naturally, I can't speak for the board, but it couldn't hurt t'try."

Hub pictured dyin' the way Ball'd described. "They ain't nothin you'cn do? Ya'can't just go in 'n chop it out?"

"No, no, no," Ball said, sittin' up and shakin' his head. "Not in here, no. We're not set up for somethin' like that."

Was that a glimmer Hub saw? A straw bobbin on the River Styx? "But it's possible?"

"Oh, yes, sure," Ball hmmphed, disgustedly, "in this day and age. Plus, if you had the money."

"How's 'at?"

"It's a shitty thing, but yes, if you had the money, there's a surgery that could possibly save your life, but, Hub, it's very expensive."

"You mean if I had th'money, I'cd get it cut out?"

"I said it was possible. It's not like taking out your tonsils or removing a toe. It's chancy, but, yes, possibly the difference between your living and dying is the almighty greenback." He stood up and patted Hub on the shoulder, then went to the door and opened it for Pickering. "Sir? He can go now."

Pickering entered, but Hub, still lost in thought, hadn't moved. "Hub," he said, quietly. Hub looked up. "Let's go," and he nodded to the door at his back. Hub stood mechanically and walked to the door.

"Dr. Wade and I'll talk to the board," Ball said.

Hub nodded, lookin' both hopeful and hopeless.

An hour later, Ball exited Warden Gordon Grundheim's office. The Warden was a well-fed, ruddy-cheeked Teuton with hands like hamhocks and legs like oak stumps.

"So," Warden Grundheim said, "I 'magine he took it pretty hard."

"Oh, yes, I know I would," Ball said. "Believe me, I've put a lot into this, and when it's all said and done, you have to go with your gut, and I believe we're doing the right thing. And like we'd discussed, you'll keep it to yourself?"

"Yes, yes, of course."

"I can't tell you how much I appreciate your help," Ball said and stuck his hand out.

"I wouldn't want to be in Hub's shoes," Warden Grundheim said, shakin' his hand. "Sit out thirty years just to have it end like that."

CHAPTER 30

One week later, Pickering escorted Hub to the Parole Evaluation Room. His symptoms had increased, he was pale, and he had shed three pounds. A week, gone. Four months (at most, Ball had said) was sixteen weeks, and the achingly slow wheels o' justice had just gobbled one sixteenth o' the rest of his life.

The Evaluation Room had the same personality as the rest o' the prison. Sterile and cold. Heartless. Soulless. Seated on the other side of a large, scarred table were the trio who would hear his plea and determine a possible different future.

The fellow seated in the middle—undoubtedly the big cheese—was a fat, bald-headed, forty-five-year-old, sweaty son of a bitch with a haughtier-than-thou attitude. He coolly nodded to the wooden chair in front center o' the table. "You can siddown." It was more an order than an allowance.

Hub's scootin' the chair back made an irritating, grating noise, shattering the ambiance. The trio's faces advertised their disapproval. Hub's showed he didn't give a shit. He figured that *You can siddown* was as close to an introduction as he was gonna get, so he gave 'em his own names. The aforementioned, rotund, ruddy-cheeked cherub would henceforth be Butter Ball. The one to his left—a buzzard-beaked, forty-year-old, desiccated spinster who probably hadn't been porked in a very, very long time (if ever), and probably wouldn't be any time in the foreseeable future— would be Hawkface. On Butter Ball's right, sat a skinny, fifty-one-year-old who'd be Go-Funny Eye, so named 'cause one bulbous orb stared directly at you while the other looked off north by northeast. He reminded Hub of a lizard-like thing he'd seen pictures of in a dog-eared *National Geographic* that could work its eyes like that. He wondered if it was possible for the fella to look at, and think about, two things at once. Or, more likely, just be continually confused.

Butter Ball flipped through Hub's file for no other reason than to make him wait. Prisoner fates rested in his chubby hands, and he was there to let 'em know it. Finally, he looked up. "Hubert Marshall Lusaw," he began, nodding to the file. " Mm mm mm mm mm Mm! Boy howdy, son, you got quite a hist'ry here. A vi'lent hist'ry." He clasped his hands, laid 'em on the folder, and looked at Hub over his half glasses. "Very vi'lent."

"Very vi'lent," Go-Funny said, confirming fat boy's proclamation.

Hawkface just pursed her lips and nodded. She didn't wanna be left out, but felt a third verbal confirmation might be overkill.

"Forty years," Butter Ball continued, "for beatin' two fellers t'death." He looked back at the file. "The Kooms Brothers."

"Komes," Hub corrected him.

All three scowled at him. It was obvious they didn't cotton to bein' corrected by anybody, and especially by an ugly double murderer with weird hair and a malformed arm.

"Komes," Butter Ball said, distinctly, acidly. "Thank you so much for settin' me straight on that." Then, "This's yer fifth p'role hearing. You's turned down on th'others due t'attitude, 'n aftah spendin all o' two minutes with ya, it's easy t'see why. You'd think with a p'role on th'line, you wouldn't be so up'ty!"

Hawkface and Go-Funny nodded in duet.

"According t'this," Butter Ball continued, tapping the file with a chubby knuckle, "yer a reeeeal hawd case. That right, Mr. Lusaw, ah you a hawd case?"

Six eyes, five aimed in Hub's direction, one toward Saskatchewan, waited expectantly for an answer that wasn't comin'. Hawkface finally cracked the silence. "You ain't tryin' very hard t'show you turned around."

Butter Ball pulled a paper from the file. "Atchur last hearin' you's asked if you's sorry for killin 'em 'n you said yer only regret waaaaaas…" while he looked for the quote, "Yeah, here we go, 'that you couldn't kill 'em but once.'" He slid the paper back in the file. "Mm mm mm, boy, that's perty cold. You still feel that away?"

"Damn right," Hub replied.

That caught 'em off guard. They were far more used to "Yes, sir" and "No, ma'am" and "Thank ya s'much." The Grim Reaper was tappin' on his shoulder and he was much more concerned about that than what they thought of him.

"Havin' t'sit in here thirty years is th'only bad I feel 'bout it. They killed my sister. Raped 'er, broke 'er jaw, 'er head, 'er nose, 'n prittnear all 'er ribs." He turned his attention to Hawkface. "One of 'em, probly Matthew, th'dumber o' th'two, gnawed off one of 'er nipples. They never found it. After goin' t'th'trouble o' bitin' it off, I doubt he just threw it away." He turned his attention to Go-Funny. "A body do that t'one o' yourn, you'd just let it go? Look th'other way? I told th'truth all 'long, 'n I'll tell th'truth now. I hope I sent both of 'em screamin' t'Hell fire." He turned blazing eyes back to Hawkface. "You want me t'tell ya what else's bit?"

Go-Funny noticed her reaction and jumped to her rescue. "That won't be necessary. Fer sure those's rotten things, but it don't give you th'call t'take th'law into yer own hands. 'At's what th'law's for."

Hub looked from one o' Go-Funny's eyes to the other. "It's all in how ya look at it, ain't it?"

Go-Funny recognized the jab.

"The law wasn't gonna be no help. Th'Sheriff was a friend o' theirs. They wasn't nothin' gonna happen t'them 'n they knew it." Go-Funny chinned to the file in front o' Butter Ball. "It says in there you waited for 'em t'come home. That's where ya got nailed with premeditation." He wanted everbody to know he could use big words.

"My bible says 'Turn th'other cheek,'" Hawkface snipped.

"Yers would," Hub said. "Mine says "An eye fer an eye." They rurnt my life s'I rurnt theirs, and you know what? I'm tired o' blabbrin, 'n if y'all think I'm agonna beg ya t'let me out, yer even stupider'n ya look. It's 'bout lunch time, 'n Wednesday's chicken 'n dumplins, 'n I'druther not miss it. It's one o' the few meals in here with any taste a'tall. You know as well's me I got a cancer 'n th'doctor don't gimme but four months at th'outside, 'n I'd just as soon die in here's anywhere. It'd be a whole lot cheaper f'th'state t'let

me out than keep me in th'hospital, so're ya cuttin me loose'r not?"
He stared 'em down.

Saturday, 9:00 a.m. Hub Lusaw stood in the middle of his tiny
cell, his tiny world, for the last time in thirty years, wearing
somethin' other than prison stripes for the first time in thirty years.
He'd already been in that same cell five years when Pickering was
first hired on as a fuckin' rookie. Next year, he'd retire, after having
put in twenty-five and rising to head bull, Captain, second only to
Warden Grundheim.

Prison's a funny place. Time moved at a snail's pace. Ever day
was an eternity. Day after day, month after month, year after year,
very little changed. Things happened on the outside Hub hadn't
been, and never would be, a part of. Bad things. Some as bad as, or
even worse than, bein' in prison. He went in in 1924. It was now 1954.
He missed the stock market crash. The Depression. The Second
World War. The Korean War. In 1924 there were bombs that could
blow you to little pieces. In 1954 there was one that could make you
and thousands of your friends and family disappear. Literally. It'd
happened. But in prison, he'd been protected from those threats.

He wore an old pair a slacks, a little shiny in the butt and the
knees; a sportcoat that didn't match; what used to be a white shirt,
collar a little frayed; one dark-blue sock and one black; and a pair o'
worn shoes with two different colored shoestrings. A suitcase with a
clothesline-rope handle sat on the cement floor beside his right leg. It
had faded and half-torn remnants of travel stickers and scuffed like
it'd been drug instead o' lugged around.

Inside the suitcase were a couple of changes of underpants, more
socks, another long-sleeved shirt, a couple of undershirts, and one
other pair of worn pants. They'd given him a tie, too, but he'd
decided that was a little much and left it draped over the bunk. He
felt silly enough already. The suitcase, everthing in it, and everthing
he had on had originally belonged to other prisoners who'd died
while under the state's protection and didn't need 'em any longer. It
looked like Norman Rockwell had painted a much older, bedraggled
version of Andy Hardy leavin' home for his first week at camp. A
camp for old, paroled murderers, dyin o' cancer. Quickly.

Pickering waited patiently outside the open cell door. "Ready?"

Hub picked up the suitcase and stepped to the door. "Ready."

Pickering pointed with his nightstick at the drawings covering the walls. "What about them?"

Hub looked over his shoulder at thirty years worth of artwork, ran his eyes over it, and turned back to Pickering. "You'cn have 'em," he said easily and tapped his temple with his fingertip. "I got 'em up here." He stepped out of the cell.

Pickering looked down the walk and called out, "Mr. Morgan?"

Four seconds later they watched the cell door roll over and clang shut.

"Fuckin' rookie," Hub said under his breath.

Pickering smiled, and they strode down the walkway with Pickering leading, for the first and last time.

After passing through six locked doors and gates, Hub stepped through the last one and watched as the guard closed it, locked it, and waved *adeeos*. Thirty years and no blaring band. No tickertape. No family waitin' with outstretched arms, tears streamin' down their happy faces. No diploma from Angola U. All they gave him was a paper that said he'd been paroled, but it didn't mean complete freedom. He'd be on probation for the next ten years. That was a good one. The only reason they let him out was 'cause he wasn't gonna see much more o' this one. They also made him promise he wouldn't beat nobody else to death. He turned his back to the gate and took in the differences thirty years had made as it paraded by on the street. When he worked on a road gang, they always carted 'em out through the back gates to work the canals and roadsides way out in the sticks. Out of eye and earshot o' the good, skittery, law abiding folk.

The prison wasn't on Mars, though. They saw some o' the life on the outside. They had access to newspapers and magazines and radio. Cars and trucks passed by the worksite, and they saw the changes made in 'em. Modern lookin' things, probly went like a bat out o' Hell. Airplanes flew overhead. Now they made 'em out of metal instead o' wood and varnished cloth. You could go anywhere in the world in one, soaring across the sky like a bird. Hub still had trouble understanding how anything that heavy stayed up in the air.

As part of his parole agreement, they'd lined him up a job working in a shoe factory. He was supposed to start the next Monday morning at 7:00, for thirty-five cents an hour. Yeah. That's what he wanted to do until he screamed to death. Make shoes. In his pocket was a hundred-and-thirty-eight dollars and eighty-seven cents. That's what he'd earned in thirty years. A hundred-and-thirty-eight dollars. And eighty-seven cents.

He'd wanted out for thirty years. And now, here he was. Out. And it scared him. From nothin' but walls, to no walls at all. From bein' watched twenty-four hours a day to nobody watchin', nobody seein' him at all. He looked to the right. Then the left. He finally picked one, the right, hefted his scruffy suitcase and started off. He got about twenty feet when....

"Hub?"

He stopped and looked around. He didn't see where it'd come from, and he surely hadn't expected to hear somebody calling out his name three minutes after he got out o' prison. Hell, maybe somebody had come to see him. Oh, crap! No. It was probly somebody inside. They'd forgotten somethin' or changed their mind and was callin' him back. Well, if they had, they could kiss his smelly butt. He was out and he was stayin' out. He started back to the gate, ready to cuss somebody out. But then....

"Hub Lusaw?"

It hadn't come from the gate. He looked across the road to the faded, rusting forty-eight Plymouth sedan with a cracked windshield, and saw a gray-haired old broad lookin' right at him. She looked a second longer, then swung a flabby arm out the window and pushed down the outside door handle with the heel of her hand. Obviously it wouldn't open from the inside. The door squealed like it was in pain, and she wrestled her bigself out o' the car. Adjusting her dress, he winced when he noticed the top of her wrinkled stockins rolled up in garters just beneath her knees. She wore what he'd always referred to as clompy, old-woman shoes. She was probly in her early- to mid-fifties, but as saggy and frumpy as she was, it was hard to tell. She reached into the car and drug her purse off the passenger side. She let the door slam, checked for traffic, and started across the street, her big ol' watery tits sloshin like hammocks in a storm. She lumbered over and stopped in front of him. He noticed she had half a dozen rubberbands looped around her wrist when she backhanded the sweat off her forehead. Her earrings were clip-ons. Yellow bananas. Her front teeth were rimmed in gold. The grin on her face said she knew somethin' he didn't.

"Who're you?" he asked, suspiciously. There was somethin' vaguely familiar about her, but it was so far removed it was far more vague than familiar. He noticed a tiny twitchy rise at the corners of her mouth and a sparkle in her eye.

"Th'mother o' yr'children."

That blew him back a step or two, and he couldn't help but look her over. All over. And there was a lot of all! Holy crap! Was that the frisky little devil he used to fuck ever chance he got? The little wifey? Ex-wifey, he reminded hisself. She gave the term *The Old Lady* a whole new dimension. If he'd had a cross or even two popsicle sticks, he woulda crossed 'em out in front of him for Divine protection. He was too stunned to try to hide it.

"Yeah, well, you don't look s'good yerself."

"You come t'greet me, Rae?" he asked, when he finally got a grip.

"T'greetcha? No. It wasn't nothin' I's lookin' for'ard to, but somethin' I felt needed doin' noneth'less. I wanted t'setcha straight on how things are. I didn know whatcha might 'r might not know. I remarried. Th'Lord's blessed me with a good husband this time."

"Well, remarried, huh? Anybody I know?" He only asked because he was still so shocked in seein' her he couldn't think of anything else.

She gave it a second, then, "Sam Dimwiddie."

"Dimwiddie?" Hub tasted, then the light came on and he took a step back. "Why, that's th'son of a bitch 'at convicted me!"

"No," she corrected him, "th'jury convicted ya. Sam just told 'em whatcha done. But yeah, he's th'one."

He looked across the street at the piece-o'-junk Plymouth, then back to her. "He must be doin' real good t'keep ya in such finery."

"He took bad sick with 'is liver a while back," she said defensively, "and th'doctor bills like t'cleaned us out, but regardless, we're gettin' back on our feet 'n I'll stick with 'im. That's more'n some do." Which was aimed directly at Hub.

"Well, 'at's a real fine piece o' information t'gimme on th'day I get out. Thank ya so much."

"If you don't wanna hear th'answers, don't ask th'questions."

"Sam Dimwiddie. Well, ain't that somethin'. I thought somebody'a shot that asshole b'now."

"Yeah, well, yer a good one t'accuse a body o' bein' a asshole. He treats me 'n th'boys decent. I feel awful guilty bein' here. He thinks I'm at m'sisters, 'n this feels like a lie. We don't live in Oledeux no more, 'n th'boys think yer dead. I told 'em that."

"How'd I die?"

"Stabbed t'death. I didn want 'em growin' up with a father in prison, so I told 'em you's kilt in a knife fight. It didn take much for 'em t'believe it."

"Does God know ya lied?"

"Yes 'n I'm sorry for it, but I had t'get on, 'n it was hard 'nough 'thout havin a husband in prison fer murder. Some years ago I let m'Lord 'n Savior, th'sweet Son o' God, Jesus Christ, in m'heart, got dunked, saved, got all m'old sins washed clean by His redeemin' blood 'n changed m'sinnin' ways," she said proudly, if a touch defiantly. "I try my damndest everday t'walk th'straight 'n narrow."

"Well," Hub said, nodding, "lyin 'r not, I'm sure God 'preciates it, but for my part, I ain't never had no hard feelin's."

As she got over the initial shock, feelings stored away for three decades started crawlin' out o' the mental woodwork. "Well, it cuts me t'th'quick t'say it," but she would anyway, "'n' sweet Merc'ful Lord God 'n Jesus Christ 'n th'B'loved Mother Mary fergive me, but I did. For a long time."

"Did what? I got lost tryin' t'keep track o' all th'one's you's askin forgiveness from."

"Hard feelin's, Hub, you smart-mouth sinner! I thought I's over 'em but I reckon not. If I thought God was lookin' th'other way, I'd spit on you! Kick you where you's always the proudest. I don't know if killin' George 'n Matthew's whatchu set out t'do 'r ya just went off th'deep end like th'lawyer claimed. It ain't my call t'say you's right 'r wrong. Th'deed just rurnt a lot o' lives. Yers, mine, th'boys. I ain't agonna tell ya where we're livin 'cause I don't wantcha tryin' t'find us."

"Speakin' of, how'd you know I's gettin' out t'day?"

"Last time I come up 'n you wu'dn' see me's when I made up m'mind t'cut ties 'n go f'th'big D. I went t'th'fella who was th'Warden at th'time 'n asked t'leave a note in yer file t'let me know if 'n when ya got out. They called me last week 'n told me. Said it was 'cause you's havin' a problem."

"Well, only if ya call dyin' a problem."

"They said it was cancer. I'm sorry 'bout that. Heard it's an ugly way t'go."

"Why'd you give a damn?"

That got her goin' again. "'Cause I's stupid 'nough at one time t'love ya, but b'lieve you me, I'm over that!" She pursed her lips shut, yanked her handbag open, and pulled out a wad o' bills rolled up in a rubber band and helt it out. "So here! It's five hunerd dollahs. I hope it helps. It's th'best I'cn do." She shoved it in his hand, and his reflexes took it.

He was totally confused. "I don't want no money from you, Raeleen." Although he did have a good grip on it already.

"Hub, th'Good Lord fergive me, but I have dreaded this day fer thirty years. Th'thought o' you's like a scab 'at itches, keeps fest'rin' 'n won't heal up 'r go away. I don't mean ya no hurt, but I was so hopin'," she pointed toward the prison gate, "you'd die in there so's I wudn hafta face ya like this. I wantchu t'take it. It'll appease m'conscience some fer any hurt I mighta caused ya. I want shed o' you, Hub Lusaw. Out o' my life, out o' my mind, 'n out o' my conscience, 'n maybe b'givin ya that money'll help do that. Don't try t'look us up, please, it'd only make things bad. I hope th'money helps ya make a new life." Then she thought about that. "Or what's left o' this'n easier." She started backing, took one last sorrowful look, and shook her head. "You used t'be good t'look at, 'n now ya just look awful. It's th'wages o' sin, Hub, sure as anything. Get down on yer 'knees 'n ask th'Lord t'wipe yer sins away 'fore it's too late. Nobody's too far gone that He can't cleanse their soul. Even yers." She looked like she was about to cry. "I'm sorry, Hub, g'bye."

She turned and waddled her wide butt across the street to the Plymouth. She opened the squealy door, tossed her purse across the seat, and got in without lookin' back. The old straight-eight fired up in a cloud o' blue smoke, and Hub watched until the car disappeared into the distance. Then he looked down at the money in his hand. In five minutes, he'd made almost four times what he had in prison in thirty years and didn't have to do anything for it. He shrugged, put it in his pocket, and started off down the road.

CHAPTER 31

It was about 4:00 p.m. when Hub came on a roadside café desperately in need of painting. Parked at the curb was a '39 Studebaker pickup that'd obviously pushed its share of stalled cohorts and pulled out more than its share of stubborn Cypress stumps. There was a cardboard sign Scotch taped in the passenger window declaring it was "For Sale, Inkwire in Lou's." Looking at how faded the sign was, he determined it'd been declaring the sale for some time. He looked at the sign in raised wooden letters over the cafe door: "Lou's Café. Fine E ts." The little *a* was in the flowerbed under the sign, leaned up against the wall, glistening with old snail tracks.

He set his suitcase on the pavement, stepped to the driver side, and tried the door. It was locked. He put his forehead against the window, cupped his hands to the sides of his face, and looked the cab over. The interior wasn't any better than the exterior. The windshield was cracked, the crack snaking from the southwest corner to the northeast. It seemed to be the day for cracked windshields. There was a dirty, butt-flattened cushion on the driver's seat, so it must be worn through, paper and crap all over the passenger-side floorboard. It had a nice suicide knob of a naked blonde, settin' back on her heels, lookin' saucily over her shoulder, her nipples concealed by her elbows. Slowly circling the heap, he looked at the bald, mismatched tires and the rusty hole in the left rear fender. The bed had rusty holes showin' through to the street, and the tailgate was missing. He went to the front, bent down to look underneath, and noticed fresh oil spatters on the road. Brushing the gravel embedded in his palm off on his pant leg, he picked up the suitcase and headed for the café.

When he entered, he saw only two patrons in well-worn coveralls and sweat-stained baseball caps in a booth in the far corner by the front window. They gave him the obligatory once over and went back to their soup. Hub set the suitcase on the floor and his butt on a red, glinty-speckled, plastic, backless swivel stool at the closest end o' the counter, just inside the front door. The floor may've felt the brush of a broom occasionally, but a bucket o' hot water and soap was obviously a rarity. If not for the eight-legged cleaner-uppers foraging after lights-out, there'd still be cracker crumbs in the corners from the thirties. The multi-colored Wurlitzer off in the corner was scratchin' out "In the Mood." Hub kinda liked it. It didn't mean to him what it meant to most people 'cause he'd spent the big band-era in state-sponsored seclusion.

In back o' the counter, Ida Mae—mid-forties, slim, amply and proudly bosomed—was poured into a tight pink and white waitress get-up with the top two buttons undone. She eyed Hub like a hungry vulture would a juicy-lookin' mouse. She slithered over and slid him a worn, gravy-and-ketchup-stained menu. "Good afternoon," oozed sultrily from a mouth too full o' bright red lipstick. She'd undone the first o' the uniform's buttons when she caught him lookin' the truck over. When he stood up after checkin' the oil stain, picked up the suitcase, and headed for the front door, she'd unleashed the second.

He looked around the café. "Kinda quiet."

She read his mind. "Don't let th'lack o' clientele fool ya. Food's good. We're just more of a lunch place. Mondee through Fridee b'tween ten-thirty 'n three, you can't find a seat, 'n that's th'truth. Close t'day at six. 'Leven t'three on Sundee f'th'after-sermon crowd."

He'd take her word for it. Besides, regardless o' how the food was, it'd probly be better than anything he'd had in a long while. He slid the menu back without lookin' at it and ran his eyes over the advertised chesty cleft. "What time is it now?"

"Five-fifteen, but don't worry 'bout it."

"You got a big steak back there?"

"Best damn steak in town," she bragged, and put her hands on her hips, daring him to take another look. "Cows're just dyin' t'get in here."

He smiled. "Mashed taters?"

"Just like th'big city," she said, flirty, pulled out her ticket book from her apron pocket and started writin' his order. She had the bright red fingernail polish to match her mouth, a jingley charm bracelet, and a wedding ring.

"Biscuits 'n gravy?"

"You ain't hungry, are ya?" she teased, grinning, under the erroneous assumption that she was the cutest thing within the city limits. It'd worked before. For years. And years. But not like it used to. Not anymore, what with the pull o' gravity and the tickin' o' the clock.

"Steak, medium rare, 'n throw some onions on it."

"You got it," she nodded, finished writing, swiveled, ripped the ticket off the pad, and slapped it on the shelf o' the pass-through window. "Gimme a moo, still kickin', tears, mashed spuds, B 'n G," she called to the cook who looked a lot like Gabby Hayes.

"It's five-thirty," Gabby reminded her. Slingin' hash was a job, not a career.

"Five-fifteen," she corrected him. "Don't worry 'bout it. I'll finish it up." She started for the back, giving Hub somethin' wiggly to watch.

"Make that with a lot o' G," Hub called out loud enough for her to hear in the back. "And a beer."

"Will do," she giggled. "Fred?"

"I heard 'im," came grumpily from the kitchen, followed by, "I ain't deef."

"What brand o' suds?" muffled up from the back.

"Cold!"

A few seconds later she slithered back with a beer and a frosted mug. She nodded to the kitchen. "Don't mind him, butcha don't wanna make th'fella's makin' your soup mad, do ya?" Then without losin' a beat, she cooed, "I like Pabst m'self." She stood with her back to the old boys at the far table, and Hub noticed the uniform was unbuttoned by one more. Two more 'n she could take it off. Subtle as a badger in heat, she helt the bottle in her fingertips, with her pinky stuck out and poured the beer slowly, givin' him time to take in the improved view. "I keep a couple o' glasses chilled in th'cooler for special customers." She slid the beer to him. "Lemme know if ya want somethin' else. Not everthing's on th'menu."

Hub wiped the greasy soppins with the last of a biscuit while Bob Wills and the Texas Playboys swung away on the Jukebox. There'd also been Eddie Arnold yodelin' "Cattle Call" and Cab Calloway sung about a Moocher named Minnie. Pretty eclectic stuff for a Looziana café. Four moods for a quarter. The cook'd muttered out his seeyatamara's half an hour earlier, and now, except for Ida and Hub, the café was empty. She'd flipped the closed sign promptly at 5:55 p.m. No one'd come knockin'.

He was suckin' the last o' the butter and gravy from his fingers when he scrunched up his face. His gut was reminding him once again of his impending demise. It was hard to get on with your life with an elephant trumpeting in your belly. He finished wiping the grease off his fingers with a napkin, then kneaded his cramping gut, pulled out the pill bottle Ball'd given him, shook one out and washed it down with the last of his third beer.

Ida'd topped off the salt, pepper, and sugar shakers, and was bussing the last table when she commented, "It's been a while since you had a good meal." She left the table, crossed the black and white tiled floor, and melted onto the stool to Hub's right. She turned in his direction, hiked her dress up above her knees, propped her right leg up on the foot rail attached to the counter's base, offering a preview of another personal product, and nervously whispered a throaty Lauren Bacall, "What were you in for?"

He gave the long leg a long look and then worked back up to her chest. Her breath caught when she felt an imaginary hand run up her skirt and another down her blouse. Her imagination also felt the rough ridges on his front teeth grinding across the base of her puckered nipple. It was like a bucket o' cold water when he nodded over his shoulder and asked, "Who's chewtabakker?"

Her seductive little act was obviously going nowhere, so she put her leg down. "M'husband's." Miss Bacall had taken a walk.

"Was 'at him? Th'cook?"

"Was 'at who?"

"Yer husband."

"Fred? Lord, no!" she said, greatly offended. "Whada you take me for?"

Surely the big lummox knew she could do better than that! She got off the stool in a huff, took her wipin' rag, and started cleaning the counter.

"My husband had t'go t'Nahlans. His mother died, which ain't no loss, b'lieve me. Been gone a week."

Not one to be easily shot down, she'd try the bastard one more time. She put the heel of her hands on her low back and pushed her front out as if stretchin', accentuating the unbuttoned blouse. "He won't be back 'til late t'marra night."

"Does it run?"

Boy! This sumbitch's been locked up way too long. "Yeah, it runs. Throw's a little oil," she admitted, "it ain't no hot rod, but it gets from one place t'other 'n back."

"Would it get me t'Oledeux?"

"Probly. What's in Oledeux?"

"You ask a lot o' questions."

"My God," she griped pettishly, puttin' on another act, "I'm just tryin' t'be friendly's all, what's wrong with 'at?"

"What's he want for it?"

"Hunerd 'n a half."

"Ain't worth that much." Then he drug up the lopsided smile he hadn't used in thirty years. "How 'bout I give ya fifty 'n you throw in th'meal?"

She ran it around for a second and then stepped around to the back o' the counter, put her forearms on the counter, bent over, and squeezed up two tittie pillows. "You gonna tell me whatchu's in for?"

Hub went from lookin' in her eyes to taking his time on her chest. "I beat two fellas t'death."

Her eyes popped open and she stood up straight. "Really? Oh, my! Ain't you a big, bad man?" That was even better than she'd imagined. "Listen," she purred, feelin' her nipples swell up, "it'll take another half hour t'close this place 'n 'at ol' truck's my transpatation home. Why don'tchu gimme 'at fifty dollars, I'll getcha 'nother beer on th'house, 'n after I lock up, you'cn take me home. I might even have some dessert there."

He thought a second, then told her, "I got a better idee."

"What's 'at?" she asked, fully prepared to be let down again.

"How 'bout I take you home, 'n you 'n me just fuck all night? You'cn pretend yer a waitress 'n I'cn be th'murd'rer just escaped from prison."

Her face lit up but before she could say okay he pushed his empty beer glass to her, got up and walked to the jukebox, and stuck in a quarter.

Then another thought entered her fevered little brain. "We's just kiddin'. Right?"

"'Bout what?" he asked, punchin' up a number on the juke box. Then he turned around. "The escapin' 'r th'fuckin'?"

Seven-thirty a.m. Warm mornin' sun shafted brightly through the lacey-curtained kitchen window and the open back door that led to the weed- and junk-strewn backyard where sat the truck. From somewhere close by, chickens clucked and a horse whinnied. Hub's ass was parked at the small faux-marble-topped dinette table puttin' the finishing touches on a hefty breakfast, wolfin' it down like a man with somewhere to go and somethin' to do.

Ida Mae stood next to him in a chenille housecoat, her hip leanin' against his shoulder. It annoyed him. The housecoat was mostly open with one saggy breast deliberately exposed. That was annoying, too. He was totally fuckered out.

She was playfully twisting a lock of his hair in her fingers. He felt like pushin' her away, tellin' her to sit down and let him eat, but he didn't. He might wanna drill her one more time 'fore he hit the road, and there wasn't any use in pissin' her off before he'd made up his mind.

"Like s'more bacon 'n eggs 'r spuds?" she purred. That close, she reeked of neglected pussy and unwashed underarms. It reminded him o' bein' hunched over her backside, jammin' it in and squeezin' her tits so hard she abused the Lord's name. She didn't look almost as good in the mornin' light as she had in the evenin's darkness. No, his stomach was full and his pecker was happy. When getting dressed this morning, he'd noticed a ring of lipstick around the base of his dick. He pushed the plate away.

"No, thanks a bunch, but I gotta make tracks."

She grabbed the coffeepot off the stove and brought it to the table. "You don't have t'be s'quick. You'cn do me agin. Or," she ran the tip of her tongue over her upper lip, "I'cd do you." He helt his hand over his cup. She set the pot on the table, untied the housecoat, theatrically flipped it open, lifted a leg over his lap, straddled his legs, ground her lace-panty-clad crotch into his, and nuzzled her chest in his face. "It's still early," she whispered, her coffee breath in his ear. "We'cd pound out one more."

What looked so good when you were hungry bordered on disgusting when you weren't. He pushed her breast from his face with the back of his hand.

"I know ya got it in ya, Sugar," she googooed, lookin' hurt.

"Yeah, I just don't want it in you no more. Git up, I gotta go."

"Ah, come on, Sugar. They's things we ain't done yet."

"Don'tchu have t'open th'café?"

"Fuck th'café," She helt on to his shoulders and rocked her pussy on his crotch. "Come on, Cowboy, let's do it again! We'cn do it rightchere on th'table if ya want. Tha'd be fun, don'tcha think?"

He reached around her, shoved the dinette table away, knockin' his plate, coffee cup, and salt and pepper shakers on the floor. He put his hands in her armpits and lifted her as he stood up.

"Now, they ain't a God Damned thing in Oledeux any better'n me!"

Hub took his coat off the back o' the chair and started to put it on.

"Listen t'me, Dammit! We'cd figger a way t'kill m'husband. I'd get th'café 'n th'house. We'cd live real good 'n just fuck like squirrels ever night!"

He stuck his finger in her face. "Yer as nutty as a squirrel!"

"No, I ain't, I'm desp'rate! I wanna man that acts like, one 'n maybe I shouldn't tell ya this 'cause it'd give ya th'big head, butchu more 'n fit th'bill! Got a weiner like a horse, and I love it you'cn keep from goin' off short o' the finish line." She let her housecoat fall to the floor, stood naked but for her panties, and gripped his lapels. "I ain't been worked over like last night in a long time 'n I betchu got ideas in yer pants I ain't never thought of, 'n I wantchu t'do'm t'me!"

"I ain't int'rested. MOVE!" When he tried to get by, she skittered to the back door and planted her palms on either side o' the doorjamb and anchored her bare feet in the corners.

"I'll letcha hit me if 'at's what starts yer engine," she purred. He was pushin' her off when she said, "No! Wait just a God Damn minute! Just answer me one question."

He stopped and rolled his head in frustration. "What?"

"Tell me who you thoughtchu's fuckin' last night."

"What's 'at mean?"

"Who's Ret?"

"What?"

"I'll letcha call me anything. I don't care! Hell, I'll change m'God Damn name if ya want! Tattoo it on my ass. Come on, tell Ret whatcha want. I'll give ya anything she can 'n a lot more." Excited by his reaction at hearing Ret's name, she continued, "Last night...y'had me on m'back, remember," she jiggled her floppy breast, "slappin' 'em around. That whatcha do? Slap hers 'round? You didn' think I'cd take gettin' fucked 'at hard, didja? You tried t'hurt me with 'at big ol' thing? Huh? Why don'tcha try it again? Maybe bite me? Huh? Make me bleed?"

The words shot a lightnin' bolt through his brain and he shoved her into the wall. Her head hit hard 'nough he thought she'd fall to the ground, out cold. Instead, she bounced back, grabbed both breasts and squeezed so hard even he grimaced. Her fingers dug into the flesh, she looked in his eyes and ordered him, "Come on, you sonovabitch, hurt me."

He pushed her off and was out the door. She followed him into the backyard. "I'm th'best ride you ever had 'n you know it," she exclaimed, gingerly skippin' after him across the gravelly dirt.

"Yer th'best in thirty years," he said without lookin' at her. His hair was standin' up on end, and for some reason, he didn't want to look at her. Scared to look at her. "But I'll do better." He pulled the Studebaker's keys from his pocket and opened the door.

"God Damn you, you bastard! Don't leave me here like 'is!"

He slid in, closed the door, and started the engine. She moved to the front of the truck, pressing her palms to the hood, figuring to thwart his departure.

"If you ain't gonna stay then take me with ya!" When she added, "You'cn putchur face under m'dress and gobble gobble gobble," he could've sworn her right eye was black as pitch and the other, slate gray.

He ruined her plans by backin' the truck up, turnin' it around, grindin' it into first, gunnin' it across the yard, and fishtailin' onto the main road. She watched him drive off, but, as the truck moved down the road, her demeanor changed, and she calmed. A smile tugged at the corners of her mouth. She drug her fingers through her hair, puttin' it back. "Run, Hub. Run!"

She looked to her left toward a weedy clump of trees in the lot across the street, then to another on the right, and smiled. "And a good morning t'you, too."

Then she swooned, threw her arms out to keep her balance, and blinked to clear her vision, surprised to find herself standin' in her backyard, all but naked. She draped her left forearm over her bruised breast, surprised at how badly they hurt, cupped her right hand to her crotch, and hopped through the gravel to the house.

She plopped in one o' the dinette chairs, wonderin' what in the world she'd been doin' in the yard? Naked? There was a plate and coffee cup on the table and another set on the floor. The cup broken. She looked up at the clock on the wall—7:52. She didn't remember gettin' up. Didn't remember comin' home. Lockin' up the café. The last thing she did remember was some fella cuppin' his face to look in the Studebaker window.

Hub drove through the streets of Oledeux and took in the changes made in three decades. Paved roads, traffic lights, neon signs. The Meeting Hall at what used to be the edge o' town was gone, replaced by a store that sold 'lectric ice boxes, washin' machines, and televisions. Radio with pictures. A couple o' old men stood on the sidewalk lookin' at 'em. Another quarter mile up the road, he came on an Army and Navy store claimin' truckloads o' World War II and Korean surplus stuff and pulled into the parking lot. Half an hour later, he exited with two bags, nudged 'em tightly in the corner o' the bed by the cab, got in, and pulled out, headin' for the swamps.

Ever mile he drove reminded him o' somethin' missed all those years, an energy that was infusing his body and mind once again. It came from the smell mostly. A Looziana blackwater swamp smelled like nothin' else in the world. Decay and rot, both tangy and sweet. To a body raised in it, it was heaven. It was like cow shit to a rancher or the farty stench o' spent diesel to a trucker. To Hub Lusaw, the swamps meant freedom and home.

Finally, he came to the end o' the dirt road he'd taken off the main. He pulled to a stop, got out, and looked around. From that point on, he'd be on foot. Ten minutes later, he was decked out in new duds from the Army and Navy, more appropriate for swamp sloggin', with a large knife, sharp on one edge and a sawblade on the other, hangin' from his belt. He adjusted a backpack and checked his bearings with a new compass. Satisfied, he started into the back country, hoping for salvation.

CHAPTER 32

Shit! The elephant was back. His gut seized up like the fist o' God, driving him to his knees. A goathead inside him was tryin' to dig its way out, scratchin', stretchin', flexin' its spiny self. When it got to where he could breathe again, he pulled out Ball's pill bottle and shook one out, his third for the day. He popped it in his mouth and washed it down with a swallow from his canteen. He was soaked in clammy sweat. Definitely the worst bout yet. Ball had told him the pain would increase gradually for two or three months? And what about the last month?

The last month, Hub, you won't die quick enough.

He sat down until the pain let up. When he felt a little better, he made camp. It was too late to keep going, anyway. The pain had weakened him so much he fell into a deep sleep seconds after he laid down. Lootie and the Little Rets let him sleep for a change.

The sun was up on the second day, and—fortified with a hearty breakfast of cold Spam, one of Ball's pills, and a few swallows o' water—he was off again. It was fairly smooth going, and along about noon he came on what was left of an old cabin, not much more than a few river rocks of what used to be a fireplace and chimney and some o' the flooring. Time and the elements had eaten away the walls and the roof, weeds and mice now being the only tenants, but even so, there was no mistaking it. It was the same cabin he'd sketched and plastered his cell wall with.

He pulled out his compass, checked his bearings, and started off again. A mile and a half futher, he spied a huge tree and, running to it, fingered a thirty-year-old hatchet scar in the shape of an arrowhead, deep in the bark. Another of his etchings. He looked in the direction the arrow pointed, verified it with his compass, and started off again. Thirty minutes later, he found hisself in a clearing. Somethin' wasn't right, though. He knew he was in the right place, had to be, but where was....

Off about fifty yards, he saw another tree, but this one was layin' on its side, propped up by some stouter branches, like a body layin' on the floor, the side of their head resting on their palm. From its condition, he determined a storm had probably felled it years before. He ran his hands over the rough bark, inspecting ever inch. There was a mark, but from what little of it he could see, it was possibly a natural occurrence...but maybe, just maybe, part of another arrowhead. If it was, though, most of it was buried under the trunk. He jiggled his backpack off, pulled out a WWII surplus folding camp shovel, got down on his knees, and dug under the trunk.

Hot Damn! It was the arrowhead, but with the tree layin' on the ground, which way had the marker pointed? He stood up and carefully, methodically, looked all around the root system wrested from the ground and splayed out like dozens of desiccated, arthritic fingers. He was trying to determine, when it went down, if it'd twisted around or fallen straight over. Noticing that many o' the roots on the side o' the trunk on the ground, although dead, still remained in the soil, givin' him his answer—it had fallen straight over. He imagined the trunk upright, and, when he finally thought he had it figured out, headed off. He remembered approximately how far it should be to the next position, and knowing that, calculated how long he'd be trav'lin' before finding it. If he had miscalculated, he'd have to come all the way back to the tree and try another direction.

He hadn't gone fifty yards, though, when he felt it comin'. He fell to his all-fours, emptied his guts on the ground, and washed down another pill. Not good. That was the third for the day, and it was only late afternoon. He'd also taken three the day before. He was reminded of Ball's warning about the danger of taking more than two in a day. He'd been so fucked up worryin' about "you won't die fast enough" he hadn't thought to ask what that danger was. He took a few minutes for his stomach to settle down, got to his feet, and started off again.

Just under an hour later, he came on a small hillock. Another o' the drawings. Pushing through the sparse trees, he saw a mound at the top, scampered up the grade, and, when he got to it, wriggled out o' the backpack, tossed it aside, and dropped to his knees. He brushed the decayed leafy material from the mound to reveal a pile o' stones. The marker! What they called a *cairn*. It was still there! Ever stone, exactly as he'd left it. Thirty years! He was as excited as a kid jerkin' off for the first time and removed all the stones to the bare ground. He pulled the shovel from his backpack, unfolded it, and started diggin' like a crazy man.

With dirt flyin' in all directions, the shovel finally slipped over a lump of rotted cloth. Canvas. God Damn! He'd completely forgotten about the canvas. All this stuff was comin' back to him! He was amazed to think that he'd had the presence of mind then to even think o' the canvas.

He was coming out o' the Komes' shack after killin' George and Matthew, when he saw the big leather satchel settin' just to the right o' the door on the porch. If he hadn't looked in that direction, if George'd left it on the other side of the door—or in the truck— he never woulda seen it.

He dug a trench around the bundle and tried to pry it out, but the cloth disintegrated in his fingertips. He dug the trench deeper and wider, then laid the shovel aside, and ripped through multiple layers of rotten material until he reached somethin' stable enough to pull on. Rockin' it back and forth, he wrestled the object from the hole and greedily peeled away the cloth. And there it was. The satchel. He caressed it like it was a woman's silky thigh, delicately pickin' off any tiny errant dirt speck, and unlatched the buckle.

Then he stopped.

Before he opened it, he wanted to take a minute, stretch it out. He'd waited for this moment for thirty long years. He wanted to remember it, wallow in it like a hot bath.

He sat on his butt, wrapped his arms around his knees, and looked around. It was quiet. The solitude, startling. Nothin' but trees and rocks and sky and swamp. He was all by hisself, and he had fifty thousand bucks tucked between his legs. The money'd waited for him. No one had put their grubby hands on it since his buryin' it. He looked at the satchel and thought how funny a thing time was. Ever day in prison had been an eternity. Yet now, here he was, and it seemed it'd been only hours, maybe even minutes ago, that he'd dug the hole and buried the satchel.

Finally, he couldn't wait any longer. He lifted the flap and pulled open the bag's mouth. It smelled kinda rank, but he passed it off to time. He reached in and pulled out a pack o' bills. Hundred-dollar bills. Then another, and another, and another. They were crisp. They were perfect. Thirty years old and brand-spankin' new. Next he pulled out a small hatchet and two guns. George and Matthew's guns. He didn't remember their bein' in there, but at the time he'd been in a hurry. Then another smaller package. Another .38. His. He didn't remember puttin' it in the bag either. He musta really been fucked up that night.

He picked up all three, one at a time, wrapped his hand over the grips and his finger over the triggers to see what they felt like. His hand liked his own the best. He snapped the cylinder open and rolled it on his forearm to check the load. It was full. He snapped it back and set it aside. He giggled, barely controlling his excitement. What an incredible experience. Everthing was exactly how he'd left it! It was like magic. Regardless of how well he'd buried it, he'd worried. He knew that however remote, there was the possibility that somebody, somehow, coulda stumbled on it and everything woulda been lost. But it hadn't. He rummaged back in the satchel and noticed another somethin', a page of newspaper rolled up. He pulled it out and unrolled it. It stunk. Bad! It was the same smell he'd detected when he first opened the satchel, but about a thousand times worse. He looked at what it'd helt for thirty years. What the Hell....

Then he spidered out o' the way. Bumps ran up his spine and he wiped his hands on his pants leg like he'd just shaken hands with a syphilitic leper. Now he knew why it smelled so bad.

Peckers! Two of 'em!

Not that he'd studied the subject at any great length, but actually having one of his very own, he knew a dick when he saw one, and they appeared to be human. Two uncircumcised human peckers! Hairy nut sacks and all! This was Matthew's shit. It reeked of him. But, where in Hell had they come from?

After he got over the initial shock, another thought entered his mind. Not wantin' to touch the things with his fingers, he picked up a couple of little sticks, and in the fading light, carefully rummaged through the grisly remains. He was lookin' for somethin' else. As much as the peckers had withered, he knew what he was lookin' for wouldn't be very big. Definitely no bigger than a cashew. Probly more like a raisin. It wasn't there. Disappointed, he tossed the detached, blackened duo off to the side.

It was time to go, so he stuffed the money back in the satchel, along with George and Matthew's revolvers. He stood up and tucked his old .38 in his belt, picked up the backpack, slipped his arms through the straps, and jostled it comfortably between his shoulder blades. Then he leaned over, picked up the satchel, turned around, and started down the slope...

And stopped...Flat! Fucking! Dead!

CHAPTER 33

Not thirty yards off stood the good doctor. Dexter Ball. Or maybe more apt, his evil twin. This one wasn't decked out in doctor clothes, and in place o' the little bottle to pee in, he had a .45 with a barrel the size of a cannon gripped tightly in his hand, his index finger curled comfortably over the trigger like it knew what it was doin'. The end with the big black hole was aimed straight at Hub's gut. At Ball's left and one step back stood One Ear, and on his right, Two Dogs—two top-drawer Seminole trackers, with eyes like eagles and noses like bloodhounds. They had feathers in their hats and pistols ever bit as big as Ball's in their hands. Two Dogs had two short lengths o' chain draped over his right shoulder. Hub recognized 'em. He'd seen 'em before. Manacles. They scared him more than the big bore overkill.

"Hey, Hub!" Ball chirped gleefully and chinned toward the bipedal bloodhounds. "Fuckers're damn quiet, ain't they?" The dark-skinned Frick and Frack smiled proudly. "You're in one Hell of a fix, boy." He caught the cold-steel look in Hub's eyes and waggled the barrel of his .45 at the satchel. "Set it down."

Knowing at the moment he had absolutely no way of running, Hub set the satchel on the ground. A jumble of thoughts rammed through his mind. The first bein' why the Hell was Ball there? Only one reason. The money. But how would he'a known? A doctor? It didn't make any sense. There had to be more. Was he gonna kill me? No. If he was, he'd a-done it the second I pulled the satchel out o' the ground. Yeah, there was definitely somethin' more.

"Boy, I wish you could see your face," Ball said, bringin' Hub out of his thoughts. "I didn't think about it until yesterdee, I shoulda brought a Brownie with me." One Ear and Two Dogs snickered.

Hub's hand made a microscopic move to his belt and the tucked-in .38. Ball flicked his gun barrel from the direction of Hub's gut to his nose, and the notched k-k of the hammer thumbin' back said everthing needin' saying. Hub felt a debilitating gloom wash over him.

"Hub? I know you're bad disappointed, and I feel for ya. I do. A little. Thirty God Damn years, and then t'have it end like this must really hurt. But, you might as well accept it, 'cause one way 'r the other, your head's goin' back t'Oledeux. Now, it's up t'you whether it goes still attached to your shoulders or carried back in a sack. I swear t'God, Hub, I'll do it. Don't fuck with me. I need proof I got you, but I'll be damned if I'll lug a whole, intact dead body back through what would be four or five days o' swamp sluggin', when I could carry out just your head in two, and I'll bet these boys feel the same way." The Southeastern Native American Aboriginals nodded their agreement. "I don't mean t'rush you into a decision, but I'd appreciate it if you could make it now."

Hub lowered his hand. Ball gestured to One Ear and Two Dogs to guard him. They moved to Hub's ten- and two-o'clock positions, far enough apart that if Hub was quick enough to get one of 'em, the other'd get him. They set their legs, raised their straight-arm gun hands to Hub's face, and didn't blink. Their intent told him he'd better not, either.

Ball waggled his gun barrel to the ground. "Take off your pack. Slow." Ball considered Hub not just a little dangerous, and if it looked like he was gonna go for the gun in his belt, he'd blow a hole right through him. He had no doubt ever move Hub made might be an attempt to get the jump on him, so he helt the .45 straight to Hub's face. Hub wriggled out o' the pack and set it on the ground. "Now, put your hands waaaaay up."

Pissed, Hub's jaw muscles worked double-time as he raised his arms over his head. It was so embarrassing.

His gun arm still helt straight out, Ball started towards Hub. When he got within ten yards, he stopped and nodded to Two Dogs. "Get the knife and the gun and chain 'im up. Take your gunbelt off first. Lay it on the ground."

Two Dogs holstered his weapon, unbuckled his gunbelt, and set it on the ground. Then he slid the manacles off his shoulders, laid 'em on the ground, and walked wide around to Hub's back. He pulled Hub's knife from the sheath and the .38 from the holster and laid 'em on the ground. The whole time, One Ear and Ball kept their guns trained on Hub's face. They were so notched up, if Hub farted, he was liable to die.

Two Dogs picked up the chains and, one at a time, pulled Hub's arms down and behind his back. He snapped the manacles around his wrists and the second set around his ankles. Now that Hub was trussed up, Two Dogs thoroughly frisked him. Satisfied, he stepped back, took a deep cleansing breath, blew it out, and nodded the all-clear. Ball took his own deep breath, and he and One Ear holstered their guns. The relief was palpable. Two Dogs brought Hub's .38 and the knife over to Ball.

"Thanks," he said, and then, "Well, Hub, I got bad news for ya. Medical news. I'm not a doctor."

"Really," Hub said smartalecky, then, "You coulda fooled me." Immediately he knew how stupid the statement was. He had fooled him. He imagined blowin' Ball's head off and shittin' down his throat hole.

"But, I got even worser news than that. You're not dyin'. Unless, o' course, you keep swallowin' those pills. They'll give you an awful bellyache. Make you feel like you're dyin'." He gestured to the Indians. "I told these boys all about you and the pills, and they just couldn't wait t'meet ya. Whada you think o' my actin' like a doctor? Pretty good, huh? The only one's in on it was Wade and the Warden. You remember the day I gave ya the bad news? Wade wasn't there? Just you and me? That dumb son of a bitch was supposed t'be in the room with us but he'd got so worked up worryin' about his actin' abilities I had t'tell him t'leave. I couldn't take the chance he'd give it away. He said he wouldn't leave, though, unless I promised 'im he could stay in the other room so he could listen in. The parole board didn't even know. The Warden told 'em t'give you a bad time, but in the end, regardless o' how they felt, they were to put their X's to your walkin' papers."

Hub was comin' out o' the ether. He grit his teeth, and the muscles in his neck roped up. "You son of a bitch!"

Faking hurt, Ball put his finger to his chest. "Me? No no no no no, sir! You made things a lot worse than they had t'be. What'd I tell you about takin' more than two o' those pills a day? I said don't do it. No matter what. Didn't I? You took three both yesterday and today, so you got nobody t'blame but yourself."

It was then that Hub figured they'd been followin' him. Watchin' him pissin' and shittin' and pukin' out his guts. Laughin' at him.

"And, too, I went easy on you. The fellas 'at gave me those things offered me some that'd give you the Hershey Squirts just for chuckles, but I turned it down. I figure you owe me for that."

"I owe you f'somethin' awright."

"You'll pardon me if I don't get overly concerned. Got you wrapped up like a Christmas ham, and I don't care if it takes a month t'get back"—he pointed to the leg irons—"those things ain't comin' off. If it's a case o' you drownin' if they stay on, then you're drownin', boy. Glug glug glug." He took another deep breath and laughed. "God Dammit, Hub, but you just made me the happiest man on Earth! I bet I get a promotion out o' this!

"Okay, enough laughs." He motioned a few feet to the side. "Move over there and siddown." Hampered by the ankle chains, Hub shuffled a few feet to a fallen log. "Get the bag," Ball told One Ear. One Ear retrieved the satchel and brought it to Ball. "Check 'is backpack. There oughta be three or four hundred dollars in it somewhere."

One Ear rummaged through the pack and found the rubber-banded wad. Ball took it and counted out a hundred in tens and twenties and handed it to One Ear. "You boys split that. Little bonus. You did a good job." He smiled at Hub and added, "We'll just say he spent it showin' the café woman a good time." Hub's eyes lit up. Ball noticed and stuck the rest o' the wad in his front pants pocket. "Shit, Hub, you ain't been alone since you set foot out the prison gate."

"What'd you mean by 'gettin' a promotion'?"

Ball smiled and pulled a thin, folded wallet-like thing out of his back pocket. "Let me introduce myself officially," he said, and flipped it open to a badge. "Special Agent Dexter Ball, Federal Bureau of Investigation. And you, Hubert Marshall Lusaw," he flipped the little wallet shut and put it back in his pocket, "are under arrest for your part in the robbery"—he pointed out the satchel— "o' that money from Southern States Security, and for your part in the murder o' the two security guards, Jack Hoff and Randolph Snodgrass."

"I don't know nothin' about no robbery 'n I didn't kill nobody," Hub said. He chinned to the bag. "I found that settin' on th'porch."

"The Komeses porch?"

"Yeah."

"How'd you think they made that kind o' money? Raisin' rabbits?"

"I didn't give a shit how they got it."

"Hub? I got you with the money. That's all I need. Anything else is just hoohaw." He looked through the trees at what little was left of the orangy-red glow in the west and told the trackers, "We're not gonna start back t'night. How 'boutchu boys set up camp and fix a little somethin' to eat." They moved to make camp and Ball told Hub, "It's gonna be a long night. Dang, I wish I'd brought my Brownie."

Long after nightfall, their butts planted on the log, Ball and the Seminoles were on one side o' the campfire, sitting on a log, and Hub on the other, sittin' in the dirt. Dinner was black beans, Spam, and pan biscuits. Hub was still chained, but his hands were now in front so he could manipulate his tin plate and spoon.

"So, I was given an old unsolved case to look at," Ball was still ridin' high, ramblin', between smacked-mouth bites. "A robbery slash murder." He'd been goin' on for a while, braggin' about his quest, equatin' hisself with other supposedly big-name FBI guys Hub'd never heard of. Ball thought he was big shit. Hub thought he was, too.

"Fifty thousand smackers gleeped, two guards murdered and mutilated, and neither the money nor the perpetrators ever found." Then, nodding to the top o' the rise, "I think that was probably Hoff's and Snodgrass's dicks you so casually flipped away up there." He wiped his sweaty forehead on his shirtsleeve and looked at the Indians. "You boys like 'em spicy, don'tcha?"

They nodded. They thought all white men were pussies, but they paid pretty good.

Ball took another bite and continued. "New bills, consecutive serial numbers, but nary a one ever turned up." He took another scoop, waved the spoon around in a futile attempt to cool it off.

"So… if the money didn't show…was it still hidden somewhere? Had it been lost? Had the robbers maybe died before gettin' the chance to enjoy it? If not, they had the patience o' Job." He popped more beans into his mouth and ignored the rule about talkin' with your mouth full. "Lookin' through a newspaper o' the time, I found a story about a fella beatin' a couple o' brothers to death." He stopped just long enough to suck some cool air over his burning lips. "Boy! They're good tonight, but sure as shit I'm gonna regret it in the mornin'. Anyway, they's killed the same day as the big robbery.

"No way to prove it, o' course, 'cause they'd been done in, but everbody figured one or both the guards was in on it. Supposedly their armored truck'd broken down, but when we went over it, there wasn't anything wrong with it. There was speculation that the bad guys killed 'em to keep 'em quiet, and then, too, that woulda been two they wouldn't have t'share the loot with. So I wondered, if the fellas that were killed…the brothers in the article in the paper…were the robbers, and if the fella that killed them went to prison…in that case you…was in on the heist…."

"I awready toldju I didn have nothin' t'do with it!"

"…regardless…it still made perfect sense why none o' the money'd never turned up. You can't spend it if you're dead and rottin' in the ground or sittin' out forty years in Angola. One and one's two. The Komes did the heist, knocked off the guards, and you knocked off the Komeses. Bingo." He took another bite.

"You're a real whiz bang, ain'tcha?"

"Yeah, I'm pretty proud o' m'self," Ball boasted. Then he laughed at another thought. "I got the best help from the ex-Mrs. Hubert Lusaw. I chased 'er down, and when I told 'er I was gonna bring charges against you, she just laughed and said 'good luck.' Said if you did have the money, I'd never get it 'cause you'd clam up out o' pure ornriness. Well, naturally, I didn't tell her, but I knew if I didn't have the money, I didn't have diddly-piddly. It still woulda been nothin' more than my word against yours. That's when I cooked up the cancer thing. I told 'er about it and said if she'd help setcha up, she might even get a little somethin' as a reward. I told 'er, too, that if she didn't throw in, I'd say she was part of it, and she'd go to the gray bar as an accomplice to murder and robbery, and I tossed in obstruction to justice just t'spice it up." He snapped his fingers. "She turned rat pretty quick then."

He gnawed off a hank of biscuit and muffled, "I wanted to make sure you wouldn't run into any trouble gettin' out here, so that money she give ya? That was my idea, too." He pruned up his face and swallowed the masticated wad of tasteless dough. "Nasty, vindictive thing, that woman, 'n uglier'n a baboon's butt. She come in handy, though. Yessireebob, boy. I played her, she played you." He took another bite o' spicy beans and shook his head, gigglin'.

KAAABLOOEE!

Looee…

Ooee…

……thundered and echoed across the swamp, and ever critter for a mile in ever direction raised a holy-helly ruckus. Two Dogs', One Ear's, and Ball's arms flew up, launchin' plates, spicy beans, greasy Spam patties, hard biscuits, and two hats with feathers, everwhere. Their heads'd snapped back and their bodies jerked off the log like God'd yanked a rope tied at their necks, flat onto their backs. The thunder rolled and tumbled until finally dissolving into the night. If Hub hadn't been lookin' at 'em when it happened, he'da thought they'd just disappeared. The only thing left of 'em, visually, were the bottoms o' their boots layin' on top o' the log.

Whatever the Hell was goin' on, he was in the thick of it—layin' on his belly with his hands clasped over the back of his head. He'd jerked his arms up as he was goin' down and forgot all about the wrist chain, and its rollin' up his face damn near took his nose off. He looked to the dark woods, where the blast had come from, wonderin' what was gonna happen next. Then, he heard footsteps off to his left, somethin' crunchin' through the woods, raised his head just enough to peek back over his left shoulder, and watched the foggy image of a man slowly coalesce in the scant campfire light. He was big, tall, probly mid-thirtyish, and smackin' on a mouthful o' gum like he was paid by the chaw. He filled out a pair o' coveralls cinched tightly over a denim shirt with the sleeves rolled up, carryin' a heavy .50 caliber Sharps rifle easily in his big right hand. Sharps were easy to recognize—more of a shoulder-mounted cannon than a rifle. Hub used to have one of his own.

The big man was followed by another fella. Balding, potbellied, and short. He had a nasty scar over his right eye that cocked the brow cattywampus. His arms were slung out to the side like he was flyin' or glidin', like an eagle. Or more appropriately, a buzzard. He stirred up the dust, scuddin' his boots across the ground as if makin' like a locomotive. But he wasn't goin' *chugga chugga chugga* or *choo choo choo* as much as *shwssshhh shwssshhh shwssshhh*. He entered the camp and *shwssshhh shwssshhh*-ed past Hub, givin' him little more than a sidewaysie glance. He dipped his left arm while raisin' his right and circled the fire. Unlike his murderous partner, he wore pants with suspenders, and under them was a bright red, long-sleeved shirt emblazoned with a home-sewn "S" insignia. Also sewn into the back at the shirt's neck was a dishtowel, hangin' down his back, flappin' in his wake. The fat son of a bitch thought he was Superman, skippin' around the campfire like a two-hundred-twenty-pound fairy. The fact o' the matter was, he'd probly just murdered Ball or one o' the Seminoles.

The Big One laid the Sharps up agin the log, stepped up on the same, overlookin' what was left o' Two Dogs' carcass sportin' a very neat little hole situated perfectly 'tween his eyes. What used to be the back of his head and brains was splayed out over a wide arc in the dirt. The Big One clapped his hands together, threw up his arms in victory, and declared, "Dead Center! God Damn, we snuck up on Seminole trackers! Godddddd Damn!" He spat out the wad o' gum and pulled a pack o' Black Jack from a front pocket, unwrapped two fresh sticks, popped 'em in his mouth, chomped on 'em like there wasn't no tomorrow, and stuck the pack back in his pocket.

The other one, Superman, finally *shwssshhh*-ed up on the other side o' the log with his legs spread, crossed his arms under his flabby tits, looked down at One Ear's body, and hissed. What little that remained of the left side of One Ear's head was badly mangled. He would henceforth be known as No Ear.

The big fella tight-roped across the log to the caped Kryptonian's end, perused the cranial damage, punched his cohort on the arm, and cackled, "You missed! Got 'im in the eye. He he he."

Finally, out o' the dark rolled the answer to Hub's question to what'd happened. There'd originally been three sittin' on the log. He'd only heard one combined blast, and unless one o' the two loonies lookin' over the log at their handiwork had sighted-up and fired from both hands, there had to be a third shooter.

And there it was.

Raeleen — in a dress that coulda form-fit a whiskey barrel, the hem fringed with dried mud — trucked into the firelight like a pissed off Marjorie Main lookin' for a carousing Wallace Beery. She had a pistol in a holster belted around her waist and luggin' a rifle in each hand.

Hub rolled into a sittin' position and declared, "Raeleen! Boy-howdy, am I glad t'see you!"

She strode past him with a hateful glare. "You just keep yr'mouth shut 'n don't move!" She stumped through the camp, straight to the spot on the log where Dexter Ball's butt had recently resided, and looked over the edge. One Ear and Two Dogs' spirits were already in the Happy Hunting Grounds sipping coffee. Their arms and legs flung out. Between 'em lay Dexter Ball, and as Raeleen had hoped, still alive and scared shitless. Both his hands were gripped tightly around his blood-gushin' throat.

Raeleen set the rifles against the log by the Sharps, nodded over her shoulder toward Hub, and told The Big One, "Keep yr'eye on him." Then she put one foot on the log, braced her elbow on her knee, and leaned into Ball. "I'm gonna letchu bleed t'death f'th'nasty things you said 'bout me."

He wasn't listenin'. He had more pressing things on his mind.

She clenched her teeth and stepped over the log, straddled his gut, planting her feet 'longside his hips, reached down, grabbed him by his blood-soaked collar, jerked him up, her nose to his, and screamed at him. "LOOK AT ME, YOU SON OF A BITCH! I wantchu t'know who killed ya! Baboon's Butt? I'll show you a baboon's butt!" She shoved him off and his back thudded to the ground. "Bastard!"

He still had a death grip on his gushing throat. She pressed her dirty right boot to his sternum for leverage, reached down and pried his hands from his neck. "No use draggin' it out, you dumb shit, just let it bleed!" Blood spurted in florid jets from the wound. His hands shot to his neck the instant she let go. She jerked his shirttail from his pants and used it to wipe her blood-spattered hands. Then stood up and looked over her shoulder at Hub. "I don't reckon he'll get that big permotion now." Then she turned back to Ball. "I sure wish you'da broughtchur Brownie."

He still wasn't listenin'.

She flipped her hands to the other bodies and told the boys, "Search 'em." She stepped over the log and started in Hub's direction, then stopped and snapped her fingers. She turned back, and while The Big One and Superman went through the Indians' pockets, she stuck her own hand into Ball's front pants pocket and pulled out the rubber-banded money wad. She tossed it in the air, caught it, kissed it, stuffed it in her own pocket, and told Hub, "He can't buy ice water where he's goin'." She stepped over the log and stood by the fire.

Hub still felt like he was part of a Barnum and Bailey sideshow and said, "I wasn't expectin' ya, but I'm awful glad t'see ya." He started to stand up.

"Did I tell you t'get up?" she asked, jabbin' a loaded, pointin' finger at his face. "No, I didn't. And if you ever b'lieved anything in yer life, b'lieve this. You don't even know how glad you *ain't* t'see me. Not a little bit. But whatchu are...is a lyin', good-fer-nothin' sack o' shit! Yer wond'rin' why I ain't killed you, too."

"Okay then," he said, almost upp'ty, "why ain'tcha?"

He'd tried bein' friendly with the bitch, and all he got for it was a smart-mouthin'. She used to be his God Damn wife walkin' behind him and keepin' her God Damned mouth shut, and he wasn't about to let her talk to him like that! The possibility that maybe she wasn't the same docile little doe she'd been thirty years ago hadn't entered his brain yet.

"You'd do better right now," she warned, "while m'blood's up, t'keep yer yap shut 'n change yer smartass attitude."

Dang! She was doin' it again. The woman who'd ratted him out to the badly leakin' son of a bitch on the other side o' the log. "What happened t'Jesus'n th'new husband?"

She just chuckled.

"You got awful hard in yer old age."

"I had a long time t'get that way," she replied, and then, "'n' for half-a-hunerd-thousand dollars, I'cn get a lot harder."

The boys'd retrieved Ball's and the Indians' guns (Ball'd been so engrossed with his condition, the thought o' pullin' the .45 at his hip'd never entered his mind), went through their pockets, and stood together on the log to watch the blood bubble and gurgle out o' Ball's throat, his mouth, dribble down the side of his face, and halo at the back of his head faster'n the ground could soak it up.

The Big One's nostrils flared. "Smell 'at?"

The caped one's nostrils flared—pulled it down the back of his throat and nodded.

"Iron. Blood's mostly iron, ya know. You like it?"

Superman scrunched his shoulders as if to say he could take it or leave it. The smell of iron rich blood was obviously a poor second to flyin'.

"You think she missed?" The Big One whispered out the corner of his mouth.

"I dunno," Superman whispered back and snuck a look over his shoulder at their rotund leader. "He made 'er awful mad with'at ugly baboon comment. She mighta wanted it like this. She's a pretty good shot."

"Is he dead yet?" Raeleen asked, shuttin' 'em up.

Ball's hands had lost their grip and crumpled off to the side, but some little blood still pulsed from the gaping hole in his throat.

"Notchet," The Big One said. "Want me t'stick 'im?"

"No, let 'im go." Then she chuckled. "He might be prayin 'r somethin."

Superman looked at the body and chuckled hisself. "He better hurry it up then."

"Mama?" The Big One said, "I got mine right smack 'twixt th'eyes."

Superman glared at him, knowing the comment was aimed at him and his screwin' up the shot to One Ear.

"I saw it. Don't gloat," Raeleen reprimanded. "Remember what I toldja 'bout gloaters comin' t'nasty ends."

"Yeah. Nasty ends," Superman said.

"Didja get their guns?" she asked. They pointed to the confiscated weaponry resting at the far end o' the log. "What 'bout th'money Ball give 'em?"

"Got it," The Big One said, pattin' his pocket.

She picked up her rifle and walked around the fire towards Hub. "Didja split it up? Give yer brother half?" She wasn't really asking. She knew he hadn't.

Superman helt out his hand 'n wriggled his fingers. The Big One dug his hand in his pocket, pulled out the money, counted out half, handed it over, and whispered, "Ain't fair. You missed." He stuffed his half back in his pocket and approached Hub and Raeleen. "That's him, huh?" he asked, insolently.

Hub started to get up.

"'At's him," Raeleen said and pushed the end of her rifle on his shoulder. "Did I tell you t'get up?"

"I wanna see that arm I heard s'much about," The Big One said.

Hub glared at him.

Raeleen nudged Hub's shoulder with the end o' the barrel. "Show 'im."

"No! I ain'tchur fuckin' monkey."

The boys snickered when Raeleen jabbed him in the forehead with the end of the rifle barrel, imprinting a little donut.

Reluctantly, Hub pulled up his sleeve, revealing the scarred, discolored, and ill-shaped forearm.

"Hoopee-do," The Big One guffawed. "That ol' woman really fucked you up!"

The well-fed fella in the Superman getup's curiosity got the best of him, and he sauntered over with his arms crossed over his soggy chest, Superman-style, spread his fat legs in a John Wayne pose, and squinty-eyed Hub. "He don't look 'at tough t'me."

Calmly, maliciously, The Big One chucked in his two cents. "Bet I'cd take 'im."

Hub looked him in the eye while pullin' his sleeve back down and buttoning the cuff. "Yeah, you might could. But I garandamntee ya you'd be bad damaged when you's done."

The Big One smiled at the taunt. "You wanna dance with me?"

Hub helt up his manacled hands. "Take these off 'n I'll teach ya some new steps."

"You ain't gonna do it now," Raeleen said, before it got any more heated, and nodded to the log. "Strip them three o' things we'cn use."

Superman started for the log, but The Big One continued to look at Hub with rattlesnake eyes. He was in the mood.

Raeleen smacked him on the butt. "Now! Go on."

He tapped Hub's leg with the toe of his boot and walked off. His version o' the last word.

"I take it th'big one's Harvey," Hub said after he left.

Raeleen looked at the boys' backs. "Yeah, Superman's a little on th'chunky side, but he gets 'is licks in."

"Didn't he usta be Henry?"

"It's a long story, but for now you'd do good t'remember when he's got th'cape out, he's Superman, 'n when it's tucked down 'is shirtneck 'n he's wearin 'is overshirt 'n glasses, he's Clark Kent. If ya forget...he'll be more'n happy t'remind ya."

CHAPTER 34

Before he'd had his brains turned to mush, Two Dogs had tossed his well-worn denim jacket over the end o' the log. The Big One, who had become Harvey, was goin' through the pockets when he pulled out a flask and waggled it in the air. "Lookie lookie lookie! Panther Piss!"

Raeleen, settin' Indian-style in the dirt beside the fire, wiggled her fingers at him. "Bring it 'n 'at bag over here." Harvey brought the satchel and bottle to her. "Superman," she called out, motioning him over. They sat on either side of her in a semi-circle with their backs to Hub. Raeleen opened the satchel, got her face too close, and pickled up. "PeeeeeU! Boy-howdy!" She looked back at Hub. "You shit in here?" Hub passed on an explanation. She helt the satchel at arm's length and fanned the mouth a few times in the attempt to air it out. After a few puffs, she took another whiff. "'At's a little better. I hope they ain't nothin' in here gonna bite me." She stuck her hand in the bag and pulled out George and Matthew's revolvers. "Goodies!" She handed one to Harvey. "One fer you."

"Thank you," Harvey responded, almost delicately.

"Yer welcome," she said sweetly and handed the other to Superman. "I know you don't need it, but he got one, you get one."

"Thank you."

"Yer welcome. Keep it as a souvenir o' th'day ya got rich. Merry Christmas."

"Ho ho ho," Superman said and they all chuckled.

Except Hub.

The boys checked the loads like pros. Harvey stuck his in his belt, while Superman put his in his lap. They were a happy, loving family.

A *deadly*, happy, loving family.

"Now," Raeleen said, shuffling her big butt in preparation. It looked so cute, the family sittin' around the campfire, the children expectant, their faces all aglow from the fire light, the mother gonna share somethin' new and exciting, and the father all trussed up like a Christmas Goose.

"In all yer life, you ain't neither one even seen a hunerd-dollar bill." Theatrically, she slid her hand in the satchel, shook it around, smiled big, and pulled out a wrapped pack of hundreds. The corners o' the boys' mouths rose and their eyes opened wide. She helt it up and showed 'em only the top bill. "Well, 'at's what one looks like." Then she fanned the pack, one bill at a time, slippin' under her thumb. "And that," she said as she continued to fan, "is what a hunerd of 'em looks like."

"That's a hunerd hunerds," Superman said.

"Ohhhh, yeah," Raeleen sighed, "but it gets better. A lot better." She closed her eyes, brought the pack to her nose, and took a big whiff, moaned, and let her breath out with a sigh. It still smelled like a sack o' cat shit, but she was puttin' on a show. She helt it out to the boys, fanned it slowly under their noses, and they took a long lungful of the imaginary scent and smacked their lips.

"Don't 'at smell good?" she asked.

Harvey and Raeleen laughed when Superman fell over like it was all too much for him. Harvey waved his hand in front o' Superman's face, and he pretended to come to and got back up.

"It stinks, but it's a good stink," Superman said.

Hub closed his eyes and hung his head in frustration.

"Well," Raeleen said, shaking the satchel's contents, "stink 'r not, they's five o' these" — indicating the pack, then the satchel — "in here." She looked at her precious little lambiekins and cooed, "We're rich."

Harvey nodded and looked from Raeleen to Superman. "Very rich."

"Super very rich," Superman threw in.

"What 'bout me?"

They turned to see Hub's expectant expression.

"You ain't," Raeleen said, coldly.

"Bullllllshit," Hub said, forgettin' where he was, who he was with, and under what conditions. Quicker than Hub woulda thought possible, and a bunch more than he'd expected, Superman jumped up and kicked his boot toe hard into Hub's sternum, emptying his lungs and knockin' him over. It felt as if his ribcage'd crumpled like a rotten pumpkin. He rolled on the ground, begging for oxygen.

Superman stood over him, red-faced and fists clenched, ready to give him another'n. "How'dju like a chunk o' Kryptonite jammed up yer hairy ass!"

Hub saw another kick comin' at his gut and used his left hand in an attempt to soften the blow. It didn't work, and he might now have a broken hand.

"That's enough," Raeleen said, hoping Superman hadn't busted a rib. Or two. Or three—and savin' Hub from another kick, one already cocked and ready to fire.

Breathing hard through gritted teeth, Superman reluctantly pulled back. "You don't talk 'at way t'my Earth Mama, you crumb bum," he growled and plopped on his abundant backside beside Raeleen.

"Hub's sorry, ain'tcha Hub," she said when Hub rolled back to his butt, wheezin' and glaring at Superman.

He wanted to rub the pain out of his hand but he'd be damned if he'd let Superfuck see it. He helt his right hand over the left and gingerly wiggled his fingers. He was surprised to find they still worked. They hurt, but they worked.

Raeleen got a headlock on Superman, rocked back and forth givin' him a noogie, and kissed his forehead. "He does love 'is Mama. Even if she don't come from Krypton." She let Superman go and nodded toward the log. "Okay, Christmas's over. Go over there 'n see if Mr. Hoover's flunky's bled outchet."

They headed for the log, brushing the dirt off their pants. Superman looked over his shoulder at Hub and gave him a look that said "I'm gonna keep my eye on you."

"FBI," Raeleen said disgustedly. "Fuckin' Blowhard Idyit. I think Idyit starts with I. Harvey! Idyit start with I?"

"Yes," Harvey answered.

Raeleen tipped her head toward Harvey. "He reads a lot. Mostly comic books 'n th'Holy Bible but words're words, right?"

Harvey pulled a buck knife from the sheath on his belt, stepped over the log, and poked Ball in the eye a couple o' times like he was testin' a baked p'tata to see if it was done. "He's finished, Mama."

"Okay," Raeleen said and wrangled her poor fat old self off the ground. Hub watched her. She looked old. Soft. Used. Wasted. Then he thought, *but so does an old rattler*. An old spider. An old scorpion. An old gator.

She wiped the grit off her hands on her dress and waved to the darkened netherworld beyond the campfire light. "Take all three of 'em outchonder som'ers. I don't wanna hafta keep lookin' at 'em." She picked up the satchel, carried it over by the log and set it down. "Either o' you find th'chain key?"

"I got it," Superman said. He pulled the small key out of his pocket and tossed it the length o' the log to Raeleen.

She caught it deftly, and Hub helt his manacled wrists up toward her. She pocketed the key. "You's changed owners's all."

"You gonna keep these on me?"

Lookin' at him like he was stupid and she wasn't was the only answer he was gonna get.

Hub watched as Harvey and Superman each took an arm and drug Ball's body into the dark beyond the camp. Earlier, he'd imagined blowin' Ball's brains out hisself, but now, watchin' his head loll and joggle and bump the ground, his ruined throat all stretched out, just about made him sick. In the last few hours, his life'd made a left-hand turn, but not just about as left as Ball's and the trackers'.

Raeleen dug her underwear out of her butt crack on her way to the bean pot suspended on a hook over the campfire. She picked up the spoon hangin' off to the side, stuck it in the pot, stirred the contents, and sang off-key. "Beans, beans, th'mus'cal fruit, th'more ya eat, th'more ya poot." She waggled her big ass like a hula dancer, looked at Hub, and chirped, "Pootie poot poot."

She thought she looked cute. Hub thought she looked stupid. A fat old woman, flat old tits rollin' around her belly, wearin' work boots and a long, ugly old dress, with a gunbelt and buck-knife sheath hitched around her wallowy acreage. He looked toward the boys, then back at her, and was reminded o' the wild tales he'd heard about Ma Barker and her murderous brood. This bunch could give the Barkers a run for their money. Yes, Virginia, there really are some nastyass sons o' bitches.

Raeleen scooped up a spoonful, brought it to her mouth, and scratched a few beans in with her teeth, took two chaws, and then waved her hand over her mouth. "Boy-howdy, they are a mite spicy." She stirred the beans and took a closer look. "I don't think they got'ny meat in there." She looked at Hub. "You knew Sem'noles was cannibals didncha" Then she called out, "Harvey! When ya get done there, gather s'more firewood. 'N Superman? You see if you'cn scare up somethin' t'go wi'these beans, they're a little lonesome on body! Then one o' you go back 'n get our stuff 'n bring it in."

She knocked the rest o' the beans off the spoon back into the pot and hung the spoon on the hook. She looked at Hub and nodded into the woods. "We's settin' out there in th'dark, I got a whiff o' this 'n my stomach commenced t'growlin so I thought fer sure th'trackers's gonna hear. We's so close th'last couple o' days we couldn' cook nothin' 'cause them Injuns got a nose like a tick."

"This's real homey 'n all 'n I just can't hardly wait t'hear th'rest of it," Hub said, smart-alecky, "but what's yer plans for me? You just gonna shoot me 'r what?"

Friendliness escaped Raeleen's face like someone slappin' a light switch. "I wish I could. I got s'many good reasons!"

"What's stoppin' ya?"

She stomped to Hub and yanked his shirtsleeve up so hard she popped the button off the cuff, exposing the scarred arm. "'Cause yer tainted soul, you good-fer-nothin' asshole, b'longs t'Lootie Komes!"

He jerked his arm back and looked at her like she was a fool. "You still b'lieve 'at shit?"

"I don't b'lieve in Heaven 'r Hell 'r God 'r Satan 'r none o' that crap, but I b'lieve in Lootie Komes! I b'lieve they ain't a minute I don't close my eyes, take a shit, get a drink o' water 'r go for a walk 'at she don't know it. 'Cause o' you, Asshole!" She clenched her fist and pounded him on the back of the head. "BASTARD!" She was as mad as a fire eater with hiccups. She hit him again. "She hauntchur dreams?" The look on his face was answer enough. "Yeah, I thought so. We's all cursed"—she hit him again—"'n donchu tell me"—hit him again—"you don't b'lieve it. We's raised th'same, 'n I know she scares th'Hell out o' you!"

He put his hand out in anticipation of another whack, but instead, she brushed the wild hairs off her reddened, sweaty face. She was almost out a breath from sluggin' him. She fished up and jerked out a small leather pouch with witchy-lookin' markings inked on it, that hung on a thongy cord 'round her neck. "Only way t'fight a witch is with a worser witch. Unforchnately, you nit, they don't come no worser'n th'one you made mad! If witches had a fuckin' pres'dent 'r a God Damn Queen, her butt'd be on the throne! I paid a lot o' money fer three o' these things. Gris-gris. They's th'best I'cd do with what little I had, 'n we ain't tooken 'em off f'thirty God Damn years!"

"And you think 'at stupid little bag keeps you alive?"

"I don't know, but I ain't takin' no chances. Last thing she said was th'day one of us's t'die, we'd allll die, 'n right now, I think I'm tired o' talkin' t'you." She smacked him one last time and huffed away. Five steps later, she changed her mind, stomped back, grit her teeth, and slapped him in back of the head once more. "Bastard!"

Harvey and Superman had lugged their packs and bedrolls up from their last campsite and were pushed up agin the log 'longside the satchel. Hub was sittin' in the dirt, opposite his captors, reminded o' the last time—not so very long ago—three other smartasses'd been perched on that same log, eatin' them same beans, and he wondered if another three-ringer might come rollin' out o' the dark to wipe them out. Maybe Pickering. Why not? The Warden'd been in on it, so Pickering's poppin' up wouldn't be any big surprise. As weird as things'd been so far, the next one could be Toad! Wouldn't that be a kick? It wouldn't be any stranger than a compassionate, tender-hearted doctor turned heartless FBI agent, or a wife and chilluns he'd written off for thirty years. Maybe Luther Knox wantin' to get even for losin' his first murder trial.

He looked hatefully at Porkyman. He wasn't the Caped One anymore. Now he was Clark Kent. Clark was fat, too. Hub wanted to say somethin' about his goin' to seed since his comic book days. Maybe later. The cape—the dishtowel—all bunched up, crammed down his neck, made him look like the Hunchback of Oledeux. Now he wore his overshirt and a pair o' lenseless glasses stuck to his face. They weren't even the kind he wore in the comics, but the cat-eye kind Hollywood movie stars wore. Did he honestly think people believed he and Superman was two different people? Hidin' behind a pair o' stupid lenseless glasses? Dumb fuck. Hub was thinkin' about askin' him where he, Clark Kent, had been all day, but that throbbing reminder in his sternum told him maybe another time. Another *maybe later*. His whole life'd been one later after another, and he was gettin' tired of it.

He and the boys were munchin' on beans and biscuits tender and flaky enough to crack a tooth. Raeleen's big butt was perched on the end o' the log, her left leg drawn up, left heel braced up on the log's end, the other on the ground. She had her dress hiked up, damn near her belly, whittlin' on her thick, yellowy, old-woman toenails with a jackknife. Ever time she moved her arm, the bag of fat hanging underneath it waggled.

Ever once in a while, Hub snuck a glance at her crotch, torn in two directions by that which lurked in her underwear. On the one hand, he figured that more than likely, because of her advanced age, and as bad as she'd let herself go ever other way, it was pretty ugly, and no doubt stunk ever bit as bad as it looked. But on the other hand, pussy was pussy, and havin' an ugly, smelly pussy to think about was better than no pussy to think about. He wished now he'd taken that last poke offered by the café woman. He spit a chunk o' rubbery gristle sizzlin' in the fire and looked at the mild-mannered reporter. "Possum th'best you could do? Greasiest God-damn animal ever was."

"Don't eat it," Raeleen barked, yankin' her dress down, folding up the jackknife, and tossin' it in her pack.

"I didn't catch it. Superman did," Clark Kent threatened, "so you better keep yer mouth shut 'r he'll jump back here 'n beat th'Hell out o' you."

"That reminds me," Hub said. "Where is he?"

"Who?" Clark Kent asked, grumpy.

"Superman."

Raeleen and Harvey shot a look at Hub, at each other, then to Clark Kent.

Clark Kent never batted an eye. "There was a comet gonna hit Argentina 'n he went t'knock it out o' th'way. He told me he'd probly be back in th'mornin'. Maybe smash th'snot outa you."

Possibly brought on by what Clark had just said, Harvey helt his plate off to the side, plugged up one nostril with his thumb, leaned over, and blew a stringy glob o' snot hissin' into the fire to keep Hub's nicely browning slug o' gristle company. He wiped what was left stringin' from his lip with his shirtsleeve. "You been spoiled b'th'fine eats at th'Angola Prison Cafay."

"It was f'damn sure better'n this shit!" Hub griped. "They ain't nothin' in here but gristle 'n grease."

"Gristle 'n grease," Clark Kent chortled.

Raeleen looked at him like he was the most precious thing on Earth or even Krypton, her younger, adopted son's home planet, and cooed in baby talk, "You think 'at's funny, huh?"

Clark Kent nodded, picked up the bottle o' Panther Piss from between his boots, and took a pull.

"You gonna drink all 'at yerself?" Hub asked, annoyed at the bad manners.

"Uh uh, sorry," Clark Kent replied and helt the bottle out to Raeleen. "Mama?"

"Uh uh, no thanks, Sugar."

He offered it to Harvey, who rubbed off the bottle lip on the front of his shirt, took a swig, and then wiped his mouth on the shirtsleeve he'd just wiped his snotty lip with, and handed it back. Wipin' his mouth across a snot-slicked sleeve was all right, but God forbid he'd stick his lips on a germ-laden bottle top. Clark Kent set it back on the ground without lookin' at the glaring poor excuse of a father figure.

"I wish you'da brought that waitress with ya," Harvey said, shovelin' a spoonful of beans in his mouth. Hub looked up, surprised. "I'da like t'had a little o' that myself. I like a moaner-groaner."

Raeleen looked at Hub. "He just might be yers."

"Whada you mean might?" Hub asked, concerned.

She let it slide.

"Ball 'n th'tribe was hid out so you wudn see 'em," Harvey continued, " 'n we's hid out so's they wudn see us, but we all heard you 'n her agoin' at it, 'n I's gettin hornier'n a three peckered Billy goat. Hell, we seen Ball 'n th'redskins rollin' on th'ground, laughin'."

"I's kinda glad t'see'm havin' a good time," Raeleen admitted, "'cause I knew we's gonna be doin' 'em in 'fore long."

"Hey, while we're on th'subject o' havin' fun," Clark Kent said and burped, "after all 'em years in prison, you have any trouble goin' in from th'front?"

Raeleen and Harvey busted up and Raeleen said, "Oh, God, Clark, you are nasty."

"See?" Hub said, noddin' to Raeleen, "'At's whatcha get usin' sex words 'round 'em when they's little."

After Raeleen and the boys had their fill of makin' fun of Hub, Raeleen had Harvey chain him down on his back, with the trunk of a small but sturdy tree firmly rooted in the ground between his shackled legs. Unless a lumberjack or hungry beaver come by, he was where he was gonna be when the sun popped up. Just about the only movement he had was puttin' his shackled hands behind his head or on his chest, but even then, the wrist bands got in the way. He'd tried layin' on his side…

clink clink clink

…but he had to twist his legs so uncomfortably to do it, in a couple o' minutes, he'd…

flip flop *clink clink clink*

…over to the left. Same thing,

flip flop *clink clink clink.*

Raeleen finally settled in for the night, and the boys trundled over, got on their knees by side her, bent down, and rubbed noses, snortin' like bugs greetin' one another.

"G'night, Mama," Harvey said with a kiss to her cheek.

"G'night, Sugar," Raeleen said with a kiss.

"G'night, Mama," Clark Kent said with a kiss. (Not long after he'd discovered he was really Superman, he asked Raeleen if he could call her Mama like Harvey, his Earth brother, did. She'd cried and told him she'd like that.)

"G'night, Clark," Raeleen said with a kiss.

"G'night, Raeleen," Hub said.

"Die in yer sleep, Asshole," Raeleen said.

Harvey giggled.

"Gristle 'n grease," Clark Kent giggled.

CHAPTER 35

The sun wasn't all the way up yet. Clark Kent was bent over a little pool about a hundred yards from the camp, washing up. He had his overshirt and caped undershirt spread out over a small bush.

"Hello, Bud, how ya doin'?" He was talkin' to a terrapin that was watchin' him with a skeptical eye. He liked terrapins. 'Specially the way his Earth mama cooked 'em up.

Back at the campsite, Harvey was puttin' their stuff together. Hub was sittin' on the ground, chained up, his back to the tree his legs'd been latched around all night. It was still early enough it was a little nippy, and he was warming his hands with a speckelty tin cup o' coffee, watchin' Raeleen.

With his lip curled up.

She was sittin' on the log, head hung low, eyes closed. She had a cup o' coffee in her right hand, tilted, ready to spill. She had her fat elbows on her fat knees, her fat legs were spread, and he thought thank goodness she had the good sense to shove her dress down 'tween her legs.

She sat up and yawned like a mule, displaying her mostly missing molars. It seemed to go on forever. She finally closed her mouth, smacked her lips, and looked across the camp and caught Hub lookin' at her. "Sleepin' on th'hard ground ain't fit f'human persons, is it?"

"Try it chained t'a tree."

She took a last sip o' coffee, slung the remains to the side, set the cup on the log, stood up, and stretched. "Awright, let's get to it. We got a long way t'go." She looked over Balls' and the Seminoles' gear. "I don't know that we need much o' their stuff. Maybe th'coffee."

"What 'bout their guns?" Harvey asked.

"Nah. We got enough. Didju see if they had any Quinine?" Harvey patted his front pants pocket. "Good man," Raeleen said, winking. "I'll finish packin' up, you go findjur brother." Harvey nodded and took off. She made sure he was gone and then asked Hub, "How'd you sleep last night?"

"Not bad, considering. Why?" Her asking wasn't just a little out o' character.

"Just wondered. I slept like a baby. First time in a long time. You dream?"

Now that she mentioned it, "No."

"When's th'last time 'at happened?" Hub just looked at her. "What's yer nightmares about?"

Hub gave it a second, then, "Her scrapin' 'at damn hunk o' wood over m'arm," he said, passing on mentioning anything 'bout all the little Rets. "What's yern?"

"Drowning."

"You think not dreamin's good?"

She let it hang.

Clark Kent was scraping a rag over the rolls on the back of his neck when Harvey called out. "Clark!"

Quickly, Clark looked to his stuff to make sure the shirt with the big S and his cape were covered by his outer shirt.

"Step on it, we're leavin'!"

Clark motioned that he'd heard and Harvey headed back to camp. Clark grabbed his stuff and started off. By the time he got back to camp, Raeleen had things pretty much put together.

Raeleen stepped to Hub and pulled out the chain key. Hub noticed Harvey kept the heel of his hand on his pistol butt while she knelt on one knee to unlock the leg irons. Finished, she stood, the chain in her left hand, impatiently snappin' her right-hand fingers. "Hop up." He did, and Raeleen unlocked the wrist chains.

"You need t'think of a better way o' keepin' me down at night," Hub bitched, rubbin' his raw wrists.

"Putchur pack on 'n shut up."

Hub wriggled into his backpack.

Raeleen waggled her fingers at Clark Kent. "Gimme th'satchel."

Clark Kent brought it over and Raeleen put the leg chains inside, then clamped one end o' the other set to Hub's right wrist, looped the other end through the satchel handles, then locked it to the same wrist and pocketed the key. "You get t'carry th'loot."

"Don'tcha think it'll get a little heavy?"

"I wudn doubt it. We'll change sides ever once'n a while." She turned to the boys before he could lodge a complaint. "Ready?" They slung their rifle straps over their shoulders and mocked a salute. "Okay, let's go."

She started off, and Hub snickered. "Dumb broad. Yer goin' th'wrong way."

"No, I ain't. We're goin' east."

"East's bout a million miles o' nothin'!"

"Not that I hafta give you a reason," and before he could dodge it, she glanced a knobby-knuckled fist hard off his satchel-totin' arm, "I don't know but what Ball ain't got somebody awaitin' for 'im in Oledeux, 'n I ain't takin' th'chance. So go!"

Harvey took the lead, followed by Raeleen. Hub fell in behind her and Clark Kent brought up the rear. Now that she was in front of him, Hub rubbed the shoulder muscle her punch had knotted-up and heard a snide cackle at his back.

"Hurt's, don't it."

They soon developed a dull, robotic cadence in their march. Harvey had the Sharps in his right hand, his backpack on his back, and Clark Kent's pack slung over his left shoulder. Raeleen wore her backpack, her rifle strap hitched over her right shoulder and Clark's in her left hand. Superman roared through their ranks ever so often, probly makin' sure there weren't any rogue asteroids or atomic-bomb-carryin'-communists lurkin' around.

"Harvey?" Hub asked. "Ain't that my Sharps?"

"Nope," Harvey replied easily, and then back over his shoulder, "I's wond'rin'. How come if ya had th'money, ya turned yerself in?"

"Reason I asked," Hub said, ignoring the question, "it looks a lot like mine."

"Hold up," Raeleen said. She laid the rifles on the ground, untied the faded and frayed handkerchief she had around her neck and wiped the wet off her face. "He didn think he'd get forty years," she said, smart-assey, wipin' her neck. "Thought they'd go soft on 'im 'n if they didn let 'im go outright, he figured he'd sit out four 'r five years for fifty thousand dollars. Ten thousand a year ain't bad money."

"I think that is my gun," Hub pushed. "I reconize a notch in th'stock."

"You got fooled, though, didncha?" she added, retyin' the rag. "Judge Parks 'n th'jury didn feel all 'at sorry for ya. I figured it out last night—in thirty years, it come t'barely over sixteen hunerd a year."

"Well, we got it now," Hub said.

Superman soared past with his chubby arms stuck out, banking from side to side, goin' *ssshhhew ssshhhew ssshhhew.*

"You'cn drop 'at *we* shit," Raeleen said, indicating the boys and herself. "Only we's us we."

"Y'know, you 'n me was close once. You usta let me tweezer out yer tittie hairs."

"I didn letcha, you made me letcha. I didn like it, it hurt. Shavin' 'em off was good 'nough for me, butchu liked doin' anything 'at had t'do with my titties."

"Well, if you think I'm just gonna walk away from it, yer nuts. You ain't thinkin' smart, Raeleen. Right now ya got me b'th'seeds. Take avantage of it, 'n let's work somethin' out."

"I ain't thinkin' smart? What is it I hafta work out? I awready got th'money. I awready gotchur seeds. What more'cd a woman want?"

Superman *ssshhhew ssshhhew*-ed the other way, and, more'n a little annoyed, Hub called out, "Hey! You! Superman!"

"What're you doin'?" Raeleen inquired, suspiciously.

"Nothin'," Hub replied, with mock innocence.

"Be careful. You scuffle with him, yer scufflin' with me 'n Harvey, too."

Superman dipped his arms to port, banked hard, and *ssshhhew*-ed back, planting his feet in front o' Hub with his legs spread and his arms crossed over the big S.

"What?"

"What? That don't sound very friendly."

"It wasn't s'posed to. I don't like you, yer evil. Whadaya want, I'm busy."

"Doin' what?"

Superman shot his arms out to the side and started to leave.

"Awright awright awright," Hub said.

Superman refolded his pudgy arms and glared at him.

"What makes you think I'm evil?"

"Yer a murd'rer. You killed th'Komes Brothers in cold blood."

"I'm a murd'rer? 'At's the pot callin' th'kettle black, ain't it? Last night, you shot one o' them Indians in th'side o' th'head." Then a nasty stroke of genius flashed in his brain. "I think you mighta been aimin' 'tween 'is eyes." Superman's eyes hunkered down. "But I might be mistakin'."

"Yer confusin' me with Clark Kent. And just so you know, Clark wouldn't miss."

"Well, you fellas do look a lot alike, but it was you I seen comin' outa th'dark, not Clark."

"I got there just seconds after it was over. Clark was still in th'woods, ashamed o' what he done." His jaw muscles danced 'round his temples. "He shot th'Indian, yes, but he told me he was very sorry 'bout it. He just felt awful. I don't think I'd bring it up to 'im."

"I see," Hub said. "Well, how come you wasn't there when it happened? You mighta saved them fellers their lives 'n poor Clark wudn have nothin' t'feel guilty 'bout."

"It couldn't be helped. I's in China. A volcano was gonna 'rupt 'n I had t'put a boulder in it t'plug it up."

"Okay then, tell me this. How come I never see you 'n Clark Kent at th'same place at th'same time?"

Superman gave it about two seconds. "Right now he's scoutin' ahead...."

"That don't answer my question."

"How 'bout it ain't none o' yer beeswax."

Hub nodded up ahead to Harvey. "How come Clark don't carry 'is own pack?"

"That ain't none o' yer beeswax either," and he took off before the Komes Brothers' murderer could ask any more of his stupid questions.

"Yeah, I know," Raeleen said. "He's fat 'n he looks perty silly in 'at getup. But if push come t'shove? He'd both kill and die fer me. As fat 'n silly as he is, he's still twice th'man you was 'r ever will be."

Their positions had changed. Harvey and Superman were up front while Raeleen and Hub brought up the rear. "I asked you yesterdee," Hub said, quietly, "what th'deal was with Henry 'n you didn answer me. He didn seem nutty when he's little."

"He drownded. When he's eight. Fell off 'at rickety little bridge over Wesley Crick, face first, 'n knocked 'is head on a rock. That's how he got th'scar on 'is eyebrow. By th'time I fished 'im out, he wasn't breathin', color o' catfish belly 'n deader'n a turd. Scared th'livin shit out o' me. I flipped 'im on 'is belly 'n pounded on 'is back 'til he come 'round. I don't appreciate yer sayin' he's nutty. He's a lot smarter'n he looks."

"He'd hafta be."

"You need t'stop sayin' things like 'at."

"He think's he's Superman."

She looked up ahead at a fully-grown, balding, overweight, thirty-three-year-old in a homemade Superman costume, his arms helt out like a buzzard lookin' for somethin' to eat. "After he drownded, he quit talkin'. Once in a great while he'd say somethin', but very seldom 'n most o' th'time, even 'at little, it wudn make no sense. They's just words. Played with bugs. Pick 'em up 'n lick 'em on th'back, 'n if he liked th'way they tasted, he'd eat 'em. Beetles mostly. They's spicy. One day he seen Superman in th'funnies, took a shine to 'im, 'n started runnin' 'round th'house like ya see 'im adoin' here. Jumpin' off things 'n tryin' t'run through closed doors. Th'day he seen 'im in th'funny papers was th'day Henry Ivanzo Lusaw died 'n Superman 'n Clark Kent come t'life."

As if all they had t'do was mention his name, Superman soared by, arms outstretched, scuffin' up clouds o' dust, goin' *ssshhhew ssshhhew ssshhhew.*

"It wudn do ya no harm t'quit tryin' t'trip 'im up. Just t'let 'im go on thinkin' it."

"I'm glad ya brought that up. I have been thinkin'…."

"I didn bring up nothin', 'n anything you gotta say, I ain't int'rested in hearing, so just keep it t'yerself."

"Don't go cuttin' me off like 'at! Just hear me out. I had time now t'think 'bout things, 'n I cain't help but see what a good job ya done raisin' Harvey 'n Henry…Clark." Then he remembered the cape was out. "Superman. And despite you havin' me shackled up, I still got a soft spot fer you 'n them. I'm thinkin' we get out o' here 'n start a whole new life, all of us, t'gether."

She turned to him, batting her eyes, smiley-faced, "D'ya honestly mean it?"

"I bare m'soul to ya, showin' my truest colors, 'n ya mock me."

"Yer true color's th'same as yer heart. Black. You know how many times I come up t'th'prison, lookin' like a God Damn moon-eyed fool 'n you never showed? Not once?"

"I's too ashamed."

"Ashamed…my…ass! You worthless, no 'count thing. You ain't never, in yer whole miserable life, felt shame. The only thing I ever meant t'you was a handy hole t'shove yer pecker in. Shame. Don't make me laugh!" She stopped raggin' on him just long enough for Superman to glide past. "The way you threw me 'n them off, like we's no more'n a holey sock, that hurt. Them little boys ast about you fer th'longest time. If you'da come down one time 'n snorted on their little faces 'n give 'em a stick o' gum—one time, Hub—it woulda made all th'dif'er'nce in th'world. He'd never admit it, but you're the reason Harvey chews Black Jack."

"Hell," Hub jumped back, "you lied to 'em. You told 'em I's killed in a knife fight."

"No, I lied that t'you jus t'stick it to ya."

"Well, I didn throw ya'off. I's locked up! What was I s'posed t'do?"

"I didn't have it so easy," she mocked. "I had t'sit on my fat, lazy ass in prison f'thirty years. *I* didn have a God Damned thing, 'n I still had t'raise Harvey 'n Clark" —Superman *ssshhhew ssshhhew*-ed by again— "Superman. Many's th'time I had t'whore m'self out t'put food in their bellies, and th'whole time you had fifty thousand dollars squirreled away!"

"Tell me. What would you adone if I'da told ya 'bout it?"

"'At's a stupid question."

"Is it? Wouldja bought food with it? With a hunerd-dollar bill? You? With a serial number th'law was lookin' for? You might as well turned it in."

"You still coulda told me 'bout it. Gimme a reason t'carry on."

"And you woulda left it alone? I couldn take 'at chance. You're accusin' me of all kinds o' things when what it boils down to is you not havin' any faith in me. And what's more, if Superman ain't mine, then you whored yerself out 'fore I went t'prison."

"If I cuda told 'em you's dead, I wuda, but I knew someday, you son of a bitch, they'd see you again 'n then they'd know I'd lied to 'em. But I did lead 'em t'blieve that maybe you wasn't their worthless father t'try t'soften th'fact you didn care for 'em. Unforchnately," she clenched up her fist, stuck out the knobby knuckle and clobbered his arm, "you sorry sack o' shit, they are yours. Both of 'em. Before you went t'Angola, yer pecker's only one ever got in me. But, I'd druther they thought I got fucked b'Adolf Hitler than t'have 'em think I's fool 'nough t'be true t'you, somebody 'at didn give a shit 'bout me!"

"You gonna tell me 'at fat thing with a dishtowel wrapped 'round 'is neck's mine?"

"He's th'spittin' image o' yer fat-fuck grandfather Cornelius! Th'fatness jumped a generation's all."

"But ya did after," he said, defensively. It was a mistake.

She knuckled him again. "I aweady toldju, t'keep from starvin'!"

"I oughta get a share," Hub said pettishly and rubbed his arm. It hurt way too much to pretend it didn't. "And I wish you'd quit hittin' me."

"A share in yer direction ain't gonna happen. I'll letcha have what was left from th'five hunerd I got from Ball. 'At's it."

"Ain't good enough. I ain't th'least sore 'boutchu sidin' with Ball. You did whatcha thoughtcha had to, 'n I understand that, but I'm gettin' at least tweny fi' p'cent!"

"No! You ain't 'n 'at's bullshit 'bout you not havin' a mad on me asidin' with him! Yer mad as Hell over it 'n we both know it."

"No, I ain't! Old age's softened me."

"Yeah, I'm sure it has."

"Well, I'll tell ya again then, ya got me all wrong."

Then he noticed she wasn't listenin' to him, but concentrating on somethin' up ahead. Superman. Weavin' like a drunkard on a tilt-a-wheel. *Maybe th'dishtowel's knotted too tight 'round 'is neck*, Hub thought.

"HARVEY!" Raeleen barked. Then she took off like a pissed-off she-bear, pullin' off her backpack in the process. Harvey turned to see her pointin' to Superman. "Catch 'im! Catch 'im!"

Superman had turned into a B-movie robot, stiff-armed and stiff-legged, fists bunched up, and the muscles in his neck stuck out like rope. His face was turning a hideous, blotchy purple.

Harvey dropped his pack on the ground, laid the Sharps on it, and jumped to Superman just in time to keep him from fallin' face-first to the ground. He eased him onto his back. Superman was stiff as a board, jaw clamped shut, arms at his side, his whole body vibrating. By that time, Raeleen had skidded to a stop and dropped her pack beside him. She plopped down in the dirt and put his head in her lap.

Hub came up and saw that Superman's eyes'd rolled up, showin' white, snarlin' and frothin', flailin' around like a puppet gone nuts. He'd bloodied his knuckles from his fists slammin' in the dirt and pissed his pants.

"What's goin' on?"

"He's havin' a fit!" Raeleen said without lookin' up.

Harvey flipped the top of his backpack open and rummaged around for somethin' inside. He found a purple-stained popsicle stick they kept for just that purpose. Raeleen helt Superman's head while Harvey tried to wedge his jaw open.

Bein' that Raeleen and Harvey were sidetracked, Hub looked hungrily at the Sharps layin' beside Harvey's pack, not ten feet away. He looked back and forth 'tween the Sharps, Raeleen, Harvey, and the guns they had in holsters wrapped around their waists and determined he wouldn't have time to get to it before bein' seen.

No, he'd pass for now. They had a long way to go. Another opportunity would show itself. Besides, if he tried now and failed, that would be it. They'd never drop their guard again.

"What can I do?" he asked, his tone drippin' with sincerity.

"It ain't nothin' new," Raeleen said, "we got it. Just stay back." Then to Harvey, "Get it in there!"

"I'm tryin'," he snapped. He didn't appreciate Raeleen snappin' at him. He was fightin' to get the stick in Superman's mouth without gettin' bit. It had happened before, and he was more than a little gun shy. Finally, he wrenched Superman's jaw open and wedged the stick in. Superman chomped down hard, growlin' like a rabid dog.

That much accomplished, Raeleen laid Superman's head on the ground and rolled over on top of him. "I got 'im, get th'jar."

Harvey picked up Raeleen's backpack, unbuckled the flaps, turned it up on end, and dumped the contents in the dirt. Then he fumbled through it until he found a small, half-pint Mason jar with awl-made air holes punched in the lid. He took a second to shake it up then squinted through the glass. "Shit, I dunno if it's still alive," he said and shook it again.

"Well, is it'r ain't it!" Raeleen growled.

"Quit yellin' at me! I ain't sure. We shuda got a fresh one. I don't think about it all th'time."

"Here!" she demanded, wagglin' her fingers to Harvey. "Hold 'im."

Harvey handed the jar to her and took over holdin' Superman down while she shook it up.

"What is 'at?" Hub asked.

"Come on, you son of a bitch. Move!" Raeleen demanded, tapping the glass with her fingernail.

Finally, it moved and she unscrewed and removed the lid. Harvey gripped Superman's head and twisted it to the left, baring his neck. Raeleen pulled his collar down and smacked the jar's mouth on it.

"What th'Hell're you doin'?" Hub asked.

Raeleen and Harvey watched the little yellow spider scuttle to Superman's neck and bite him. "There she goes," she said.

Superman never felt it. Raeleen pulled the jar away, slipped the lid over the top, shook it up, and slapped it on his neck again. "One more. Come on, one more…." The spider bit again. "There ya go."

She pulled the jar off, screwed the lid on, and stuck it in her pack.

"He," Harvey said.

Raeleen looked at him, confused. "He what?"

"The spider. It's a boy one. You said 'there she goes.' It's a boy spider. Girl spiders're a lot bigger."

Raeleen started laughing. There they were...in the middle o' nowhere...sittin' in the dirt, tryin' their best to keep somebody dressed up like Superman alive by gettin' a spider mad enough to bite him in the neck. While white-haired Hub stood off to the side, shackled, holdin' a leather bag with fifty thousand dollars in it. And Harvey was givin' her lessons on the differences between girl spiders and boy spiders.

"Lift 'is head," Raeleen said. She reached for Harvey's backpack and noticed that in his hurry, he'd left the Sharps within Hub's reach. She looked up at Hub and Hub just looked at her as if he'd never thought of goin' for it. Placing it out o' reach, she pushed the pack's contents around to make an indentation and placed it under Superman's head. He was already startin' to wind down.

"Well, 'at's 'at," she said, groaning to her feet and brushing off the dirt. "We ain't goin' no futher t'day." She fished the manacle keys from her pocket, gave 'em to Harvey, and nodded to a small tree. "Fix 'im up over yonder, then come back here 'n help me with Superman."

"I'cn help ya," Hub said.

"You got but two jobs," Raeleen said. "Luggin' th'money 'n keepin' yer mouth shut."

Harvey unlocked the manacles and removed the bag, and Hub rubbed his wrist. "Take yer pack off."

Hub took it off, and Harvey led him to a small tree and chained him up.

CHAPTER 36

Three-thirty a.m. Hub was off by hisself, layin' on his back, his manacled legs wrapped 'round another tree, sawin' logs. Raeleen and Harvey were side by side. Superman was ten or twelve feet to Raeleen's left and opposite the fire from Hub. The full-blown seizure, combined with the effects of the venom, had knocked him out. Raeleen had tucked him up good and tight with a blanket over his shoulders and under his chin. He hadn't moved a whisker since Raeleen and Harvey carted him into camp. His breathing was slow and deep. Ever once in a while, he'd kinda moan or whimper.

The night was fairly pleasant. Night birds, crickets, and bullfrogs chirped and sang. The campfire had burned down, leaving orangy-yellow ghosts to bob up and down, peekin' out o' the embers. Over the last few minutes, a soft wafting breeze had come up, sniffing and feathering in soft, pillowy waves through the camp. At first, it was barely enough to disturb the snakey tendrils of smoke from the campfire, but as it grew in intensity, it also grew warmer.

Hub opened his eyes. He didn't move, though. Somethin' was wrong. A dry, staticky somethin had rolled over the camp like a gauzy shroud. The somethin' wrong was in the breeze. It had come with it. Like it was hiding within. Like a gator under the water. Hub watched the tree limbs around him slowly lean over and back. Then he looked to the stars. But they were gone. It wasn't clouds, though. There hadn't been a cloud in the sky all day, and hadn't been when they turned in.

Now, the breeze began to sound like voices, whispering. He was sure of it, but he couldn't make out what they were sayin' or exactly where they were comin' from. The words grobbled in his ears like pebbles rollin' in a creek bottom. Shivers ran up and down his spine. He wondered briefly if he might not be fully awake. God knew he had experience in dreams. He squeezed his eyes shut and opened 'em again. Still no stars.

The breeze whispered again, nearer this time. There was a whispery, breezy response from the camp's other side. Then he heard another, from another direction.

Suddenly, he shuddered and sucked in a lungful of the warm air. Something, feather-soft, had touched his left cheek. Either that, or it had passed close enough to stir the air right at him. It was that soft. He was paralyzed with fear. Not just 'cause o' that, though. There was a...presence. He tried to listen for a clue that would give him an idea of what it was, but his heart was pounding so hard, it was all he could hear. His nutsack was wrinkled up tight. Then he come conscious o' the fact that he could hear nothing. His breathing, yes. His heart, still, yes. But that was it! It was if everthing but the visual had died.

The breeze picked up, stronger and warmer. He watched tree limbs movin' but he couldn't hear 'em! He looked at the fire—although small, it was still burning, but it offered absolutely no light outside of itself. If he stood up, he wouldn't cast a shadow. If he put his hand to it, it wouldn't burn him.

Then...

to his side! Something moved! Black on black, but so quick he couldn't tell what it was. The next second, it was next to him, on his left, to the side of his face, low to the ground, like it was crouched. Then, instantaneously, it was over his face, hovering, weaving back and forth, back and forth, like the head of a cobra. Just as suddenly, it was back by his left cheek, weaving, serpentine, lookin' at the corner of his eye. Close. Very, very close.

An image popped in Hub's mind. Floating like that snakehead by his ear. Hairless with huge, goggly eyes that took up most of its face. It didn't have a nose to speak of, just two narrow slits. Small, pointed ears and teeth like needles. It was either a dark or grayish-green, the size of a small dog with a bulbous head. It was lookin' at him, grinning hideously, daring him to move, hopin' he would, and if he did, it'd pounce. He might not be able to see it, but it was real, a thing…with purpose and intent. Evil, dark intent. As sure as Hub knew his own name, he knew its sole purpose was pain and hurt.

The only other times in his life he'd been this frightened was in his nightmares with the witch. This thing had to be either her, or of her, but Lootie's only other form had always been Ret. Although…if she could be Ret, why not this thing.

He was brought back when he felt its breath puffin' on his cheek. But then he realized that whatever it was, breathin' wasn't somethin' it did. It didn't require breath. No, it was just somethin' to remind him it was there. He could feel the heat. It was that close.

Then…it was moving again, around his body, jerking quickly but with the ease of thought, glaring at him, full of hate, pain, and evil hunger. Hateful, hungry, and warm. And it never stopped lookin' at him. Grinning. Grinning. Grinning. Staring. Glaring. It wasn't concerned that Hub knew it was there. In fact, just the opposite. It wanted him to know. It wanted to frighten him. It had succeeded. It knew that, too. It knew exactly what he was feeling, gorging on his terror.

The warm breeze grew to a hot wind, now roaring like a hurricane, and as it rolled hurly-burly through the camp, it swirled around Hub's body, wrappin' around him like a spider cocooning a June bug. He wanted to scream, but he was either too scared or somehow paralyzed. The thing, whatever it was, both did and didn't want him to move. His not moving meant it could drag the moment out, make it last, 'cause when Hub did move, it'd attack, and the game would be over. He also knew the attack would be short and it'd hurt.

A lot.

He felt the warmth of its face moving along the contours of his body, then returning quickly to the side of his face, always back to the left, to see his reaction. A cat playin' with a mouse.

Then it stopped. He and it detected some other thing at the same time. Something was coming. Something even more hideous than this thing. IT was bringin' it! It had….

I'll take the younger one first whispered deep in his brain, and immediately the silence let go. The roaring wind assaulted his ears like pouring boiling water on a cold hand. The new thing was just beyond the camp. Hub heard it over the wind. It was real. Not something the goggle-eyed demon had planted in his brain. Son of a bitch! The goggle-eyed Thing! It was Her! The Witch! She'd created a diversion. He knew he was right, 'cause when the thought entered his mind, he felt the heat bristle beside his face. She wanted to keep his mind on her and not on what was outside the camp.

Unbeknownst to Hub, Harvey and Raeleen had been going through the exact same experience. The thing beside their face, the heat, the glaring, the floating, and now—the new presence of the somethin' else prowling outside the camp.

Suddenly, she was gone! Her objective had been achieved, and now it was time for the next show. And there it was. A deep snuffling, grunting, snorting just beyond the camp. Their paralysis over, Harvey's and Raeleen's hands slid to their weapons layin' beside 'em, and quickly they jumped up, guns at the ready. And that was it! From all around the camp came a deafening, horrendous, screeching wail, and with it, a hot, gale-force wind.

Hub was terrified. He'd heard that same human, yet inhuman wail before. In his nightmares. The only way he could sit up was facing the tree, and with his legs wrapped around the small trunk, he hollered into the raging wind to be cut loose. Harvey and Raeleen paid him no attention, too busy pointin' their weapons outside the camp. All around. The howls and yowls was everwhere, but they could see nothin' other than large, dark, shadowy shapes crashing through the brush and the trees, circling the camp like a bunch of wild Indians around a wagon train. Insane with fear, Harvey couldn't take it any longer and fired into the dark. Shootin' at somethin' he couldn't see was better than waitin' for somethin' he couldn't.

As if his shot was just the spark they'd been waitin' for, the camp was filled with monstrous black forms crashing through the camp, trompin' the fire's embers, scatterin' sparks like maddened fireflies. One o' the beasts had actually stomped Hub's right leg when it charged past him. Terrified, he had no room for thought, only action, and hugged up tight to the little tree, but at eight or nine inches across, it wasn't much of a shield.

Superman's arms shocked straight up over his body, rudely awakened by a pistol's explosion and thundering cloven hooves. He sat up groggily, lookin' through bloodshot eyes that refused to work in tandem, tryin' to make sense of a senseless situation. Lacking the many hours of slumber needed to purge his system of the seizure and venom, he had no idea of what was goin' on, when suddenly his upper body was bashed by a four-hundred-pound hog from Hell. Absolutely unprepared, he never saw it coming.

The animal's gaping, scimitar-tusked maw hit him flat in the chest, emptying his lungs and slammin' him on his back. While the monster stood on his body, a second animal shoved up from behind and clamped its massive jaws on Superman's lower right leg. A sharp jerk of the beast's head dislocated the leg from the hip and tossed him, flailing, eight feet through the air. A third monster seized his midsection before he hit the dirt. A dozen crazed, coarse-haired, tusked behemoths snorted and grunted to get at him. They looked like twelve starved hogs tryin' to eat from a two-hog trough.

Packs of wild swine, javelinas or peccaries, the size of large dogs, roam the backwoods of Southern Looziana, and they can be deadly, but they were nothin' compared to these things. In a matter of seconds, they'd all shared in ravaging Superman, pushin' one another aside to get to him, tearin' him apart.

Hub kept yelling to be cut loose, but Harvey and Raeleen had their hands full firing at the tusk-wielding horde. Because most o' the animals seemed to be coming from Hub's direction, that's where most o' the bullets were going. Hub darted to the other side o' the little tree like a crab scuttlin' around a rock. Bullets plicked and plocked the ground and chipped bark off the tree. One clipped the tip of Hub's left shoe.

The hogs roared, squealed, and pushed one another out o' the way, all wantin' a piece of Superman, and all the time, the screeching wail permeated everthing. Raeleen and Harvey fired and fired and fired at anything that moved, and that kept Hub on the far side o' the treelet. After the first half dozen or so'd flowed around both his sides like water around a rock, he realized they'd never even looked at him. They weren't payin' any attention to Raeleen or Harvey, either. They were so close that their gun barrels actually pressed into the creatures' bodies when they passed. Raeleen and Harvey fired until they ran out o' ammunition, then they reached for their rifles. The things had showed no concern whatsoever as the weapons exploded time after time.

There was no question about it; they had but one goal— Superman. They weren't interested in, didn't even see, anything else.

The battle seemed to go on forever, but in less than a minute, as quickly as it started, it was over. What was left of the demonic herd thundered off into the dark, the pounding of their massive hooves fading. The hot wind and the screeching wail rolled into the distance, following the herd, and finally dissolved to nothin'. The only sounds left came from two damaged and squealin' hogs their comrades had left for dead, Raeleen's, Harvey's, and Hub's raspy breathing, and Superman's gurgling moan.

Hub grabbed the ankle manacles and ratcheted the chain up and down the tree trunk, rasping off bark and lookin' around, fully expecting the demons to catch their breath, get a drink of water, and come back for a second round. "Get me out o' these fuckin' things!"

Three of the huge beasts lay scattered around the camp, dead, the other two still kickin', tryin' to get up. Harvey finished 'em off with vengeful shots to the head. Raeleen allowed her rifle to slip from her hand and scurried to what was left of Superman. He was torn to pieces. Literally. His colorless, bloodless right arm lay five feet from his body. The left, also torn asunder, nowhere to be seen. The monsters had played a lethal game of tug-o-war, and Superman had lost.

It hadn't been a rogue herd o' swine lookin' for somethin' to eat. They were messengers, and the message had been delivered.

Falling to her knees, Raeleen tried to pick Superman up to cradle him, but he shrieked in pain. Scared to death for his brother, Harvey bent over him and was shocked beyond words at the ragged, bleeding ends at his shoulders where his arms used to be. There was a bloody flap of scalp hangin' down almost to his cheek that hid his right ear. Harvey carefully, lovingly, pushed it back and tried to press it to his head. After two attempts, he gave up—it just wouldn't stay put. The muscle high on the left thigh showed through his shredded britches, and there was a huge, jagged slice on his left side below the ribcage, exposing some kind of ropey internal part. Because the night negated all color, it looked as if the blood pulsing casually, rhythmically from the wounds was black. Even in the weak light, it was obvious he couldn't survive.

Harvey bent down, his face to Superman's, and tenderly brushed the back of his finger over his undamaged cheek. One of the few parts still intact. "I'm sorry for ever time I ever hitcha."

"Don't tell 'im a thing like 'at!" Raeleen growled.

Superman looked at Raeleen. "No, Earth Mama, 'at's awright. I'm Superman." Then, as if a switch had been flipped, his eyes saw no more. Superman, The Man of Steel, last remaining citizen of Krypton, was as dead as dead could get.

"No no no no," Raeleen wailed, pulling her dead baby to her sloshy breast. "My poor little boy." She rocked, cradling his head to keep it from flopping, and pushed stray hair from his color-drained face. She turned the body to look at the damage, and, when her gaze passed over his chest, her mouth fell open, staring at his bloody shirt with the trashed S. Putting careful and tender aside, she ripped away what was left of his tattered shirt.

No hex bag.

He'd left it hangin' on the bush at the creek that morning so it wouldn't get in his way while washin' up, and later, when he discovered it was missing, he'd been fearful of telling Raeleen. Not only would he have had to put up with gettin' whacked and yelled at, but they woulda lost precious time havin' to go back to retrieve it. And she woulda gone back. And he woulda got yelled at. And he woulda got whacked on. Then, after retrieving it, they woulda got back to the place from whence they'd started, and she woulda whacked him again to remind him of how much time they'd lost. Then she'd whack him again and tell him how careless he'd been for takin' it off in the first place, and threaten to whack him again if he ever took it off again. What few times, when he was little, he'd taken it off, she'd yelled at him and riddled his fat little legs with welts from a keen switch she flicked like a whip. He was much more fearful of a red-faced, butt- and face-whackin' mother he could see and feel than the fearful witch he'd never seen, that the bag was supposed to protect him from.

"No no no no," she moaned, angrily, pounding Superman's inert body. Then, in mid-pound, she stopped. Her body stiffened, and she turned and looked wild-eyed across the bodies of five dead hogs that had just killed her baby...to Hub, still tethered to the tree. "It's started," she said. She'd seen the light. Like the Good Book said, the writing was on the wall. "You did this!"

"Me?"

"Yeah. You. You 'n th'witch. She said she'd take mine fer hers 'n now she's done it." She chinned to the mangled body in her arms. "Which one'd he pay for ya think, huh? George 'r Matthew?"

Hub thought he was actually watchin' somebody lose their mind.

"We're dead," she said as if it'd already happened.

"Bullshit!"

"All of us!"

"Well, you lay down 'n die if ya want, but I ain't goin' with ya," Hub said with a lot more bravado than he felt. He grabbed the leg irons still wrapped around the tree trunk and shook 'em violently. "Unlock these God Damn things."

Raeleen let Superman's body ease to the ground, wrangled herself up, and stood on shaking legs, her dress soaked with her son's blood. She picked her rifle up off the ground and aimed the business end at Hub.

"You gonna shoot me?" he asked, tryin' for time to head her off. "What 'bout th'curse? You gonna help Lootie out b'shootin me? 'At's nuts! You got one son left. If ya wanna live," he pointed to Harvey, "if you want th'one ya got left t'live, we gotta get out o' here. Out o' th'swamp."

She looked at Harvey. He'd taken up her position when she got up, bent over Superman's blood-soaked body, tears runnin' down his cheeks, snot runnin' over his lip, and blubberin', "I'm sorry, I'm sorry, I'm so sorry." She looked back at Hub.

"Don'tcha see?" he pursued, "'at's egzakly what she wants ya t'do. She had t'slip up on us when we's asleep. Don'tcha see? 'At's th'only way she'cd do it. We wasn't expectin' it, 'n our power was down. But now, we know what she's up to 'n we'cn fight it. We gotta stay strong, though, stay t'gether, fight 'er off. The fewer of us they is, th'better chance she's got." It made no sense at all, a stone-cold bluff, but it was all he had. "If we got any chance a'tall, we need t'get out o' here."

She looked like she was thinkin' it over.

"Rae! We gotta go!"

She was thinkin' that maybe he was right. Besides, she could always kill him when they got out o' the swamps. "Get up," she ordered Harvey. "It's almost sunup. We're leavin'."

Harvey couldn't believe it. "What 'bout Superman? We can't just leave 'im like this. We gotta bury 'im! He's my brother!"

"No!" She stomped to him, grabbed him by the back of his shirt, and hoisted him off the ground. "Not no more! Now he's just dead! Getchur stuff t'gether, we're goin'!"

"But, Mama, they'll eat 'im."

"No! Move! Now now now," she growled, spraying curds of spit, and with each *now* he turtled up his shoulders as she pounded him on the back, pushin' him to action. Then she grabbed his shoulder, yanked him around and ripped his shirt open, exposing the hex bag hangin' around his neck. She thrust an accusatory finger at Superman's armless body. "Now d'ya understand? Is it funny now? Huh? Is it still somethin' t'give me a hard time on 'n laugh about? He took it off 'n that's all it took!" Before he could say anything, she pulled him to her, wrapped her arms around him, gave him a quick hug, pushed him off, and gestured toward Hub. "Get that bag on him 'n let's get out o' here."

Harvey's first order of business was to take a big breath and calm down. It was hard to do with most of his brother's body layin' in one place, another part a few feet away, and yet more gone. He picked up the satchel, carried it to Hub, unlocked the ankle manacles, took 'em off, and dropped 'em in the satchel. Hub stood up and Harvey unlocked the wrist chains. "Putchur pack on."

Hub picked it up, put his arms through the straps, and settled it between his shoulder blades. Harvey clamped one end o' the chain to Hub's wrist. Then he picked up the satchel and slipped the end o' the chain through the handles. He started to clamp the end down when he felt somethin' hot and sticky. Blood. Tricklin' down Hub's forearm, off his fingers, onto the satchel. Hub pushed the sleeve up. Blood was seeping from the scar.

"They getcha?" Harvey asked, nodding in the direction the hogs'd disappeared. Hub shook his head. Harvey unlocked the chain and put it on Hub's right wrist, through the satchel grips, back on his wrist, and pocketed the key. Raeleen and Harvey put on their own backpacks.

"What're we takin' with us?" Harvey asked, nodding to the camp goods.

"Nothin'," Raeleen said. "Nothin' that'd slow us down."

They picked up their weapons, and Harvey took one last look at Superman's body. "I wish we'da stayed home 'n never started this shit."

Raeleen wrapped her arm around his waist and squeezed. "I doubt it'da made any dif'ernce. I think maybe if it hadn't been hogs, here, it'da been somethin' else, som'ers else." She pushed on his shoulder. "Let's go."

Harvey took point, then Hub. Raeleen brought up the rear, contemplating shooting Hub in back o' the head.

...Th'day th'first dies...

CHAPTER 37

The sun was still fairly low on the horizon when they came on a creek, burbling peacefully, cut deeply in a gully, maybe fifteen, sixteen feet across, hemmed in on both sides by a steep, gravelly, rocky wall. Floods had scalloped a wall along the far side. A tangle of broken timber, debris from past floods, was wedged in ever so many yards. A fallen log straddled the gap, both ends wedged in tight. Water coming on the high side flowed through a gap only about a foot deep between the creek bed and bottom of the log, then became a small waterfall. The drop was six or seven feet below this natural bridge.

Harvey kicked at the log's end a couple of times to test its stability. Determining it wasn't going anywhere, he started over, carefully, but about halfway acrost, his foot slipped on the spongey, slippery moss and he slud off the lee side. Going down feet first, he thought he was gonna be all right, but with the added weight of his backpack, the Sharps, and bein' off balance, he landed hard and his left foot glanced off the side of a slime-smeared stone like it was ice. He crashed onto his left side, bruisin' his hip badly on a sharp rock. The rifle clattered across the stones and settled in the water.

"Get over there!" Raeleen barked, nudging Hub away with the end of her rifle. Hub moved off, and Raeleen set the rifle on the ground, adjusted her holstered .45 in case she had to go for it, and carefully, but quickly, walked the log just over Harvey. There he sat, on his butt like a baby in a playpen, water flowin' over his legs.

"You okay?" She'd just lost one son and was suspicious of anything happening to the other.

Harvey pushed the wet out of his hair and rubbed it back. "I ain't sure," he said, more embarrassed than anything. "I didn break nothin', but I mighta fucked up m'foot."

"Gotchur bag?"

He pulled it out from under his shirt and waggled it at her.

She looked back over her shoulder at Hub to make sure he was being good.

"I ain't goin' nowhere," he said, reading the look.

She turned to face Hub so she could keep an eye on him, got down on the log on her all fours, reached down, and wiggled her fingers to Harvey. "Come on."

While he was pushin' hisself up out o' the water and gingerly testing his foot, Hub was lookin' around. The wind was comin' up. A familiar wind. All too familiar.

"Yeah, shit," Harvey said, testing his ankle, "I hurt it some."

"Well," Raeleen said, "they ain't nothin' we'cn do but keep goin', come on." Harvey started to bend to get his rifle. "Leave it!" Raeleen blurted. "We got others."

Harvey grimaced from the pain it took to hobble under the log, and reached for her hand.

"Rae?"

She looked up to Hub. He nodded to the sky.

"You better hurry."

She followed his nod and saw the darkening clouds boiling overhead and the treetops swayin' back and forth. She looked back down at Harvey. "Gimme yer hand. Quick!"

He did, and as he started to pull hisself up, his chest slid past a short stub protruding off the log's low side. After pullin' his hex bag out of his shirt to show Raeleen, he'd neglected to tuck it back. It snagged the stub, ripped off, and plopped in the water. Harvey tried to get it, but with the bad ankle, a wasted effort. Dumbstruck, they watched it tumble downstream, sluicing through and over the stones, until it disappeared.

Then they heard it.

The screeching, the wailing, approaching like a thundering locomotive from Hell. Harvey pictured Superman and what the hogs had done to him and wondered if it was his turn for somethin' as bad—or worse.

Raeleen lay flat on the log, wrapped her right arm around that side, leaned to the left, and reached for Harvey. "Move!"

Harvey had no more than reached up when he jumped back and looked down to see a two-foot-long cottonmouth hangin' from his pants leg, its fangs hung up in the fabric. He'd been bitten. Then another got him. And another. Another. In seconds, they were all over, like they'd popped up out o' thin air. They were slitherin' out of holes in the gravelly creek walls.

Hub watched one wriggle right between his own two feet, slide down the bank, and splash into the water. It had no more interest in him than the hogs had. It undulated in the water with its kin, straight to Harvey, and bit him. Raeleen jumped up as one wriggled past her on the log and dropped over the side. Cottonmouths, rattlers, and copperheads slithered through the water, ever one of 'em bound for Harvey. He reached down and squeezed hard with both hands, squishin' somethin' inside his pant leg. A writhing serpent fell out. He swooned, pressed the heels of his hands to his temples, and fell back in the pool. He looked like a six-foot-two, two-hundred-and-forty pound child, sittin' on his butt in a wading pool. The venom taking effect, he looked at the squirming multitude, confused and bewildered. He picked one up and brought it to his face as if to look at it, and it bit him in the cheek. He looked up at Raeleen and whimpered, "Mama?" Then his lip curled, his eyes rolled up, and his body crumpled as if his bones had turned to butter. He flopped back, smackin' his head, hard, splittin' the back of his skull on the sharp edge of a rock, and the water turned the prettiest pinkish-red. His body spasmed, sickeningly, a byproduct of the venom. Finally, it stopped, but even in death, the serpents continued to bite.

…Th'day th'first dies…

Nature exploded while Raeleen struggled to stand up on the log. She turned around and pulled Hub's revolver from her belt. "Well, asshole," she yelled over the storm, "it's over. It's done. They're dead. I got nothin' t'lose now."

"'At's CRAZY," he hollered back, his eyes squintin' from the rain and wind. "We still got a chance," but all he saw looking back at him was the gun's big black hole, and in back of it, a face that'd lost all reason.

Lightning cracked. The thunder was deafening. Hub ducked as if it'd been thrown at him. Raeleen never flinched. All she felt was her finger crooked around the trigger, and all she saw was the look of fear on Hub's ugly face.

"What d'I care?" she laughed, crazily, through gritted teeth. "She's got both m'babies now. I ain't gettin' out alive, 'n I'll make damn sure you don't! Like you said, maybe me killin' you's part o' her plan all along. I don't know 'n I don't much care. It's awright with me." She raised the gun, helt it out at arm's length, and thumbed the hammer back.

Hub looked down the barrel where the hot lead slug was gonna come screamin' from and put one o' those neat little holes in his forehead, blowin' out the entire back of his skull, brains and all. That was the picture he saw. Nothin' else. Obviously all that bullshit 'bout your life flashin' through your brain was just that. Bullshit. He did notice, however, that her hand wasn't shaking. Not a'tall. She looked happy. She wasn't gonna get talked out of it this time. It was gonna happen. She pulled the trigger.

click

He rocked back a step but caught hisself before falling over. He'd been fully prepared to die, and it was a shock that he hadn't. He wasn't disappointed, but he was surprised.

So was Raeleen. She looked at the gun, then at Hub. He started to move to her, but she snapped the gun back up.

He stopped.

She thumbed the hammer back—again. Aimed—again. Pulled the trigger—again.

click

Again.

Hub leaned back and howled. "It's empty! You dumb bitch! You forgot t'reload it!"

Quicker than she could get out o' the way, Hub jumped to the log, swung the satchel with both hands, and clobbered her upside the head. The blow knocked her in the water on the log's high side. She righted herself, but before she could shake it off, he jumped off the log, wound up and swung the satchel like an Olympian in the hammer throw, and hit her again. The blow spun her around. She fell flat on her face in the water, but before she could get up, Hub was on her, straddlin' her back. He leaned for'ard with all his weight on the back of her head, grinding her face in the gravelly bottom. Gathering all her strength, she pushed herself up onto her all fours, Hub ridin' her like a hobbyhorse. He got off on her left side before she could get to her feet and kicked her, hard, in her left saggy tit.

It felt as if her breast had exploded. The kick emptied her lungs, and the pain emptied her stomach. Lumpy globs a' vomit flowed downstream as she grabbed for her ruined breast and rolled over in agony to her back. Except for the excruciating pain, her mind was a blank.

Hub jumped on her, astraddle her gut. She bucked and tried to push him off, but she didn't have near the strength on her back she had on her belly. He pounded her in the same tit, and when her hands went to protect it, he hammer-fisted her face and shattered her nose. Bright red blood flowed over her lip. Temporarily stunning her with a hard blow to her left cheekbone, he lifted the heavy bag over his head and smacked it flat in her face. Blood gushed from her broken nose and a gash over her right brow, down her cheeks, and into the water.

They were both so consumed with hate and rage they didn't notice the air was filled with Lootie's screech. Hub finally weakened Raeleen to the point where he could grip her throat with both hands. He leaned for'ard and, lockin' his elbows out, straight-armed all his weight into it, helt her head under the water. She thrashed desperately, trying to pry his fingers loose, but it did no good.

Then Hub noticed her hex bag bobbin around in the water above her throat. She gasped for breath when he yanked her head out o' the water just long enough to let her watch him rip it off her neck. He pressed the sodden bag to her busted nose and ground it in the blood, then tossed it in the water. She watched it flow under the log. Laughing, he leaned into her again, forcing her head under the water. Raeleen's fingers dug into his, but it was useless. She finally let go, and Hub figured she was finished.

He figured wrong, though, because under the water, she was groping for the knife in the sheath on her belt. She pulled it out and jammed the blade into Hub's side, hard. He gnashed in pain and almost let go, but came to his senses and, if anything, squeezed harder. She stabbed him repeatedly in the hip and thigh, anywhere she could stick it—under the circumstances, she wasn't particular. But still he didn't let go, his fingers buried in her throat. Then it hit him, that with his fingers clamped around her throat, she'd probably last longer than if she took a lungful o' water. He pushed her head down as far as he could and then let go. As he'd hoped, she took advantage of it and sucked, hard. He helt her face under the water, allowing her to take all the water her oxygen-depleted lungs wanted. Then he rewrapped his hands around her throat....

Lookin' up through the watery distortions, Raeleen saw her killer. There was no mistaking the long, scraggly hair, the scar's discoloration, and the eyes, one inky black, the other....

...and this time he squeezed so hard he felt somethin' snap in her throat. Immediately, her body went slack, and the knife rolled from her dead hand to the gravelly creek bottom.

...Th'day th'first dies...

Raeleen was dead, but unlike Henry's end, the hot wind didn't subside and just blow off. The dark, menacing clouds kept boiling and thunder rolled. Blood pulsed from his wounds when he rolled off Raeleen's body, exhausted. He stood up, and although hampered by the satchel, unhitched his pants and pulled 'em down far enough to check the wounds. They were bleeding, but other than burnin' like Hell, he didn't believe they were anywhere near life threatening. Most of 'em had hit him in the hip and upper thigh. Nothing vital. He hitched his pants back and, bending to Raeleen's body, searched her pockets for the key to the manacles. Then he remembered. Harvey had it. He remembered his puttin' it back in his pocket after chaining him up that morning.

He hobbled along the crumbly creek bank. He'd been so busy throttlin' the life out o' Raeleen, he hadn't noticed how the creek'd risen. The water that'd been flowin' under the log was now lapping over it. Raeleen's lifeless body was wedged under it, helping to dam it up. Standing in water now almost knee high, he looked into the lower part o' the pool where dozens of snakes continued to wriggle and slither over Harvey's lifeless corpse.

He picked up a cantaloupe-sized rock out o' the water and tossed it over the side to scare 'em off. It hit Harvey square in the sternum, forcing water to spout from his mouth. His arms and legs jerked skyward, his eyes bugged open, and he screamed as if bein' ripped from a horrendous nightmare.

Hub screamed!

If the writhing, squirming mass'd had the capability, they woulda screamed too, but instead, they took their shock out on Harvey's already venom-saturated body, all over again. Then, as quickly as it'd started, it was over. Harvey plopped back in the water. Dead.

Again.

The miraculous reanimation had stirred the wrigglers up but hadn't scared 'em off as Hub'd hoped. He looked at the blood runnin' off the tips of his fingers. Blood that wasn't comin' from the knife wounds but his scarred arm. Rain pelting his face, he looked into the boiling sky and shook his fist. "It'll take more'n this, you old bitch!"

Then Hubert Marshall Lusaw started off, the satchel with fifty thousand dollars still chained to his wrist.

Two hours later, Hub was still sloggin' through the stormy swamp. The water was only up to his nuts, but the silty bottom was like walkin' in wet cement. He alternated holding the satchel over his head, on his right shoulder, or snugged to his chest. He woulda given a thousand dollars for a ten-cent hacksaw blade. Suddenly, he stopped and cocked his ear. Was it just part the storm or, no…a motor! Comin' his way. He quickly waded to a large cypress.

Slicing slowly but deliberately through the storm-agitated water was a dented aluminum skiff with two big black men, Bob McDonald, in his low sixties, and Phillipe LaRue, in his low fifties. Cowering under a yellow slicker, Phillipe was at the tiller while Bob sat in the bow, on the look-out for flotsam that might damage the hull. In the skiff's belly lay the carcasses of half a dozen three- and four-foot gators.

Hub watched from around the tree when they passed not more than fifty yards from him. He assumed they were poachers and, therefore, wouldn't wanna have any more to do with him than he did with them. It woulda been difficult for them to see him with the storm, but with their bein' hunkered down under their slickers, it was almost impossible.

When the skiff motored out o' sight, Hub started off in the same direction. He was unfamiliar with this part o' the swamps and figured the boat's inhabitants might be headed for some semblance of civilization. If not, he'd still find his way, eventually.

No more than thirty minutes later, a grin spread across his face as he neared the edge o' the swamp where the trees started to thin out. He looked at the raging, boiling, bruise-hued clouds and shook his fist. "You lose, you fuckin' bitch. You're good at sneakin' up on abody with snakes 'n hogs, but how'd ya do agoin' toe t'toe with me! Come on, you ol' whore! You ain't gonna give up on me now, are ya? I wish ya had 'nother idyit son I'cd throttle th'life out of!"

Lightning flashed and thunder crashed as if in reply. He looked all around the sky, searching for her ugly face. "'At th'best ya got? Noise? Quit hidin'! Come on, just once, show yerself!"

Instantly, the screeching wail ceased. Right along with his smartassey attitude. The silence was deafening. The black clouds still boiled, which should make some kind o' sound.

But it didn't.

The wind blew, which shoulda made some kind o' sound.

But it didn't.

The small storm-tossed waves lapped at him, which shoulda made some kind a sound.

But they didn't.

The branches in the trees rocked with the wind, which shoulda made some kind o' sound.

But they didn't.

It was like somebody'd turned a glass bowl over him, upside down, and inside, the lack of sound was all there was. Then...he did hear somethin'. A grumblin', rumblin' that he felt more than heard. Then, in his head...

"I'm here."

Slowly, he turned to find he was face to face with the biggest alligator he'd ever seen. In truth, he didn't know gators got that big. It was as if it'd materialized out o' thin air. Thin water. All that was stickin' out o' the water was a little o' the snout, the eyes, and some o' the dinosaur-like knobblies. It looked like a God Damn log with eyes. Hub coulda parked his ass between that snout and the eyes and not touched either one. He could only imagine how much more there was under the water. It didn't move, but just looked at him. It coulda been a log for all the life it displayed. Except for the eye. Hub's blood ran cold as he recognized the discoloration that ran from the middle of its upper jaw, up through the blue-blind left eye to the middle of its monstrous skull. The other eye was jet black and depthless.

She hadn't snuck up on him at the last second with a herd of swine. She hadn't snuck up on him with a pool of wriggly cottonmouths.

Like he'd challenged, she was gonna go toe t'toe. The sound of the raging storm rolled back at full volume, and the alligator's glassy black eye filmed over. Then the monstrous body tightened spring-tight, and the dinosaur flicked its enormous tail, one time, hard, catapulting itself clean out o' the water. Its cavernous mouth flew open, it twisted to the right, grabbed Hub around the middle, and snapped shut. As with Raeleen's throat, somethin' popped. A bunch o' somethin's.

The gator squished all the air out of Hub's lungs. It also squished up his gullet what little was still in his stomach from the meager meal consumed the night before. What'd already been digested was squished out the other end. It felt like his eyes were gonna pop out of his head. Then the beast went into its death roll, and Hub's body and the satchel flailed, slappin' in the water with each pass. The beast spun like a rubber band on a kid's balsawood windup airplane, but each time it rolled Hub out o' the water, it was like time had stopped and he had all the time in the world to see the bright red blood flingin' through the air like somebody flickin' thinner from a paint brush. Then he was back under the water. He didn't have time to pick and choose when he sucked in badly needed air, and half the time it was green, brackish water.

Finally, he was jerked to the surface one last time, and tried to pull air into lungs that were squeezed almost flat. The way the thing had him, he was layin' on his back. He and the monster managed one last look. Hub watched its eye roll back and the eyelid close, then it slowly slid under the water, while Hub, blood slobberin' from his mouth, valiantly but worthlessly pounded on the gator's rocky face, fightin' to the last. Bloody bubbles rose to the surface and burst, flickin' the prettiest little flumes of pinkish water.

...you all die.

The wind subsided, thunder and screeches faded into the distance. Buried deep in the screeches was somethin' that sounded like a cackly laugh.

Finally, Lootie Komes could go to Hell in peace.

CHAPTER 38

The dented, scuffed aluminum tub with the tiny outboard motor was pulled up high on the bank and tied off with a clothesline rope to a dead tree stump. A scruffy, slap-em-up, lean-to campsite'd been hurriedly constructed, and Bob and Phillipe had their skinny black butts planted on two upturned galvanized buckets, their coat collars turned up, warming their arthritic hands with their coffee cups. A cast-iron skillet lay on a grate in the middle o' the fire with half a dozen thick slices o' fatty bacon sizzlin' and spittin' grease. Bacon, beans, and coffee—the breakfast of poachers the world over. During working hours, the buckets served as fish-gut containers. Smelly fish guts was catnip to gators. Gatornip.

It was a beautiful morning…a bright blue sky, and not a sign of clouds. A damn sight better than the day before. Normally, they woulda felt a storm coming and prepared for it, but that son of a bitch yesterday had come up so quick it caught 'em unawares and nearly blew the camp away.

Two huge, near-feral, slat-sided mongrels lay off to the side, chained up, their slobbery jowls resting on criss-crossed front paws, concentrating on the skillet. The smell of all that bacon fryin' would've aroused most dogs, but those two knew that whimperin' and carryin' on wouldn't do any good. The best they could look for'ard to'd be gator or fish innards.

The reason there hadn't been much put into the campsite was 'cause they had no intention o' stayin' in one place for more than a day or two. A permanent, traceable residence was an unrealistic luxury in the life of gator poachers. In fact, they were waitin' for another pair, Coozie and Gerard, so they could break camp and move on. They shoulda been there the day b'fore. Probly got caught in the storm. They hoped Coozie and Gerard's luck was better than theirs. There were seven skins, stretched tight on boards at the edge o' the camp, dryin' in the sun. It was a pitiful lot. They'd pulled in almost enough to pay for the gasoline and supplies it took to survive that week. Profit wouldn't make an appearance.

Bob set his cup down, leaned in, and helt his tin plate next to the skillet with his left hand, grease spitting on it, and with the knife in his right, poked two bacon strips, pulled 'em on to the plate, and sat back to wait for 'em to cool. The knife's handle was longer than the blade. It was old and had been honed so many times, it was worn down to a nub, but it was one sharp son of a bitch. No tellin' how many times the rough leather wrapped around the handle had been replaced.

He never used it that he wasn't reminded of where it'd come from. It was the same blade the ol' witch, Lootie Komes, had jammed into her chest bones the day Hub Lusaw was sentenced to forty years in Angola Penitentiary for killin' her sons, George and Matthew. God, what a day that'd been. He and Phillipe had been paid two bucks apiece to pick up her body, put it in back of the cop's truck, and unload it at the morgue. It'd creeped him out how little she'd weighed—nothin' but skin and bone. How somethin' so evil could weigh so little, still stumped him. That day, on the way to takin' her body to the morgue, he'd looked around to make sure nobody was lookin', reached over, and pulled the blade from 'tween her ribs. When they got to the morgue, he and Phillipe lifted her out and lugged her inside. All the cops wanted to do then was get away, so they never looked at the body, and the people at the morgue never asked anything about where the tool was she'd used to kill herself. They probably figured the cops had it.

At the time, he thought it might be good luck. He'd asked hisself no tellin' how many times since then, though, how in the world the knife that had put the finishing touches on one o' the nastiest witches he'd ever heard of could bring anybody good luck, but when he was in the back o' the truck, something told him to pull it out. Even when he was doin' it, it was like he was watchin' from a distance. In the three decades since, it'd poked many a slice o' bacon and gutted many a gator belly, but that was about as far as good luck'd gone. It hadn't brought him riches, that was for sure.

He stuck the blade in the end of a bacon slice, helt it up and let the fatty end drop in his mouth. It burned his tongue and he sucked in air to cool it off.

"Hot?" Phillipe chuckled.

Suddenly, the dogs jumped up, hackle-backed, growlin' real low and lookin' into the swamp. Bob and Phillipe looked in the same direction. Then they heard the motor. Movin' as quickly as only skittery gator poachers could, they set their cups and plates on the buckets, snatched up their rifles—.22 single shots that wouldn't do much more than make a little noise—and scanned the swamp 'til they saw the familiar pair approaching in another skiff. They waved and re-stowed their implements of minor destruction.

Coozie LeGrange, thirtyish, and Gerard Boot, in his early twenties, waved back. Laid out in the bottom o' their boat was the same pitiful take Bob and Phillipe'd garnered the day before—half a dozen three-to-five-footers. Gerard tossed a rope tied to the front o' the boat to Phillipe, standin' on the bank. He caught it, and after he and Bob pulled it as far up the bank as possible, Gerard and Coozie jumped out and helped beach it higher.

"What took ya s'long?" Phillipe asked. "We 'spected ya las' night."

"Had t'wait out th'stoam," Gerard replied.

Bob looked over their catch and shook his head. "Watah dogs."

Gerard looked at the catch stretched out on the boards. "You oughta know."

Gerard and Coozie waded back into the water. "Gimme a hand ovah heah," Coozie said. He reached in the water for a rope trailin' from the back o' their skiff.

"Whatchu got dere?" Phillipe asked.

Gerard said nothin' as he untied the rope, slung it over his shoulder like he was about to haul a barge upriver, and started for the bank, but there was somethin' in the little smirk. Bob and Phillipe met him and took aholt o' the rope.

Phillipe felt the weight when they started haulin' it in. "Watchu got tied up 'ere?"

Slowly, the carcass of an eighteen-footer surfaced. Bob's and Phillipe's eyes popped open.

"Oh, my God," Bob said, "where you get a subm'rine?"

"Yestadee, we seen 'im on the bank, gettin' a tan, layin' in a sun," Coozie said, beaming. "He slud in a watah 'n it took us all day t'fine 'im agin. When we do, he dead." He shrugged. "Dunno why. We look 'im ovah but din see nothin' 'at kill 'im. But, 'at's fine wi'me, as big's he is, I wudn wanna hafa fight 'im nohow."

Gerard wrapped the rope in his hand. "Les get 'im up b'foe a big one come 'long 'n wanna eat 'im."

They all pulled what they could to shore, but quite a bit still remained in the water. Phillipe looked it over. "I ain't nevah seed a beast 'at big my ho'life."

"You gotta go waaayyy out t'get 'em like dis," Coozie said, "but dis ol' man only 'bout foah mile back." He affectionately ran his hand over the carcass. "Jus look a'dat! 'Cept f'da scahs on 'is head, he damn neah pufec. Nobody gonna wanta head nohow."

They all admired the hide, then Gerard rubbed his hands in anticipation of the work ahead. "Well, les get 'is clothes off!"

They put their backs into it and with the use of leg, back, and ropes, rolled it over, belly up.

"Mm mm mm," Phillipe said, tappin his boot toe on the fat tail, "some good eatin' 'ere."

"Gimme yer knife," Gerard told Bob.

Bob walked to the fire, picked up the short-bladed knife, brought it back, and handed it to Gerard. Gerard got down on his knees, stuck the blade in the anus, and started sawin' up. "Dis gonna make a lot o' hanbags," he laughed.

"How ol' you tink he is?" Phillipe asked.

"Ohhhhhh, my," Gerard said, givin a learned observation, "I dunno, t'irty, mebbe more. Watchu tink, Cooz?"

"Yeah, mebbe eben fohty."

Phillipe, Bob and Coozie were still lookin' the beast over when Gerard exclaimed, "Wat d'...." He used the point of the knife to lift one side o' the incision, then jerked his arms up like he'd been shocked. "Oh, Lawd...." He sat there lookin' at the incision.

"Wat?" Coozie asked, big eyed.

Gerard used the blade to lift the flap again. He tilted his face to look underneath. "Wat d'Hell..."

He lifted the flap enough that he could stick the fingertips of his other hand just inside the incision and pull out a bundle of blood-stained hundred-dollar bills, still bound in a wrapper. The others eyes popped open in conjunction with their mouths. Again, using the blade to open the incision, he leaned to the side and peeked inside the bloody cavity. He slipped his hand in again, and, one at a time, pulled out three more bundles, and it was Coozie's turn to voice the required and appropriate, "Wat d'Hell...."

Putting his fear aside, Gerard continued to probe for more.

"Da bank dohn have dat much money," Phillipe said.

The other three laughed but they were nervous laughs. When Gerard scrunched up his brows, the other three spidered back. They knew it'd been too good to last. Then their own brows scrunched when he pulled out a chain, slowly, carefully, one link at a time.

"I's tooken a lot o' tings outa gatah bellies," Coozie said, "but...he et a chain?"

"Maybe a whole boat!" Gerard said, continuing to pull the chain, when suddenly, he jumped back and crossed hisself. "Ohhhhhh, Sweet Blessed Mudda o' Jesus, hep me!"

Coozie couldn't take the suspense any longer. "Well, come on, wat is it?" He looked back and forth between Gerard and the hundred-dollar-bill-spewing-monster.

Gerard inched back to the gator, poked the tip o' the knife in one o' the links and lifted it out. Slowly, there appeared...a scarred and deformed human arm. Phillipe, Coozie, and Bob moved off with a full round of chest crossings and *Lawdy, hep me*'s.

Both ends o' the chain were still locked to a wrist rubbed raw from the struggle at bein' consumed, and what was more, the fist on the end o' the arm had a death grip on two leather handles. Having pulled out the entire arm and chain, Gerard flipped it to the dogs. Immediately, they commenced tearin' it apart.

"...and th'lowest o' th'low'll fight over yer bones."

Bobby Norman's literary career began as an actor. A member of the Screen Actors Guild since 1991. Black Water is his first published book. He graduated from Santa Ana High School the same year as The Chantays and Diane Keaton. He lives in Norco, California, horse capital of the United States, with his wife, Ilene, and a varying number of furry and winged critters. One of his goals is to have dinner with J.K. Rowling and Stephen King. And they buy.

BLACK TIDE

• A MATT ROWLEY NOVEL •

PATRICK FREIVALD

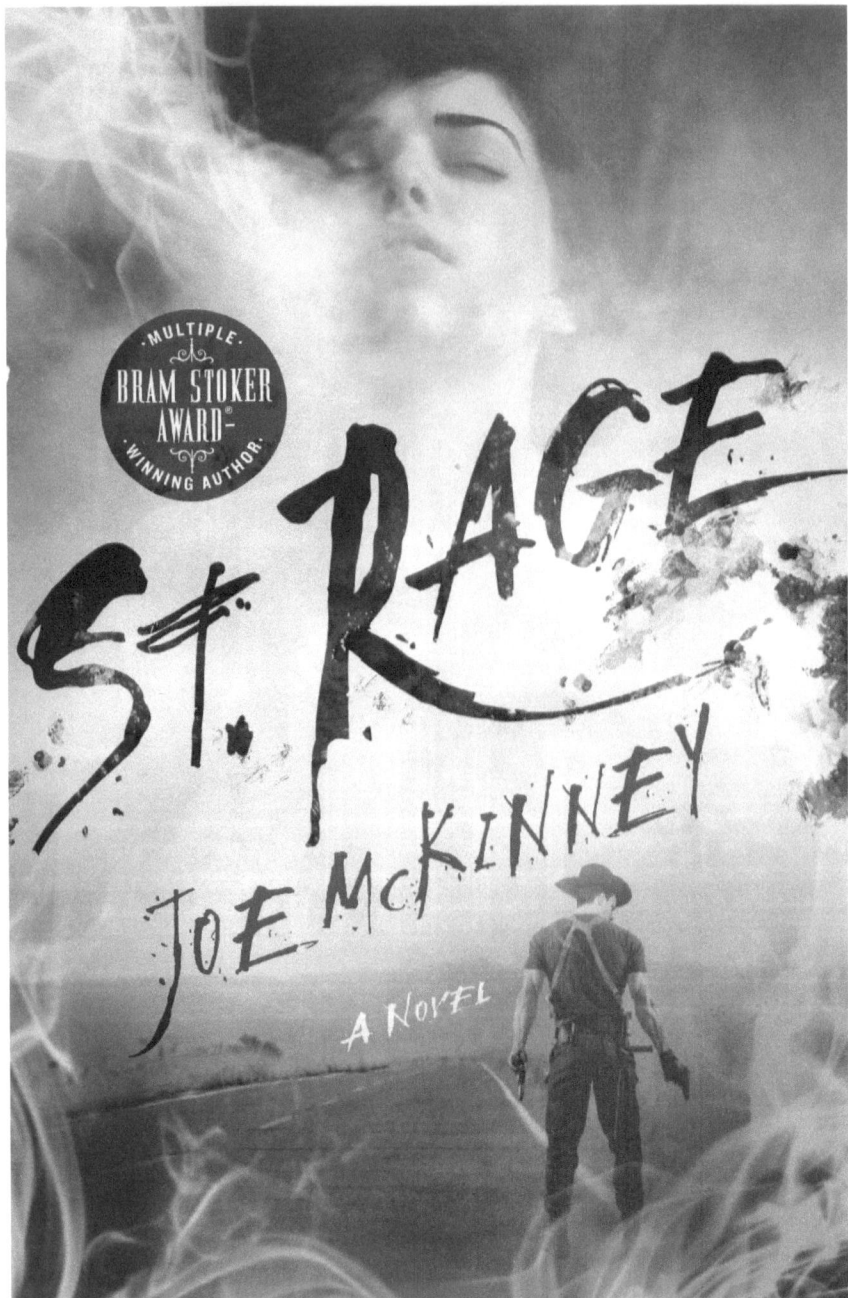

St. Rage

JOE McKINNEY

A NOVEL